Penny Mirren is the pen name of Samantha Pennington. Sam writes light-hearted, uplifting fiction and romantic comedy. She was selected for the inaugural Kate Nash Literary Agency Mentorship programme in 2020 and is a member of the Romantic Novelists' Association. Sam lives in North Essex and when she's not writing, enjoys being first mate on her husband's tiny fishing boat and reading books for her wine club.

# the Un-Retirement

## Penny Mirren

avon.

Published by AVON
A division of HarperCollins*Publishers* Ltd
1 London Bridge Street
London SE1 9GF

www.harpercollins.co.uk

HarperCollins*Publishers*
Macken House
39/40 Mayor Street Upper
Dublin 1
D01 C9W8

A Paperback Original 2024
2
First published in Great Britain by HarperCollins*Publishers* 2024

ISBN: 9780008694166

Typeset in Minion Pro by Palimpsest Book Production Ltd, Falkirk, Stirlingshire

Printed and bound in the UK using 100% renewable
electricity at CPI Group (UK) Ltd

For three remarkable women – Mum, Nan & Babs

# *Prologue*

## *Two Years Ago*

On a day of poignant 'lasts', it came as something of a surprise to Maggie when she pushed open the door to The King's Head to find Colin Neville on the threshold, glass of Buck's Fizz in hand. In over thirty years of after-work drinks and pub lunches, Colin had never once set foot inside, which made this a first. His expression, though, akin to that of someone with their genitals in a vice, betrayed the fact he'd never felt less comfortable.

He cleared his throat.

'Maggie. Just a few of us, from the office, ah, that's to say, we, wanted to raise a glass and wish you well.'

Maggie smiled back at her boss with fondness, whilst also appreciating that she would never again have to divert her gaze from his egg-splattered tie or the gingery slice of hair that regularly broke free of its comb-over to waft gently in the air-conditioned breeze of the district council offices.

'Gosh. How kind, Colin, I'm not sure what to say.'

Although, of course, she did – she'd even prepared a speech. And this was by no means unexpected. Actually, she had helped Pam (who gave a comedy wink when Colin turned his back) to plan the small shindig about to take place. Maggie liked to be prepared, especially if the alternative would have meant leaving her last hours of gainful employment in Colin's clumsy hands. She had a perfectly nice mantelpiece, thank you, which was in no need of a carriage clock.

And so, feigning delighted astonishment at the sea of faces beyond, she followed dutifully after Colin and Pam to a table laid with finger food and champagne flutes of fizz. A helium balloon hovered above a ribbon-tied gift bag, which she suspected contained the silver watch she and Pam had ogled in the posh jewellers in town. Pam had been unusually effusive over the window display, oohing and aahing and pointing at all the lovely things, which Maggie had later realised was likely a ruse.

A boisterous cheer erupted from her friends and colleagues, and she allowed herself a fleeting moment, just the tiniest taste of sentimental whimsy for the end of an era, before chasing it swiftly down with a gulp of – hmm, Cava. *Shame on you Colin*, she thought.

In truth, it was rather difficult to feel sad about it all. Not with so much to look forward to.

'I'm going to miss you, Maggie,' said Martin from tenant services; a forty-two-year-old Warhammer buff who still lived at home with his parents.

'You're going to miss her sausage rolls, more like,' said Pam.

'Charming!' said Maggie, though she suspected this was

true. There had even been a rumour that last year's relocation of the planning department to the second floor had been a strategic move to muscle in on the famed flaky pastry.

Pam threaded her arm through Maggie's and gave her a squeeze. 'I really am going to miss you though.' Her voice wobbled. 'Seventeen years we've sat next to each other.'

'We're having coffee next Saturday, you daft thing. And I'll see you at WI.'

'It's not the same. Who's going to fight for the quilted toilet paper? Or Nescafé Gold Blend? And I bet you a Chelsea bun we're back to long life milk by Tuesday.'

Oh, the glamour of an administrative career. Still, it hadn't been all bad, and she had made friends for life over the years, many of them there in the room today.

'*Speech!*' called out Gary, who was brandishing a fresh pint of lager in one hand and a half-empty glass in the other. That was the trouble with these sorts of events, they tended to deteriorate rather quickly once the petty cash came out.

'Yes! Speech!' echoed Samira, smoky eyes freshly made up with liquid eyeliner flicks. She began to chant, 'Maggie! Maggie! Maggie!'

Gary began bongo-ing the bar top.

Even Colin, in an uncharacteristically sociable move, perhaps owing to the fizzy drink, clapped his hands in encouragement.

What was a girl to do?

Maggie put down her glass and surveyed the room.

'First of all, I'd just like to say, thank you everyone for

coming along this evening. It was such a wonderful surprise!' she lied through her teeth and pointedly averted Pam's gaze. Pam had just polished off a Bacardi and Coke and was on the cusp of melodrama. 'It's no secret I've been counting down the days to this moment and that's no reflection on any of you. Some of us have been colleagues for more years than I care to remember, some for only months, but we've all been part of the family serving this fine community most of us call home, and for that, I feel immensely proud.'

A round of applause swept through the room and Maggie truly hoped the sentiment had struck home, though secretly she had her doubts. The new hybrid model of working from both home and office, since the disastrous days of Covid, had changed something fundamental, something human, about the job. She stole another quick glance at Samira and wondered how she was faring. It was now three months since she'd found the poor lass sobbing her heart out in the ladies' loos and taken her off to a private meeting room for a strong cup of tea and a chat. Samira had hardly been in the office since then and such enquiries were not for the likes of a work email.

A movement caught Maggie's eye and glancing at the doorway, her spirits soared. Even after forty-one years of marriage, Geoff could still surprise her. His own retirement party wasn't for another fortnight, which meant he must have left work early today. He still had his bicycle cuffs on, had come straight from the station. He grinned and gestured for her to continue.

'Here he is,' called out Gary. 'The lucky guy who gets

to enjoy Maggie's Victoria sponge for eternity whilst the rest of us are starved of cake.'

Maggie laughed, along with the others. 'I can assure you right now, I have absolutely no intention of spending our retirement slaving in a kitchen. We have plans, my dear, and most of them include far-flung shores and a taste for *new* experiences, not a Victoria sponge in sight.'

On cue, Geoff moved to stand at Maggie's side.

She smiled up at him. 'Didn't expect to see you here, love.'

'Wouldn't have missed it for the world,' he replied, eyes sparkling with pride.

'There you go, Geoff,' said Pam, plonking a glass in his hand. 'Let's have a toast, then I want to hear all about this fancy campervan of yours.'

Geoff slung an arm around his wife, and beamed as glasses all around were raised.

'To Maggie, and Geoff, and a retirement filled with adventure!'

# Chapter One

## Maggie

*Now*

'Granny, why are you wearing a Santa hat *and* a bikini?' asked Alice, forearms flat on the table, bottom in the air.

'I think the question should be, why *are* you wearing a bikini, Mother?' retorted Hannah, craning her neck to see the picture her daughter was looking at.

'I'll have you know your father said I looked as good in a two-piece there, as I had back on our honeymoon, so watch your cheek,' chided Maggie.

Hannah gave a woeful sigh. 'You always did have a good bum. Why couldn't I have inherited your bum? Mine's like a flat cushion, only no amount of plumping gives it any more bounce.'

'All bottoms are lovely, darling, isn't that the message we're going for these days?'

'It most certainly is,' agreed Hannah, giving her daughter a light tap on hers. 'Sit down properly, my darling, you'll wear the knees out on your school tights.'

Maggie pointed to the photo her granddaughter was

still examining. 'That was two Christmases ago. Grandad and I were on holiday in Australia – they have their summer during our winter.'

There may as well have been a comic book think bubble above Alice's head in the seconds before she spoke.

'But what does Santa wear then? Doesn't he get all hot and sweaty in his big red coat and boots?'

Hannah stuck her tongue out at Maggie, as if to say, *my daughter's smart, what did you expect?*

'I'm sure he has both a winter suit *and* a summer suit, for warmer climates. Santa is a very resourceful man; he'd be prepared for anything. Anyway,' added Maggie, thumbing back through the pages of the album, 'what do you think of this one? Isn't Grandad silly?'

The photo, one of Maggie's favourites, was taken on the Spanish leg of their grand European campervan trip. They'd stayed on a lovely little site just outside Lloret de Mar, on the Costa Brava, and had taken the bus to Barcelona for the day. Geoff, being Geoff, had wanted to stop and watch the street entertainers on the busy Las Ramblas and in this picture, he was striking the same pose as a human statue, frozen in mid-sprint. He'd tried everything to get the young man to crack a smile, but only succeeded in sending Maggie into fits of giggles instead.

'Oh, Mum,' murmured Hannah, giving her shoulder a quick squeeze.

She hadn't quite reached the stage Maggie was at, who found comfort in these memories. Hannah still wouldn't talk about her dad much at all. Perhaps it was simply that these weren't *her* memories.

Their year of wanderlust was one of the best she'd ever had, and it couldn't be torn away from her too. Not now, not ever. The memories were so recent, they played out in her head in technicolour. If she tried hard, she could almost believe Geoff was simply away for work and that within a few days they'd be packing their suitcases again, ready to cross off the next destination on their bucket list. They still had Turkey to explore, most of Greece and Cyprus. That had been the plan for this year. That had been their plan.

She remembered, as she studied the photo again, how they'd stopped for a tapas lunch in a café, just out of shot. 'Best patatas bravas I've ever tasted,' Geoff had declared. He'd said that a lot. You might have said he was easily pleased, but Maggie knew better. He was simply pleased. Happy to be together, living out their dream. She remembered reaching across to wipe a speck of sauce from his beard.

'You'd think someone who'd spent so much of their time in five-star establishments would have learned to use a napkin by now,' she had said, or something like it. He'd just grinned. What she'd give to see that mucky, cheeky face again now. But this was all she had left. Photos and memories.

In *these* photos, she looked the same as she did now, more or less, a little more tanned maybe, perhaps a few contended pounds heavier. It wasn't like looking at the old albums, where the passage of time had suspended them somewhere unreachable, somewhere where smooth skin and supple limbs distanced them from the here and now. In *these* photos, Geoff was almost within reach.

Deciding to lighten the mood, Maggie abruptly stood. 'Who fancies a spot of apple crumble before you head home?'

'Me, me!' cried Alice, her hand shooting into the air like a firework.

Perhaps of all her roles past and present – trainee chef, wife, mother, administrator, member of the PTA, and the WI – this was one she enjoyed most: unrepentant spoiler of dearly beloved grandchild.

'Just a little bit then,' said Hannah, snapping the album shut and putting a full stop to their reminiscence. 'I need to get this one home for her bath.'

Maggie reached into the cupboard for three bowls and paused at the sight greeting her from beyond the kitchen window.

'Good grief. What's the daft old fool up to now? He looks like a garden gnome. Are those . . . *bells* on his legs?'

Hannah rose and came to join her at the window.

'He's a similar age to you, Mum. And that looks like a Morris dancing costume to me. Good on him for giving it a go.'

'Four years older actually, Hannie. But you know what I mean, he's *old*. He walks funny.'

'He has arthritis, Mother, as you well know. And at least Oscar's getting the most out of life, which is more than can be said for many. I think it's admirable.'

'I hope you're not referring to me.'

'Of course I'm not referring to you.'

'Yes, well, there's a big difference between cramming every conceivable hobby into every waking hour and doing something meaningful with your life. I know which I'd rather be doing.'

Hannah was quiet whilst Maggie spooned warm, gooey crumble fresh from the oven into the bowls. But she couldn't hold her tongue for long.

'Maybe you *should* take up a hobby? Get out a bit more, mix with people. You were always so sociable before you retired. Why don't you see if Pam fancies doing something with you? You haven't seen her in ages, have you?'

Maggie barked a laugh. 'Is this another one of those conversations where you suggest things that might be good for me, Hannah? You can save your breath if you're going to try and convince me to listen to waterfalls at bedtime again. I was up half the night peeing.'

With an exasperated sigh, Hannah went to the freezer for the ice cream and began scooping it into the bowls.

'I seem to remember suggesting Monty might be good for you. I assume there's no arguments there?' she challenged.

'That's different. Monty needed *me* as much as anything.'

As if anyone could have walked out of that cat rescue centre without wanting to take them all home. If it wasn't for the fact that Monty hated other cats, Maggie would have happily embraced the moniker of crazy cat lady and lived out her days drowning in fur and Dreamies. But, as it was, Monty had made his human selection clear, striding to the bars of the cage as Maggie passed by and lifting one white-socked paw in a clear high-five. They'd been the firmest of pals ever since.

'Black olives are good for you too, Granny,' interjected Alice. 'Mummy says they make your pupils bigger, which means you can see more in the dark.'

'Isn't that carrots?' questioned Maggie. 'Crusts to curl your hair, carrots to see in the dark?'

'Don't be silly, carrots look nothing *like* eyeballs, Granny,' giggled Alice.

Maggie looked to Hannah.

'What? Don't look at me like that; I just don't want her growing up to be a fussy eater, that's all,' Hannah whispered behind her hand.

'Oh, far better to sound thick as mince, but have a bourgeois palette, I quite agree,' muttered Maggie, rolling her eyes. She handed Alice her bowl. 'Thank you, sweetheart, I'll bear that in mind, especially as my optician keeps blathering on about varifocals. But what Granny *really* needs isn't pointless hobbies. I'm thinking of getting a new job.'

Hannah paused with her spoon halfway to her mouth. 'Seriously?'

'Perfectly serious. Why wouldn't I? I'm only sixty-five, not dead. There's plenty of life in the old dog yet.'

'Are you getting a dog, Granny?' asked Alice excitedly. 'I *really* want a doggy.'

'It's just a way of saying there's still lots I can do, sweetheart. Perhaps I'll find some volunteering work, do something useful.'

Hannah smiled and nodded along. 'I think that's a great idea, Mum. Really.'

'Granny,' said Alice, an ice cream moustache lending her an authentic air of wisdom, 'you should get a job as a cook, because you're very good at it you know.'

Maggie bent and planted a kiss on the top of her granddaughter's head. 'Thank you, darling.' To Hannah, she added, 'Of course, I'll still be around to pick Alice up from school and look after her until you're home from work, love. I wouldn't change that for all the tea in

China . . .' Maggie pre-empted the inevitable question, '. . . That means there's not enough delicious cups of tea in the world, Alice, to tempt me away from our fun afternoons.'

'And you *really* like cups of tea,' maintained Alice, who had clearly got the gist.

'Right then, little miss,' said Hannah, placing her bowl in the dishwasher, 'we'd better get off home. Say goodnight to Granny.'

Maggie watched from the doorstep as Hannah bundled Alice into her Volkswagen Golf, waving as they pulled away to drive across town to their new two-bedroomed home. Hannah's own recent status as a single parent, while juggling childcare and a legal career, had doubtlessly contributed to her decision to move back to her hometown, and Maggie couldn't have been happier to have them both close by. She only hoped it wasn't out of a sense of duty. Yes, she was now a widow, but she had no desire to be a burden. When they had disappeared from view, she closed the front door and made her way back to the kitchen where she flipped on the kettle to make another *tuppa-tea*, as Alice had called it until quite recently, the memory bringing a smile to her lips.

Once the kettle had boiled itself into a crescendo, the house sank back into a heavy silence.

She took her tea to the table and lowered herself onto a chair, not yet ready to retire to the lounge, to a sofa undinted by the weight of another body, to a television brimming with everything, yet nothing, she wanted to watch.

Instead, she slid the photo album back towards her and opened it at the first page. To the very first day of their journey, two years ago. At the top of the page, Maggie had written the words in bold: Maggie and Geoff's Big Adventure.

Below, were two photos.

One had been taken at her retirement party in The King's Head. She wore a curious expression of joy mixed with anticipation and had been snapped just as she'd opened the small gift box containing her shiny new watch, which lurked unworn in her bedside drawer, a memento from another life.

The other picture had been taken at Geoff's own retirement. A different beast entirely. One might have called it a busman's holiday, treating a top chef to a five-course meal at a Michelin-starred restaurant. But Maggie hadn't been complaining. She had enjoyed every minute on his arm, taking it all in and savouring every bite. This photo had been taken at the precise moment Geoff's former employer had presented him with a set of hand-engraved Japanese knives, the most expensive money could buy. At the time, she and Geoff had secretly joked about how he never intended to cook again, how they'd live off takeaways and toasted sandwiches. As it happened, they were jolly handy knives. She'd used one only this evening to chop the red peppers for their stir fry.

What would Geoff have made of her idea to go back to work, she wondered? But she guessed it was a moot point. If Geoff were here, she'd have had no such thoughts. If Geoff were here, she wouldn't be searching for ways to fill her endless, purposeless days.

In the picture, the Michelin-starred chef, who Geoff knew well, had come out to shake his hand. Geoff hadn't quite reached those dizzying heights of fame, but he had enjoyed a long, prosperous career in a profession he loved.

It was a profession she'd loved too, once upon a time, before motherhood and marriage changed the course of her life. Newly qualified in catering, she'd been working in a busy hotel kitchen, when she'd fallen unexpectedly pregnant with Hannah. When she returned to work some years later, it was to a part-time office job more conducive to parenting, owing to its flexible working hours and proximity to home, for when Hannah came out of school. And that was where she'd stayed, quite contentedly, right up to her retirement.

There was the familiar clatter and snapping shut of the cat flap in the back door, as Monty returned from his evening constitutional. He was a stickler for routine: dinner was at six (fish cuts in jelly being the only acceptable meal choice), followed by a lengthy groom on the rug before a perambulation that usually saw him home by eight. He sauntered over to where she sat and jumped onto the neighbouring dining chair, offering her a friendly miaow which might have meant 'honey, I'm home,' but more likely meant 'fuss-time, thanking you kindly.'

Idly stroking Monty, she glanced back down at the photo. If things had been different, might she, too, have shaken the hands of revered fellow chefs in starched whites, having earned their mutual respect throughout an illustrious and successful career? Might she then have retired safe in the knowledge of her potential having been fully reached? As Geoff had, before it was cruelly severed short. And as her brilliant, clever daughter would one day too.

Perhaps it wasn't to be contemplated, the paths not

taken. If he hadn't worked a fifty-hour week for most of his working life, if she'd made him see the doctor about his heartburn.

Did anything good ever come from wondering, *what if?*

Monty, who always chose to sit upon a book, or an important document, rather than in the vacant space beside it, sprung onto the table and settled himself down upon their likenesses for a nice thorough lick of his undercarriage. His message seemed clear: so, what are you going to do about it then?

## Chapter Two

## *Hannah*

Before Alice was born, none of this would have been an issue. It would have been majorly *annoying*: who wants to be hauled into their boss's office at half past five on a Wednesday afternoon for a new client briefing? But it wouldn't have meant the difference between grabbing a precious hour with her daughter before putting her to bed or forcing her five-year-old into another late night because Mummy was delayed again. Five years ago, she had only her unwavering ambition to progress from associate solicitor to senior partner. Before she'd become a single mother.

If this was going to be a regular occurrence, she guessed she could sound out her mum on having Alice sleep over. It wasn't ideal, but surely better than the constant disruption to her routine, and far better for Alice to be looked after by her own grandmother than childminders or nannies, as would have been the case if she'd have stayed in London.

'Hannah, take a seat,' said Richard White, indicating the plush leather sofa in the corner of his office.

The offices of Tucker, Farraday & White were in the prestigious WC2 postcode of Westminster, an address easily reached on the District line from her former apartment in Fulham. A home that had also housed Darren, the husband who'd assured her, when they fell pregnant with Alice, that her career need never suffer. She'd barely been back from maternity leave when she discovered his first indiscretion. Now, her commute to north-west Essex took an hour and a half, door-to-door, on a good day.

'Bit of a juicy one for you here,' said Richard, twisting his laptop for her to see. 'Deceased hedge fund manager with a contentious will. Quite the kitty too. Client is one Caitlin Gallagher, you might have heard of her, one of those influencer types.'

When Hannah had chosen to specialise in wills and probate, she'd hoped it might offer a more interesting range than the work of her colleagues in property, or corporate law, for example. She hadn't been far wrong. It was simply astonishing, the skeletons that leapt from closets, once clients were in the ground.

Forty-five minutes later, Hannah left Richard's office with a groaning inbox of case files and dialled her mother's number as she marched down the street.

'Mum, sorry, got caught up. I'll be on a later train, is everything OK?'

'Not a problem, darling. We're both fine, aren't we, Alice?' Hannah heard her daughter call out 'Hello, Mummy' in the background. 'I'll plate you up a dinner, love. Take care.'

Hannah couldn't even remember the last time she'd cooked anything. A bacon sandwich maybe? Not that she was ungrateful, her mother's food was amazing, and Alice was well looked after. But, just for once, she'd love to be home in time to pick her up from school herself, take her home and spend time with her. Like her own mother had when she was little.

Clearly, it was too much to ask for a seat on the train, so Hannah crowbarred herself into a corner by the door, scowling at the guy who had abandoned a 100-litre backpack in the aisle for others to trip over before taking himself off for a nice sit-down. She glared at him across the carriage for a bit, then took out her phone and typed a message.

*Just checking you're still coming on Friday. Remember to collect Alice from Mum's house, not mine.*

Communicating with her ex-husband was never something she enjoyed, so it was just as well she was already in a sour mood.

A reply came back surprisingly quickly.

*I don't even know where you live, Hannah. And of course, I'm still coming.*

There was no 'of course' about it. This would be Darren's first night with Alice in nearly six weeks. Twice, he'd postponed, citing the 'stresses of moving house' as an excuse. Flaky tosser. He knew *nothing* about stress. The decisions he made daily were rarely tougher than whether a logo looked better in shades of blue or green. He had absolutely no idea how easy he had it, working from home and pissing about on Photoshop for a living. Granted, graphic design wasn't in her own particular skillset, but that was beside the point. As far as Hannah was concerned, this was it. If he bailed again, she'd see him in court.

The train rattled into a station, and she glanced up.

Tottenham Hale. Only a full eleven stops to go then . . . Marvellous.

But, in a stroke of luck, the exodus of four passengers, one of whom nearly fell through the doors when his foot caught in the giant rucksack, freed up a nearby seat. She slumped into it with the weariness of someone who'd known as she'd slipped on her four-inch Karen Millens this morning, there would be regrets. Tomorrow, she resolved, she'd become one of those commuters who changed their shoes when they left the office – it was time to embrace the skirt suit/white adidas combo.

She pulled out her laptop and angled it away from her fellow passengers before opening up the file on Caitlin Gallagher. It didn't take long to get the gist. Well-heeled Bronte Gallagher had been the sole heir to her father's considerable fortune, right up until lovechild Caitlin popped up six years ago and was now contesting the will. She'd worked on cases like this before, but never with such eye-watering sums of money involved, or such media attention. Using her phone as an internet hotspot, Hannah typed the sisters' names into Google, returning several pages of results for Caitlin Gallagher and numerous pictures of her playfully pouting for an Instagram account that professed to have over half a million followers. Bronte was a different kettle of fish. Her internet presence appeared to be limited to charity dinner appearances and an editorial feature for *Hello!* on the ghastly chrome and glass kitchen she'd apparently designed herself. She was the polar opposite of gregarious Caitlin: angular, haughty and oozing superiority. Hannah sighed and closed her laptop, too tired to delve into the case right now.

When the train pulled into Audley End, Hannah hopped off and paced towards her car. Lord knew how her father had found the energy to then cycle the last couple of miles home at the end of a long shift, but that's exactly what he'd done for over thirty years. The only thing that would stop him was snow on the ground in winter.

Driving through Saffron Walden, she ran through a mental checklist of chores to be crammed in before embracing the oblivion of sleep. There were the documents to be read before a 9 a.m., meeting tomorrow; she could do that on the train. There was Alice's reading book to check, a story before bed, the washing to fetch out of the tumble dryer and . . . *shit*. She'd forgotten to unload the washing machine last night. It hadn't even made it to the tumble dryer. It would have to be washed again. And the bread was stale – she couldn't give Alice mouldy sandwiches in her packed lunch tomorrow.

Wearily, she pulled into the parking bay of Allsave, which was more a legalised extortion store than one of any convenience, but she hadn't the stomach for Tesco.

It felt like being fifteen again, entering the shop. Except, instead of giggling in the aisles with her best mate Laura and stocking up on Pringles, she had a basket containing a sliced wholemeal loaf, a bottle of laundry detergent and two bananas.

'*Hannah Lawford?*' a voice said, emphasising both the Hannah and the Lawford.

The words cut through her dilemma over whether Alice would prefer ham or cheese in her sandwiches. It was entirely contradictory that it took ages to get used to a married name, but then just as long to revert to your family name again.

She spun around to see a woman she vaguely recognised. It took her a few moments to place her.

'Karen?' she ventured.

'Oh my God,' enthused Karen, who was sporting an unflatteringly severe bob. Unfortunate choice really, considering what her name had come to represent. 'I didn't know you were back here.'

'Yep. Just couldn't seem to stay away,' quipped Hannah, with really only the mildest trace of sarcasm. Barely noticeable. She schooled her mouth into a friendly smile and tried to forget how tired she was.

Had she been friendly with Karen? She might have been at a sleepover party with her once or twice, possibly a school trip. What was her last name? It totally escaped her. In the six months she'd been back here, this kind of encounter had become a surprisingly common event. Oh, for the anonymity of a noisy London suburb and the bountiful offerings of Deliveroo. In the old days she could have had her groceries delivered along with a poke bowl and a bottle of plonk without seeing a soul. This would just take a little getting used to, she supposed.

After the minimum of compulsory small talk, Hannah made her excuses, paid for her shopping, and got back in her car.

By the time she unlocked the front door to 11 Bridge Lane, her childhood home and pivot for everything in her life now, it was almost ten past eight.

The warm, chocolatey sound of her mother's voice drifted from the lounge at the end of the hall and halted

Hannah's trajectory to the kitchen, which was the usual hub of the 1930s' semi.

Hannah paused at the doorway, heart floating in affection at the sight of her daughter, all cosy under a blanket, her head on a cushion and her feet in Maggie's lap. As Maggie did the voice of the Gruffalo, Alice's nose crinkled in exactly the same way her grandmother's did when she laughed – they were like two different-sized peas in one very special pod.

Alice spotted her first.

'Mummy!'

'Hello, chicken. Have you been good for Granny?'

'She's been a delight, as ever,' said Maggie, removing her reading glasses and sliding out from under Alice's legs. She patted the space she'd just vacated. 'Sit yourself down and I'll fetch your dinner. It's chilli and rice, is that OK?'

'Sounds lovely, Mum.'

In truth, she'd gone past being hungry, as was so often the case these days. She was simply too tired to care much about food, but there would be no arguing with her mother, even if she'd had the energy. She kicked off her crippling shoes and reached across to run a hand through her daughter's silk-soft hair. 'How has your day been, sweetie?'

'We're learning about dinosaurs, and I made a gobblersaurus out of an egg box. I'm going to colour it in tomorrow. I think I'll do it . . . purple and red.'

'A gobblersaurus, huh? I'm not sure I've heard of one of those.'

Alice grinned. 'That's because I made it up. It's a bit like a stegosaurus, but instead of eating leaves it eats *absolutely* everything. Even poo. *And* belly button fluff.'

Maggie re-entered the room with a steaming hot plate and a tea towel for Hannah's lap. 'I could do with one of those gobblersauruses around here, save me putting the vacuum cleaner round. Honestly, it's a wonder Monty isn't bald as a coot, the amount of fur clogging up my Henry.'

Hannah gently lifted Alice's feet from her legs. 'Let Mummy just eat this then we'll get you home to bed.'

As the blanket moved, it became apparent Alice was already in pyjamas, cute white and yellow ones with a giraffe print all over. 'Where did you get these lovely jimjams?' she asked, knowing they weren't from home.

'Oh, I bought a couple of spare bits to keep here, just in case,' said Maggie, moving a crumpled magazine from an armchair and folding herself into it. 'I hope that's OK, love. And I popped Alice's uniform in the wash and got it dried, so it's all nice and fresh for tomorrow.'

If it wasn't for the food on her lap, Hannah could have sprung from her seat and hugged her mum. But if she'd done that, she might have cried. And if she cried, she might not stop.

Instead, she picked up her fork. 'You didn't have to, Mum. But thanks, that's really helpful.'

As the first mouthful of rich, spicy chilli exploded on her tongue, she decided she was hungry after all. 'This is delicious, Mum.'

'All Granny's dinners are delicious, Mummy, that's why she's going to get a job as a cook. Just like I said.'

Hannah glanced up and found Maggie watching her, with a self-satisfied, probing expression on her face. Hannah knew this look of old. It was the same look she'd had about her when she'd declared war on Malcolm and Sylvia Fields.

Not war, in the literal sense, but whatever the equivalent was in planning terms. Politely worded letters at dawn, perhaps. In her mother's mind, there had been no conceivable outcome that would have led to the erection of the two-storey, light-blocking monstrosity they'd proposed across the road, which wasn't so much an extension as an entombment. Hannah had scant knowledge of how the planning department of local council worked, but she did know that back in those days, just before she'd left for university, there had been a vigorous level of home baking each day. Diabetes-inducing quantities, in fact, for only the small customer services team Maggie worked in. Her mother was a woman whose wiles knew no bounds.

'Really, Mum?' she asked, unsure what to make of Alice's statement.

Maggie smiled like the cat who had got the cream. 'Really. I have decided I would like to get back into catering. I always wanted to run my own restaurant, back before you were born. Your dad was an executive chef, which was more about management than anything, brought into high-end kitchens to turn them around, whereas I always enjoyed the hands-on cooking. Now is precisely the right time to chase that dream. Not to *own* a restaurant, per-se. Well, not to start with anyway,' she chuckled.

'But—' began Hannah, promptly cut off before she could continue.

'But what? I've given it plenty of thought. Why would I go and volunteer at a charity shop, for example, when I have the skills to work in an industry I loved? I may have worked in admin for over half my life, but it was never really me. Not in the sense I could throw my heart and soul into the work.' She hitched forward in her seat. 'When I cook, Hannah, I feel *alive*.'

Hannah put down her fork.

'That's great, Mum, and you *are* a fantastic cook. Everyone thinks so. But have you thought about what sort of place you'd like to work in? I mean, are we talking one of the tearooms in town, for example? I could see you working in Mrs Pepperpot's Pantry, their scones are to die for, and you'd get to chat to so many people.'

Maggie shook off the suggestion, with a familiar and stubborn determination Hannah hadn't seen in her for some time. Not since losing her dad.

'That's not cooking. Besides, they buy all their cakes in, everyone knows it. No. I want to work in a proper kitchen, with a proper menu and the tummy-whooshing anticipation before service starts and then fifty covers flood into the pass.'

Hannah stared at her mother, incredulous. Had she lost her mind?

'You can't be serious. When have you ever worked anywhere like that?'

Her mother's eyes glittered with challenge. 'You'd be surprised. Have you forgotten where I met your father?'

'Where *did* you meet Grandad, Granny?' asked Alice, twirling her hair sleepily around her finger.

'They met at college, right?' Hannah picked up her fork and resumed eating.

'We did. I was on a two-year catering course, after passing my Domestic Science O Level. And your father, who already had an apprenticeship in a kitchen, was on day release. We were in the same classes on Tuesdays.'

'Did you and Grandad sit next to each other?' asked

Alice, yawning. She'd be overtired if Hannah didn't get her home soon. Then would come the tears. And almost certainly a night spent cramped into Alice's single bed, flat up against the wall, which would mean little sleep for her, and she *so* needed sleep.

Maggie smiled broadly. 'Sometimes. And sometimes we paired up for our practicals.'

'Ooh-er,' sniggered Hannah.

'You're far too intelligent for smut, dear, it doesn't suit you. But to cut a long story short, Grandad and I started dating. Then, when we finished college and got our catering qualifications, he continued with his classical training apprenticeship, and I began working in various London hotel kitchens as a junior chef. It turned out I was rather good at it.'

'And then did you and Grandad get married?' asked Alice, who was far more interested in the romance part of the story than the career Maggie was wistfully recalling. It occurred to Hannah then, these sorts of conversations were important, to help Alice to remember the grandad she'd had such precious little time with.

'Yes, sweetheart. We did. And then we had Mummy, and we moved here, to Saffron Walden, to be near to Grandad's family and lots of open space.' Maggie offered them both a tender smile. 'It was a lovely place to bring up a family, and Grandad could still get to work on the train. Mummy's grandparents loved spending time with her, just like me and Grandad Geoff did with you, darling, whenever you came to stay.'

Alice said to Hannah, 'And now you don't have a grandad anymore either, do you, Mummy? *Or* a daddy.'

Hannah's heart twinged at Alice's astute observation. 'No, darling, but I have lots and lots of lovely memories of our time together, just like you do. And I was a very lucky little girl, because my mummy was always there to look after me.'

Hannah gave her mum a grateful smile. If she was being honest, she'd never truly stopped to think about the adjustments Maggie had made for them. Had her mum really sacrificed her own dreams, so her dad could pursue his?

Those, Hannah suspected, were truths Maggie would never acknowledge. Certainly not out loud.

Hannah pondered her next words carefully. Didn't she owe it to her mum to champion her in the way Maggie always had with her? Would she have got to where she was now, without the unwavering belief her parents had in her that she could do anything she set her mind to?

'Mum,' she ventured. 'You know, if you're really serious about getting back into catering, let me help. With a bit of thought, we can create a CV to really emphasise the professional start you had in life, whilst playing up the decades of home catering experience you have. I don't know anyone who can feed a crowd as well as you can. That's all in your favour.' She found her stride, suddenly wanting to help. Maybe this wasn't a crazy idea after all. Her mum needed a sense of purpose again; this could well be it. 'And, if you want to get some more up-to-date experience, maybe I could get you a few practice shifts at Fiesta? You know, the Mexican place in town, Laura's husband's restaurant? I'm sure he'd be only too willing for an extra pair of hands, it could even be voluntary, if paying you was an issue. It's not like you need the money.'

She hoped she wasn't overstepping the mark here. Marco Garcia was a great guy and he'd do anything for Laura. Which, by extension, she hoped would include her, his wife's oldest friend.

Maggie's face was passive. A raised eyebrow and a twitch of the mouth acknowledged the suggestion, as if to say it wasn't a terrible idea. But with Mum, you could never tell.

Hannah yawned and pulled herself to standing, forcing her feet back into the hateful shoes. 'Let's talk about it again soon.'

'Leave that,' Maggie chided as she bent to pick up her plate from the coffee table. 'You both get yourselves home to bed. I've all the time in the world for dirty dishes.'

Alice's long, thick eyelashes fluttered briefly as Hannah scooped her off the sofa. She buried her face in her hair, which smelled of strawberry shampoo and something else that niggled nostalgically at her memory. Something wheaty . . . Playdough?

*I'm missing out on so much*, thought Hannah, picturing her mum making the homemade modelling material, and adding food colouring to the mix, just as they had done together when she had been Alice's age. But there was no use complaining; she'd just have to get on with it and be grateful she earned enough to provide them both with a nice home.

She kissed her mum goodnight and carried Alice to the car.

# Chapter Three

## Maggie

Sleep was no longer something Maggie seemed to need. Not in the quantity she'd enjoyed previously, when bedtime was something to be savoured. That precious time at the end of a long day when she would put down her book and switch off her light, Geoff climbing into bed beside her, smelling of toothpaste and Imperial Leather – the cooking smells of his day, scrubbed and showered away.

These days she woke frequently. Often by her bladder, one of later life's many irritations. She had reluctantly eliminated her bedtime cup of chamomile, to no avail. May as well chug it down regardless, she would only wake up anyway.

During the early hours of Friday morning, two days after declaring her intent to return to catering, Maggie had an idea. It began as no more than the seed of a thought, a vague notion that began to grow as dawn broke, flexing its fingers tantalisingly into the gap between her curtains. Maybe the time had come to stop licking her wounds. Maybe the time had come to act.

The bedside clock showed 5 a.m. Ten whole hours until she needed to collect Alice from school. Hadn't the Battle of Waterloo been fought and won in less? She threw back the covers decisively.

After a breakfast of toast and marmalade and an all-important cuppa, Maggie pulled on a lightweight jacket, gathered her shopping bags from the cupboard under the stairs and stepped out into the waking, spring warmth of a late May morning.

She chose to drive to the out-of-town supermarket, as there would be more than she could carry on foot. Later, when it opened, she'd walk to the butchers for the finest minced beef and lamb that money could buy. If she knew one thing when it came to taste, it was this: quality is paramount.

An hour later, she returned home with five bags of shopping and a large bunch of peonies which she arranged in a vase on the kitchen windowsill. The sight cheered her and spurred her on with the next stage of her plan, which involved sitting at the table with a strong coffee, a chocolate croissant and her laptop.

### Margaret Lawford – Curriculum Vitae

She typed the words in Times New Roman, then changed her mind.

Deleting her name, she retyped in Comic Sans.

### Maggie Lawford – CV

The last person to call her Margaret and been her Auntie Flo, twenty-five years previously. She wasn't answering to anything other than Maggie; may as well get that straight from the off.

It didn't take long. Forty-seven years of employment neatly wrapped up in just four or five jobs. She faltered at the part where a YouTube tutorial had indicated she list her hobbies; should she add something to make her sound terribly interesting, like Batik or Tango? Briefly, she indulged in a daydream that saw her tripping the light fantastic around a stainless-steel kitchen, as waiters in black tie twirled past brandishing her crème brûlée. Then sanity prevailed and she typed: travel, baking and the WI (Women's Institute).

At exactly 8.30 a.m., Maggie was first through the door of the butcher's. Juicy haunches of beef hung in the quaint shop window, tempting hungry shoppers as they passed by. She exchanged a good many English pounds with the butcher, for some fine, locally farmed meat, then popped into the greengrocers for vegetables and herbs the dear buyers at Tesco had clearly never heard of. Such a pity it wasn't market day, but when inspiration strikes, one simply has to act.

Her last stop was the library, where she hastily printed twenty copies of her brand-new CV and fielded questions from Pam, who was in there renewing her Danielle Steels. This was trickier than it should have been as she'd postponed their last coffee morning – OK, maybe she had postponed a few – and Pam had a considerable volume of gossip to impart.

Maggie shielded the printer and fibbed a bit, said she was running an urgent errand for Hannah. In a way, that was true. Why would she trouble her incredibly busy daughter with tasks she was perfectly capable of performing for herself? Not to mention that the idea of Hannah grovelling to her friend for trial shifts at Fiesta had given her the willies. She wasn't *quite* at the care in the community stage just yet, thank you very much.

Back home, she ransacked her cupboards for Pyrex dishes, saucepans, casseroles and baking trays. This wasn't hard; with a large extended family on Geoff's side, Maggie had been used to catering for a big crowd over the years and had amassed quite the kitchen arsenal.

Then, taking her apron from the hook on the back of the kitchen door, she fastened it with a decisive knot, and set to work.

After ninety minutes of peeling, slicing, chopping, frying, simmering and stirring, and a period of co-ordinated oven rotation, Maggie carefully retrieved three steaming shepherd's pies and four bubbling lasagnes from the oven. She covered them with clean tea towels and opened the window wide to clear the hot, steamy room.

There was just enough time for a freshen-up, whilst the food cooled.

After a quick wash, Maggie stood at the large triple wardrobe housing only her clothes, Geoff's having been relegated to a cupboard in the spare room until she had the stomach for it, and pondered which outfit might make the best impression. Should she choose the layered silk tunic she'd bought in Italy, throw on a pair of dangly earrings and exude bohemian vibes? Or perhaps a more formal approach was needed. After all, Maggie's planned excursion would be tantamount to a job interview. Maybe the green Hobbs dress she'd had for Geoff's retirement do? She delicately fingered the smooth viscose, memories surging through her like a sugar rush. *You look a million dollars tonight, Mags. I'm the luckiest guy in here.* She recalled how he'd found her hand and tugged her gently back towards him, before they'd taken their place at the table with the others. *I couldn't have gotten here without your support, and I can't wait to be retired with you. It's our time now, just you and me.* No, the green dress wasn't quite ready for another exciting outing.

Her gaze alighted on a practical garment she'd bought on a whim a few summers ago, one she had worn tirelessly on their campervan adventure due to its ability to make her feel thirty years younger. This, she decided, studying her reflection as she buttoned up the denim-blue chambray jumpsuit, was the Maggie she recognised of old. She teamed it with a pair of comfortable brown sandals and omitted any jewellery. You didn't wear trinkets in a hot, busy kitchen. You just got on with it.

There was one last thing to do. And it was here that Maggie threw up a silent prayer of thanks for the relentless merry-go-round of Tupperware parties she had been forced to endure in the eighties and nineties. Nobody warned you being a mother would mean endless and pointless guilt-purchases, every day of the week. If it wasn't school fundraisers, it was a Betterware party, or maybe The Pampered Chef. One friend might be doing Avon, another Oriflame. Occasionally someone with looser morals arranged an Ann Summers party instead, which spiced things up nicely. Maggie might have liked a speedy peeler as much as the next cook, but life was *so* much more fun when she got to watch Pam mime unthinkable acts with a banana. Well, she *would* gulp down those Cinzano and lemonades as though they were orange squash.

In all, she filled nineteen Tupperware containers with generous portions. There would have been twenty-four, a nice even number of each, but she was damned if she could find the missing lids and there wasn't time to spare. The shepherd's pie had come out particularly well, oozing rich, boozy gravy with every spoonful, the fragrant aroma of rosemary complimenting sweet shallots and roasted garlic. The King Edwards had mashed to perfection, the creamy, buttery topping having crisped beautifully in forked peaks.

A quick taste confirmed it was up to her usual standard. She only hoped everyone else thought so.

Typically, as often happens when time is in short supply, Maggie stepped from her front door clutching the heavy plastic laundry basket she'd called into service for transportation, her car key between her teeth, and walked straight into the path of Oscar.

'Let me help you with that, Maggie,' he said, dropping his own belongings to the pavement and wrestling the basket from her before she could object.

Fortunately, she'd placed a towel on top or he'd be wanting to know the ins and outs of a gnat's wotsit, as well as where she was going with nineteen Tupperware containers of food. Perennially cheerful, Oscar was perfectly harmless – endearing, one might say, in his own inimitable way – but with the best will in the world, there simply wasn't time for a casual neighbourly chat.

'Blimey. What you got in here then? Severed limbs?' he laughed raucously at his own joke.

'Got it in one, Oscar. Best keep your wits about you.' Maggie zapped her car key and opened the door, standing back so Oscar could get to the back seat of the small hatchback she now drove, since trading in Geoff's Nissan X-Trail. As he leaned across, she was treated to an insufficiently covered Lycra-clad behind. Not quite *all* bottoms are lovely, perhaps.

'You always have been funny, Maggie,' he said, grinning widely. 'How have you been keeping?'

*Oh, for goodness sakes, not now!*

'Very well, thank you, Oscar. The little one keeps me on my toes. Incidentally, must dash – there's somewhere I need to be.'

She slid into the driver's seat, as Oscar bent down to pick up what she now saw was a rolled-up foam mat.

'Me too,' he chirped. 'Yoga for the over-sixties at the community centre.' And then, quite unnecessarily, he performed a daring, and rather wobbly lunge, as though Maggie had no idea what yoga was and needed a visual clue. 'You should come along some time. You'd be home in plenty of time for the school run.'

'I'll bear that in mind. Lovely seeing you,' she called out, pulling the car door shut. *And I'd rather that laundry basket contained my own severed limbs than be around a bunch of old duffers like you, all grunting, groaning and farting*, she decided.

Parking in the town centre was always a challenge and today was no different. But maybe someone was looking down on her, because just as she debated ditching on a double yellow line, a space just big enough for her small Peugeot appeared ahead.

She had timed it perfectly. It was 1 p.m. on a Friday lunchtime, and each one of the establishments on her hit list should be rushed off their feet. Precisely the right time, she predicted, when busy owners with pound signs in their eyes might consider taking on extra help.

First up was Maison Rose, a boutique establishment serving modern cuisine with a continental bent. She retrieved one of her CVs from a plastic sleeve and a sample of each of her dishes, which she placed into a brown paper bag for maximum professionalism, then made a beeline for the restaurant.

Inside, at least half the tables were occupied, with customers waiting to be seated. Maggie waited patiently in line, until the server approached, a youthful beauty who appeared to have been vacuum-packed into her revealing blouse and leggings like a sous vide duck.

'Hi,' pre-empted Maggie before the server could deliver her welcome spiel. 'I would like to speak with the manager please, or, indeed, the chef?'

The server looked back at her blankly, before shaking off her confusion with a smile.

'I'm so sorry, but we're rather busy at the moment. Maybe come back a little later after the lunchtime rush?'

Maggie matched her smile. 'It's OK, I won't take up any more than a couple of moments. It might well be worth their while.'

'Is this about last Wednesday?' asked the young woman cautiously.

'No idea what you mean.'

*Last Wednesday?* Maggie had noticed her memory wasn't quite what it was, but she was pretty sure she would have remembered a dinner to set her back just shy of a hundred pounds.

'The lawn bowls luncheon?' the server narrowed her eyes. 'Weren't you the lady with the . . .' her voice lowered to a whisper, '. . . the fishcake issue? Because we can assure you it won't happen again. In fact, we've taken them off the menu. And you *were* partially refunded.'

Maggie wanted to be outraged that she looked as though she filled her days playing lawn bowls, but her brain had lodged on the words 'fishcake issue'. Could it be that all was not well in the kitchens of Maison Rose?

'I'm afraid that wasn't me, no. I'm here on other business. *Official* business,' she added for good measure. That should get the management's attention.

Sure enough, the server whisked Maggie into the restaurant and deposited her to a row of stools at a polished walnut bar, then, ignoring the puzzled expression of the bartender, nipped behind and mumbled into an intercom. Maggie looked to a waiting couple in the queue and offered them a 'you just can't get the staff' shrug.

It was a matter of seconds before an achingly attractive young man with jet-black hair and facial stubble in a three-piece suit appeared at her side.

'Madam?' he enquired, getting straight to business. 'Jacob Green. Restaurant owner. How can I help?'

Maggie felt her resolve begin to trickle away. Jacob had the kind of piercing grey eyes that shot straight to the heart (or groin, depending on personal preference), a predatoriness which, for a younger woman, might have been flattering. Personally, she'd always preferred the cheerful, openness of Geoff's ruddy, bearded face to any brooding Don Juan types. A chiselled jaw was seldom to be trusted.

'Pleased to meet you Jacob, I'm Maggie,' she said, thrusting out her hand. When he shook it, she realised his soft pampered skin had never seen a hot griddle in its life. 'And I'm hopeful it might be *I*, who can offer some help to *you*.' She reached into her bag for the CV and was embarrassed to find her fingers trembled as she passed it to him. 'I'm a qualified chef, looking for a new position in a professional kitchen. I'm fully trained in knife skills, butchery and pastry, with something not many of your younger applicants might have in abundance – almost five decades of catering experience.'

Satisfied she'd delivered her speech without stumbling over her words, she waited as he skimmed the page, heart slowly sinking as she registered a hint of amusement creep across his features.

He gave a slight shake of the head.

'Wow. I mean, this is all awesome stuff. And I'm just so flattered you thought to try Maison Rose, but unfortunately,' he waved an expansive hand as he spoke, 'we're fully staffed at the moment. But I'll certainly keep your details on file, if that's OK? Should anything crop up.'

Maggie felt the heat of an embarrassed flush creep up from the collar of her jumpsuit. A sensation she hadn't felt for more years than she cared to recall.

'Of course, I understand. Oh, I almost forgot. This is for you.'

Maggie handed him the brown paper bag and watched as he peered in, confusion crumpling his brow.

'Sorry, what is this?' he asked.

'Samples, for you to try,' said Maggie, immediately wishing she had just thanked him and left.

'Samples?' he asked with trepidation, as though she'd just handed him several plastic pots of wee.

'Of my food. There's a portion of my top-secret shepherd's pie recipe and my family's favourite lasagne, although, of course, I can adapt to most menus. But generally, I find good old comfort food tends to be the best way to . . .' she trailed off. She had been about to say to a man's heart, and she'd been thinking of Geoff. Of the excited way he'd clap his hands together when he'd enter the kitchen and smell something delicious bubbling in the oven. 'The proof is always in the pudding, I find.'

'I see,' said Jacob, his eyes sliding from hers to those of the bartender. 'That's very, er, forward thinking of you. Thank you,' he said, before handing her back the bag. 'I'm sure the food is delicious, but I'm afraid I'm unable to accept it. Company policy.'

'Right, well, thank you for your time,' said Maggie, sliding from the bar stool, aware something in the air had shifted; that most probably, she was being mocked.

She began to move away, then turned back just in time to catch Jacob twirling a finger at his temple, indicating to his employee this granny was batshit crazy.

Momentarily she was transported to another time and place, to others who had undermined and underestimated her. If only she had known then what she knew now, after sixty-five years of lived experience. But these were different times.

With a magnificent smile, she said, loud enough for

the closest diners to hear, 'I do hope you iron out your fishcake problem, such a shame to lose them from the menu. The secret is to cook the fish and seafood first, before you pan-fry them. The only time you want to be eating raw fish is when you're enjoying sushi, but I'm sure your chef knows that. Toodle-pip.'

Outside, Maggie allowed herself a brief chuckle, before making her way back to her car. Next on her list were Giovanni's (Italian), The White Lion (traditional pub grub), and Cheese & Cheer (trendy new bistro). She would make a point of avoiding Fiesta, if only because Hannah might be upset to find she went to her friend's restaurant without her.

This time, when she pushed open the door of Giovanni's, she tried a different tack.

'Hi,' she said to the approaching teen – why were all the staff barely out of nappies? 'I'm looking to get back into work after a year of travelling,' that was what the youngsters did these days, wasn't it? Went off to *find* themselves before knuckling down? Well, she'd just done it in reverse, and the only thing she'd found was that no mattress was as good as your own, and in Aruba they ate Dutch cheese, a bonus since Gouda was her weak spot. After all, she'd already had everything else in the world she had ever needed. 'I realise you might not be hiring right now, but I'd like to leave some complimentary samples of my work and my resumé for your chef's attention?' *Oh, that sounded good.* Far more professional – Hannah would be proud.

The young woman fluttered her voluminous lashes and Maggie swore she felt a breeze.

'Uh, I know we're recruiting for a pot washer?' she said, her voice going up at the end of each sentence as though *she* were asking Maggie. 'I think interviews are taking place on Monday? I could pass on your details to my manager if you'd like to be considered?'

Interviews, for a pot washer? Maggie struggled to keep the surprise from her face.

'It's more the catering side I'm interested in.'

'Sure,' said the girl, unphased. 'Sorry we couldn't help. Openings just don't come up very often I'm afraid, but I can take your CV just in case?'

Maggie left Giovanni's and tried to push down her disappointment. There were plenty more establishments to try, and perhaps she would have more luck in a good old-fashioned pub.

She checked the time; another hour and a half before Alice would need collecting from school. Perfectly doable. Darn it, she had promised Alice they'd make jam tarts today and she'd used up all the butter, she'd have to buy some more. This kind of multi-tasking would become perfectly normal, she told herself, once she'd gone back into work. Although she was starting to wonder if getting any kind of job might be harder than she'd first envisaged.

# Chapter Four

## Maggie

There had been a well-used motto in the Imperial Hotel kitchens, circa 1997, repeated by Chef as frequently as he tossed his hot saucepans and playfully thwacked Maggie's backside with the tea towel: do it right or do it twice.

It drifted back to her as she watched Alice at work with sticky fingers and the concentration of a surgeon. These tarts wouldn't be perfect, indeed some of them resembled roadkill, but they would taste like heaven, for they had been made with love, and lashings of strawberry jam.

Fresh from polytechnic with her City & Guilds in Catering, there had been one particularly gruelling shift when Maggie was made to bin seven platters of prawn vol-au-vents and start again from scratch because her sauce hadn't been 'quite the right shade of pink'. One learns from one's mistakes – and today she had learned a new lesson. In forty-seven years, everything, and nothing, had changed in the world of catering.

What was it Baz, landlord of The White Lion, had said,

with a condescending sneer? 'You should try the day centre, love. The old folks there will lap up your "special shepherd's pie".'

She'd treated him to a megawatt smile (greatly enhanced by her recently whitened denture) and wished him a pleasant day. The same smile she had flashed almost five decades ago after one bottom-whip too far, before suggesting Chef stick his job somewhere he'd have to retrieve later with buffet tongs. As she recalled, her and Geoff had celebrated the occasion with a trip to the pictures that evening. Fortunately, Baz hadn't been hiring, or she suspects a similar denouement may have been on the cards.

This had been a disappointing discovery. There simply weren't many jobs. And even if there were, nobody was interested unless you could fillet a seabass with one hand and mop the floor with the other, all whilst filming it for social mania, as Geoff had called it. In her day, just as in Hannah's, when her daughter had earned her first wage washing dirty plates in Piccolo's, you hadn't needed a marketing degree, simply to enter the kitchen.

'Granny, are we having a party?'

Maggie looked to her granddaughter, whose enormous blue-grey eyes were studying her suspiciously.

'No, sweetheart, why?'

'You've made *millions* of jam tarts. I don't know *exactly* how many because I can only count to thirty in my head.'

'Oh sh – ugar.'

Maggie swept up the pile of circles that had been steadily accumulating as she'd stabbed them out with her pastry cutter. 'Silly Granny,' she said, squashing them into a ball and re-rolling the pastry. 'I got a bit carried away. I'll make a pie for Mummy to take home with what's left over.'

A key sounded in the lock, followed by the click clack of heels in the hallway, announcing Hannah was home from work.

'Mummy! I'm making jam tarts.'

'Hello, darling. Hi, Mum.' Hannah swooped in to plant a kiss on her daughter's rosy cheek before heading straight to the cupboard for a wine glass and pouring a generous glug of Sauvignon Blanc from the fridge.

'Bad day?' asked Maggie, resisting the urge to comment on her daughter's apparent thirst; the poor love looked exhausted.

'*Long* day.' Hannah delivered her response between sips. 'Packed train. Wedged between two sweaty bankers all the way from Liverpool Street. And then I drove my car from the station with a pizza-delivery flyer flapping around under my windscreen wiper. Imbeciles. Out-of-town takeaway, otherwise I'd be giving them a piece of my mind.'

A narrow escape indeed, decided Maggie, taking the tray of tarts from a kitchen table that had seen three generations of delicious culinary industry, and sliding them into the hot oven.

'Granny had a bad day too,' piped up Alice.

'Oh? *Bargain Hunt* finished, has it?'

Maybe Hannah spotted the trace of hurt pass briefly across her mother's face, because she sighed and put down her glass. 'Sorry, Mum. Come on, tell me about your day.'

But before Maggie could speak, Alice helpfully explained: 'Granny cooked lots of food and took it to people. But they were all ungrateful bar stewards and didn't want to try it. What's a bar steward, Mummy?'

Maggie coughed loudly, gathering up utensils to load into the dishwasher.

'Just someone who serves drinks,' said Hannah through gritted teeth. She was at Maggie's side in one stride. 'What have you been up to? And what on *earth* have you been doing with all this Tupperware?'

Bugger. It was useless hiding it now. She'd forgotten the dishwasher was rammed full of it. All that time and food, wasted. All gone in the bin.

Maggie tucked a loose silvery strand behind her ear and swallowed down her wounded pride.

'I took matters into my own hands, Hannie. All your talk about practice shifts and helping me do a CV. I worked for the council for thirty-odd years, what did you think I've been doing all that time? Shouting down a tin can tied with string? Sending messages in Morse code? I typed up my CV on the laptop, printed it off at the library, then visited a selection of Saffron Walden's eateries with samples of my tastiest dishes. What could be better than putting your money where your mouth is and *showing* what you can do?'

Hannah looked incredulous and opened her mouth to speak, then closed it again. Eventually she blew out her cheeks. 'I'm guessing it didn't go to plan?'

'Let's just say it's become clear the ability to cook is now a second-rate requirement. I'm not twenty-three with sketched-on-eyebrows and a "TikTok following", ergo I'm invisible. At least that's what the gentleman with a bun atop his head in Zen Lounge implied.'

'Zen Lounge? Isn't that the new veggie place?'

'So it would seem. Honestly, everything these days is vegan, gastric, or orgasmic—'

'It's gastro, Mum, I'd be miffed if I'd paid for something that gave me gastric. And I *know* you know it's organic . . .'

'Don't split hairs, Hannah, and believe me, when you get to my age, food jolly well should bring you pleasure – there's precious little else.'

Hannah gestured wildly at the back of her daughter's head to remind Maggie who was listening, just as the doorbell chimed, sending its metallic trill echoing along the parqueted hallway.

Maggie set down her tea towel to answer the front door, still thinking about the establishments she'd called on today. Even the humble beefburger on the bar snack menu in Cheese & Cheer had been skewered into brioche and tarted up with nonsense like goat's cheese and baconnaise. What was wrong with a slice of cheddar and a dash of tommy sauce, for heaven's sake.

When Darren followed her back to the kitchen, Monty, who had been preening himself upon the ancient, unused Aga, bolted in a black and white blur across the room to wind his way protectively around Hannah's legs.

'Phantom still hates me I see,' said Darren.

'He's not called Phantom anymore, silly,' supplied Alice.

'No? Since when?'

'Since Mum adopted her irritating habit of shortening names and adding a 'y'. Not the best look when your elderly mother stands on her doorstep calling Phanny home,' Hannah said, gathering up Alice's schoolbag, overnight bag, coat and shoes.

'You do exaggerate,' tsked Maggie.

'Really? Then why do you insist on calling me Hannie, even though you know I hate it?'

'I gave birth to you, darling. I have inventor's rights. Besides, it's only a sign of affection.'

'I don't remember you ever shortening my name, Maggie,' said Darren.

Maggie turned her back on him so he wouldn't see her grimace. 'No, funny that.'

Oblivious, Darren asked, 'What's it called now then? The cat?'

'Monty Don was doing something wild with wisteria at the time on *Gardeners' World*, so we went with that. I'd only had him a few weeks, so I'm sure he didn't mind,' answered Maggie, though in truth *she'd* minded. He definitely resembled Michael Crawford with that white patch across his face.

'He's called Wisteria? Cool.'

*What the devil did my daughter ever see in this twerp?*

Somehow, Maggie refrained from voicing her thoughts.

'No, Daddy,' giggled Alice, impervious. 'He's called Monty.'

Whilst Hannah helped Alice to wash her hands, Maggie retrieved the cooked tarts from the oven, flooding the kitchen with an intoxicating aroma. Then she wrapped some up in tin foil, found the only clean Tupperware container left in the house and handed it to Darren. 'A gift, from your daughter,' she said sniffily.

Five minutes later, with a final 'Be good for Daddy,' Maggie heard the front door close, before Hannah returned.

'I was going to make a pie for your dinner,' she said, from where she sat at the table, disheartened from the day's events. She jerked her head towards the abandoned rolled out pastry. 'What do you fancy, chicken and leek?'

There was a long pause.

Had she upset her by steaming ahead to seek work by herself? She suspected her daughter often found her difficult, which wasn't a pleasing thought. She loved Hannah beyond measure and only ever wanted to be a help, not a hindrance, in her busy, stressful life.

'Do you know what I fancy?' said Hannah at length.

Maggie looked up.

'A curry. Let's go to The Golden Crocus and make the most of Darren having Alice tonight. After all, it could be weeks until he makes a reappearance.'

The Golden Crocus. One restaurant she *hadn't* visited today in her quest to find employment, partly because she had nothing of value to offer towards Raj and Gita's sensational culinary repertoire, and partly because she wondered if simply crossing the threshold would bring back memories too painful to bear.

'I don't know, Hannie,' she began, before adding, 'you must be tired. Don't you want to get off home?'

Much easier to divert attention away from herself.

Hannah, shrewd as ever, was having none of it.

'If Dad was here, he'd be grabbing his jacket faster than you can say chicken biryani and a garlic naan.'

At the mention of Geoff's favourite dishes, a smile tugged on Maggie's lips.

'Well,' she ventured, 'perhaps by the time I've fried the chicken off, it might be getting on a bit.'

Hannah patted her mum's hand. 'Go and put some lippy on.'

It was approaching 7.30 p.m. when Maggie and Hannah, who was still in her work clothes, strolled down into the high street. Such a pretty part of the medieval town, where timber-built cottages huddled together, and their lime-plastered walls, in fruity pastel shades, glowed in the evening sun.

'Do you miss London terribly?' Maggie asked her daughter.

'Sometimes. It's a bit weird, bumping into people from school whenever I pop to the shops. But there are worse places to live and I'm so grateful Alice has you. We both are, what would we do without you?'

Maggie hooked an arm through Hannah's. 'We're lucky to have each other.'

Having the pair of them around the corner had been her lifeline this last year. Perhaps, in a way, she'd been Hannah's too. Yet she knew she still had more to offer, *more* she could do.

When they reached the corner of Queen Street, where the Indian restaurant occupied prime position in a Grade II listed building, they stood and took it in.

'Could do with a lick of paint,' commented Hannah.

She wasn't wrong. In the thirty-five or so years she and Geoff had frequented it, the place had never looked so tired. Perhaps Raj and Gita were beginning to struggle with the day-to-day upkeep. This pricked at Maggie's conscience. Gita was a friend. She should have looked in on her before now.

Bolstering herself for a tsunami of memories, she stepped through the flaking door held open by Hannah.

But rather than sprightly Raj, with his cheeky banter and trademark red waistcoat, they were approached by a gangly teenager sporting a full, curly mullet that Maggie was sure had gone out of vogue in the nineties.

'Have you boo ataybbl?' he asked, his words trailing off inaudibly.

Maggie blinked and looked to Hannah. The boy looked at the floor.

'Sorry, I didn't catch that?' said Hannah.

'Have you, um, booked a table, with us tonight?' he repeated, exerting a fraction more effort to enunciate his words and revealing a set of shiny braces on his teeth.

'No, sorry, we haven't,' said Hannah. 'Is that a problem?'

Maggie did a quick sweep of the room; Roger and Sandy Beresford over by the window, she gave them a brief nod. A large group of yummy mummies wading noisily through a gallon of Prosecco – was that Samira from work? She'd pop over to say hello later, such a lovely girl. Otherwise, it was empty. And there, at the back in the corner, was *their* table. Hers and Geoff's. Vacant.

'We'll take the table over there,' she said, shimmying past the boy and leaving Hannah in her wake.

For donkey's years the tables had been covered in ruby red linen and laid with starched white napkins. Now, the tables were bare, exposing years of scratched veneer.

'Could do with a spot of beeswax,' noted Maggie, checking her sleeves for grime.

'Perhaps they're going for a modern feel?' offered Hannah, taking a laminated card from between the salt and pepper grinders. 'Oh, hello. The menu's changed as well.'

'Really?' Maggie dipped into her bag for her reading glasses and took one for herself. 'Sirloin steak? Chicken kyiv? But where's the curry? I was having a lamb balti!'

Hannah frowned and rubbed her eyes, a sign Maggie knew from experience meant she was running on fumes, and her heart contracted. Even as a child, she'd always refused to give in, always wringing that little bit more out of a game, a toy, a day.

'No, here you go, over the page. Chicken korma, chicken tikka masala or vegetable bhuna.'

'No lamb?' Maggie studied the plasticky sheet, aghast. 'No samosas?'

'Ladies!' came a familiar baritone, prompting them both to look up. But the voice did not, as Maggie expected, belong to Raj.

'Sav!' exclaimed Hannah. 'What a nice surprise, didn't I see on Facebook you're doing something important with cyber-security these days?'

He'd altered since Maggie had last seen him, which had to have been, gosh, nearly twenty years ago, possibly longer? Now, he was a thirty-eight-year-old man, the same age as Hannah. Raj and Gita had regularly spoken of their only son with pride, a sentiment Maggie had reciprocated.

'Usually, yes. But I'm on an unexpected sabbatical at present,' he said, brown eyes twinkling, just like his dad's.

'Are your parents out back?' asked Maggie, though she was getting the distinct feeling she already knew the answer.

'New Delhi. Went back for my aunt's funeral, then Mum

had a fall, broke her hip,' he winced. 'She's just had surgery but it's a lengthy rehabilitation, so they're stuck there for a bit. I've stepped in to help out. Can't let the family business down, can I?' he said, as one of the squiffy women called out, 'Excuse me, we've been waiting ages!'

Sav began to move away. 'I'll take your order in a tick.'

Seated at the rear of the restaurant, they were adjacent to the swing door leading to the busy kitchen. On many an evening gone by, once service had finished, Raj and Gita would emerge with coffee and Gita's sublime Nankhatai biscuits, to join Maggie and Geoff for a chat among friends. Maggie had often tried, and failed, to wrangle the recipe out of Gita for the butter-rich cardamom cookies, but it remained her closely guarded secret. Today, however, they were privy to the sound of something heavy clattering to the floor within, followed by a steady stream of expletives.

The mumbling adolescent loped past carrying two full plates of food and headed *into* the kitchen, which was never a good sign. Further expletives ensued.

'Hmm, I'm not sure Jamie Oliver will be popping back anytime soon,' said Maggie, jerking her head to the elaborately framed picture upon the wall. Sandwiched between a proudly, beaming Raj and a clearly smitten Gita, was the man himself.

'I don't think that's on the cards anyway. He was only seen in here once.'

'That's not what Raj told your dad. Apparently, Jamie said it was the best Indian food in the area, visited regularly.'

'Perhaps that was before he became a multi-millionaire

and one of Britain's best-known chefs. Honestly, anyone would think you knew him personally, just because he grew up round here.'

'Actually, I corresponded with his parents once. Replacement wheelie bin.'

Sav whizzed back past like a typhoon, joining the commotion in the kitchen. There followed something that sounded a bit like a sob, and the plaintive cry of 'I can't do it'. The group of women, who should have known better, commenced an off-key rendition of 'Why Are We Waiting', and then a smoke alarm joined in.

Perhaps it was the knee-jerk reaction of a mother sensing a floundering child within her midst, or perhaps she was just being nosy. Whatever the reason, Maggie Lawford pushed back her chair, and to exclamations of 'Mum? Where are you going?' she crossed the room and elbowed her way through the swing door marked 'Private – Staff Only'.

# Chapter Five

## Hannah

Hannah stared at the door as it swung closed.

Five seconds later the alarm stopped wailing, along with the caterwauling. The room was plunged briefly into silence, until a guffawing snort that morphed into hiccups, shattered it. Now she thought of it, where was the music? Didn't restaurants normally have ambient background music to create atmosphere and warmth?

She looked at the group of women. Proportionally speaking, there was a very strong contingent of ditsy print dresses and denim jackets. It had been the spring/summer uniform for untold generations of women, evolving over time from burlap to rayon, from polyester to viscose and full circle to organic Fairtrade cotton (the jacket occasionally supplanted for a button-up cardigan). This entire table could be a poster advert for White Stuff. All that was missing from the scene was an allotment, a bicycle and a wicker basket of everyday essentials: artisan bread, charcuterie and a bunch of bluebells. If Hannah hadn't moved to London, she may well have been seated among them, but as it was, her mother knew more of the mums than she ever would through being there at the school gate. Her only real friend in the area was Laura Garcia.

At the thought of Alice, she reached instinctively for her phone. Darren had recently moved to Hertfordshire, to be closer to his family apparently, or, perhaps to her. It wasn't far, just thirty minutes by car, but it was far enough away for her to feel an underlying anxiety. What if something happened? What if Alice got upset and wanted to come home? She didn't think it likely, as Alice had been excited about seeing her dad's new house. Thankfully she was blissfully unaware he was a complete and utter dick, who had put said straying appendage before either of them at least twice before, that she knew of. There were no messages, no missed calls. She'd have to trust all was well. Besides, if he bothered to stick to the new arrangement, she'd have to get used to this.

Five minutes passed as she sat there feeling awkward. What was her mother *doing* in there?

And what would Sav think at her barging in like that? It was Jessica Holt's ninth birthday party all over again. Didn't Mum realise that just because you could, didn't mean you should? How was she to know Jessica's mother hadn't intended to serve burnt pizza all those years ago? Perhaps in their house, they *liked* burnt pizza, had happily embraced all known carcinogens in a blatant two-fingered revolt against science.

It had been so weird seeing Sav again, for the first time in what? Twenty years? No, it was slightly more recently than that. He'd been in the pub one Christmas

Eve when she'd been home from university. But *hell*, had he changed.

When she'd last seen him, he'd been just as gawky and wiry as ever. Arms too long for their sleeves and trousers three inches above the shoes. His ears had always stuck out a fraction, emphasised by the thick crop of hair cut too short at the sides. But his smile was infectious, a toothy, cheeky grin that sparkled in his eyes.

Now, his shapely jaw was covered in thick stubble. His clothes, head-to-toe black, were well fitting, and his hair had grown wavy, curling at the nape of his neck. Today his smile hadn't *quite* reached his eyes, despite his obvious delight at them being here. He'd looked a little bit stressed, which was understandable under the circumstances.

Breathing in a sigh of resignation, Hannah got up from her seat. She crossed to the kitchen door and pushed on it a fraction.

The scene inside the kitchen resembled a cross between animated children's movie *Ratatouille*, and cult horror classic *The Texas Chainsaw Massacre*. A large, grown man in crimson-splattered chef's whites, who looked decidedly familiar, stood with his face in his hands, whilst Sav crouched on the floor trying to ladle puddles of gloopy sauce back into a dropped pan. The awkward teen was drying a stack of plates and Maggie was stationed at a chopping board, sleeves rolled up to the elbows, slicing white onions.

'Ah, Hannah. Make yourself useful and wash up the pan in the sink, would you?'

Hannah blinked, unsure if she'd heard correctly.

'Chop, chop,' said Maggie, tapping the blade on the

57

board in emphasis. 'Now – Ben – wasn't it, dear?' she enquired of the boy.

He nodded mutely, his impressive flop of eyebrow-skimming dark curls bouncing to attention.

'Sav will give you twenty pounds.' She turned to Sav. 'You have some cash I presume?' He patted his pocket, pulled out a wallet and extracted a crisp note. 'Good. Ben, take this and slip through the back door. Run to Allsave and purchase four jars of tikka masala sauce. Best quality brand they have, understood?'

Ben nodded again, this time seeming vaguely bemused. 'Yep. Got it.'

'Quick as you can.'

Hannah watched as the lad bolted out the back, faster than she'd have imagined possible just ten minutes earlier.

'Joe, love. Do you have poppadums, bhajis, pakoras? Anything at all we can give the ladies as an appetiser?'

The chef withdrew his hands from his bearded face and Hannah realised it *was* someone she knew, Sav's best friend from school – Joe Butler. This was turning into a real blast from the past.

He gave a miserable shake of his head.

Sav began to explain. 'We didn't imagine the whole group would order Indian food. We sold out earlier. There's garlic bread though. And plenty of mushroom pâté.'

Hannah let out a snort of incredulity. 'This is an Indian restaurant! *Of course,* they're ordering Indian food. *We* wanted Indian food.' She muttered under her breath, 'Doesn't look like *that's* happening now.'

Maggie shot her a look, one that when she was a child would have meant *Do I have to come over there and make you?* and so she reluctantly trotted to the sink and picked up the filthy, oily pan with thumbs and forefingers. Her shirt was going to get ruined.

As soon as the pan was scrubbed clean, she passed it to Maggie who plopped it straight over an open flame and began frying the onions.

Then something seemed to click inside Joe, and his demeanour changed. 'I'll get the chicken,' he said, heading over to the tall fridge.

'We have lots of pistachio nuts,' Sav suddenly remembered. 'Sacksful, God knows what Mum did with them.'

'Excellent,' said Maggie. 'Hannah, would you help Sav find some suitable receptacles for the nuts and, I'd suggest, perhaps a bottle of something on the house.'

Sav grimaced.

'This is now about saving your reputation, rather than enjoying a profitable night. I don't know much about social media, but I counted fourteen women out there and I can't imagine it will be a good thing for The Golden Crocus if they leave here unfed. Got the chicken, Joe? Excellent now get it sliced and into the pan then crack on with the sirloins. And get that pan of korma heated back up, add water if it's grown too thick.'

Hannah loaded a tray with the dishes of nuts, all the while marvelling at her unflappable mother. She'd somehow taken control of a scene of total chaos, where even the head chef seemed to have forgotten his own name.

Plastering the look she reserved for her most troublesome clients on her face, Hannah stepped back into the restaurant and approached the long table of women.

'Chef sends sincere apologies for the minor delay with your food. Your main courses will be with you shortly, but in the meantime, please enjoy these complimentary pistachio nuts.'

You can often tell a ringleader, simply by the way others look to them for guidance. In this case, Hannah spotted three sets of eyes all slide to a horsey-looking woman with corkscrew curls. She also clocked a pretty girl she thought might have worked with her mum – what she'd give for hair so lustrous and straight. Her own thick brown locks were usually scraped back into a ponytail for a smart, easy maintenance hairstyle. Wearing her hair like this gave her one less thing to think about, the finding of clean knickers and unladdered tights (for herself as well as Alice) being quite taxing enough of a morning.

'Nuts?' repeated the horsey woman. 'We've been waiting for,' she checked her phone screen, 'well over an hour. It might take more than a few *nuts*.'

At that very moment, Sav arrived with not one, but two chilled bottles of Prosecco, which he ceremoniously uncorked before topping up glasses. 'Terribly sorry about the delay, ladies. Electrical fault in the kitchen, all sorted now. We'll have you fed in no time. Fizz is on the house, of course.'

There were several loud whoops.

'And the bottles we've already drunk?' asked horsey.

Sav looked to the four empty bottles and true to a fault, he mimed being stabbed in the heart.

'Ladies. You're killing me.'

One of the women giggled and another looked him up and down.

*They fancy him.* He'd get away with anything, if he really laid on the charm. She could even see why, which irritated her. Why did she care, all these years later?

As they moved away from the table, Hannah pulled Sav aside and whispered, 'It's like a morgue in here, can't you put some background music on?'

Sav stared at her as though she'd just explained the laws of gravity.

'I *knew* there was something missing. Leave it with me.'

Back in the kitchen, Ben had arrived with four jars of Patak's sauce, which were now simmering with the chicken and onions. A steak was resting on a board, another was on the griddle, chips were fizzing in the fryer, halloumi and aubergine skewers were browning under the grill and there were saucepans of rice and vegetables on the stove.

'Let's start plating,' said Maggie.

Joe drained and sieved the rice and passed it to Maggie, who used a teacup to mould it into sophisticated mounds on the plates. She sprinkled chopped coriander for decoration then spooned on the curries. Meanwhile, Joe began plating the eye-wateringly juicy-looking steaks, with mushrooms, tomatoes, onion rings and chunky chips.

'Service,' Maggie called.

Although, to whom, it was hard to tell.

'That means you, young man,' said Maggie to Ben, who was doing his best to shrink into the corner. 'The plates are warm, so use a clean tea towel, Hannah will help.'

*Will she indeed*, thought Hannah, although secretly she was now invested in wanting to wipe the sneer from horsey's face, and the food looked good. Even if some of it was out of a jar.

Within minutes, fourteen hot dinners had been delivered to the table and the sound of generic instrumental music drifted from wall-mounted speakers. Hannah was surprised by the choice of playlist – personally, she would have chosen the authentic sound of a sitar rather than a panpipe rendition of Britney Spears' greatest hits – but then nothing about tonight had been as expected.

Leaving Sav to remain on the restaurant floor, she slipped back into the kitchen, where the clean-up was underway.

It was after 10 p.m. when the customers left, none the wiser they'd eaten Patak's finest, and further sated with an incredible lemon cheesecake Joe had made earlier in the day. She taste-tested it before what was left of it was whisked back into the fridge, and her stomach wailed with hunger so loudly everyone in the kitchen looked up. Sav reached into his pocket for his wallet again and rifled through it.

'Ben, mate. Do you need to get off home or are you OK to hang on a bit longer?'

Surprise registered on the boy's face, along with apprehension. He obviously expected to be sent on another errand.

'No school tomorrow, so I can be home as late as I like,' he said.

'Excellent, in that case, could you go and set up a table for five please? Joe, leave all that,' he waved a dismissive hand at the remaining pots and pans still waiting by the sink. 'Please go to the bar and fetch these ladies whatever they would like to drink. And get yourselves something, you've definitely earned a beer.'

Joe, who looked tired, but no longer on the verge of a breakdown, saluted. 'Yes, boss.'

Sav checked his watch. 'Right, well it's the kebab shop or the Chinese takeaway. Take your pick.'

A laugh spluttered out of Hannah. 'I'm sorry,' she said, 'it's just so crazy. We came in here tonight for a curry. And now we might be sitting down with a Chinese takeaway instead.'

Sav's face broke into a grin. 'Yep. But I sure as hell don't think anyone here feels like firing up the stove again tonight. So, what'll it be?'

Ben winced. 'I don't really like Chinese.'

Joe looked to the younger boy in horror. 'What? Not even pancake rolls? Everyone loves pancake rolls. Oh, and crispy duck, with plum sauce and cucumber.' He began making appreciative noises.

'Beef in black bean sauce is my favourite,' Maggie contributed. 'But I'm partial to crispy duck too.'

'My dad always gets sweet and sour, which is as bad as when people put pineapple on pizza, why does anyone *do* that?' asked Ben with feeling. It was more words than the lad had spoken all evening, and he seemed to have lost some of his initial self-consciousness. He also seemed to have an easy rapport with Joe, which Hannah could relate to, he had such a gentle way about him.

Hannah's tummy grumbled and an image of a greasy doner kebab, packed with pickles and salad imprinted itself on her brain.

'Couldn't say why, because I've not eaten one since I

63

was about seventeen years old, but is it terrible that I've got a hankering for a dirty great kebab?' For some reason, she looked to Sav as she said it. Although, to be fair, he was paying.

'It's only terrible if I don't get there before they close, because I really want one too,' said Sav, reversing out the door. 'Three kebabs and a selection of Chinese dishes coming up.'

Within half an hour, as Hannah was reaching the bottom of a large glass of white wine, Sav waded through the restaurant carrying three loaded bags.

Joe jumped up to help dish out the food, and a peaceful quiet fell as everyone dug in hungrily.

'Thanks for this,' said Hannah, rescuing a piece of meat that had fallen to her plate. 'You really didn't need to.'

Sav's eyes widened. 'Oh, believe me, I did. Tonight would have been a complete disaster if you hadn't both stepped in. Maggie, you are an absolute legend.'

Joe made a noise of discomfort at his side and Sav reached around and hugged the big man to him. 'Hey, mate, I meant no disrespect to you. I blame myself entirely – I should never have put you in this position.'

Maggie, who had polished off the best part of three duck pancakes and an entire portion of black bean beef and rice, put her fork down.

'Do you mind if I ask what the situation is with your parents? Is this a temporary *arrangement*?' She said the words as though the arrangement had been one of organised self-destruction. 'Or will normal *service* resume when they return, if you'll excuse the pun?'

Sav shook his head. 'I honestly don't know. They'd been

arguing a bit about retiring lately. Mum wants to, Dad doesn't. I think I just need to keep things ticking along until they come home and get their affairs in order. The only problem is, we can't offer the usual menu because Mum made everything herself, as you know. And don't ask me if I picked anything up over the years, because I can tell you her lentil dhal is one of the best things you'll ever taste, but I've *no* idea how to make it. I'm used to writing software, not menus.'

Sav put down his unfinished kebab. 'Joe was out of work, and he'd trained in catering after school, before then going into the building trade instead. Do you remember, Hannah? When the rest of us did A Levels, Joe went off to catering college.'

Hannah did remember. She also remembered taking ju-jitsu classes around the same time but couldn't tell you the name of a single move now, less still perform one without rupturing her spleen.

'So, I said to him he should come and work here for a bit. Kill two birds with one stone.'

Joe piped up. 'Gita posted some of her recipes and I thought I'd almost mastered the korma and tikka masala. If I hadn't gone and dropped the bloody thing on the floor it would have been fine. Well, apart from the fact the most people I've ever catered for in one sitting before this is six on Christmas Day. But we can't turn away group bookings – we need the business.'

'We figured if we had a couple of good curries, we could expand the menu to include food Joe could easily cook,' Sav resumed. 'Plus, there are now two other Indian restaurants in town, so why shouldn't we offer something different?'

Now it was beginning to make sense. Sav had been doing a mate a favour, but in the process, stitched himself and the restaurant up like a kipper. If they carried on like this, the place would be a laughing stock by the time Gita and Raj returned.

From the way her mum was frowning, Hannah could tell Maggie thought the same.

Ben picked at the label of his bottle of Cobra, in a way that indicated he was no stranger to the drink, despite being clearly underage.

Joe sighed and wiped his fingers on a napkin.

*Wait for it*, thought Hannah, who had a pretty good idea what was going to happen next.

Never one to disappoint, Maggie sat up straight.

'Sav, I'd like to make you a proposition . . .'

# Chapter Six

## Maggie

Maggie was buzzing.

If she thought about it, she hadn't felt levels of excitement to rival tonight since, well, at least since in the days leading up to her and Geoff's big trip. And even then, the warm tingly feeling you got with the anticipation of something good wasn't the same as the blood-roiling adrenalin you felt with the pressure of a ticking clock and a dozen simultaneous tasks. The knowledge that if you got one thing wrong – burnt onions, undercooked chicken, overcooked steak – the whole thing would have to be done again. Profits wasted, customers impatient, employers intolerant. It had come back to her like muscle memory, from those early days at the Imperial Hotel and subsequent kitchens, when she had just been starting out.

Of course, she cooked most days. Although, in truth that was mostly because she had Alice to feed. In the long, unbearable days in the wake of Geoff's sudden, fatal heart attack, Maggie had subsisted on buttered toast and the occasional tin of soup. Left to her own devices, even one year on, she rarely bothered with more than a jacket potato at weekends, when Alice was home with Hannah.

To Maggie, it was obvious. She'd wanted to find a way back into catering and here was a restaurant very much in need. But a certain amount of 'sensitivity' was required as Joe was already chef in that kitchen. He was also an old friend of Sav's. She had no desire at all to stampede all over the poor man's ego and suggest he wasn't up to par. Besides, that simply wasn't true. Once he'd got a handle on his anxiety and focused on the task in hand, it had become obvious he had a flair for food. His cheesecake had been divine! What Joe needed was confidence. And a good brush-up on the basics. This was an area in which Maggie felt she could help.

Sav had listened with interest as she'd laid out her thoughts.

'I wouldn't want wages. I'd just like to help out for a while. Help Joe here find a rhythm.' She had tossed it out casually, as though she hadn't just spent the day trudging the streets of Saffron Walden seeking paid culinary employment. This was different. Raj and Gita were old acquaintances of whom she thought very highly. They also formed part of the rich tapestry of her shared life with Geoff and she wanted nothing to taint it. Certainly not the sustained decline of their livelihood whilst they were otherwise indisposed.

'You'd do that?' asked Sav, looking from Maggie to Joe. 'Would that be OK with you, Joe?'

Joe, a big bear of a man with a scruffy ginger beard and kind eyes, had nodded vigorously, 'I will take *any* help. Seriously, I was on the verge of losing it this evening. I'm sorry, I don't know what came over me.'

Maggie had reached across and patted his hand. 'Panic, love. Pure and simple. Happens to us all. Best way to deal with it is to be prepared. I can help with that.'

And so, it had been settled. Starting from next Friday, Maggie would begin working in The Golden Crocus's kitchen.

Hannah had messaged Darren to check he could collect Alice at 5 p.m. sharp from now on, rather than whatever arbitrary time suited him. Given he worked from home *and* for himself, as she'd pointed out, it shouldn't be difficult. She had also reminded him, though Maggie hadn't been privy to the particular vocabulary used, should he let anyone down, he'd find himself on the unfavourable end of a sole custody application.

Maggie switched off her bedside light and hugged the duvet to her. For once, she didn't lay lost in the maze of her memories, flipping her pillow occasionally to enjoy the cold side, as night turned steadily into day. Instead, with the tang of curry still clinging to her hair, and a bone-deep tiredness, she drifted into a deep and contented sleep.

When the doorbell rang at 5 p.m. on Friday, Maggie breathed a sigh of relief. A breath she felt she had been holding all afternoon, trying to keep her doubt from Alice who excitedly chattered about Daddy's new dog Keith – *a cockapoo named Keith, for heaven's sake?* There was every reason to doubt her ex-son-in-law and she wasn't sure the forced air of civility she'd mustered thus far could be maintained if he let Alice down. Not to mention that if he didn't show up, she would be letting the restaurant down on her very first day.

But, sure enough, there he was. Standing on the doorstep, hands clasped behind his back as though awaiting his gold star. All the intelligent, academic and witty men of integrity Hannah must have encountered over the years, and for reasons unknown, she'd settled on this drip.

'Bye, Granny,' said Alice, flinging her arms around Maggie's waist. 'Good luck cooking in the rester-room!'

Darren frowned.

'Rest-au-rant,' Maggie corrected, not particularly enjoying the image of toilet pans, rather than saucepans, which must have passed briefly through Darren's mind. 'Bye, sweetie, I love you.'

Not giving him opportunity to converse further, she closed the door on them abruptly. Give them a couple of minutes to drive away, then she'd set off for The Golden Crocus just in time to help prep for the evening shift.

She grabbed her bag from the kitchen counter and then faltered as her eyes fell on the knife block. Should she take Geoff's Japanese knives? They were better than anything she'd found in the restaurant's kitchen and were intended for just this purpose. But what if she lost one, or Joe severed his thumb, or met some other awful fate? Eventually, deciding she was overthinking it, she retrieved their original case from the cupboard and wrapped them up inside. Then, she placed a saucer of food down for Monty and left the house.

One of the things Maggie loved most about living in Saffron Walden was that within a matter of minutes, and relatively little footwork, you could experience leafy wide-open spaces, *and* a vibrant, bustling town centre. Her home in Bridge Lane was situated to the west of the town, backing onto the 6,000 acre Audley End Estate, owned by English Heritage. But within a stone's throw, you were in the narrow, ancient lanes of the medieval town centre, with its imposing church – the largest in the county – and the ruins of a twelfth-century castle. From here, it was a mere ten-minute walk to Alice's primary school, and a further ten to the new estate north of the town, where Hannah and Alice now lived. After growing up in the London suburbs, it had taken some getting used to, but now Maggie couldn't imagine being anywhere else. Especially at this time of year, when the beginning of June brought with it long days, light evenings and the scent of honeysuckle that spilled over walled cottage gardens. She breathed it in deeply as she walked into town, nodding Good Evening to those she passed, and enjoying the feeling of having somewhere to walk *to*, on such a beautiful Friday evening.

She ducked off the high street into Queen Street, and stopped halfway down when she reached the familiar crooked building on the corner, at the end of a row of handsome period properties that housed a café, a pizzeria and a gift shop.

'Maggie,' greeted Sav, in obvious relief when she pushed open the restaurant door. 'You came.'

'Of course I came.'

In the kitchen, a blaring radio competed with the extraction unit, and Joe was stirring a pan. The fragrant aroma of spice filled the room, making Maggie's mouth water. He looked up as she entered and smiled. 'Hello, Mrs Lawford.'

71

Sav, who had followed her into the kitchen, crossed the room and turned down the radio to a less headache-inducing level.

'Is there anything you need me to do? Or would you rather I left you to it?'

He looked anxious, Maggie thought. Almost jittery. Like he had the weight of the world on his shoulders.

Conscious of the very truthful adage about too many cooks in a kitchen, Maggie had a different task for Sav.

'I was wondering, does your payment system have a record of the previous few weeks' service? Are you able to look at, for example, which dishes were ordered the most?'

Sav grimaced. 'My parents don't have anything anywhere near that high-tech I'm afraid, despite my constant nagging to upgrade. These days most cash registers are computers with sophisticated EPOS systems, but Mum and Dad were still using an old till and handwritten bookkeeping. It's taken me a while to get my head around it.'

'What did you want to know?' asked Joe. 'Because I can tell you that in the couple of weeks I've been here, no-one has ordered the chicken kyiv But there's a box in the freezer, just in case.'

*No, no, no,* thought Maggie. It was the jars of sauce all over again. Gita would have a fit.

'Are you really surprised?' she asked, levelling them both with an incredulous frown. Pussyfooting around the issue wasn't helping anyone.

'Most loyal customers will not be expecting to find chicken kyiv on the menu, or sirloin steak for that matter. This has been an Indian restaurant for over forty years – one of the best in the area, thanks to your mother's incredible cookery. And any new customers will have reached that conclusion for themselves, simply by looking at the place.'

Sav looked pained.

'I appreciate that. But surely offering a range of food we *can* cook, rather than a three-page menu of dishes we can't, is better than closing until my parents return?'

Maggie shrugged.

'Maybe, maybe not. But I do worry about the restaurant's reputation. In this industry, word of mouth is everything.' At the stricken look on both Sav and Joe's faces, she decided that throwing negativity around at this stage wasn't going to be hugely helpful. 'Perhaps we can all put our heads together on the menu, sort something out,' she said, rubbing her hands together. 'But right now, there's work to do, so where do you want me?'

Joe pointed to the large pans on the stove. 'I doubled up on the quantities today. We should have enough of the curry dishes, *if* I don't drop them, that is. But I could do with a hand on veg prep? And we need to make our soup of the day. I over-ordered on tomatoes, so maybe cream of tomato?'

'Roger that,' replied Maggie, setting the case of knives down and reaching for a chopping board. Gita's kitchen was ordered and tidy, with everything in its place. A shelf spilled aromatic herbs from mismatched ceramic pots and she reached to rub a frond of dill between her fingers, bringing the zingy, aniseedy scent to her nose and breathing it in. She spotted several dog-eared pieces of lined writing paper tucked between the coriander and the mint and nosily peered at one. She saw at once they were handwritten recipes. These must be the ones Gita had sent. Her writing was precise and neat, with each step numbered for ease. Maggie loved collecting recipes, she'd amassed hundreds over the years, cut from magazines, hastily copied down from the television or borrowed from a friend. She'd ask Sav if she could make copies of these too; she loved a traditional curry.

Unlike the kitchen, which looked to have been modernised, at least in the last decade, with stainless steel cabinets and clean white tiling, the storeroom was a cool, dark space filled with old-fashioned Formica wall cabinets and humming chest freezers. Maggie spotted the boxes of overripe tomatoes and tried not to flinch at the idea of serving cream of tomato soup in an Indian restaurant, instead putting on her sensible head. In a profitable kitchen, you wasted nothing. You adapted the menu to what you had, to what was plentiful and seasonal. She made a mental note to speak to Sav about how they did their ordering and carried a box back to the kitchen, an idea beginning to take shape.

'Joe, point me in the direction of Gita's spices. We're going to give this soup a little Indian kick.'

Just before 7 p.m., Ben arrived for his shift. It might have been Maggie's imagination, but he seemed to stand a little straighter and was dressed a little smarter since she'd first clapped eyes on him one week ago. If he suffered with shyness, he was certainly in the right job to conquer that malady.

'Have you had a good week?' she asked, whilst peeling a potato.

He screwed up his nose. 'Not the best. Had my Geography exam today, totally messed it up.'

*Of course.* He was likely in the midst of his GCSEs. She remembered Hannah's only too well. The late-night cramming and the mood swings. Always so driven, even when her friends were out partying or hanging around with boys – for Hannah, those things were put on hold until she'd sat her final exam. And even afterwards, she'd been so focused on A Levels and university, followed by another four years of studying law, Maggie wasn't sure she'd ever truly let her hair down.

'Perhaps it didn't go as badly as you thought it did, love,' offered Maggie supportively.

'Oh, it was *bad*. Really bad,' replied Ben wryly, but with none of the angst Hannah would have displayed. 'I think I've properly screwed up. Not that I have the faintest idea what I want to do, but so long as it doesn't involve school, I'm all good.'

'I feel you, kid,' piped up Joe. 'I hated school. Is that old relic Mr Harding still there? He seemed ancient back then.'

Ben's face lit up mischievously. 'Yep, I reckon he's been cryogenically frozen since 1939. He says things like *jolly good*, and *chaps*, and wears knitted tank tops. Is that what all the teachers were like back then?'

'Oi, you cheeky fucker, I'm not that old!' cried Joe, then clamped a hand to his mouth. 'Oops, so sorry, Mrs L. It just slipped out.'

'Heavens above. Do you think I've been living in a cave? Let me tell you, when I worked in professional kitchens, I learned words to make even you youngsters blush. And, please, stop calling me Mrs Lawford, it makes me sound like my mother-in-law, who was nearly a hundred when she passed.'

'Well, I worked on building sites for the best part of twenty years, so I'm pretty sure I've heard it all,' laughed Joe.

'No-one could be as bad as that chef guy on the telly,' said Ben. 'He's a complete arsehole, excuse my language. I don't know why anyone works for him.'

'Hugo Wick? Yes, he's a complete tool. I quite agree,' nodded Joe. 'He makes Gordon Ramsey seem positively angelic.'

'My friend Tom says it's all an act, but I'm not so sure,' added Ben.

Maggie watched the back and forth between them with interest. She knew exactly to whom they referred, of course. She'd encountered the delightful chap herself through her role within the council when he wrangled three entire street closures. He'd been filming for a TV show about the origins of culinary ingredients and had been exploring the town's historic connection to the exotic spice saffron. Closing roads was normally a feat less likely achieved by most local townsfolk than flying to the moon, even for jubilees and carnivals. But money *always* talks, never mind the livelihoods of the businesses affected. Rumour had it he'd been so taken with the area he'd since moved here. Lucky, lucky them. Long before she'd even had the pleasure of liaising with the awful man, Maggie had heard tales from the kitchen, thanks to Geoff. Hugo Wick's reputation had very much preceded him, and not in a good way.

The door to the kitchen swung open.

'Right then guys. You're up,' said Sav, slapping a ticket down on the counter. 'First table of four are here.'

## Chapter Seven

## *Hannah*

Technically, Hannah was supposed to finish at 4 p.m. on a Friday, but an overrunning meeting meant she was on a later train than usual. She trudged along the platform, seeking an empty carriage to no avail, before settling herself down opposite a smartly dressed woman absorbed in her phone. The woman glanced up briefly, her eyes sliding down Hannah's form to the trainers which had revolutionised her commute this week, a grimace of distaste passing across her face.

Hannah was immediately transported back to the mediation meeting that had made her late, and specifically to Bronte Gallagher. Slight and sinewy, as though she spent far too long in the gym, Bronte bore little resemblance to her sister. Whereas Caitlin was brash and loud, with an obvious affection for cosmetic enhancement, Bronte seemed only to observe with quick, shrewd eyes, as though she'd already thought out every possible move in a game you didn't know you were playing. Even her solicitor had looked scared of her.

Caitlin, Hannah decided, was by far the nicer of the two sisters. Hannah was sure that Caitlin would've been judged for her pillowy lips and permanently startled expression, but she didn't seem to care what other people thought.

'What we are trying to determine, Ms Gallagher,' Hannah had said, addressing Bronte, 'is to what extent your father had intended to make reparation to Caitlin, for his absence in her life. His intention to make such reparations, despite never finalising his change of wishes is not in question, because as you will know from document thirty-three, section 5.1b, there are witnesses to this effect. The omission of these reparations from his will at the time of death is being contested on the grounds of proprietary estoppel, that is to say – a broken promise. Now in the case of contentious probate, it is our job, with the help of the court, if necessary, to get to a satisfactory resolution for all parties.'

'How about,' began Bronte, so quietly Hannah had to lean closer to hear her, 'we begin with the fact that this . . . *woman*,' she hissed the words so viciously, it was a wonder Caitlin didn't vault the table to punch her, 'has been misusing the Gallagher family name for the past six years to advance her own career and it is my intention to win back every single penny of it. That common gold-digger is *not* my sister, and she will not get as much as a blade of grass from my late father's estate. It is *I* who intends to take *her* to court, *Ms Lawford.*'

There had been a brief period of Freudian debate among her university friends whether Hannah's ambition to become a lawyer had anything to do with her family name, in much the same way Dickens' characters so often lived up to theirs, the draconian Thomas Gradgrind being her particular favourite.

Perhaps there *was* something in it. Or, more feasibly, rather like her mother, she just rather enjoyed wiping smug smirks from entitled person's faces at any and every opportunity.

'I believe you refer to her use of your family name on her social media accounts. As your father only accepted his paternity six years ago, her change of name is completely lawful. Furthermore, I must advise that Caitlin is perfectly willing to take a DNA test, to allay any doubt over her parentage.'

*Then, just maybe, you might learn that despite Daddy showering you with ponies, country club memberships and Chanel handbags, your own flesh and blood has been wilfully rejected since birth until a cancer diagnosis gave him an unexpected and somewhat late dose of contrition,* Hannah thought.

Just another day in the life of the monied and moronic, it really was eye-opening this business, the lengths people were prepared to go to when it came to either the protecting or claiming of inheritance. Hannah sighed inwardly, glad the week was over, and gazed out of the train window at the countryside flitting past, a glorious patchwork of rapeseed gold and luscious shades of green. If she was being honest, she was glad to be leaving the city too.

She mentally catalogued the contents of her fridge and briefly wondered how women like the Gallagher sisters would be spending their Friday evening. Bronte probably had some kind of manservant to feed her Fortnum & Mason truffles whilst she pampered herself in a jacuzzi. Caitlin would be dolled up to the nines and out somewhere swanky, pouting at her iPhone. Well, she had a date herself – with a bubble bath and a book, and what was wrong with Maltesers anyway?

Later that evening, when her skin had wrinkled and the bathwater had cooled, Hannah pulled herself from the tub and tugged on a robe.

She'd picked up a pepperoni pizza on the way home, which she shoved in the oven, then went upstairs to get dressed. She had no plans for the evening, other than to walk down to The Golden Crocus and surprise her mum at the end of her shift, partly to walk her home, and partly from curiosity to see how things had gone. There had been no point telling Maggie of her intention because the stubborn woman would invariably have found a way to render her redundant.

When 9 p.m. arrived, Hannah set off.

She told herself the new indigo jeans she had picked up from Zara at lunchtime were because her old ones were going through at the knee. And it felt so nice to have her freshly washed hair loose about her shoulders for a change, to shrug off her professional persona and embrace the weekend.

The arrangement, presuming Darren continued to behave like a grown-up, was that he would have Alice every Friday from 5 p.m. to Saturday lunchtime. In theory, this would give her Friday nights, to, what, go out? Go out where? This was her old stomping ground, so she knew from experience there was a considerable lack of scope. Besides, she'd not been 'out' in so long, she wondered what it entailed these days, but suspected it would necessitate Spanx and so was minded not to even bother. A date with the sofa and *Love Island* was novelty enough these days, and anyway, there simply wasn't the energy for more.

Having said that, she *was* meeting Laura for a drink the week after next, but owing to her friend's own small children and a husband who worked in hospitality, they'd had to settle for a low-octane Wednesday night, when Marco had a night off from work. Maggie had been only too happy for Alice to sleep over, and Alice was excited too because she would get to sleep in Mummy's old room. Fortunately, Hannah's fourteen-year-old self's wall art of choice – posters of The Back Street Boys and Leonardo Di Caprio – had been replaced with a tasteful cornflower blue colour scheme.

As Hannah strolled into town, she gazed anew at the familiar streets and found herself peering through the tiny leaded windowpanes of The Cross Keys Hotel. Inside, the Elizabethan hostelry was abuzz with diners and drinkers. It looked cosy and inviting and like somewhere she'd like to while away an evening, over a bottle of wine.

Back when she'd been an A Level student, and as each of her friends turned eighteen, they'd frequented all the bars in town, enjoying the novelty of being officially old enough to drink. Not that she'd ever been a wild child or a tearaway teen. She'd always been happier having a pint in one of the local pubs than trekking into the nearby city of Cambridge, in search of nightclubs and boys like so many of her friends had preferred. Somewhere along the way, she seemed to have forgotten that. Had replaced those formative memories with visions of a boring hometown, where nothing interesting had happened in her life until she'd moved to the city.

It didn't look dead right now. It was the exact opposite. She cut down one of the tiny lanes that linked up the old Market Rows; relics from the original medieval market stalls that still hosted bakers, butchers and artisan shops, passing several small bars and eateries as she went, most of them busy. The mild evening air hummed with the refrain of chatter and the appealing smells of garlic and spice, as well as the unmistakable aroma of fish and chips wafting from a paper bag carried by a passer-by.

When she reached Queen Street, she slowed, wondering whether she should wait outside, rather than get under everyone's feet. Last thing she wanted was to be roped into serving again. From this direction, as she approached the restaurant from behind, the building looked even more run-down. The sun had set, but a nearby streetlamp dimly illuminated the peeling paint and grubby guttering. One of the ground floor windowpanes was cracked, which had to be a security risk. And in the gloom, she couldn't quite tell, but was that a massive pile of *rubbish bags* blocking the fire exit? Surely that was illegal, never mind dangerous.

Just as Hannah was about to pass by, she caught a movement out of the corner of her eye and leapt three feet into the air, as the rubbish bags sprung upright.

'*What the f–!*'

'It's just me, Hannah.'

Hannah put a hand to her chest, to calm her rapid breath.

'Bloody hell, Sav. You frightened the life out of me. Why are you hiding out here?'

She stepped closer, her eyes adjusting in the dim light and taking in his black suit jacket, black shirt, black trousers, inky dark hair, vast brown eyes. He held one arm behind him, concealing something. The other hand he thrust into his trouser pocket.

'Going for the Matrix look, are you? Is that a machine gun in your pocket, or are you just pleased to see me?'

Sav grinned sheepishly, and then she saw it, the thin trail of smoke drifting up and past his shoulder.

'Tut, tut. And I had you down as clean-living boy. Aren't you full of surprises?'

'Temptation calls to us all. And I've had a truly shit day. Just don't tell my mother, she'll be praying away my impurities from now until her deathbed.'

Hannah gave a knowing laugh. 'Tell me about it. I'm sure my mum thinks I'm a raging alcoholic, from the look she gives me each time I reach for a glass of wine. The truth is, I'm a solicitor. If I didn't destress some days, I'd be drafting wills in my sleep.'

'Perhaps you just need to find other ways to unwind,' he replied. Was it her imagination or was that a suggestive smile?

'How's it going in there?' she asked, deciding to change the subject.

'Great,' said Sav with feeling. 'Your mum is something else. It's gone like clockwork tonight. Although we did have one table walk out because we didn't have jalfrezi on the menu.'

'I'm not saying anything. Nothing at all about chicken kyivs on an Indian menu.'

She looked up and down the street.

'Well, come on then.'

Sav looked puzzled. 'What?'

'Give us one of those. Unless you need to get back inside?'

Sav pulled the crumpled cigarette packet from his pocket and grimaced. 'I promised myself I'd dump these after this one. Only bought them an hour ago, first time in ten years.'

'Well,' said Hannah, sidling up to stand next to him in the dark doorway. 'Let's make this the last ciggy we ever have. For old times' sake. And then we'll dump them.'

He plucked one from the packet and handed it to her, then she waited for him to strike the lighter and leaned into the flame. The first puff sent her into a coughing fit in much the same way it had when she was fourteen and had tried one in the park for the first and last time. It was vile, just as she remembered. What on earth had possessed her to attempt it again. It was almost as though just being around people from her childhood had caused her to regress by twenty-four years.

Sav lit one too and they stood in the quiet with their backs to the door. Suddenly Joe's voice came from somewhere just behind them, causing Hannah to flinch.

'There's no custard left, Maggie!' he bellowed, pausing to listen to the faint sound of Maggie replying from deeper within the building, then Joe called back incredulously, 'Fresh? We usually just use tinned. OK, well, what ingredients do we need?'.

They were standing just outside the storeroom. Hannah glanced at Sav, who had his fingers to his lips, and almost burst out laughing. He looked like an errant school kid, afraid of being caught behind the bike sheds.

'I won't say anything about serving custard in Indian restaurants, nothing at all,' she whispered.

With the sound of a door closing somewhere inside, Sav deemed it safe to speak.

'They're getting on like a house on fire, your mum and Joe. It's done him wonders already. I honestly don't think his confidence could have handled another knock. He's had a rough time lately, poor bloke.'

'I remember him from school – he always was a gentle giant, soft as anything,' said Hannah.

Sav nodded.

'I'd been hoping when my parents returned, I could persuade them to keep Joe on. Give Mum a chance to take a step back, once she'd trained him up.'

'Sounds like a *great* idea. But you make it sound like maybe that won't be happening?'

Sav rubbed at the skin between his eyebrows.

'I'm not sure if there is going to be a restaurant for Mum and Dad to come back *to*.'

Hannah twisted to face him. Saw the deep grooves of worry etched into his features. She took another shallow drag of a cigarette she didn't really want, before stubbing it out on the ground with her shoe. 'What's happened?'

'Between you and me, I had a meeting with the accountant today,' sighed Sav. 'Second meeting in under a week. Let's just say he's made it abundantly clear the restaurant has been struggling for quite some time.' He shrugged, took another drag of his cigarette. 'A combination of the effects of the pandemic and the new Indian that

85

opened in town last year, probably. But, as the accountant so delicately put it, if the business bank account were a patient, it's already bled out and is laying stiff in the morgue.'

'Yeesh,' winced Hannah. 'Tactful chap, then.'

'I just really wanted to keep things ticking over, you know? This place has been my parents' life.'

'Have you talked to them about it? About what the accountant has said, I mean?' asked Hannah.

'I've tried. They said Simon's always been overdramatic. That it's *just his way*.' Sav pulled off such an uncanny impression of his father's accent Hannah couldn't help but smile.

'So, what's next then? I mean how long do you think the restaurant has left?'

Hannah knew how these things worked. Sooner or later the Kapoors' creditors would come knocking, and whilst they might own the premises outright, there would be business rates, utility bills, suppliers, not to mention the staff.

Sav turned to her then. Took a long, resigned breath.

'Well, that's just it. The accountant has given us six weeks, until the 14th of July. Six weeks to turn it around, or he recommends the business is struck off. But there is also another option . . .' he trailed off.

'Which is . . .?' Hannah prompted.

'We've been made an offer. One I am going to suggest my parents accept because,' he gave a humourless laugh, 'I really don't think they'll get a better one.'

'O-*kay*,' said Hannah, 'like an offer from an investor? Or do you mean a buyer?'

86

Sav nodded. 'Hugo Wick. He's also one of Simon's clients. He's made an offer on the premises. Apparently, he's been after a prime location like ours for a while, but they just don't become available that often. I mean, I'd rather burn it to the ground than see it in the hands of *Huge Prick*, but it's my parents' business. It's their decision. And as much as it pains me, I just can't see another option.'

Sav scrubbed a hand through the back of his hair, miserably. Hannah felt for him, and not just because that tit off the telly was involved. She could only imagine how he must feel, being left to deal with a situation like this whilst his parents were halfway across the world.

'Hey,' she said, giving him a friendly punch in the arm. 'It'll all work out for the best. Whatever happens.'

'Thanks, Han. I appreciate you lending an ear,' Sav said. No one had called her Han in years, other than Laura. He gave a small shrug, one nowhere near strong enough to dislodge the weight of his mood, then he crossed the small courtyard and lifted the lid of the black bin and tossed in the packet of cigarettes.

# Chapter Eight

## Maggie

With a final flourish, Maggie wiped the last of the crumbs from the counter and rinsed the cloth in the sink.

'I do believe that's a wrap,' said Joe, beginning to unbutton his chef's jacket. 'Not bad for a Friday night; we're usually here until eleven clearing down and washing up.'

'I don't know why they don't get a dishwasher,' grumbled Ben who had just finished putting away the cutlery.

'And put you out of a job?' said Maggie. 'Because from what I can make out, there's no shortage of applicants in this town.'

'I meant, like an electric one. Look at the state of these.' He held up ten wrinkled and sodden fingers.

'I know you did, dear. And I was pointing out that jobs aren't easily come by these days, so perhaps it's just as well you're needed.'

Ben said, 'I know, I'm not complaining, I really like working here. I just thought I'd be doing a bit more with food, rather than serving and washing up. That's all.'

Maggie eyed the young lad with interest. 'So, you like cooking?'

'Yeah,' said Ben, removing the hairband that had been holding back his floppy mop of curls whilst he'd scrubbed. 'I cook a lot at home, just easy things like stir fries and stuff. My dad's a greengrocer, so we've always got like a ton of vegetables in the fridge. Which is handy since I'm a veggie.'

He grinned and Maggie noted what a lovely smile he had. Perhaps once he'd had his braces removed he would be inclined to do it more often. There was something vaguely familiar about him too . . .

She studied him again. 'Hang on a minute. Your dad doesn't have a stall on the market, does he?'

'Yep. The smaller one.'

There were a couple of fruit and vegetable stalls at the regular market and Maggie knew exactly the one he meant; she'd visited Vernon's stall many times. He sold the best cauliflowers for miles around; they didn't go black the minute they hit your fridge like the ones from the supermarket. Revelations really were around every corner. They were even hiding away beneath ridiculous hairstyles.

'Well, I'm sure Sav wouldn't mind if you came in a little earlier next time and helped me and Joe with the prep? Would you like me to ask him?'

Ben shrugged in a way that indicated he was ambivalent about the suggestion, but Maggie could see right through it, all the way to the small child beneath, who had probably loved to bake jam tarts and gingerbread men, just as Alice did now. Although, seeing as Ben hadn't mentioned anything about his mother's cooking, perhaps she didn't cook, maybe his dad was the chef in the house.

Sav poked his head around the door. 'Visitor for you, Maggie.'

Another face appeared. Hannah's.

'Hello, love,' she smiled at her daughter, who somehow looked a little different. More relaxed, and her hair was down. She couldn't remember the last time she'd seen all her beautiful chestnut brown hair loose, wild and wavy. Hannah had been naturally blessed, not that she'd agree – she had always hated her thick, unruly mane. Nothing like Maggie's own hair, which had always been poker-straight and, since she had turned fifty, soldering-wire silver. 'What brings you down here?'

'I wanted to hear all about your first proper shift.'

There had been a minor disagreement with Sav, when Maggie had first offered her help. He had insisted she would be paid, like any other employee. She had argued it was a favour, a purely voluntary gesture. It had gone on like that for several minutes, until reluctantly, Maggie had acquiesced to accept some small recompense. A mere pittance really and certainly less than minimum wage. But it had never been about the money. Not for her.

'Fifteen covers,' said Joe proudly. 'All served fresh, hot food. No jars or packets around here, thank you very much.'

Ben gave a dramatic cough.

'What?' asked Joe.

Ben coughed again, this time disguising the word 'custard', as he did so.

Joe rolled his eyes. 'Yeah, yeah. Well, I know how to make it from scratch now. And it tasted just as good as my nan's.'

Maggie chuckled and looked up just in time to catch Hannah elbowing Sav. As if they were sharing a private joke. How curious.

'Not that I'm saying you're like my nan,' Joe hastily added. 'My grandmother's ninety-seven and thinks Harold Wilson's still prime minister.'

'Maggie's a kitchen *diva*,' said Ben, waving showbiz jazz hands. A touch over the top, thought Maggie, but honestly, the transformation in him, now he'd lost his initial shyness, really was quite something to behold,

'Agreed,' said Sav, folding his arms. 'That's why I'm appointing Maggie as my G.E.O.'

Everyone looked to him in confusion, all except for Hannah who buried her face in her hands and began slowly shaking her head.

Then Joe groaned. 'Oh, please. Mate.'

Sav grinned.

Then the penny dropped. Not a CEO, but a GEO, *Grandma Executive Officer.*

'I think you might need to brush up on your comedy routine before you use it on the customers, young man,' said Maggie, feeling secretly rather pleased with herself. Who knew getting older could garner you such a fan club? 'Right, shall we head off then, Hannie?' she asked. 'Leave these jokers to it? I'll make us one of those nice bubbly hot chocolates with the marshmallows on top when we get home.'

'Ahhh, now you're talking,' said Joe. 'All I've got waiting for me is *Gogglebox* and a Dr Pepper.'

'I love *Gogglebox*,' said Ben. Maggie decided to extract herself, before Joe went off on another long tangent (she'd already been briefed on the plots of no fewer than five *Mission Impossible* movies this evening). She picked up her case of knives, hooked her handbag over her arm and wished everyone goodnight.

As they opened the front door to leave, a young woman almost fell through it. She looked like a packet of Starburst, positively fizzing with energy and sporting a neon pink and yellow bomber jacket.

'Hey,' she said, her face splitting into a wide, infectious grin. 'You must be Maggie. Ben's told me all about you.'

Slightly taken aback, Maggie realised the girl was a similar age to Ben. Fifteen or sixteen at most. She had a rather pretty, tiny blue nose piercing. Were they allowed those at school? They wouldn't have been when Hannah was at school.

Without waiting for a response, the girl bowled towards the kitchen. 'He's out back, yeah? Catch you later.'

In her wake, Maggie exchanged a bemused look with Hannah, then they stepped into the cool late evening.

'I really didn't need walking home you know, love,' said Maggie. 'I've been doing it quite successfully for years.'

'I know,' replied Hannah. 'I just fancied some air.'

Well, *that* was a lie. Hannah had been quite content to live in a giant exhaust fume bubble for nearly twenty years without expressing such wholesome wants or needs.

'I expect that was Ben's girlfriend,' said Maggie. 'Not quite what I'd have imagined.'

'Definitely not what I imagined,' replied Hannah, with a hint of amusement in her voice.

Before Maggie could ask what was funny, they rounded a corner and saw a commotion ahead.

'Wonder what's going on up there,' said Hannah.

A police car was parked diagonally across the road, its silent blue light intermittently filling the night sky.

'Someone with too much drink inside them, I expect. That's usually about the limit of misdemeanours around here.'

'So did you enjoy yourself tonight?' asked Hannah.

Maggie answered without even thinking. 'I loved it. I mean, the kitchen is ill-equipped; the menu, quite frankly, is ridiculous and Gita's knives are as blunt as butter spreaders, but Joe's a sweetheart and super keen to learn. I was a bit nervous about letting him loose on these, mind,' she lifted up the case as she spoke, 'but everyone survived. No trips to A&E.'

Hannah stopped dead, her arm popping out like a boomerang and halting Maggie in her tracks.

'Whatever's wrong?' asked Maggie, registering the concern in her daughter's eyes.

Hannah hissed, 'I can't believe I didn't notice. *Please* don't tell me that's Dad's set of knives you're carrying.'

Maggie looked down at the black case in her hand. 'Yes, why?'

Hannah blinked. '*Mother*. That is over a thousand pounds worth of folded Damascus carbon-edged steel, sharpened to Samurai levels of lethality. I don't like them even being in your house, and you're carrying them through the street? In a rolled-up scrap of canvas?'

Maggie made a *pfft* sound. 'Don't be so dramatic, Hannah. What do you think's going to happen? Will a filleting knife wriggle its way out like a homing pigeon and implant itself in the nearest prime rump? This isn't Harry Potter.'

Hannah narrowed her eyes and spoke in such a low, urgent tone Maggie couldn't possibly mistake it.

'Mother, you could receive up to four years in prison for carrying a knife with more than a three-inch blade. You have *fourteen* of them in a case not fit for purpose. And there are two police officers, *right* there.'

Maggie stared at her, nonplussed. 'But . . . your father often brought his knives home from work. Particularly if he wanted to sharpen them.'

'But Dad was a chef! By trade. And he kept them in a locking case. There *are* exceptions, but not just any old Tom, Dick or Harry can flounce around the streets with dangerous weapons about their person!'

Oh well, that was alright then. For a moment there Maggie had been slightly concerned, but as usual, it was just her pedantic daughter crossing t's and dotting i's.

*She gets it from you, you know*, came Geoff's voice in her head. *Iron-willed and stubborn as a mule, just like her mother.* Yes, love, but she cares. She gets her kind soul from you, and that's what makes her someone to be reckoned with.

Maggie resumed walking, a rebellious smile tugging at her lips. 'Good, because I *am* a chef. And I have a job in a kitchen. Come along, dear.'

Near the end of the high street, it became clear why the police were in attendance. Someone had driven into a lamppost, which was now keening at a sorry angle right across the road. There was no sign of the offending vehicle, however.

The police radio crackled into life as they walked past the wound-down windows of the police car, sticking to the opposite pavement. Maggie could feel Hannah tightening her grip on her arm, as though she feared her mother might break into song and dance and flash her contraband goods about.

'Maggie?' came a nasally, authoritative voice. 'Mrs Lawford?'

Maggie glanced at the person in the driver's seat of the car.

'Christopher! How lovely to see you. Got you working the graveyard shift, have they?'

Behind her, Hannah audibly let out a strangled moan.

'Hannah, this is Pam's nephew. Remember I told you he recently transferred from Kent Police?' Maggie pushed her forward as though she were presenting a debutante at court. 'This is my daughter, Hannah. She's a top solicitor.'

Christopher nodded an acknowledgement.

'Hello,' ground out Hannah, through her teeth.

A fine first impression. Why did she even bother?

'Well, this is a bit of a mess,' said Maggie, looking to the limp lamppost.

'Yes, it is, and I rather suspect the perpetrator's vehicle to be in a sorry state, as they seem to have left most of their paintwork behind.'

Hannah cleared her throat impatiently.

Ignoring her, Maggie tutted. 'Drink driver, do you think?'

Christopher tapped the roof of the car. 'Could be. CCTV should tell us more,' he said, pointing to the camera above the Maison Rose shopfront. 'You both take care now. If you see anything suspicious, report it right away.'

'We certainly will, Officer, goodnight,' called Hannah, already half-dragging Maggie along the street.

Once out of earshot, Maggie rounded on Hannah. 'Did you have to be *quite* so rude? I was hoping to introduce you properly.'

'What? Wait a minute,' said Hannah. 'Were you seriously thinking about my love life back there?' Her eyebrows had disappeared under her hairline.

'No,' said Maggie as innocently as she dared. 'Of course not. I've met him a few times, he seems a decent enough chap – and you *could* do with some more local friends.'

'For goodness' sake, Mother. Next time you want to introduce me to someone, could you wait until you're not committing an offence that could see you incarcerated? In fact, please could you refrain from introducing me to anyone at all? I'm *not* interested.'

'Alright, alright. Keep your hair on,' muttered Maggie, rummaging in her bag for her door keys. 'Now are you coming in for hot chocolate, or is that too reckless for a Friday night? Do you need to get home and pair your socks or something?'

'Very funny. Yes, I'm coming in. There's something I want to tell you about.'

Twenty minutes later mother and daughter were seated at the kitchen table with large mugs of thick, frothy chocolate drinks when Hannah dropped the Hugo Wick bomb.

'I can't believe it,' said Maggie in astonishment.

Well, maybe she could believe it, she could believe almost anything these days, but she certainly couldn't accept it.

'Not in a month of Sundays can that self-entitled, arrogant fop be allowed to railroad the Kapoors from their home and business.' Maggie put her mug down with a thud.

'I'm not sure it's necessarily railroading, if they're going to lose it anyway?'

Maggie snorted. 'If that man sets his sights on something, he'll keep going until he gets it. He's the sort. What does Sav say about it all?'

'Well obviously he doesn't want to see his parents' livelihood fail, but he doesn't see a way to save it. I can't see how it could possibly be turned around in just six weeks. Can you? The 14th of July feels so soon. Especially if Gita isn't going to be well enough to get back in the kitchen. Anyway, please don't mention any of this to anyone. Sav told me this in strictest confidence, so, unless he tells you about this himself, you didn't hear anything from me, OK?'

Maggie traced a finger around the rim of her mug. She gave a vague nod.

It *used* to be profitable. She knew it. She'd spent evenings in there when you could practically smell the twenty-pound notes as they leapt into the till. Maggie wasn't an idiot. She knew things had changed, the pandemic had seen to that, what with rising energy prices and the cost of living. But this was an affluent town. There was money here, and the other restaurants were busy. The Golden Crocus simply needed to adapt – Sav hadn't been wrong when he'd said it – it's just he was going about it in quite the wrong way.

Sensing her daughter's eyes upon her, Maggie looked up.

'What?' she said.

Hannah pursed her lips. 'You've got your Del Boy face on.'

'What's that supposed to mean?'

'You're smirking. Thoughtfully. What are you scheming, Mother?'

# Chapter Nine

## Maggie

By the time Maggie set off on Monday afternoon to collect Alice from school, she'd quite forgotten what it was to have endless hours to fill. She had helped at the restaurant on Saturday as well as Sunday, which was when she'd cooked up her latest plan.

'Granny! Look what I made!' Alice emerged from the classroom clutching a paper plate smothered in yellow poster paint and dancing about in a manner suggesting she was either very excited or might not make it home before needing to visit the toilet.

Today, however, they were not going home.

'It's lovely, sweetheart,' enthused Maggie, divesting her grandchild of her school bag and searching for a tactful way to ask what, indeed, *it* was. 'Very colourful.'

'I'm calling her Sally. Can we put it on the fridge?'

All of life was a trade-off really, wasn't it? One unwieldly, sellotaped-together cereal packet 'gobblersaurus' relocated to Hannah's clutter-free kitchen. One yellow paper plate-type thing about to take its place in Maggie's far more rustic space, which, it seemed only yesterday, had played host to Hannah's own school projects.

'My real sunflower's nearly this big now,' boasted Alice, indicating a space between the ground and her knee.

'Ah, it's a sunflower! I see,' said Maggie, spotting the crude orange and yellow paper petals protruding from the plate. Alice's class had all sown their own sunflower seeds a few weeks back and the progress of these specimens had been the cause of much rumination.

'Of course it is, Granny,' tutted Alice, thoroughly unimpressed. 'What did you *think* it was?'

'Well, perhaps my optician is right about those varifocals after all, love.'

Alice nodded sagely as she took her hand, and they exited the school gates. 'You should eat more olives,' she said.

At the end of the street, when they turned left instead of right, Alice didn't miss a trick.

'Where are we going, Granny?' This was swiftly followed by, 'I need the toilet.'

'Well, today, we're doing something a bit different.' *Something I hope Hannah won't mind*, thought Maggie, who hadn't yet had chance to update her. 'We're going somewhere fun, it's not far.'

As they traversed the high street at toilet-needing speed, Maggie noted the injured lamppost had now been truncated to a hazard-tape swaddled stump and wondered if the perpetrator had been caught. Bloody imbeciles driving at breakneck speed through these narrow streets, they wanted locking up. What if they'd hurt a person, instead of a chunk of metal? Just the thought of it had her gripping Alice's hand tighter, as in her mind's eye the scene played out.

When they reached The Golden Crocus, Maggie pushed the doorbell and prayed the others were already here, before the jigging at her side ceased for all the wrong reasons.

Fortunately, within seconds, there came the sound of a bolt sliding home, followed by the turn of a key in the lock.

'Hey Maggie,' said Joe, smiling. He crouched down to Alice's level. 'Hey Alice, I'm Joe.' He handed out his giant hand for her to shake, a tender gesture that did something gooey to Maggie's innards.

'*I'm* going to wet myself,' replied Alice, in greeting.

Joe looked startled, but rapidly stepped aside as Maggie practically swooped Alice off the floor and hurried her to the ladies' loos.

Disaster narrowly averted, and almost giddy with relief, Maggie and Alice exited the bathroom into the gloomy restaurant. It was a bright, warm day outside, but inside, the small windows and low ceilings allowed in little natural light. This wasn't aided by the ancient, patterned wallpaper and dark wood furniture. The restaurant had always remained closed from Monday through to Wednesday, offering welcome rest days for Raj and Gita. Which made today the perfect day for practice, which in a flash of inspiration Maggie was coining Method Monday. If it went well, perhaps there'd also be a Tuition Tuesday and even a Warm-up Wednesday.

In the kitchen, Joe had prepared five workstations around the central prep table, and he'd brought in one of the stools from the bar.

'This alright?' asked Joe, placing clean tea-towels and aprons at each station. 'I wasn't sure how much equipment we'd need, so I've brought in extra from home, just in case.' He indicated a carrier bag on the side, bulging with potato mashers, slotted spoons and whisks.

'Perfect,' said Maggie. 'Now we just need the rest of our students.'

'Granny, is this your rester-room? Where you do the cooking?' asked Alice, taking in the stainless-steel fittings and the enormous oven.

'Rest-au-rant,' Maggie corrected again. 'And today, darling. You're going to be doing some cooking too, just like we do at home.'

Alice's eyes widened to the size of saucers. 'But Granny, I can't cook dinners! I don't know how to.'

The sound of the doorbell chimed in a box high up on the wall and Joe, smiling at Alice's reaction, left the kitchen.

Maggie took advantage of the moment alone with her granddaughter to lift her up onto the stool and wrap her into a hug. Into her ear, she whispered, 'You're a marvellous cook darling. Now, together, you and me, we're going to show our new friends a few tricks. What do you say?'

Alice considered for a moment. 'OK,' she nodded, 'maybe I could show them how we prick the lemon cake all over to make it more drizzly, they probably won't know that will they, because it's our secret trick?'

Maggie kissed her forehead. 'Exactly. See, you're already an expert.'

Ben followed Joe into the kitchen, dressed in black jeans and a t-shirt that hung off his lean frame.

'No school today, Ben?' asked Maggie, who'd half

102

expected him to be in his uniform, fresh from the school gates.

'Exam leave,' he replied. 'If I start saying things like doth and thee, it's because I've been revising Macbeth all day. It's doing my head in.'

'God, I hated Shakespeare,' sympathised Joe, who then snatched up a large mixing bowl and nearby wooden spoon and began stirring demonically, his features scrunched into a hideous gurn. '*Double, double, toil and trouble; fire burn and cauldron bubble*,' he crooned in a ridiculously high-pitched voice.

Alice giggled loudly, whilst Ben and Maggie exchanged a look that said *what the hell did I just witness?*

'Right then, children,' she said, calling her class to order. 'No Sav today?'

Joe put down his props and smoothed down his apron. 'He said to start without him, he's gone to the cash-and-carry. Shouldn't be too long.'

Maggie nodded.

'OK, today we're going to strip things right back to basics and start with making bread. Then whilst the dough is proving, we'll practice a few knife skills and prepare a simple roux-based soup. A roux, as you may be aware, is the base of many sauces and an essential catering skill.'

Joe and Ben nodded along, each standing at their stations awaiting instruction and Maggie felt a premature wave of pride at the eagerness in these two, very different men, giving up their own free time to learn.

'But,' she said, offering a sidelong glance to Alice, to keep her included in proceedings, 'before we begin, what is the very first thing any chef must do?'

A stupefied silence reigned.

'I know, I know!' cried Alice, bouncing up and down on her stool so animatedly, Maggie feared she'd fall. 'Wash our hands, Granny!'

An hour later, after a messy period of mixing, kneading and stretching, three scored loaves and a child-sized bread roll lay proving under tea towels. Maggie had broken away a small piece of her own dough for Alice, with which she had studiously attempted to replicate Joe's every move. It seemed the big man had a fan.

'Now, remember we've used instant yeast as a cheat here, the normal process for making the tastiest, fresh-baked bread would take closer to three hours, but the principles are the same, we've merely eliminated some of the rising time.'

Ben had surprised her by exercising some creative flair and adding nigella seeds to his loaf. Gita's store cupboard boasted a menagerie of spices, seeds and ingredients, many that even Maggie hadn't heard of, and each of them as exciting to her as pick 'n' mix to a child.

'So sorry, guys,' came Sav's voice as he appeared at the door. 'That took longer than expected. Wow, it looks like you've been busy,' he added, peering under a cloth. Then, when he spotted Alice, drowned in an adult-sized apron, and looking ghostly under the layer of flour coating her cheeks, he remarked, 'and you must be Maggie's sous-chef. I've heard lots about you.'

Alice met Sav's kind smile with an indignant hand on her hip. 'I'm Alice, not Sue.'

Maggie chuckled to herself.

As Sav took up his place at the counter, after washing

his hands as instructed by Alice, Maggie moved on to the next stage of her lesson, knife skills. She'd been a good girl and not risked Hannah's wrath by carrying Geoff's knives back to the kitchen again, even though they were missed. Joe had since sharpened Gita's knives, which although not a patch on Geoff's, were now at an almost acceptable standard, Maggie noted. She was thankful Sav had selected the bluntest of the bunch when one of the potatoes he was chopping, slipped from his fingers, shot across the kitchen island and ricocheted into the sink with a splash.

Later, Ben stirred his roux, under the guidance of Joe who'd nailed it first time.

'Always remember, lads, a watched pot *doesn't* boil over,' called Maggie when they stopped to look at a funny video someone called Tom had sent to Ben. He'd mentioned this Tom rather a lot – a school friend, Maggie supposed. Maggie had even seen that Ben had a photograph of himself and Tom with their arms around each other as the background on his phone.

Sav, in an effort to catch up, was kneading his bread as urgently as though administering CPR, and she hoped to God he was never called upon to resuscitate anyone; they'd be crushed as flat as a naan.

Maggie took out her phone and sent a quick message to Hannah.

*We're at the restaurant, could you collect us on your way home? Don't worry about supper, we have it covered! Xx*

Whilst a simple leek and potato soup wasn't exactly the most inspiring of evening meals, let alone seasonal, Maggie knew better than anyone this rich and creamy dish accompanied by a fresh, warm, crusty loaf could be the finest of any feasts. And that was what this session was all about. Cooking simple food, well.

At the sound of a melodic rap on the window above the kitchen sink, Ben moaned. 'Oh, crap.'

The bright, smiley girl with the nose piercing was waving through the glass, trying to catch his attention. He turned and held up his splayed fingers, mouthing *I'll be five minutes*.

'Somewhere you're meant to be?' asked Maggie, bemused by the expression of doom writ across his face.

'I forgot I promised Jade I'd help with her media studies project.'

'Well, that's not terribly charitable, is it, leaving a young lady standing outside? Let her in, she can wait whilst we finish up.'

Ben sighed and passed his spoon to Joe, then went through to the storeroom to open the fire door.

Sav sniggered. 'Why do I get the impression Ben *conveniently* forgot?'

Seconds later, a rainbow-coloured whirlwind blew into the kitchen. Everything about Jade, from her pink eyeshadow, down to her bright yellow Converse, was cheerful.

'What's up!' she sang, whilst seemingly not requiring a response. 'Smells *divine* in here.'

'That will be the bread,' remarked Maggie, crossing the space to open the oven door. 'So effective they use it in supermarkets to make us hungry whilst we shop. But this,' she said, removing one of the golden loaves, 'should taste better than anything shop-bought.'

'Soup's done,' said Joe, turning off the gas. 'Shall we try it?'

'Always try a dish before serving, to check for seasoning.'

'Can I have some?' asked Alice, who had been so good, helping to peel potatoes and watching and listening.

'We're going to take *ours* home to share with Mummy, darling,' said Maggie with a wink.

'I really don't think I'm cut out for this,' said Sav, exasperated. His dough had turned as solid as a house brick, from being vigorously overworked and the only chance it would be rising was if it levitated off the worktop. If this man was ever in charge of the kitchen, the place would be doomed.

'You can share mine, mate,' said Joe, grabbing a couple of soup bowls and a bread knife.

'This is so awesome,' enthused Jade, pulling out a glitter-covered phone and taking pictures of the food. She zoomed in as Joe bent over the loaf and carefully sliced it open, the cut bread springing back beautifully under the applied pressure. Then Jade showed them the short video she'd created in just moments; it looked so professional, and mouth-wateringly inviting.

Maggie was impressed. 'What are you doing with that?'

'Oh, I just posted it on Insta. Everyone loves pictures of food, right?'

Did they? Well, she supposed it was no different to ogling the mouth-watering recipes in her weekly *Good Housekeeping* magazine.

As the others slathered butter onto warm bread and slurped at their soup, Maggie decanted hers into a tub ready to take home.

'How is it?' she asked, though the expression on Jade's face as she licked a spoon clean, then double-dipped it into a disgruntled Ben's bowl, said it all.

'Bloody hell, Jade,' he grumbled. 'I was kind of enjoying it *without* your saliva.'

She paused, as though considering his point, then ditched the spoon for a hunk of bread, which she plunged into the soup leaving a trail of gently bobbing crumbs in its wake, then stuck her tongue out at him.

'See,' said Jade, angling her phone for Maggie to see, 'it's got twelve likes already.' Another one popped in as she watched.

*Indeed.* And whilst Maggie had just spent the best part of two hours coaching her very willing students in the art of cookery, it had taken a mere thirty seconds to share the results with the world. Well, perhaps not quite the world, but as far as Maggie was concerned, even a cute snap of Monty liked by her five Facebook friends was a viral sensation. It seemed the hippy fellow in Zen Lounge may have been right. Things really had changed.

# Chapter Ten

## Hannah

By the following Wednesday, it had become clear Maggie was on some kind of mission. To what end exactly, Hannah was unsure. What she did know was that since embarking on her Mary Berry impersonation at The Golden Crocus, she'd seemed somewhat distracted. At one point, Alice claimed silly Granny had put her bowl of strawberries and cream on the floor and Monty's pongy cat food in front of her on the table. Then there had been the day Hannah had received a call from Alice's Year 1 teacher to ask if Granny was still coming to collect her because she appeared to be running late. Naturally, a panicked Hannah had immediately called her mother, who answered, breathless, saying, 'I'll be there in two mins,' before hanging up. Then, this evening, when she'd dropped Alice's bag round after work ready for her overnight stay, Maggie seemed to have *entirely forgotten* Hannah was going out and was virtually pushing the pair of them out the door, not a morsel of dinner in sight.

'Alice is sleeping here tonight, Mum?' she'd said, holding up the bag. 'I've brought her pyjamas and clean clothes for tomorrow. I'm going out with Laura, remember?'

A crestfallen look had washed over Maggie before she quickly righted herself. 'Silly me! Head like a sieve.'

Hannah left not knowing whether her mother had been disappointed with herself for forgetting, or dismayed at the forgotten arrangement. Either way, it didn't sit right. Because for whatever the reason may be, Hannah was left feeling as though they were becoming an inconvenience. Or even worse, a burden.

'She'd probably just forgotten and made other plans,' reassured Laura when Hannah expressed her concerns.

They were standing at the bar in the busy White Lion pub, waiting to be served.

'I don't think so. Since Dad died, Mum doesn't really go out much,' said Hannah. 'She used to be heavily involved in the WI, but she's not mentioned that in ages. I don't think she even sees her friend Pam much these days, and they used to be so close. It's more that lately, she's become . . .' Hannah paused, searching for the right word. 'Unpredictable.'

Laura cocked an eyebrow. 'You don't think . . .'

'What?' frowned Hannah. 'I don't think what?'

'You don't think she's started dating? What about that guy two doors down?' Her stage whisper was as subtle as if she'd leapt onto the bar in her bra and pants and run a teaspoon along the optics.

Hannah gawped at her friend, speechless.

'What can I get you ladies?' asked the beer-bellied landlord, who had miraculously appeared in front of them.

Magic. It would be all around town by nightfall: Maggie Lawford and Oscar Wright, who'd have thought it? And what with her husband not even gone a year.

'No, Laura,' she said, once they'd placed their order and Baz had slunk off to the cellar for their inconvenient beverage request – shocking, who dares to order wine in a pub? 'I can categorically assure you my mother has not started dating. And whilst I've nothing against the idea of my mother finding love again one day, her and Dad . . .' she sighed, exhausted by the very idea, 'they were soulmates. In every sense of the word. Mum may as well have lost a vital organ.' She shook her head and picked at a beer mat. 'But *something's* changed. She's got a bit of her old spark back. Which is bloody great, I just don't want to extinguish it with all the responsibility I'm heaping upon her.'

Laura shook her head. 'Nuh-uh. Don't even think it. Your mum loves having Alice.'

'Well, the feeling's mutual. I still can't believe Darren, the useless ball sack, has actually managed to show up two weeks running, I keep waiting for him to let Alice down. And then he won't know what's hit him.'

'Han,' said Laura in the tone of voice she usually reserved for persuading one of her twins not to pummel the other one's head in, 'I do agree with you. *Total* ball sack. Worse, as I'm not sure there's anything half as productive as sperm inside his miserable carcass. *But*, you know, maybe he's genuinely trying. Perhaps he's finally grown up and realised what he's been missing out on. I mean, he's decorated a bedroom for Alice in the new place, didn't you say?'

Hannah scoffed. 'Yeah, it's *Frozen*-themed. *So* five years ago. And I'm still not convinced there isn't a new floozy on the scene. Someone he's sneaking in once Alice is in bed, so she doesn't tell tales on him.'

'But you don't know that. You don't *actually* know if he's been seeing anyone since you kicked him out, do you?'

When Hannah had got wind of his first indiscretion, a one-night stand on a lads' night out, she'd been prepared to put it behind them. Not in the *I forgive you, I love you, I can't live without you* sense; no, it was more that with a newborn baby preventing anything more than two hours' sleep, leaking boobs during client meetings and a tiredness so severe she fell asleep on the tube and ended up in Richmond three times in one week, she couldn't face doing it alone.

The second time, however, had been a more visceral experience. The kind where a cancelled meeting sees you unexpectedly heading home at lunchtime in relatively good spirits, only to find your husband in flagrante with the cleaner, in the (presumably, uncleaned) bath.

'Right, here we go. One bottle of *dry* white wine, as requested by Madame. I take it that will be two glasses? Or shall I just pop a straw in?'

Baz, who had run this pub since Hannah and Laura were students and who had not aged nearly as well, chortled at his own wit. It really was a wonder the place was so busy, but it just so happened to have the nicest beer garden around, which was where they headed.

'Sea salt and cider vinegar,' Laura squinted at the packets in her hand, 'or cheddar cheese and pickled onion?'

'I didn't have time for dinner, so all of the above. Get them bad boys open,' replied Hannah, minded to rip them open and bury her face inside.

'Oh, this is nice,' sighed Laura. 'It's so wonderful having you on the doorstep, Han.'

Hannah smiled at her friend and clinked their glasses together. 'Cheers to that. So, this is new,' she indicated the twinkling fairy lights draped artfully around the walled garden and the colourful hanging baskets. 'Doesn't look like Baz's handywork.'

Laura leaned in conspiratorially. 'He's got a new woman – Hayley. She *was* working for Marco and defected to this place when she started dating Baz.'

Hannah grimaced. 'They say there's someone for everyone. How is Marco? Busy as ever?'

Laura blew out her cheeks. 'He's so busy I hardly see him. I feel like a single parent half the time. Do you know what Connor said the other day? He said, "Mummy, are you and Daddy going to get another house like Freddy's parents have? And will I get another Mummy too?" Honestly, Han, he was as excited as when he writes his letter to Santa. Perhaps that's exactly what he was thinking about – double the bloody presents. I know Marco can't help it and he's just trying to provide for us, but at what cost? That's my worry.'

Laura took a miserable sip of her wine and Hannah had a visceral flashback to her own childhood. To the countless nights she'd lay awake in bed, determined not to fall asleep before her dad got home. She knew when she heard the door click softly shut, even though he was silent as a burglar, he'd always creep up the stairs and peer into her room, just in case. To Hannah, bedtime without a goodnight kiss from her dad wasn't bedtime at all. It just meant she'd usually wait, for as long as it took.

'The hospitality business can be so gruelling, especially on relationships and families. But Marco adores you and the kids; he's just trying to build you a future, by doing what he does best.'

'I know that,' said Laura, with a small smile. 'I just wish he wasn't missing out on so much. *And* I wish I had something I was even half as passionate about, as he is about that place.'

'You're passionate about being a mother. Don't knock it!'

'Really, Hannah? Some days the most adult word to leave my mouth is toothpaste. If I don't get back into work soon, I'll have forgotten how to speak, let alone interact with other adults.'

'Is that what you want? To go back to work?'

'I don't know,' Laura shrugged. 'I feel like I should, but I honestly don't know how we'd manage as a family. We'd become even more fractured than we already are.'

Exactly the choice Mum faced, thought Hannah, guiltily. And thanks to her, she hadn't been forced into a similar one. Although lately, whilst the shine hadn't gone off her career exactly, the spotlight *had* shifted slightly, and it was illuminating an empty space next to it where she increasingly wanted to be.

'Hello, hello, hello,' said Laura, smirking over Hannah's shoulder. 'Here's a couple of faces I haven't seen in a while – it's like being back at high school all over again.'

Even as Hannah turned briefly to glance behind her, an anticipatory glow warmed her cheeks. Sure enough, stepping through the open doors into the garden, bottles of chilled Corona in hand, were both Joe and Sav. She turned back around, inexplicably embarrassed.

Before a couple of weeks ago, she hadn't seen this man for over fifteen years, and now he was everywhere.

Laura waved frantically, as though they'd been saving them a seat at a football game.

Unable to see what was going on behind her, Hannah mentally catalogued her appearance. She'd come pretty much straight from work, only stopping at her mum's to drop off Alice's things, before driving her car home and walking straight back into town. She hadn't even gone inside the house. Was still wearing smart trousers and a high-necked silk blouse and jacket infinitely more suited to the courtroom she'd been in today, than a twinkly pub garden in early June. Her sleek ponytail was giving her a headache and she wasn't sure her armpits were as fresh as she would have liked.

Sav, on the other hand, as he appeared at the picnic bench before them, was in washed-out chino shorts, a fitted linen shirt and slip-on canvas shoes, looking for all the world like a man on his summer vacation.

'Good evening, ladies,' said Joe cheerfully. 'Gosh, Laura, haven't seen you in a while. I heard you've got twins! Bet they keep you on your toes?'

'Honestly? Some days it's like keeping Pennywise and the Joker from killing each other, and other times as joyful as watching puppies play in toilet roll. No two days are the same.'

As the two men laughed, Hannah's eyes slid to Sav's, only to find him watching her.

She picked up her wine glass. 'Not out dodging bullets and freeing enslaved humans from the mainframe today, I see, Neo?' she said, motioning towards his casual attire.

Sav acknowledged the jibe with a grin.

'It's a Wednesday. Middle of the week, no-one has the energy. Maybe that's why you're here of course? Offering legal counsel to brow-beaten villains and vigilantes on their day off, from, you know, vigilante-ing. Are your robe and wig under the table?'

Hannah smiled into the rim of her glass. *Touché.*

'If you must know, I came straight from the office. And I'm a solicitor, not a barrister, we don't play dress-up. At least, not for work.'

*Blimey Hannah. Where did that come from?*

A bemused smile danced around the edges of Sav's lips.

'Um, did I miss something?' Laura said. Her forehead was crumpled in confusion.

Hannah hadn't got as far as updating her friend on the situation with The Golden Crocus, or her mother's involvement in the kitchen, or indeed her recent interactions with Savinder Kapoor. As far as Laura knew, these two hadn't seen each other since school. And of the four of them, only Joe and Laura had stayed in the area.

'Oh, not much. Only Hannah's mum being a superstar and my new kitchen hero,' said Joe. 'Hey, do you mind if we join you?'

'Of course not! Sit down.' Laura moved her bag from the space beside her and Joe, with as much grace as a pantomime horse, squeezed into the spot, one leg under the table, the other jutted out at a right angle. These types

116

of garden picnic tables were simply not designed with six feet and four inches of skeletal frame in mind.

'I'll go and get some more drinks,' said Sav. 'Han? Laura? Another bottle?'

'I shouldn't really, the twins will be jumping up and down on my head when the sun comes up, which is never fun with a hangover,' giggled Laura, 'but this is the first time I've been out with real adults in such a long time I feel like letting my hair down.'

Sav gave a decisive nod. 'Another bottle coming up.' He raised his empty bottle of beer and motioned to Joe. 'Same again?'

'Please.'

'Another thing that maybe we *don't* mention to my mother,' said Sav to Hannah, eyes sparkling, before he turned on his heel.

'Well,' said Laura abruptly. 'We won't see him again for a good half hour, by the time Baz has slogged back down to the cellar.' She narrowed her eyes. 'So that should give you both plenty of time to tell me what's been going on.'

As Joe briefed Laura on the evening he henceforth referred to as his mini meltdown, and Maggie's subsequent assistance, Hannah felt a warm glow of pride. There are some who may have found her mother's interference patronising or meddlesome, but it was clear from listening to Joe, he had a genuine respect and fondness for her. In the week that had passed since she had started offering cookery lessons at the restaurant after school, they'd had quite a few more sessions.

'You should have seen the caramel tuile your Alice made yesterday,' said Joe, laughing. 'I tell you, that little girl is going to be cooking you five-course gourmet meals by the time she's ten.'

'It's all she talks about,' grinned Hannah. 'She used to say she wanted to be a doctor when she grows up, but now she insists she wants to be a "chef, like Joe". I think you have an admirer.'

Joe's kind face crumpled with pleasure. 'She's a great kid. You must be really proud.'

Hannah felt a rush of love. 'I am. But truthfully, it's Mum who's her biggest influence.'

'So how come you got back into catering, Joe?' asked Laura. 'The last time we bumped into each other you were renovating period properties. Change of heart?'

Joe's face fell, but he recovered himself quickly. 'Dad sold the firm and emigrated to New Zealand with wife number four. Always thought I'd take it on eventually, but there you go . . .'

Hannah had known Joe was unemployed when Sav asked him to work for him, but not the circumstances. That seriously sucked, to have dedicated nearly two decades of your working life to a family firm, believing you would be carrying it forward to the next generation, only to have it pulled from under you. Even worse, it looked as though the very same thing might be about to happen again.

'But you know what,' added Joe, brightening, 'I'm really loving it. Made me remember what drew me towards catering all those years ago, before Dad persuaded me to go and work for him instead. I should have ignored him and followed my heart. I think this is where I'm meant to be.'

'That's brilliant,' said Laura. 'I'm really pleased for you.'

Discomfort bloomed in Hannah's belly. It didn't sound like Joe had any inkling the restaurant was doomed. Why hadn't Sav been honest and told him about it? Was he really going to stitch up his oldest mate by not warning him he could be out of a job again in a matter of weeks?

When Sav returned with their drinks, he sat beside Hannah. He slipped in next to her with infinitely more grace than Joe had, and for some reason, even though there was a foot between them, it felt intimately close.

Laura, who had managed to polish off the first bottle almost single-handedly, began topping them both up from the new one and gave a sudden, hiccupy giggle.

'What's funny?' asked Hannah.

'Nothing. I was just remembering the last time I saw you two sitting together like that. Shelley Dunn's house party after our GCSE results, ring any bells?'

Hannah's cheeks flamed.

'Ha!' exclaimed Joe, remembering. '*Oh my God.* I'd forgotten all about that.'

Hannah wished, with all her heart, she could too.

An unwelcome flashback of her and Laura dancing to Kylie Minogue's 'Can't Get You Out of My Head', wearing white tea towels on their head in as close an approximation to the star's iconic costume as could be found in Shelley's parents' kitchen had her curling her toes under the table.

'How old were we then?' asked Joe.

'Sixteen,' replied Hannah. It was seared into her mind. Sixteen years of age and the first time she'd ever kissed a boy.

'I don't think I remember that?' said Sav.

119

Hannah's mortification intensified.

'Course you do. Her parents went away and the whole of Year 11 gatecrashed her party in that big posh house,' said Joe.

It was also one of the first times Hannah had drunk alcohol. She was only tipsy really, uninhibited enough to dance and join in the fun, and enough to know when she'd found Sav in the garden on his own, he'd been waiting for her. He'd been sitting on a garden bench, looking out at Shelley's parents' immaculate lawn. Or, at least, it *had* been immaculate, until fifty drunk and rowdy teenagers took a dip in their pool and the police were called.

She remembered sitting down next to him, still hot from all the dancing. Remembered the way he'd glanced sidelong at her. At how thrilling it had felt.

'You've got a better memory than me,' said Sav, his tone light and dismissive.

*How could he not remember?*

'What about when you were sick on our school trip to Normandy, Joe?' asked Hannah, deliberately changing the subject.

The conversation moved on to safer territory, which was to say, the gentle teasing of Joe, and Laura gave her a knowing smirk. The same smirk that been on her friend's face when Hannah and Sav had pulled apart from that kiss to find her standing on the patio before them, two bottles of WKD Blue in hand.

## Chapter Eleven

## Maggie

Maggie was dressed for the kitchen, in what she had come to think of as her work uniform. A comfortable pair of cotton trousers, her lightweight memory-foam trainers, and a breathable, linen top. She only became aware she was pacing when Alice asked if she was trying to get her steps up, like Mummy did. On the one hand, it was highly amusing to think of her daughter doing circuits of her matchbox-sized lounge in an effort to please her Apple watch. But on the other, how sad Hannah hadn't even the time to get out in the fresh air and enjoy such a simple activity as walking.

'Yes darling, that's right. Only a few more to go. Got to try and keep fit.'

It was a fib, but better than saying, 'No, darling, it looks as though your useless father isn't coming, he isn't answering his phone, and I was supposed to be at the restaurant an hour ago.' Never mind the fact she'd spent *so* much time on her feet this past couple of weeks, she'd given herself bunions.

From where she sprawled on the sofa, Alice reached out and changed the channel on the TV remote, switching off the inoffensive chirruping of an animated mole on CBeebies and replacing it with an ITV trailer for a cookery programme, featuring none other than the gloating face of Hugo Wick.

Everything about the man, from his foppish, shaggy hair, to the way he stood, shoulders back, legs a stance, screamed privilege. You didn't need Wikipedia to tell you what came out in his mannerisms; he was a public-school bully who belittled, degraded and bulldozed his way through everyone in his path.

'Think you can cook? Well, I'm here to tell you you're wrong. Forget everything you think you know, tear up your recipe books and chuck out your air fryers. Tune in tonight at 9 p.m. to see how it's *really* done.'

'Arrogant arse,' muttered Maggie under her breath, worried Alice would do her usual trick of repeating her choicer phrases, racked her brains for a distraction and amended in a too-light tone, '*I was going to ask*, would you be a poppet and run upstairs to fetch Granny's watch? Thank you, darling, it's in my bedside table drawer.'

As soon as her granddaughter skipped from the room, she stabbed at the remote control, vanquishing Hugo's smug scowl from the screen and then she dialled Hannah's number.

'What shall I tell her?' she whispered, hating how angry Hannah sounded. 'And he hasn't contacted you either? Right, OK. I'll think of something. See you when you get here, love.'

Maggie hung up and immediately rang the restaurant,

dismayed when it went to the answerphone message advising the restaurant's opening hours. She didn't have the personal phone numbers of either Sav or Joe and would just have to hope they managed without her. The restaurant would be open for business by the time Hannah got home, which, thanks to a railway incident, wouldn't be her usual early Friday finish.

'Here you are, Granny,' said Alice, delivering the good as new retirement gift to her. Watches seemed so redundant in these days of mobile phones.

'Thank you, darling,' said Maggie, slipping the pristine timepiece onto her wrist and fastening it. Perhaps it was time she started wearing it, it looked rather splendid on. 'Now, I've just heard from Daddy, and he's very sorry but it looks as though he's not going to make it today after all.'

Alice's face fell and Maggie's heart tugged. She hugged her into her side. 'How about a game of Guess Who, until Mummy gets here, how does that sound?'

'But I wanted to see Keith,' replied Alice, a tell-tale quiver in her voice foretelling tears. 'Mu-mmy bought me some treats to give him. They're in my bag.'

'Oh, sweetheart. I'm so sorry. But you can give him the treats next time.' Maggie stroked her hair and inwardly cursed her ex-son-in-law. She'd dared to hope he might have bucked his ideas up. Clearly sticking to a routine was too much to ask.

'But I really wanted to play with him,' she said, her breath coming in shallow little half-formed sobs.

It didn't go unnoticed to Maggie that Alice was more upset about the prospect of not seeing Darren's dog than not seeing Darren himself. Thank goodness for the fickleness of a child's wants. Though she was no fool, knowing only too well how carefully young children disguised their disappointments. Had seen it herself countless times when Hannah was young and Geoff had missed school nativities, parents' evenings, mealtimes.

'I've got an idea,' she said, bending down to her granddaughter's eye level. 'Seeing as you have a bag of treats and I happen to have a surplus of flapjacks, how about we pop along and see Banjo for a few minutes?'

Alice wiped her eyes with her cardigan sleeve. 'Is, is, is that the old man's dog? The white fluffy one?'

Maggie tried not to baulk at the reference to the 'old man'. As Hannah had pointed out only recently, the difference in their ages was negligible.

Seemingly placated with the new plan, Maggie fetched a plate of flapjacks from the kitchen and took Alice by the hand, then they trotted two doors down along the street and rapped at number thirteen.

She had to hand it to him; he kept his small front garden neat and tidy, the path swept, and the lawn cut. Her own, she'd noticed, was looking rather tatty. Another small way in which the gaping hole Geoff had left in her life could be both seen and felt.

'Maggie, what a nice surprise,' beamed Oscar, throwing open the door. 'And how lovely to see you too, little Miss.'

A sombre Alice clung to Maggie.

'Drowning in flapjack,' said Maggie, thrusting the plate into his hands without further explanation. 'And we wondered if we might say hello to Banjo whilst we're here?' She widened her eyes and looked down at Alice, hoping he would take the tearful child-sized hint.

As his dark, wiry eyebrows worked, almost comical in their contrast to his shock of white hair, she could see the cogs grinding. They appeared to be in need of a little WD40, so she added, 'Alice *so* loves dogs.'

Eventually the penny dropped. He furtively checked behind him, then hesitated for a moment, before saying, 'Now, would you believe, it's time for Banjo's walk, what clever timing is that? Would you like to take him to the park?'

Maggie discreetly checked her watch. There was another half an hour at least before Hannah's train got in. Plenty of time for a quick turn about the park. More bleeding steps she really didn't need.

'Can we, can we?' gushed a much merrier Alice, all thoughts of Keith forgotten.

'Of course, darling, if it's OK with Oscar?'

Oscar nodded enthusiastically. 'You'll be doing me a favour. Now, wait here and I'll fetch him.'

To Maggie's surprise, Oscar stepped back inside and firmly closed the door, which felt oddly like having the door slammed in their faces. Perhaps he was concerned Banjo would run off. Although she'd seen the little dog trot meekly along beside him off the lead, many times before.

Within seconds, Oscar reappeared with a very excited Banjo, complete with baby blue collar and lead.

Alice looked as though she might combust with happiness as the cute Westie nuzzled against her leg. She bent to stroke his head and he panted appreciatively.

'Well, he certainly seems to like you,' said Oscar. 'I'd keep him on the lead, as it's your first time walking him.

He's usually a very good chap but I wouldn't want you to panic if he did a vanishing act.'

'Understood,' said Maggie, taking the lead, whilst Alice skipped in front. 'Thank you,' she mouthed, shielding her face so only he could see.

'Happy to help. You know, I'm starting a new pottery class tomorrow at 2 o'clock, if you fancied having a go, or – should that be *a throw*? I'm pretty sure there are spaces available.'

*Give me strength.*

'Lots on at the moment, Oscar. Another time perhaps,' she said cheerfully, letting the little dog lead her away.

By the time they returned from a scoot around the small park closest to home, Hannah's car was parked in the street. They quickly returned Banjo to his owner and let themselves in.

Alice had completely forgotten she was ever meant to be going to her father's and was still buzzing from her time with Banjo. Hannah, on the other hand, was so rigid with temper, you could have used her as a spirit level.

'Sorry,' said Maggie. 'Hope you haven't been waiting long. We just took Banjo for a quick walk.'

'I thought you had to be at the restaurant,' said Hannah, an icy edge to her tone. 'I took a taxi from Stansted Mountfitchet to get me home quicker.'

Shoot.

'Well,' began Maggie, with caution. 'I'm sorry about that, but Alice was a little . . .' she hunted for a word to convey her granddaughter's upset without starting a blazing scene about Darren in front of her, 'disappointed. About not seeing Keith.'

Hannah sucked in air through her nose, her entire face taught with tension.

'And who's Banjo?'

'Oscar's doggy, Mummy. He's really cute. And he licked my knee.'

Hannah narrowed her eyes in a way that caught Maggie slightly off guard. What the heck was wrong with that? Banjo was a fluffball soft as blancmange, not a snarling, rabies-infested Pit Bull.

'Often walk Oscar's dog, do you, Mum?'

Oh no, no. Maggie did *not* like the tone her daughter was taking. And she also knew better than to engage with her when she was in one of these moods. Her gripe was with Darren, not her. Best not to give rise to it.

'Right. Well, I'll be getting off. There's a quiche in the fridge if you want it, Hannah. Alice and I ate earlier. Lock up after yourselves.'

She kissed the top of Alice's head, shot a *behave yourself* look in her daughter's direction, then scarpered before she could react. She wasn't that brave.

Service had already begun, by the time Maggie arrived at the restaurant.

She made an apologetic face at Sav, who was serving drinks behind the bar and filed past a mere handful of diners into the kitchen, where Joe was plating their starters.

'Everything alright, Maggie?' he asked with concern. 'We thought something must have happened.'

'No, but give it time. I'm fearful for my ex-son-in-law's life. I suspect the only thing stopping my daughter from

127

driving straight to Bishop's Stortford and murdering him on the spot is the fact I'm here and unable to look after Alice. So hit me up with some jobs.'

Joe grimaced. 'Not much to do. We've only got two bookings tonight. Sav even told Ben to take the night off.'

Maggie's heart sunk. Two paltry bookings on a Friday night. This place wasn't going to make it through another month and even *reach* 14th July. Not that she could voice her thoughts because it was blindingly obvious Sav had chosen not to enlighten his best friend, or Ben for that matter, on the predicament he was in.

If she didn't set her plan in motion, it would be too late. She only hoped Sav would go along with it.

'Joe,' she began. 'Have you finished the order for the wholesalers? Are we still expecting a delivery tomorrow?'

He frowned. 'Yes we are, but I haven't finished it yet. Why, did you want to add something?'

'Er, just a few extras.'

She squirmed, knowing that might just have been the understatement of the century.

## Chapter Twelve

## Maggie

What Maggie had planned was, if she was being honest, ever so slightly manipulative. But drastic times called for drastic measures and if there was even the slightest chance of saving The Golden Crocus, then surely it was worth it.

At 7 a.m. on Saturday morning, she telephoned Hannah.

'Mum. What's up?' There was a cool edge in her voice, and she sounded tired.

'Nothing, I'm fine. Are you?'

There was a long sigh on the other end of the phone. 'Yeah. Apparently, Darren forgot. Can you believe it? Was in the cinema of all places with his phone on silent. Or so he claims.' Her voice cracked with a fizzing rage. 'How can you *forget* you have a five-year-old waiting for you to pick them up?'

'Hmm,' was all Maggie could offer. Fanning the flame of Hannah's anger wasn't going to help anyone. 'Is he collecting her today instead?'

A loud snort of fury had her pulling the phone away

from her ear. 'Mum. He isn't going to be picking her up ever again. Not if I can help it. And I'm *sorry* if that's inconvenient for you. We'll just have to make other arrangements.'

Maggie recoiled a little from the stinging remark but told herself it was nothing personal. Hannah was hurting on Alice's behalf. A sentiment she could relate to.

She deftly changed the subject. 'I was wondering if you and Alice had any plans this morning?'

'Not unless you count weeding my patio. It's starting to look like a scene from *Jurassic Park*. I keep expecting to be ambushed by velociraptors whenever I hang out the washing.'

Maggie smiled. This was more like Hannie.

'Well,' she ventured, 'if you have nothing more pressing, I wondered if you and Alice could pop along to the restaurant. Say, 9 o'clock?'

'Really?' She sounded exasperated. 'It's hardly feeding the ducks, is it?'

'Alice likes it there.'

'I know she does, Mother, and sometimes it would be nice if she liked being *here*, too.'

Maggie reeled. Although if she thought about it, she supposed it was true. Alice did spend far more time at Maggie's house – and, lately, in the restaurant kitchen after school – than she did in her own home. But there wasn't time to address that right now.

'Look. I could do with your help. I have an idea to share with Sav and the others, and I think Sav might take it more seriously if you're there too.'

There was a sound much like a fart from the other end.

'I don't see what bearing I could possibly have on anything to do with Sav,' retorted Hannah. 'You're very much mistaken, if that's what you think.'

Most interesting. It seemed she'd touched a raw nerve.

'Oh, I don't know. Call it strength in numbers then,' tried Maggie.

After a beat, Hannah said. 'OK, Mum. We'll be there. Should we bring anything?'

Maggie considered for a moment. 'Your appetites.'

As she hung up, she looked around the kitchen, at every surface covered with defrosting Tupperware containers. It was a good job she hadn't got rid of the chest freezer in the garage, which rarely held more than a bag of ice and several emergency pizzas, because over the past week it had finally come into its own.

At 8.30 a.m. on the dot, her doorbell chimed, and she smiled in satisfaction. Teenagers today got a bad rap, but they weren't all lazy so-and-sos.

'Morning, Ben love,' she said, throwing open the door onto a hazy, bright day.

He'd been surprised to hear from her when she'd called him last night but didn't seem to mind at all that Joe had passed on his number. And, when she'd explained what she wanted, he'd been only too happy to give up his Saturday, which Maggie couldn't decide was admirable or marginally sad. A boy of his age should be busy with a million things, schoolwork aside.

'Morning,' he said, an element of shyness creeping back in outside the familiar kitchen space.

'Are you OK with that one and I'll take this?' Maggie asked, pointing at the large box on the floor in the hall. It

131

had seemed much more sensible to walk down than try to park on market day and Ben had youth on his side. Though personally, she thought he could do with a bit of feeding up.

'How are the exams going?' asked Maggie as they walked along the street.

'Had my last one this week. That's it now, *a-ll* done.' He almost sang the words, so jubilant was he.

'Well done. That must be a relief.'

'Er, I'm not sure about that. Pretty sure I'll have to retake Maths. But for now, I'm glad it's over. And I'll be able to do more hours at the restaurant, which is a bonus. Me and Jade are saving up for a trip to Leeds.'

Maggie ignored the flicker of guilt. Positive thoughts only.

'Leeds? What's in Leeds? I thought you were going to say Alton Towers or even Amsterdam. That's what you youngsters do these days isn't it, pretend you're going for a mooch around Anne Frank's place when all you're interested in is the wacky baccy?'

Ben laughed. 'We're only sixteen, Maggie. I don't think my dad would allow me to go to Amsterdam yet, even though that would be super cool. No, Jade wants to go to Leeds because that's where she hopes to go to uni. It's one of the best places to study journalism.'

Maggie was surprised. 'Doesn't she have another couple of years before university?'

'Yep. But this is Jade we're talking about. She's even planned the names of her future babies, which she'll have when she's thirty-five, mid-career. Apparently.'

'Gosh. And how do you feel about that?'

Ben shrugged and laughed. 'Nothing to do with me.'

'Well, I think it's fabulous she's so ambitious. I was at her age. Hannah too, and look at her now, a successful lawyer. Just remember to have some fun along the way, you kids, it's just as important.'

When they reached the restaurant, the front door was unlocked, and Sav was sitting at one of the tables with his laptop. He barely looked up.

'Hi guys, go on through. Joe's just taking in the delivery out back.'

They manoeuvred past with the bulky boxes, which Sav didn't even register, he was so engrossed in whatever he was doing.

Beyond the kitchen, the fire doors were open, and Joe was hauling crates into the storeroom, aided by a jovial ruddy-faced chap.

'Morning, Maggie. Morning, Ben,' called Joe when he spotted them. 'This is Ivan, from the wholesalers.'

'Eh-up,' greeted Ivan. He placed a crate of vegetables on top of a freezer and adjusted his flat cap. 'So, this is the lovely young lady I've heard so much about.'

'Oh please,' scoffed Maggie.

'I'm very pleased to meet you,' said Ivan, with broad Yorkshire charm. 'Your name seems to come up a lot in places 'round ere.'

Maggie stifled a groan of embarrassment, picturing her fruitless job-hunting day. She was probably a complete laughing stock among the town's catering establishments.

'I'm not sure why. I keep myself to myself.'

'Well, Marco Garcia in Fiesta speaks very highly of you. And so does the butcher when I deliver his pickles and chutneys. I get about, me.' He gave her a fat wink.

'Quite,' said Maggie, unwilling to be sucked in by his shameless flirtation.

She turned her attention to Joe, who was checking off a delivery note. 'Is everything there?'

'Looks like it.'

''Course it's all there,' said Ivan. 'We'd be a *part*salers if it wasn't now, wouldn't we?'

'What's this?' asked Ben, pulling a small, green, tapered vegetable from the top of a brown paper bag.

'Okra,' replied Maggie. 'Sometimes known as lady's fingers.'

Ben and Joe exchanged a look and suppressed childish snorts of laughter.

'Something you wouldn't know much about Ben, mate,' laughed Joe.

'Probably more than you.'

Ivan laughed out loud and picked up an empty plastic crate. 'On that note I think I'll leave you to it. Laters, folks.' He tripped out into the street and jumped into his parked van.

'OK, boys, are we going to stand around all day making puerile jokes, or get on with some work?'

'Sorry Ma'am,' Joe saluted. 'Where do you want us, Ma'am?'

This prompted another snigger from Ben.

'Joe!' came a squeal from the kitchen and Maggie turned to see Hannah and Alice had arrived, accompanied by Sav, who looked tired and drawn.

'Ah-ha, here's my favourite little chef,' said Joe, as Alice ran and jumped into his arms.

'Are we going to make more bun shoes?' she asked, bright-eyed with anticipation.

134

'Choux buns,' he corrected, referring to the last cookery lesson Maggie had given, in different types of pastry. 'I don't know yet what we're making today.'

Maggie experienced a sudden wave of nerves, deep in the pit of her belly. She knew, today, she was pushing the boundaries of what was required of her. Quite possibly she was overstepping the mark. Yet, with all the staff assembled and on behalf of her friends Gita and Raj, she knew she had to try.

'What *are* we making today, Maggie?' asked Ben, who hadn't even questioned what was in the box he'd carried.

Here goes nothing.

'Right, well. Firstly, Sav, I'd like to apologise. I'm afraid I embezzled your cousin's phone number from you a couple of weeks ago under false pretences.'

Sav pulled a face in confusion.

'Obviously, I did want to speak to your mum, ask after her and wish her a speedy recovery. But I also wanted to put something else to her entirely. You see, whilst I've been coming here in the afternoons and providing lessons in the basics of most classic cookery, I've also been taking lessons myself. With Gita. In the art of Indian cooking.'

Hannah looked puzzled.

Sav said, 'What? How?'

'Over Skype! Isn't it amazing? I've never used it before but with a bit of trial and error and some help from your lovely cousin Pritha, we sussed it. I've been getting up at 4 o'clock most mornings, to allow for the time difference, spending a few hours with Gita in the kitchen, working on my own recipes in the day, then squeezing in a quick spot of housework before collecting Alice from school and heading over here.'

'Shut the fridge door!' exclaimed Joe.

Hannah gawped.

'But, Mum, you must be exhausted! And there I was, thinking . . .'

Maggie tilted her head in amusement. 'Yes?'

'You just seemed so distracted, not to mention forgetful. I was beginning to wonder if . . .' She didn't seem to be able to articulate what Maggie knew she'd been starting to suspect.

'If I was copping off with the old duffer next-door-but-one? Is that what you were thinking? Don't be so ridiculous. I've seen him in *lycra*, Hannie. The man has no shame.'

Sav's face contorted as he attempted to keep it straight.

Hannah went a shade of pink.

'So,' Joe began, bringing the topic nicely back around to the reason for all this, 'does this mean you've learned the recipes from the original menu? Are we going to be a proper Indian restaurant again?'

'Well. That's what I wanted to put to you all. I *have* learned most of the recipes, yes. But I don't think that's what we should be offering. I have a different idea.'

'Go on.' Sav sounded dubious.

'Ben, love, help me unload these boxes.'

He moved to where they'd placed them on the worktop and they began unpacking the Tupperware containers, Maggie arranging them into rows.

Then she turned to Sav. 'The Golden Crocus has always been an Indian restaurant. A very *good* Indian restaurant.'

'Yeah, didn't Jamie Oliver used to come here? There's a picture of him on the wall,' piped up Ben.

'He did,' answered Maggie. 'Though the frequency of his visits is a matter of some debate.' She smiled at Hannah.

'But these days it has competition. There are two other Indian food restaurants in this town now, as well as Chinese food, Mexican food, Spanish food, you name it, it's out there. But what could set this place apart is excellent feel-good, comfort food, cooked with an Indian twist. Authentic home-cooked flavours, just as Gita would create, no additives, no *packets or jars*,' she emphasised, 'but also the kind of food you enjoy at home. Great dishes, cooked well. Memorable food. And, with the greatest of respect, neither myself or Joe are adequate substitutes for Gita in the kitchen, and nor would we wish to be. If she *is* thinking of taking a step back from the cooking long term, then this could be a perfect solution.'

Joe started nodding. She could see the cogs whirring, the chef in him already creating. 'Wow, we could make pies, but like instead of steak and kidney it could be, I don't know, beef madras or chicken balti or something.'

'*Exactly* my point,' replied Maggie. 'And I've spent quite a bit of time devising some dishes, over the past couple of weeks, as I've learned new skills and techniques and flavour combinations. I've brought them in for you to try, and, if you like them, which I really hope you will, I've er . . .' she paused, knowing this was the part where Sav could really take umbrage, 'I've adapted this weekend's produce delivery, so we can kick off with a brand-new menu tonight.'

A pained expression fell across Sav's face.

This had been a risk. She was backing him into a corner, and she knew it. Forcing him to lay it on the line in front of everyone. *What will it be*, she wondered, *sink or swim?*

'Ah, Maggie. Look this is really great and everything, but . . .'

'I think it's a brilliant idea!' blurted Hannah. 'Sav, think about it,' she said, spinning around to face him, fixing him with the full force of a lawyer's conviction. 'Not only is it a totally awesome USP for the restaurant, but a fresh shot. How often do you get the chance to reboot a forty-year-old business? And I presume your parents are on board with the idea, right, Mum?'

Caught off guard, Maggie coughed, 'Gita seemed quite taken with some of the dishes, yes.'

It wasn't a lie. She just wasn't revealing the full extent of their conversations around the subject of the restaurant.

Something unspoken passed between Sav and Hannah. If Maggie didn't know better, she'd have said it was a challenge. But when had Hannah and Sav ever been close enough for such games?

'I can help you with the menus if you like,' offered Hannah. 'We don't have anything else planned for today, do we, Alice?'

'I wanted to go and see Banjo again,' came a small voice from the corner.

'We can still do that, sweetie,' said Hannah, unwavering. 'We'll all need a break. I've a feeling it's going to be a long day.'

The kitchen fell quiet as Sav battled with whatever was going on behind those busy, dark eyes. Doubtless a mix of guilt, for not being straight with the others about the restaurant's dire outlook, as well as a feeling of defeat. If there was one thing Hannah was exceptional at, and there were many, it was setting out a case.

Eventually, despite the slight tic in his jaw, Sav let out a long, resigned breath.

'OK. Let's taste these new dishes then.'

# Chapter Thirteen

## Maggie

Maggie held the freshly printed sheet aloft and Joe read it out loud.

'Food you love, with an Indian twist. Evening Menu . . .'

Sav, with some interference from Hannah, had done a fantastic job. It looked professional, upmarket and unfussy, just as she'd hoped. Sav had even driven out of town to a large stationer for a ream of high-quality, thick cream paper and fresh ink for his printer. After much persuasion, Maggie had eventually convinced him laminated menus were the stuff of greasy spoons and kindergartens, designed purely for splattering with unidentifiable substances and not conducive to appetites. Besides, the flexibility of a changeable menu at the press of a button was invaluable and allowed for last-minute alterations.

By far the most popular dish in the morning's taste test had been her keema shepherd's pie, as she'd suspected it would be.

By then, in her sessions with Gita, Maggie had come

to understand the crucial importance of a good ginger and garlic paste, which formed the base of so many Indian dishes. The tangy aroma as it was added to sweet, softened onions was intoxicating. But it was only when she began to add the minced lamb meat to the pan, breaking it up with her wooden spoon as it browned, then adding salt, chilli, turmeric, coriander, cumin and fenugreek, as per Gita's keema recipe, that she realised, here were the bones of one her family's favourite home-cooked meals. Geoff's favourite, actually.

By the end of that morning, Maggie had adapted her usual recipe and created a spicy, rich, perfectly browned keema pie that looked and tasted divine. OK, so it was a deviation of the traditional north Indian dish, but the essence of it was there, cooked into the food in the same way Gita and Gita's mother before had done countless times over the years.

That was how the idea had started, until, within days, her kitchen was overrun with ingredients, pots, pans, plates, spoons and jar upon jar of spices, seeds, pastes and nuts, her enthusiasm for experimenting knowing no bounds.

It had taken quite some doing to clean and clear each day before heading to school for Alice, and a considerable amount of fresh air to blow through the cooking smells. She couldn't have said what made her want to conceal it from her daughter. Perhaps a fear of failure, or worse, foolhardiness. Hannah would question why she was getting so deeply involved, and she didn't even have an answer, not really.

But the more time she spent with Joe and Ben, each of

them so eager to learn and create, both of them passionate about food and taste and texture, the more she realised the amount of potential right there under Sav's nose.

'Happy?' she asked Joe.

He nodded and grinned. Though it was too late to back out now. There was an industrial-sized tray of keema pie in the oven, a dish of lamb shanks marinating in tandoori spices in the fridge, puff pastry cases ready to be filled with balti chicken, sweet potatoes peeled and sliced, ready to be fried. A tray of dark chocolate brownies cooled on the side, ready to be served with the freshly made pistachio kulfi Maggie had shown them how to make. The sweet, dense Indian ice cream had gone down a storm with everyone, even Sav, who, used to his mother's version, had tasted it then tipped his head in approval. Everyone had set to work that day, chopping, peeling, grating and whisking.

Hannah had taken Alice home around mid-afternoon, for a much needed rest. Then they were going to see if Banjo was up to another walk with his new human friends.

Maggie wasn't sure what was keeping her from collapsing on the spot. Sheer adrenalin, probably. Her right hip ached, her knees were screaming in protest and her bunions felt like cobblestones had been placed inside her shoes.

'Right then,' said Sav, who somehow looked fresh as a daisy. He was wearing a clean shirt and trousers, and smelled like sandalwood. 'Let's get this show on the road.'

As Sav went to open up, Ben came back into the kitchen. 'Tables are all laid.'

'With the linen?' asked Maggie, who'd also persuaded

Sav the sticky, tired tables needed either burning or covering. Covering seemed preferable.

'Yep. It looks about fifty years old, but better than before.'

'The food is the main event,' assured Maggie. 'Everything else is mere garnish.'

From where it sat on the worktop in the corner, Maggie's phone began to ring. Her *Ski Sunday* ringtone was deafeningly loud in the sudden quiet that had descended over the chaos. Like the lull in a storm.

Fully expecting it to be Hannah, Maggie answered it, without the scrutiny of her reading glasses which would have told her it was Pam's name, not Hannah's, lit up on the screen.

'You're not dead then, Maggie. I was starting to wonder.'

Drat. She didn't have time for this right now.

'Pam! So lovely to hear from you. Unfortunately, you've caught me at a bad time. Can I give you a tinkle tomorrow?'

'Is there ever a good time? I've been trying to get hold of you for weeks.'

What poppycock. OK, there had been a couple of texts she'd not yet responded to. And she hadn't felt up to WI last month, had made some excuse about Monty being under the weather. But that was before.

'Are you OK, Maggie? I'm worried about you.'

The concern in her friend's voice caught her off guard. Guilt stabbed at her conscience. Why *had* she been avoiding her oldest friend? In the weeks after Geoff's death, Pam had been her rock. Whilst Maggie had somehow managed to plaster on a mask of strength and resilience for her daughter and granddaughter, in her private moments, it was Pam who had seen her through it. Always on the other end of the phone or perched at the kitchen table with a teapot and biscuits.

She couldn't have said when things changed, she only knew they had. That, at some indefinable moment, sympathy and support felt like gifts she no longer wished to receive. A kind of watershed for the intimacies of her old life. A gradual realisation she was on her own. It was only Maggie who could look after Maggie. There was comfort to be taken in the caring for others, of course. Without Hannah and Alice and Monty, her life would have felt rather meaningless lately. But there was work to do on the redefining of oneself. She just wasn't sure anyone else would understand.

'I'm quite alright, Pam. Absolutely nothing to worry about. Just been a bit busy, you know how it is. Let's get a date in the diary for coffee, text me when you're free.'

Pam was always free. Nothing she liked more than an excuse to chuck cream cakes in her gob. Although, to be fair, that might have had plenty to do with escaping her husband Dave, whose idea of scintillating discourse was 'gems he'd found at the tip', most notably the burgundy leather recliner, which he was disinclined to leave between Friday afternoon and *Match of the Day 2* on Sunday. She supposed he must possess at least some charm, as their marriage had survived thirty years.

She realised with shame, that for quite some time, she hadn't asked Pam how *she* was doing.

'Are *you* OK, Pam?' she asked gingerly. 'And Dave?'

'Fine,' came the curt response. 'I'll let you get back to whatever it is you're so busy with. See you.'

Maggie stared at the phone screen. Pam had cut her off.

'Everything OK?' asked Joe.

'Oh, yes, just a friend checking in,' brushed off Maggie as breezily as she could.

The situation would have to wait, although Maggie suspected it might take a little more than a cuppa and a slice of coffee and walnut cake to make amends. She'd been a poor friend, no two ways about it.

When nearly an hour passed and no orders had been put through to the kitchen, Maggie felt the stirrings of panic.

Where were the customers? Sav had said there were at least three bookings for tonight and usually plenty of walk-ins.

Joe was busying himself with a peach and pomegranate tart he'd devised himself, the sweet shortcrust pastry and layers of thinly sliced fruit perfectly balanced with zingy lime zest and flaked almonds.

The door swung open. It was Ben.

He looked at their expectant faces and shrugged.

'One cancellation and two no-shows so far. There's a table of four booked for 8.15.'

'Jeez,' muttered Joe. 'They'd better be hungry.'

Behind Ben, the door opened a crack.

'Alright if I come in?'

It was Jade.

'Thought I'd see how it was going,' she said to the room. 'Ben told me about the new menu. Sounds *amazing*. Like, when he told me about the aloo gobi cauliflower cheese I was drooling, guys. Cauliflower cheese is the *best*.'

'Well,' said Maggie, arms crossed with tension. 'It looks like it might be your lucky day Jade, love, because there's a vat of it prepped, and not a single customer.'

Next through the door was Sav, with a face like thunder.

'That's it. Last table has cancelled, heard "better things" of our competitors, apparently. Bastards. Who does that? Reserve a prime table on a Saturday night and cancel ten minutes before their booking.' His jaw was set rigid as he swept an arm around the room. 'Sorry folks, looks like you've all given up your day for nothing.'

As if they were all involved in a new version of how many people can you fit in a Mini, or in this case, a kitchen, the door swung open again and into the cramped room slipped Hannah, with Alice in her arms, already in her pyjamas.

'Sorry,' she whispered, though there really was no need. There were no customers to hear her and no cooking to disturb. 'Alice wouldn't go to bed without coming to say goodnight.'

'I wanted to see Joe's special tart, he said I could have a taste,' said a shy and sleepy Alice, into her mother's shoulder. 'I've never tried a pommygranny.'

Nobody corrected her.

Everybody looked to the luscious tart, glistening on a cake stand.

'What's going on?' asked Hannah, her smile fading.

'No-one showed up,' said Sav, matter-of-factly.

'There's still time,' said Hannah, checking her watch. 'It's only 8.30.'

Sav gave a sarcastic laugh. 'This isn't Brick Lane, Hannah. Perhaps you've lived away so long you've forgotten, but most folks around here are tucked up in bed by 9 p.m. with a cocoa.'

Maggie stifled the urge to pick him up on his tone. She

knew the pressure he was under. Also knew she'd ambushed him today. Spent restaurant money on produce and a whole day of everyone's free time.

Maybe it was Alice's presence tempering her normally fiery daughter, but Hannah merely shrugged.

'Didn't look that way to me. The town is busy, there is money being spent and people young and old are out there having a good time. They're just not in *here*, having a good time. Different scenario entirely.'

Sav returned her direct gaze. For a moment it looked like he would argue his point, but then something in his demeanour changed and his shoulders seemed to visibly drop.

'Look. There's something you guys should know.'

So, here it was then. This was the face of defeat.

Sav continued. 'I was hoping not to have to do this, God knows I've tried. *We've* tried, all of you, and I'll be forever grateful. But the truth is this restaurant hasn't made money in years, the accountants are quite certain it's the end of the road and whether my parents were standing here or not, the fact remains – The Golden Crocus will probably have to close.'

Joe began shaking his head. A look of hurt passed across his eyes.

'How long?' he asked.

'How long have I known? A couple of weeks, longer. The books show how unprofitable the business has been. I was just hoping it was a blip, that things would pick back up.'

Joe ground his teeth. 'I meant, how long have we got. But it's nice to know you've been sitting on this news as we've all been working our arses off. Sorry,' he muttered to Hannah, though Alice was too tired to notice.

Maggie looked to the ground. Wasn't she just as responsible for keeping secrets? OK, so Hannah had told her in confidence, but still, she'd ignited in Joe a passion for this kitchen, whilst knowing it could be snuffed out at any moment. Perhaps that had been cruel.

Sav cleared his throat and tried to channel a professionalism he clearly didn't feel. Joe was his best friend, after all.

'Look, we've been made an offer. An extremely lucrative offer. Hugo Wick wishes to purchase the premises, fixtures and fittings and all; he's been looking for somewhere for a while, apparently. Mum and Dad are on board.'

Maggie's head snapped up.

Well, that was a lie. They damned well weren't 'on board'. Raj would still be smiling at the door in his red waistcoat as the building fell down around him, and as for Gita . . . Well, she was stuck in India with a newly fitted titanium hip and not a chance of running a kitchen for months. What choice did they have if Sav wasn't going to fight their corner?

'Hugo Wick!' exclaimed Joe, slamming a tea towel to the counter. 'You're going to let that gigantic pr—'

'Ahem,' interrupted Hannah, eyes widening in warning.

'You're going to let that vacuous idiot take over a core piece of our town centre and turn it into a poncy bistro. He'd serve up a solitary fish finger and charge you a fortune for the privilege.'

Sav sighed. 'If he's that determined, he'll find premises somewhere, even if it's not this one. But at least if it *is* this one, I won't have to worry about my parents starving in their old age.' He sounded tired and ratty. This conversation wasn't going anywhere.

'So, what's the deal?' demanded Joe. 'I mean, why go through with this whole charade today if the cards are already on the table?'

'*Because*,' hissed Sav, 'I hoped we might still turn it around. I hoped I might be able to save this place and hold my head up high when my parents return and say, "Hey, so I know I didn't go into the family business like you'd hoped, but I've managed to keep it trading."' He dragged his palms down his face. 'It's not a done deal. The accountants have given me until 14th of July to make this business profitable, or they've advised we sell. I decided *I'd* give the restaurant until then too, before going back home to my own business. I can't leave my partner in the lurch forever.'

Ben perked up, from where he'd slouched against the sink. 'That's still like four weeks away.'

'Does it really matter? Look I'm sorry, I really am. But to think we could turn this around in such a short time was probably always just a pipe dream.'

Then he addressed Maggie. 'And I'm really sorry, Maggie, you've worked so hard and I've barely even managed to pay you minimum wage.'

Maggie flapped a hand at him, dismissing any such concerns. 'I told you from the outset, you don't need to pay me. I'm happy to help.'

'Er, guys?' said Jade, from where she sat on the worktop, scrolling through her phone and swinging her yellow shoes against the cupboard doors in a most unhygienic fashion.

Ben sighed and muttered, 'Not now Jade.'

Poor lad looked as deflated as Maggie felt, and completely unequipped to deal with Jade's particular brand of effervescence right now.

'But wait. You need to hear this.'

She plucked a mini poppadum from a dish on the side and crunched down on it loudly. 'This place has a website, but it's *old*, man. Like I don't think it's been updated in a decade. The font's in Comic Sans, for God's sake.'

Maggie reeled. Was that where she'd been going wrong? What was wrong with Comic Sans? Was it code for, '*You're a dinosaur from the last millennium, steer well clear*?'

'Yes, I made it for them a long while ago. It's basic but does what they wanted, displays the restaurant's opening hours and contact number. What's your point?' said Sav.

'My *point* is, even if customers wanted to find out more about you before they made their dining choice, there's nothing out there, no socials at all. I've just checked, no Instagram, no TikTok, there's not even a Facebook page!' She delivered this statement as though the Saxons had stupidly cooked with fire, when they'd had electricity all along, if they'd only known how to harness it.

Sav rolled his eyes. 'Of course there aren't any socials, Jade. My parents are in their late sixties and have only just embraced the microwave.'

'*Mum* has a Facebook account,' countered Hannah, proudly.

Maggie decided now wasn't the time to admit she'd only ever used it to check the opening times of the fish and chip shop and make Monty jealous with all the cute cat videos.

'So, what's your excuse, Sav?' challenged Jade. 'This is you, isn't it: @sosavthelad?'

Hannah spluttered a laugh, then stroked Alice's hair, as she stirred.

'And . . .?' Sav sounded exasperated.

'So, *you* could set up some socials for the restaurant. Share pictures of all that awesome food, do offers and giveaways, the sort of thing *other* restaurants do when they're trying to attract new customers.'

Maggie had to hand it to the girl – she didn't mess about. She was dismantling Sav's flimsy protests as though he were the sixteen-year-old, and she the adult, even if she was skirting on the boundaries of cheek. A career in political journalism was perfectly suited to her, decided Maggie; she was a budding Laura Kuenssberg.

Sav held up his hands. 'I created that account over ten years ago, I never go on it.' He paused for a moment, then sheepishly added, 'I only set it up to follow Joe's restoration building projects.' He side-eyed Joe, who visibly mellowed at this sweet confession.

Suddenly it was as clear as day to Maggie.

She didn't know why she hadn't seen it before. The answer had been staring them right in the face.

'Jade, dear,' she started. 'Am I right in thinking you've finished with your exams?'

'My last one was yesterday. Why?'

Maggie looked to Hannah, who encouraged her with a nod. She'd thought the same thing, obviously.

'How would you feel about becoming this restaurant's dedicated social media manager? Starting tonight. We have an entire menu catered for, lots of fresh, delicious, colourful food just crying out to be snapped, blogged, dumped and bumped and any other torturous-sounding procedures you'd suggest.'

Jade plucked up another mini poppadum and jabbed it first in Maggie's direction, then at Sav.

'I think, *that* sounds like a plan. Let's get the word out there. The Golden Crocus is right here, very much in business and with exciting new food not to be missed. We need to stop with the bitchin' and get promotin' this kitchen.'

She sat back, looking pleased with herself.

Sav, who wore the expression of a railroaded father, cajoled into organised fun by his unruly family, merely held up his hands in surrender.

'Fine,' he said. 'Fine.'

## Chapter Fourteen

## Hannah

Wednesday morning had begun with a dispute over the ownership of a Mocha Frappuccino leading to Hannah's eventual departure from Starbucks with half of it on her trousers. This was not ideal, but at least her trousers were black, so she'd come off infinitely better than the arrogant wanker who'd tried to wrestle the drink from her hands. His expensive shirt may have been white when he stepped through the door, but he left looking like a dalmatian. That was the trouble with Westminster: an incredibly mixed bag sharing common spaces, which might be wonderful if accompanied by common courtesy.

Things had barely improved with her first meeting of the day, a client seeking lasting power of attorney over his muddled, bewildered wife. Considering Hannah dealt in the business of mortality, there were some aspects to her job she never quite got used to.

By lunchtime, she'd sat in on another two meetings, drawn up a will, filed two applications for probate and fielded no less than seventeen emails from Bronte Gallagher's solicitor. If she didn't get out of the office, she was likely to type Bronte a short note explaining some simple economics – the longer she pissed about, the less money in the pot there would be and the more in the bank account of Tucker, Farraday & White. Not that it should matter to her, she was well overdue a bonus, and a promotion for that matter, but she did hate waste.

After she'd decamped to a bench in St James' Park with a Pret-a-Mortgaged sandwich, Hannah tilted her head to the sun and took several long, slow breaths. The park was a luscious, green pocket of tranquillity amidst the madness and mayhem, yet it was still impossible to escape the constant noise of the city. Since moving back to Saffron Walden, a place she'd happily turned her back on for the sake of her career, she increasingly found herself yearning to spend more time there. To take slow walks in parks with Alice, even though she now constantly pleaded to get a dog like Daddy's or Oscar's. She wanted to make things with her daughter, get messy and sticky from painting, cooking, cutting-out and glueing. Not to hear about it all second hand.

Thinking of home, she took out her phone and opened Instagram.

She'd created the account on Sunday morning, after a surprisingly fun Saturday evening.

With Alice settled on a row of chairs pushed together, and with Joe's hoodie for a cushion, Sav had bolted the doors and they had set to work. Firstly, they had heated and plated the food, with some surprisingly artistic touches from Ben, who had taught himself to carve crocuses from radishes. That boy was a revelation. Next, Jade had snapped away at the dishes from every angle and filmed some Insta-worthy moments, like Joe cutting into the peach and pomegranate tart. Unfortunately, she *hadn't* been filming when Ben shoved a forkful in his mouth, then looked down his nose through Maggie's borrowed glasses and adopted a Gregg Wallace accent.

'Ah, mate,' he said. 'It's summery, it's sweet, it's fresh and gooey. It's like getting a great big hug from a pomegranate.' Everyone had fallen about in hysterics.

There was also some classy footage of Sav, carrying plates into the restaurant. The background was blurred but the delicious food was in sharp, mouth-watering focus. Amazing what she'd achieved with an iPhone. The overall effect had been professional, fun and exciting.

Lastly, once each item had been presented and catalogued, they'd all sat down together and feasted like kings. Poor Alice had snoozed through the whole event, which was probably for the best, for the sake of Hannah's Sunday morning. But the food . . . had been incredible. Even now, as Hannah scrolled through some of the reels, set to punchy, catchy music and inviting the viewer to click in those first few crucial seconds, she glanced down at her limp ham and cheese sandwich and her tummy gave an involuntary gurgle.

Hannah wasn't one for social media; she was with Sav on that score. But she could certainly see the benefits, particularly after being privy to Caitlin Gallagher's bank balance and seeing quite how well influencing paid. She had no need of a share of her father's estate, although Hannah was quietly confident she would win her claim, and could potentially be catapulted onto the country's rich list.

With that thought in mind, Hannah had impulsively created an account of her own and shared some of Jade's reels from the brand-new official @goldencrocusfusion account. After finding a few old schoolfriends and colleagues to flesh out her account, she'd then immediately followed Caitlin and sent her a cheeky DM: 'The restaurant I told you about on Monday . . .'

Caitlin had been waxing lyrical over the phone about a chic new place in Kensington and so Hannah had happened to drop into conversation she'd had one of the 'best meals' in her life at a boutique, Indian fusion restaurant in the sticks of Essex. Caitlin loved words like 'boutique', and she was also an Essex girl through and through.

*Wow*, thought Hannah, refreshing her feed. *That girl has sway*. Her post had been shared three thousand times and now she had seventy-five followers, most of them called Elon Musk. Hannah was desperate to know if any of this buzz had translated into bookings, but without the cover of her mother, she didn't feel quite able to contact Sav directly. Not that she had his number, and she had a feeling he checked his Instagram messages about as frequently as he wore pink.

If she was honest, Hannah was still reeling from the revelation that Sav did not recall that moment twenty-two years ago, in Shelley Dunn's back garden.

It had been just a kiss between teenagers, one they'd immediately ignored as though it never happened at all. But oh, it had also been so much more than that. The kind of kiss she had not seen coming, and would never have imagined in a million years, certainly not with Sav. Most girls at her age had been swooning after the sixth formers, not the boys in their own class. But in that moment, as though gunpowder had been lit in her belly, everything had changed. Not so, for him, it seemed.

*Why the hell does it matter?* she berated herself. Did she remember every kiss she'd ever had? Maybe not. But she certainly remembered that one.

She had to stop thinking about it, especially when she was with Sav. And she could have killed Laura for bringing it up the other day.

Anything she was doing to help the restaurant was more for her mum than it was for anyone else. Because the truth was, for the first time in over a year, Maggie was more like her old self. The passion with which she'd immersed herself in cooking and in the plight of The Golden Crocus was how her mum had always approached life generally: with gusto and guts. This facet to her character had been swamped by grief for the past twelve months, shoved into a corner whilst she soldiered on with Alice's childcare needs and pecked at her hens.

Hannah missed her dad so much she ached, but her schedule had simply never allowed for grieving. After the phone call that had torn her world apart, she'd taken two weeks' compassionate leave from work, during which time she'd delivered Alice to her reception class daily then hotfooted it to Saffron Walden to assist with the funeral plans and support her mum, before returning to London.

Hannah had limped numbly through the next five months, right up until the day she'd happened upon

Darren's soapy session with the cleaner. In his defence, he'd said, as he sobbed and begged for her forgiveness, she'd become distant and he was lonely, as though it had been *his* father found collapsed on the bathroom floor, toothbrush still in hand.

If there was ever a blessing to be found in the sudden and tragic passing of one's beloved and cherished dad, it was that Darren's transgressions then paled into insignificance. She simply hadn't the capacity to care for him or his excuses. It had been almost cathartic, the cutting of him from her life. Like the treatment of an infected wound. She'd been weak and in pain, but she would recover. Possibly, she realised, blinking away the moisture building around the rim of her eyes, she was on that path already.

The following morning, Hannah woke before her alarm. This was a rare occurrence, as the relentless 6 a.m. ringtone usually felt like a middle-of-the-night air-raid siren, wrenching her from deep unconsciousness. She'd had a fitful night's sleep; panicked, anxious dreams punctuated with snatched images of her dad. She'd woken, almost expecting to find him sitting on the edge of her bed, bringing with him the smell of kitchens and bicycle chain oil, before realising she was in her new home, and her dad would never be coming.

She rubbed at her sore, gritty eyes and prised herself from the covers, preparing to begin another finely tuned morning routine. First, she slipped silently downstairs in her dressing gown and closed the kitchen door to boil the kettle for her first and only caffeinated coffee of the day.

Next, she made Alice's packed lunch: a sandwich cut into triangles, sticks of carrot or celery, cherry tomatoes and some pieces of cut apple. At this stage, it would be just as easy to make herself some lunch, but for some reason she never did. She loaded washing into the machine and pre-programmed it to come on later, loaded the dishwasher, and then had a quick scan of the news whilst glugging down her coffee with a slice of toast. This usually took her to 6.30 a.m. and was Hannah's only quiet time to herself in her entire working day. She'd tried getting up half an hour later, in those first few weeks of commuting, before quickly realising how crucial the extra half an hour to herself was.

Next, she went for a shower, no longer creeping around. The process was economical: shower cap on, quick lather, rinse off. Clothes were laid out the night before. Make-up was minimal and professional. It was already gearing up to be a stiflingly warm day. Birds chattered away in the tall trees across the road from her uniform street of new-build homes, where established trees and gardens were another decade away. She'd like to throw on a skirt and sandals, instead of packaging herself into a suit, but she was in court today and was destined to broil like a trussed-up brisket on the underground, which was no place for bare toes.

'Mummy! I can't find Snowflake!' yelled Alice with a tell-tale note of hysteria, assuring Hannah her daughter was awake and about to lob a plush toy-shaped spanner into the well-oiled works of the morning.

'He can't have gone far. When did you last see him. sweetheart?' asked Hannah, pulling her thick hair through an elastic band as she wandered into Alice's room. She was racking her brain to picture whether Alice had been cuddling him last night, among the other dozen or so soft toys frequently rotated in terms of popularity. Snowflake, the cute polar bear toy she'd come back with from Darren's two weeks ago, was currently trumping them all, even the purple Care Bear she'd begged for her birthday in April. Had he been there last night, when Hannah had read *The Owl who was Afraid of the Dark* at bedtime, her own eyelids drooping and a case file still to be read?

Alice had dragged her duvet off the bed and was in the process of auditing her bedroom with one leg of a pair of tights pulled all the way up, and the other leg trailing behind her like a tail as she shuffled around the carpet.

'Darling, let's get you dressed first, then we can look together. It's going to be warm today, I don't think you'll want tights.' Hannah turned and began to rummage through Alice's drawers for a clean pair of white socks, when a bump preceded an ear-shattering scream.

Hannah spun around to see Alice's feet poking out from under the bed.

'What are you doing under there? Come on, wriggle out,' coaxed Hannah amidst the heaving sobs. When Alice showed no effort to move, she resorted to pulling her out by her ankles.

'Let me see, did you bump your head?' asked Hannah, pulling her into her lap and inspecting her daughter's tousled hair.

Alice nodded, her little chest shuddering as she tried to speak. 'Snnnn . . .Snnnowflake is t-t-trapped. I tried to pull him out, but the bed fell on me.'

Hannah interpreted that to mean one of the poxy bed slats had sprung out of its plastic holders again, useless things.

'Oh dear,' comforted Hannah, kissing her forehead. 'Where does it hurt, sweetheart?'

Alice reached up and touched the back of her head, her bottom lip trembling as the tears streamed down her face.

Hannah parted her hair and saw a pink patch of skin, but no cut, or sign of swelling. She slid Alice off her lap and got down onto her belly to look under the bed, where sure enough, one flimsy piece of plywood dangled free, not heavy enough to have done any serious damage. And there at the far end, trapped between the bedframe and the wall were Snowflake's white fluffy paws.

Seeing the immediate triage required, Hannah pulled herself up and bent across the bed, tugging it away to free Snowflake, whom she placed in her daughter's arms. A quick glance at her watch confirmed they had ten minutes to get out of the house and into the car – if she was to get Alice to breakfast club and herself on the train in time for her first meeting.

When Alice's sobs had subsided enough to allow the removal of her tights and yesterday's dirty knickers in favour of clean ones, she announced she wasn't going to school because you weren't allowed to take toys to school, and she wasn't letting Snowflake out of her sight again. The jut of her jaw and the scowl on her face was enough to convince Hannah that plans would rapidly need changing this morning and that good old Granny might have to come to the rescue once more.

'Carry on getting dressed, darling. Mummy's just going to make a quick phone call.'

Forty-five minutes later Hannah zipped through the narrow streets as fast as the traffic conditions and parked cars would allow – what was it with rural drivers saying thank you to you, for saying thank you, whenever *they* gave way. In London she'd been happy simply not to be rammed. She swung into the train station carpark to find it completely full.

*Oh, come on!* She was just half an hour later than usual and getting the next train; how was it possible that every single person in the neighbourhood was also getting this train?

She did two circuits and was about to give up, when she spotted a tiny space at the end of a row. Presumably everyone else had ignored it owing to the need to exit one's car through the roof once parked. But Hannah was a determined woman, with a backside not necessarily suited to seductive, wobbling twerks, but absolutely made for squeezing through tight gaps.

With one leg, her bum and one boob squeezed free of the car, she had only to feed her laptop and handbag through the letterbox-sized gap in her door. It was at this precise moment she watched in complete astonishment as a young lad with a satchel leaned across her bonnet and tucked a green and white flyer under her windscreen wiper.

What the . . .

'Oi!' she called out. 'I am literally *right* here.'

The lad ignored her and moved on to the next car.

Irritated, late and thoroughly fed up, Hannah yanked

her bag so hard one of the handles snapped, and the contents of her bag scattered to the tarmac. *Oh, for f . . .*

That was when she heard the familiar rattle of the train approaching the platform, which was at an unreachable distance, even if her broken bag had contained one of Mary Poppins' flying umbrellas.

Fighting the urge to scream, she calmly bent and began scooping up tampons, lip balm, pens, a packet of tissues, a button from Alice's school cardigan she hadn't got round to sewing back on, various receipts and bits of paper that were almost certainly unnecessary but which she never had time to sort through. She ground her teeth against the sound of the short beeps indicating the closing train doors and rose to standing, then leaned across to rip the offending and, frankly, littering, flyer free.

Deb's Dry Cleaning
Five items for just £3 each
Quote discount code LL216

She screwed it into a ball. Did people seriously take any notice of this crap? Didn't everybody curse the ground these litterbugs walked on and simply toss the rubbish into the nearest recycling bin? Obviously not, since this was becoming an almost daily occurrence. Either the businesses who employed these kids to do the equivalent of windscreen fly-tipping genuinely saw results from it, or they were eternally optimistic.

Then, still smarting from her ordeal, she plonked herself down on a bench to wait for the next train and had the stirrings of an idea.

## Chapter Fifteen

## *Maggie*

On Thursday afternoon Maggie collected Alice from school and, instead of heading home, took her back to Hannah's instead. Her daughter's pointed comment about Alice not spending enough time at home had struck an uncomfortable chord with Maggie, who had given some thought to how she might help redress the balance. And after Alice's little episode that morning, the solution had seemed obvious.

Whilst Maggie's home was larger, and more homely in many respects, it seemed likely Alice was struggling with all the disruption. The poor mite was constantly shipped between her grandmother's, her dad's and the restaurant. So, Maggie would ensure Alice spent as much time at home as possible. Hopefully she would begin to associate the fun things she did with Granny with her own home, and of course it gave Maggie the opportunity to provide covert support to Hannah, the odd bit of laundry and a whip round with the vacuum cleaner. Nothing too obvious, or she'd be accused of interfering, such was the thin line between nurturing and meddling.

The new arrangement was not without its challenges, of course. For example, Maggie brought with her the ingredients to make a spaghetti bolognese, only to find her daughter possessed neither a cheese grater nor a sieve. And the only seasonings in the food cupboard, besides salt and pepper, were a jar of kalamata tapenade and a bottle of soy sauce – hardly everyday essentials.

'Doesn't Mummy cook at the weekends, Alice?' Maggie asked gently.

'Of course, she does,' admonished Alice, engrossed in a crayon drawing of Banjo she planned to present to Oscar. Although Maggie wasn't sure Oscar would recognise his prized pup from the depiction, as it looked more like a decapitated yeti. 'We have Em-an-em's ready meals,' she added firmly.

Maggie didn't usually credit herself with being down with the kids, musically. She was more of a Fleetwood Mac kind of girl herself. But on this occasion, and mostly owing to Gary at her old job in the council, who was quite the fan, she was thrilled to know exactly to whom Alice referred. 'Gosh, I didn't realise he'd brought out a food brand too. They're all at it these days aren't they, even Kylie Minogue makes rosé, though I can't imagine she's ever so much as walked through a vineyard, let alone crushed grapes. So what sort of food does a rap star make? Hip-hop dogs?'

Maggie chortled at her own wit, whilst Alice stared back at her warily as if she'd morphed into Miss Trunchbull.

'Mostly, we have something like macaroni cheese,' she said with caution, 'but it's not just *any* macaroni cheese, though, Granny, it's very yummy.'

'Ah,' realised Maggie, glad nobody but her granddaughter had witnessed the crossed wires. 'You mean Em-and-Ess,' she spelled out slowly. Marks & Spencer. Not Eminem.' *Of course*, not Eminem, you ridiculous woman.

'Yes, Granny,' said Alice, exasperatedly going back to her colouring.

So, her two favourite ladies were subsisting on microwave dinners of a weekend by the looks of things, which she could hardly blame Hannah for. It wasn't as though it was ever worth doing a proper shop, now Maggie cooked for them in the week.

On Friday, however, Alice came back to Maggie's. It had taken some persuading for Darren to be given another chance. Hannah had finally acquiesced when Maggie appealed on his behalf that Alice loved spending time with him and her needs should be put first, above any wish to punish the man for his repeated shortcomings.

'You must have loved him once, love, he can't be all bad?' she'd asked gently.

Hannah had made to argue, but instead huffed out a sigh of defeat.

'No, he's not bad, Mum. I just thought he might grow up, but he never did. Far more interested in gaming than adulting. We were never good together, and that's as much my fault as his. I expected too much of him, settled for something less than we both deserved.'

Maggie had shaken her head. 'Oh, love. The *least* you

can expect is love. Promise me you'll never settle for anything less than that again.'

Hannah had given a dismissive *hmph*, as though she'd long ago given up on the idea.

And now, Maggie was nervously waiting for Darren. Nervous because she wondered if he would show up, and because she was cooking at the restaurant tonight and had no idea if Jade's social media efforts had brought in new bookings, or whether the team would face another wash-out service.

At 4.45 p.m., while Alice was in the bath, Maggie's doorbell rang. Perhaps Darren was trying to make amends, by being inconveniently early.

'Granny, I've got soap in my eyes!' hollered Alice from the open bathroom door, her voice carrying down the stairs and out into the street to where a couple walking their dog turned their heads to look.

'You'd better come in for a minute,' said Maggie to Darren.

'Thanks,' he said, stepping into the hallway. 'I'm sorry,' he said awkwardly, when Maggie put one foot on the stair, 'about last week.'

There were a good many choice words on the tip of Maggie's tongue, but with her granddaughter in earshot, her vocabulary was sadly restricted. 'I think you'll find it's not me, or even Hannah, to whom you should be offering your apology, Darren.'

He looked at the ground. 'I know. I've just been struggling a bit. You know, with the new set-up.'

'I thought you were settled in your new flat now. Alice loves her room,' said Maggie.

He raised sorrowful eyes. 'That's not what I meant. I meant having her,' he jerked his head towards upstairs, 'without her.' A nod that could have been directed at the lounge, or the woman next door, but which Maggie took to mean Hannah, from where she beamed in a frame on the mantelpiece, an arm slung around her dad at his birthday party five years ago.

Maggie removed her foot from the stairs, turned around and folded her arms.

'I know, I know,' he said, holding up his hands. 'I have no right to miss her. But I do. And I want you to know, I regret everything that happened. I don't know what I was thinking.' He gave a small, nervous laugh. 'It all just got so much, with Hannah always working. She didn't have time for me anymore, I know it's no excuse. Pathetic, really. I hope one day she might find it in her heart to forgive me, but for now, I am just going to be 100 per cent focused on Alice.'

Maggie nodded once.

Absolutely no point in telling him he was wasting every last one of those pinned hopes. He'd be far better off concentrating his prayers on discovering the key to eternal life or a lottery win, but it wasn't her place to say it.

'Graaaannnny,' called Alice, more urgently. 'It's really stingy.'

'Coming, love.'

She gestured to the lounge. 'Go and take a seat. We won't be long.'

After drying Alice and dressing her in clean pyjamas and fluffy bunny slippers, she and Darren left in his car, and Maggie set off for the restaurant.

She tapped on the fire door, nerves fizzing in her tummy. This would be her first shift since showcasing the new menu, although the restaurant had been open yesterday. The restaurant would usually have opened last Sunday too, but Joe and Ben chose to spend a day practising the recipes instead, which didn't upset Sav, given how quiet The Golden Crocus had been on the Saturday night before. Maggie had been wondering for the last twenty-four hours how their first service had gone, or more to the point, if there had been any customers. And what if no-one showed up tonight? After all that work. It was an unbearable thought.

'Evening, Maggie,' beamed Joe, flinging open the door. 'Am I glad to see you.'

Maggie followed him through the storeroom as he updated her.

'We had eighteen covers last night! Normally it's dead on a Thursday.'

Maggie eyed him with concern. How had they managed? The menu was still so new, the dishes barely learned.

'Ben asked Jade to come and help Sav serve so he could stay in the kitchen with me. It was amazing, Maggie. We were like a machine.' He strong-armed the air for emphasis.

Joe was so obviously pleased with himself it was infectious.

Maggie grinned. 'That's brilliant, Joe, love. And you remembered all the dishes.'

'I've been practising all week, not just Sunday,' he said. 'We've got a freezer full of biryani-stuffed peppers and saag fritters if we need back-up. I've pre-mixed a tonne of garam masala,' he said, pointing to a tub on the side, 'and I've minced the ingredients for the pastes and refrigerated them. Oh, and the lamb shanks been marinating overnight. We had to get an urgent delivery from the wholesaler this morning, and I've another coming tomorrow.'

Maggie took in the work surfaces, vegetables all laid out ready for prep with knives, dishes and utensils. Onions were sweating pungently in a large pan on the hob and as Joe hooked a metal spoon off the rack on the wall and began to stir, she experienced a wave of pride at the change in him. He was animated, energised, organised and – above all – excited to be cooking. Exactly how any chef should be.

The door swung open, and Sav marched in, greeting Maggie as he reached for the cutlery carrier. 'Are we ready for this then, guys?'

Maggie felt the familiar and galvanising thrum through her veins as nerves turned to adrenalin.

'How many covers are booked in for tonight?' she asked tentatively.

Sav grinned. 'Thirty-seven so far. I swear, Jade has achieved nothing short of a miracle with her social media accounts. Although, bizarrely, lots of the callers said something about a 10 per cent discount code, which was news to me. Must have been something Jade set up. A *tad* cheeky if you ask me, but hell, it's worked! We've got bookings coming in for tomorrow too.' He glanced up at the clock on the wall. 'Where's Ben got to? He should have been here half an hour ago.'

Maggie looked from Sav to Joe, who was already chopping potatoes into neat cubes, ready to be roasted with cumin. 'He'll be here,' said Joe with confidence.

'Bloody hellfire,' muttered Maggie, mentally flexing her stamina muscle to check it would see her through. When Hannah had been young, they'd regularly hosted Geoff's entire extended family and she'd fitted eighteen around her kitchen table once, using pasting tables as extensions. But his parents were now long gone, nieces and nephews grown up and moved away, and it had been quite some time since she'd catered for such numbers. 'Right, then, where do you want me, Chef?'

The next hour whizzed past in a flash, lost to the reflex actions of simmering, draining, baking, slicing, blending, mashing, stirring and tasting. The menu was compact, but strong, as only the best menus were – great ingredients, tasty dishes, all home-cooked from scratch. Gita had been able to offer such a vast range of dishes as so many of her sauces began with a common base, combined with many years of experience. But currently The Golden Crocus's fusion menu offered only six starters, eight main courses and four desserts, as well as optional side dishes. At least two of each option were vegan. This made the entire offering manageable and able to be cooked fresh each service. Some of the dishes, such as those Joe had mentioned, could be cooked ahead and frozen, which was a huge time saver in busy periods.

At Maggie's suggestion, there would also be a special of the day, a dish easily adapted to utilise any surplus of produce or to trial a new idea. This kept a chef creative and allowed for moments of inspiration. Tonight's special, improvised by Maggie and owing to some beautiful seasonal asparagus and sugar snap peas, would be a bright, summery, saffron-infused risotto, Indian-style.

Ben arrived at five to seven, just as the restaurant was about to open. He was trailed by Jade, who had toned down her iridescence, which was to say, her sunshiney sneakers were replaced with black Doc Martens and her sequins swapped out for a t-shirt emblazoned with the words 'woman up'. As Joe went to open his mouth, presumably to berate Ben for being late, Jade widened her eyes and gave a slight shake of her head. The meaning was clear, *not now*.

Curious. Perhaps they'd had a lovers' tiff, thought Maggie, noticing the dark circles around Ben's eyes. She didn't fancy anyone's chances in a stand-off with Jade.

Joe looked thoughtful for a moment, before tossing Ben an apron.

'We need you in here tonight, Ben. You OK with helping out again, Jade?'

She gave him a look. 'Depends on whether I'll get paid this time?'

'Not my quarters, you'll have to chase Sav. But we'd appreciate the help.'

Jade sighed, 'I'd figured as much anyway.'

She exited the kitchen for the restaurant floor, and Ben went to the sink to wash his hands.

'Everything OK?' asked Joe.

'Fine,' mumbled Ben, not meeting his eye. 'Sorry for being late.'

As service got going, and tickets piled up on the side, the kitchen buzzed with activity. Maggie and Joe fell into the harmonised steps of a routine they'd developed over the past few weeks. Joe took care of starters, the grill and desserts, whilst Maggie focused on sauces, baking and plating. The melancholy that had hung over Ben when he first arrived seemed to lift a little as he worked, until he began second-guessing both Joe and Maggie's needs before they even had to ask, racing off to the fridge or storeroom, washing and drying pots, pans and plates, helping with garnishes and salads.

Joe caught Maggie's eye as Ben delicately topped a brownie with a perfect quenelle of pistachio kulfi, something notoriously hard to get right, and they exchanged an impressed nod.

'You're really good at that, mate,' said Joe.

Ben gave a self-deprecating laugh. 'Glad I'm good at something then, because I certainly wasn't good at school.'

'I'm serious, Ben. You're a natural in the kitchen – have you at least thought about going to catering college?' He added, 'If you like, I could help you look into it, see what the entry-level requirements are, that sort of thing?'

Ben blushed at the compliment but gave a small nonchalant shrug. 'Cheers, yeah. Maybe.'

He didn't give much away, but Maggie recognised the way he came alive when he worked with food. Perhaps he didn't want to get his hopes up; perhaps he feared he'd messed up his exams so royally there was no point in making plans. Either way, she was pretty sure the seed had been planted long before Joe had spoken the words aloud.

The swing door became a conveyor belt of dishes going out, scraped-clean plates coming back in and the occasional shouts of 'more lemons for the bar', from Sav as he and Jade moved like greased lightning to serve customers their hot food. If Maggie didn't know better, she'd swear the man was enjoying himself.

'Man, I'm so hungry,' groaned Jade, swiping a sweet potato fry from a tray Joe was holding and stuffing it in her mouth.

'You know, for someone so concerned with appropriately gendered speech,' Maggie commented, pointing at the slogan on her t-shirt, 'you bandy about the terms "man" and "guys" somewhat freely.'

Jade rolled her eyes. 'It's just lingo, Maggie. It's neutral language. Earlier, someone on table seven called me 'Waitress', and I was like, *dude*, nobody says waiter or waitress anymore. See what I'm saying?'

'Mmm,' said Maggie, not entirely sure she did, but quite certain Jade knew exactly what was what. She'd have to pay closer attention.

At one point, Sav came into the kitchen brandishing an orange piece of paper. 'Does anyone know anything about this?' he asked, confusion wrinkling his forehead.

Maggie took it from him.

The logo for The Golden Crocus was reproduced in a close approximation to the sign above the door and there followed a series of statements in shouty bold capital letters.

**SAFFRON WALDEN'S FINEST INDIAN RESTAURANT BRINGS A WHOLE NEW WORLD OF FLAVOUR TO YOUR DOORSTEP. CHECK OUT OUR BRAND-NEW FUSION MENU, AVAILABLE NOW. AS RECOMMENDED BY @CAITLINGALLAGHER. BOOKING ESSENTIAL.**

**QUOTE THIS CODE FOR AN EXCLUSIVE 10%
DISCOUNT: GCNEW123
OFFER ENDS SUNDAY.**

'One of the customers out there said it was stuck under her windscreen wiper, can you believe? Said her and her girlfriend had never been in before because they'd always assumed we'd closed down ages ago. I mean I know the place needs a coat of paint, but *derelict?*' He looked stunned.

Maggie looked at the flyer, with the sneaky suspicion this might be the work of her daughter. And if so, why on earth hadn't she mentioned it?

## Chapter Sixteen

## Hannah

As cowardly as it may have been, Hannah hadn't dared to turn up at the restaurant on Friday night, even though Alice was at her dad's. Instead, she had taken a bottle of wine and a pizza round to Laura's.

'But I don't get why Sav would be angry at you for using your initiative and helping to market the place?' Laura said, trying to wrestle a pyjama top over Connor's bucking head.

'Mummy! Can you wipe my bottom,' bellowed Charlie from along the hall.

'Alrighty,' said Hannah, happy to be free of said delightful task now that Alice was older. 'You take the one with the business end issue and I'll see if I can work out if this one . . .' she paused to tickle Connor's belly, '. . . has an off switch.'

'I've checked all over, Han, believe me. I think maybe they should go back to the shop.'

'We didn't come from the shop, silly Mummy!' cried

176

out Connor. 'We came from your bum, like a big fat smelly poo.'

An hour and some dark sorcery later, Laura had both boys tucked up in their matching single beds. The nightstand between them held a mesmerising nightlight designed to look like an aquarium, with bright, colourful fish bobbing around peacefully. Hannah reckoned if she lay down on the rug and stared at it, she'd have been zonked out in moments too. Instead, she crept downstairs whilst Laura read them a story, and busied herself in her friend's messy kitchen with loading the dishwasher, switching it on and pouring them both some wine.

Once they were both curled up on the sofa with slices of pizza and a box of Maltesers which Laura had, again like a magician, produced from a hidey hole high up on the bookcase, she resumed her line of questioning.

'So, the way I see it, if the leaflet resulted in customers, why on earth would Sav be mad?'

'Maybe because I offered a 10 per cent discount,' admitted Hannah, wincing at the memory.

It had been the work of moments at her laptop during her lunch hour on Thursday, once she'd finally arrived at work two hours late. Then, instead of taking her normal route back to Liverpool Street that evening, she detoured via Farringdon to a same-day print service she'd found on Google.

'And,' argued Laura, 'what's 10 per cent when it comes to saving the business? Marco is constantly running those sorts of campaigns, especially in quieter periods. It's what businesses do, adapt and change.'

'That's just it though, isn't it? It's not Sav's business. And

I get the distinct impression he'd rather just sell up whilst his parents aren't around to fight him over it, or fight each other.'

Laura took a huge bite of pizza, then tried to hasten her chewing so she could talk. It was obvious how starved of adult attention she was, by the way she barely drew breath. 'So, what's the deal with you two anyway?'

'Sorry, who two?'

'You and Sav, you muppet. Your eyeballs were practically on bungee cords that night at the pub. You were trying so hard, and failing, not to look at him.'

Hannah spluttered out her wine. 'What? I've no idea what you're talking about. I was probably just miffed they came and gatecrashed our evening; it was you I was meeting up with, not boys we went to school with.'

'*Boys* we went to school with,' said Laura slowly, as though she were trying out the words on her tongue. 'Han, I hate to break this to you, babe, but another twenty years has passed since we all left school. I've got the grey pubes and bingo wings to prove it, even if you don't.'

Hannah laughed, and then did what any woman in need of a diversion would do and got up from her seat with the empty plates. 'You stay there, I'll take these out and make us a cuppa.'

Before Laura could protest, she scarpered to the kitchen.

'You fancy him, don't you?' came Laura's voice behind her.

*Bugger.*

'I know you, Hannah Lawford. There's no way on this green earth you'd be wasting even one brain cell on that ancient old relic of a place unless you had good reason.

You're high-flying Hannah, legal wonder woman extraordinaire, who doesn't even have time for a skincare routine, let alone saving a poxy restaurant. How do you do that by the way?' she said, pulling her own skin taught at the sides of her eyes. 'Fresh as a flipping daisy, without so much as a facial. Whereas I order everything I can find with retinol in the title and my face still looks like a wrinkled scrotum.'

Hannah shrugged. 'Years of wearing high ponytails? Maybe when I let my hair down I have the sagging jowls of a Saint Bernard.' She sighed, knowing she was avoiding the subject. 'The restaurant is important to Mum. It was her and Dad's favourite place, on the rare occasions he had weekends off. It's given her purpose again, Laura. I haven't seen her this motivated about anything in so long – I just want to support her.'

Laura nodded along. 'Uh-huh. And Sav being back here and looking hotter than jalapeños in hell, has nothing to do with it at all. I see.'

Hannah gave a snort of laughter.

Laura side-eyed her. 'Don't tell me you haven't noticed. You'd actually have to be blind.'

'OK, yes. I've noticed. But it's not about that. It's just . . .' Hannah searched for the right words. 'I guess being there in the kitchen with the gang, and having Alice there too, it's made me realise how little fun I have, Laura. And it has been *fun*, hanging out with them and getting to know them all. And Mum's cooking's done that, I'm really proud of her.'

'Right,' agreed Laura, nodding away effusively. 'And the fact you and Sav have history *and* a level of sexual tension

179

which could create something extra spicy in that kitchen is purely incidental. Come on, Hannah. We might not have seen as much of each other as we'd have liked over the past few years, but you're forgetting I *know* you. Even if you won't admit it to yourself, you have feelings for him. It's plain as flipping day.'

Later that evening, Hannah texted her mum to ask what time she was finishing and extricated herself from Laura's inquisition to walk down and meet her.

She made sure to wait at a distance, not particularly wanting to bump into Sav, at least not until she'd had a chance to probe her mother on the evening's success. Although from the steady exodus of cheerful customers from the restaurant, things looked hopeful.

Eventually, Maggie's head appeared, between the parted front door, whipping from left to right as she scanned the street.

'Mum!' called Hannah, giving a little wave from where she sheltered behind a parked car.

'What are you doing over there?' Maggie squinted into the dark. 'Aren't you coming in?'

'I'd rather just get back?' she called, painfully aware of the open window above her head. Any minute now there'd be another head peering above the parapet, and it would be like a scene from Monty Python, with cries of 'Halt! Who goes there?'

'Don't be ridiculous, Hannah. Sav's pouring me a Baileys, get yourself in here.'

'Mum, I'm tired, can't we just go home?' Hannah heard the pleading tone in her own voice and grimaced. Then the window above her head slammed shut, the occupants clearly not caring *who* goes there, merely that they get on with the *going*.

'Your little stunt worked, if that's what you're worried about,' called Maggie. 'And there is one happy but utterly exhausted team in here, whom I'm going to enjoy an after-service drink with before going home, whether you're coming in or not.'

Then, Maggie disappeared back inside.

Hannah stood for a moment, with the strangest feeling of déjà-vu. Only, she was sure in the scenario she was remembering, it was *her* refusing to go home with her mother when she came to pick her up from a party – not the other way around. And she'd been about ten.

Eventually, she galvanised her feet into action and crossed the road to the restaurant. She opened the door to find her mum, Jade, Ben and Joe all seated around a table. Joe had his feet up on a chair and was making short work of a pint, whilst Ben and Jade were bent over her phone, sipping from bottles of coke. Sav was at the bar, pouring a dark liquid into crystal tumblers.

'Aha, just in time,' he said, shooting her an amused look. 'Indian rum on the rocks for the secret marketeer? Maggie's braving it.'

'Is she now?' Hannah raised her eyebrows at Maggie.

'Changed my mind about the Baileys – OK with the fun police?'

'Bloody hell . . .' Hannah trailed off under her breath. Then she added with forced enthusiasm, 'Yes please, Sav. I would love to try your Indian rum. With plenty of ice, please.'

She slumped down into a chair next to Jade and peered across at the pictures she was editing on her iPhone.

'Was that tonight?' she asked, in surprise.

'Sure was. This place was *buzzing*, man! I've got loads of great content for the socials. There'd have been more if I hadn't had to keep stopping to clear tables. You're seriously going to need to think about employing more staff if things really take off.'

Hannah looked to Joe, who merely put down his pint and tugged on an imaginary chain. 'Boom,' was all he said, with a cheeky grin.

'And everything went OK?'

Maggie made a *pfft* sound. 'It went more than OK, Hannie. And contrary to Jade's observations, I've seen Raj single-handedly serve this entire restaurant on many an occasion back in the day, and tonight it was at half-capacity.'

'It's true,' nodded Ben. 'I was usually washing up; he rarely wanted my help out front. But I prefer being in the kitchen anyway, it's much more fun.'

'We were on *fire*,' said Joe with a slightly dreamy expression. 'I've never experienced anything like that before. I can't wait to do it again.'

Sav handed him one of the tumblers. 'Well, I'm glad about that, Joe, because we're doing it all over again tomorrow.' He switched his attention to Hannah. 'Isn't selling tables in your local curry house a bit below your paygrade, Han?'

'You'd be surprised what falls under a soliciting remit,' she countered, then regretted the ill-advised joke when her mother choked on her rum.

Joe suddenly sat up straight. 'Er, folks. What's the time?'

Maggie checked her watch with a yawn. '10.22.'

'Shit. Eight minutes to finalise the order for tomorrow morning – I'm going to have to double everything. Be right back.'

He pushed back his chair and ran to the kitchen.

'Double,' echoed Sav ponderously, to no-one in particular, then he downed his drink in one.

The next morning, thanks to her mother's sneaky installation of ingredients in her fridge, Hannah enjoyed a leisurely breakfast of scrambled eggs on toast whilst watching *Saturday Kitchen*. She knew jolly well, for instance, that not one of Maggie's meals this week had involved eggs or lean, smoked bacon. The new routine seemed to be working out well. OK, so it wasn't as convenient for her mum, having to relocate to Hannah's, but Alice seemed much more settled, and, she had to admit, it was great to drive straight home from work without an extra stop. And always to a plated-up dinner.

Her phone lit up on the coffee table with an incoming call from Darren. She pounced on it immediately.

'Darren? What's wrong?'

'Hello to you too. Nothing's wrong, why do you assume anything's wrong?'

Hannah swallowed down a retort about his track record, and instead asked, 'What time will Alice be home?'

'That's what I wanted to ask. There's a charity day at the local petting farm, bouncy castles and stuff. I thought I could take Alice, then bring her home teatime instead?'

Hannah's instinct was to say no. That he needed to show

he could be reliable before thinking about changing the routine, but the image of Alice's excited face at the prospect of seeing the animals stayed her tongue.

'Does Alice want to go?'

'I wanted to ask you first, before I got her hopes up. But you know how much she loves that sort of thing.'

Yes, I know what our daughter likes, you moron. However, this was a more adult approach than she may have expected and showed a modicum of consideration for those involved.

'And you'd have her back by 5?' she asked.

'Promise. Or I could give her tea first?'

'No,' snapped Hannah. 'We have plans.'

They didn't have plans. But she had precious little time with Alice as it was and wasn't about to forfeit any more of the weekend.

'OK, well, thank you, Hannah. I appreciate it.'

What was he up to? Now she almost felt guilty, like she'd made him grovel for the scraps off her plate. This was their daughter they were talking about.

'Have a fun day, both of you,' she said, ending the call.

By mid-morning, Hannah was bored. She spent her entire working week chasing her tail and wishing she could be at home, then when a whole day without responsibilities stretched out before her, she found herself looking for ways to fill it.

She took a mug of tea out to the patio and placed it on the small bistro table she'd ordered from Ikea, along with two chairs, one for her and one for Alice. She got down on her hands and knees and tugged at clumps of long grass sprouting between the paving slabs, the sounds of summer drifting over the fence from other back gardens, squabbling siblings, a lawn mower, the rushing of a hose. Her mind went where it often did when she found herself alone. To her own childhood. To a memory of her father setting up the sprinkler, then running through it fully clothed, laughing. *Come and try our upside-down shower HanHan.* How did her mum bear it, the ambush of memories at every turn, in every room?

She abandoned the weeds, drained her cup, then got ready to go out.

'I'm pretty sure that's a thistle you're attempting to prune there, Mum,' she said, startling her mother where she knelt in the small front garden with a pair of secateurs in hand. Great minds think alike. Healing ones, too.

Maggie held a hand to her chest. 'Goodness, Hannah, don't creep up on me like that, I thought you were Oscar.'

'Morning, Maggie!' called Oscar cheerfully from the pavement. 'Just been chatting with Hannah and hearing all about your star turn in the restaurant. Will we be seeing you on *Bake Off*?' he chortled.

Maggie plastered a neighbourly smile on her face and pulled herself to standing.

'Never been a fan of having my edibles fondled before they go in my mouth,' said Maggie, to a short, sharp snort of laughter from Hannah. Maggie tutted, 'Oh, you know what I mean, all that sculpting and shaping, you'd think they were playing with plasticine, not baking cakes.'

'It's great entertainment,' said Oscar. 'Though of course, it's not the same without Mary.'

'Oh, I don't know, Prue's just as good.'

'Mm,' agreed Oscar. 'Although, I er, meant my Mary.'

Maggie grimaced, as though remembering too late the giant turd on the lawn into which she'd just planted her slippered foot.

'Yes, of course,' she said.

A solemn silence fell.

Hannah decided to rescue her mum, announcing cheerfully, 'Wondered if you fancied a spot of shopping, Mum, and a late lunch?'

If actions could speak louder than words, then the gusto with which Maggie removed her gardening gloves and slapped them down on the nearest fencepost screamed *take me anywhere and take me now*.

'Sounds wonderful, darling, it's too hot for gardening today anyhow. No Alice today?'

'She's spending the day with Darren, so I'm all yours.'

'You know, Maggie,' piped up Oscar, the usual jollity back in his tone, 'I could lend a hand to get this all ship-shape.' He pointed to the borders which used to be home to vibrant fuchsias and verbenas. 'You've enough on your plate and it would keep me out of mischief, eh?' he winked, and Hannah saw her mum physically flinch.

Maggie shook her head vigorously, 'No, no. No need, but thank you for the offer, Oscar. Give me five minutes, Hannie, and I'm all yours.'

With that, Maggie disappeared inside and Hannah gave Oscar a grateful smile. 'Thanks, Oscar, that was really kind of you. Perhaps Alice and I could walk Banjo again tomorrow, if it's OK with you?'

'Anytime, love.'

Oscar patted her arm and continued along the lane to

his own front door, his stoop a little more pronounced than usual.

Thirty-five minutes later, because Maggie had wanted to change into something cooler, have a wee, feed Monty, change handbags then have another safety wee, they stepped back out into the warmth of day.

'This is nice,' said Maggie, as they walked through the teeming streets. The town was always busy on Saturdays, when tourists flocked to the medieval town to shop in its historic market square or to look at the castle ruins or visit the museum. 'I can't remember the last time we went shopping together.'

'Probably when you came to stay in London, and we went to see a show. Remember, we spent hours scouring the length of Oxford Street so you could get an outfit for Dad's retirement do?'

'Oh, I remember it well, Hannie. Ghastly place. Couldn't live there now. Give me Saffron Walden any day. I could probably have found something just as suitable on my own doorstep.'

This was undoubtedly true. The small town was peppered with independent boutiques and interesting shops, as well as a scattering of high street names. And if what was happening at The Golden Crocus had taught them anything, it was that shopping local mattered.

As if she'd read her mind, Maggie pulled her to a stop outside the bookshop.

'Would you mind if we made a quick detour to the restaurant? Just to check everything's on track for tonight? Two minutes, tops. I'm sure they have no need of me yet, but . . .'

'Mum, of course. It's fine,' she smiled. There must be an invisible string joining Maggie to that place. Hannah didn't admit how often she thought of it too.

As they approached the restaurant, Maggie pointed out the transit van half up on the pavement, 'Oh, Ivan's here, the wholesaler, you'll like him. Thinks himself something of a Casanova.'

The fire door was propped open, so they filed in, through the storeroom to the kitchen, calling out a cheery hello, only to find Joe leaned up against the sink, arms folded across his chest and a grim expression on his face.

*This doesn't look good*, thought Hannah.

A kind-looking man wearing a flat cap stood opposite. He threw them an apologetic smile.

Sav could be heard on the other side of the connecting door, talking urgently to someone in the restaurant, or rather *at* someone, 'I know. Yes, that's right. But if we could just have a few more days . . . Right. I see.'

'What's going on?' asked Maggie.

No-one replied.

'Joe?' she asked again gently. 'What's happened?'

He breathed in deeply and then let it out in a long, weary sigh.

'We're on stop.'

Maggie nodded.

'What does that mean?' asked Hannah.

The other man, Ivan, spoke up. 'Boss won't let 'owt else go. Account's three months in arrears, thought I'd tell yous in person, like.'

From beyond the door Sav ended his phone call, and shouted loudly, 'FUCK!'

There followed the sound of a thwack as something was kicked or lobbed.

The four of them stood looking at each other, none of them quite sure what to do.

Hannah was about to investigate when Sav came through the door. When he registered Maggie and Hannah's presence, his face fell even further.

'I'm sorry,' he said, his voice hoarse with exhaustion. 'I've tried everything. There's nothing left. Not another penny I can borrow. It's all gone.'

Maggie stepped forward, 'Sav, love. What do you mean?'

Hannah frowned. Surely it was obvious: there was nothing left in the pot. Hadn't they known this already? OK, so perhaps it was worse than they'd thought if the supplier hadn't been paid for three months.

Maggie stepped closer still and lay a tentative hand on Sav's arm. 'When you say there's nothing left *you* can borrow, love, I hope you don't mean . . .?'

Joe looked up, caught the inference of Maggie's words and turned his head.

'Sav?' he asked.

'I'm so sorry,' replied Sav, his jaw set hard with controlled emotion. 'I should have been more honest. When I first stepped in to help Mum and Dad, I thought there must have been some mistake . . .' He stopped talking for a moment and visibly composed himself before continuing, 'If you could see upstairs . . .'

Hannah experienced a crawling sensation across the back of her shoulders.

'I don't know how they've been managing,' he added miserably.

Maggie rubbed at his arm in a soothing fashion.

'I had some savings, so I used them to pay for the essentials, the electric, the gas, the business rates. Thankfully wages were up-to-date, though if I know my parents, they'd have sold the clothes off their back rather than owe the staff,' he gave a small laugh. 'Though I'm not sure they haven't already, sold the clothes off their backs, that is.'

# Chapter Seventeen

## Maggie

The first Skype with Gita had been a stop-start affair, interspersed with spells on mute and unflattering close-ups of Sav's cousin Pritha, as she offered patronising advice such as, 'You look like a decapitated mule, Auntie. Maggie doesn't want to see your bosom.'

By the second call, Gita had worked out how to superimpose herself onto a backdrop of the Sahara and in between cookery tips was sharing her screen to show Maggie baby photos of her great nephew. In return, Maggie had learned how to record their sessions, with Gita's consent, of course, so she could revisit the methods and recipes.

All of which is to say these were two perfectly capable women.

During their conversations, Maggie had come right out and asked Gita about her long-term plans for the restaurant, once she was mobile enough to fly home. Gita had shrugged and said, 'I don't know what else we would do? It is our home. Raj and I have poured our hearts and our souls into it.' Then she'd sighed and checked over her shoulder. 'I am not a fool, Maggie. I know we can't go on forever. Things have to change, and Sav being there is a good thing. He can talk some sense into my husband. He is a *real businessman*, you know?'

Maggie hadn't liked to enlighten Gita that being good with computers and numbers doth not a restaurateur make. When it came to food, Sav was about as qualified to bake a tarte Tatin as the MP for West Suffolk was to perform a vasectomy, just because he'd been appointed health minister once upon a miserable time.

As Maggie had listened to Sav and seen the wretchedness etched in his face, Gita's words came back to her. *He can talk some sense into my husband.* How bad had things really got?

'Sav,' she began as tactfully as she could, aware Ivan still stood there taking everything in. 'When you say, you should see upstairs . . .?'

Sav looked up, his sorrowful brown eyes finding hers.

'Well, if you guys don't need me for anything else . . .' cut in Ivan, taking his cue to leave.

'No, thank you, Ivan. Sorry,' said Sav.

Ivan gave a reassuring smile. 'Hey, if I had a quid for every time a customer fell behind on their account, I wouldn't be driving a van for a living, let's put it that way. I'm sure you'll have it sorted in no time, pal.'

He nodded goodbye and left.

A loaded silence descended. Joe picked at his thumbnail and Hannah stood awkwardly like a spare part.

Eventually, Sav said, 'Alright. I'll show you,' then he turned and exited the kitchen.

Hannah moved first, flicking curious eyes to Maggie, before shrugging and following after him.

Maggie touched Joe's shoulder. 'Come on, love. I've a feeling Sav could do with a friend right now, more than he could a chef.'

Joe unbuttoned his jacket and for a moment Maggie feared he was going to leave, but then he bundled it up and placed it on the counter and indicated for her to lead the way.

The Kapoors' private quarters were accessed through a locked door adjacent to the toilets, near the entrance to the restaurant. Maggie had never been upstairs before, her social interactions with Raj and Gita having been mostly when she and Geoff had dined here or bumped into one another in town. She imagined low ceilings, exposed beams and crooked floors, like so many of the period properties around: small, cramped rooms, old-fashioned décor (if downstairs was anything to go by) and perhaps a good deal of clutter.

What she hadn't imagined, as she followed Hannah and Sav through the door at the top of the stairs, was the large, empty chasm confronting them.

An ancient sofa faced an old-fashioned electric bar heater that had been placed in front of the fireplace. In the corner was a low pine corner unit, its surface covered with newspapers. 'That's where the TV used to be,' said Sav, pointing to it. 'And that,' he added, gesturing at a glass display cabinet, empty but for a biscuit tin and two or three dog-eared paperbacks, 'used to house my great-grandmother's Indian tea set, a much-prized possession brought out for every visitor and every occasion, as well as a full set of Britannica encyclopaedias, and my dad's vinyl collection.'

'I remember the tea set,' said Joe, subdued.

Sav crossed the large room, into a corridor, where he flung open another door.

'Kitchen. Minus any actual food.' He opened the cupboards, revealing half-empty packets and jars and lots of empty space.

'Bedroom,' he announced, opening another door and Maggie flinched. She was not entirely comfortable with looking at Raj and Gita's private sleeping quarters, but the grim expression on Sav's face propelled her forwards.

There was a double bed, neatly made with crisp sheets. But the wallpaper was coming away and the pink curtains were so faded in places by the sun they looked to be tie-dyed.

Sav crossed the room to a tidy dressing table. There was a mirror and a small cream stool and several bottles and lotions. He flipped open an ornate box. 'Unless Mum wore every piece of jewellery she owned to fly to India, this is looking somewhat emptier than I remember.'

Maggie became aware of Joe at her side, fidgeting.

As they made their way back to the lounge, Sav pointed at other doors. 'My old room, bathroom, office, nothing much to see there.'

'Mate. This isn't right. Where's all the furniture?' asked Joe. 'Where's the enormous dining table and chairs gone? And your dad's armchair? All the ornaments and pictures on the walls? It was like a museum in here.'

*Of course*, realised Maggie. Joe had been Sav's childhood friend; he had probably spent many hours in this apartment.

Sav rubbed at his temples. 'It's all happened so gradually. When I was here a few months back, I asked where the table had gone, and they said they were getting new furniture. Another time I noticed some other bits and bobs were missing and Mum said she was decluttering. Then on the last few occasions, we've eaten downstairs in the restaurant as they were only flying visits. I haven't been home as much as I'd have liked, with the business and everything. Of course, now I know they were deliberately keeping this from me. But I'm their only son – I should have known something wasn't right.'

Hannah seemed to be last on the uptake. 'Wait a minute. Are you saying your parents have sold everything?' She looked aghast and added in a much softer voice, 'Sav, I thought they'd been burgled.'

'Hmm. Does look like that, doesn't it?' He gave a mirthless laugh. 'So, do you see the quandary I'm facing? Either I insist they sell up, knowing my parents haven't a leg to stand on right now (in my mother's case, quite literally). Or try my damnedest to make their sacrifices worthwhile and turn the place around, seeing as I've been so far up my own arse I haven't even seen what's been happening under my nose.' He sunk down into the creaking sofa. 'I thought if I took a couple of months off work, I could sort this all out.' He gestured helplessly around him. 'I had savings. But it still hasn't been enough.' He looked at Joe. 'Everything's gone, and I don't even have enough to pay you anymore. Or Ben, or Jade, or you, Maggie, not even for one more day.'

A lump formed in Maggie's throat, as instead of being angry, Joe paced over to Sav and threw an arm around

195

his neck. It was more of a wrestling headlock than a hug but was touching none the less.

'Your poor parents,' muttered Maggie, looking about her. This room, particularly, felt as though the soul had been ripped out of it. There were faded patches on the walls where pictures had hung; only a posed family portrait of the Kapoors, with a very young Sav in best shirt and trousers, remained.

Sav followed her line of sight. 'They were oil paintings mostly, Dad always brought one back when he visited his parents. I hated them as a kid. Thought they should have black and white prints from Habitat like all my friends' parents did. I can't believe they let things get this bad and said nothing.'

'Never underestimate pride, love,' said Maggie, understanding only too well what the Kapoors' motivation will have been. 'It can be the greatest motivator or the harshest jailer. Your parents built this place from nothing and enjoyed thirty years of success. That can be a hard thing to let slip through your fingers.'

And wasn't that partly why she'd been avoiding Pam? Much easier not to sit and listen to all the gossip from the old office crowd whilst she festered away in an empty house, often not bothering to dress until it was time to pick up Alice.

Pride had abandoned her on the day she'd lost Geoff, only to be replaced by endless waiting.

Cooking had saved her. Or was it these people? The lines had blurred now.

'Sodding Covid,' moaned Hannah, who had seen her fair share of its impact. Her department had never been so busy than in that first awful year.

'We can't blame it all on the pandemic, this place has been stagnating for years. But you know what makes me mad?' said Sav, his eyes dancing a fine line between fury and despair. 'It really looked like things were starting to turn around. We're fully booked all weekend, and if we'd have carried on like this, the projections would have been along the lines of what the accountant was asking for. With just under three weeks to go until the 14th of July, I was starting to think we might make it. And now I'm going to have ring all those customers back and cancel them.'

Joe looked thoughtful.

'Is that really necessary?' he said. 'I mean, I can't talk for the others, but I'll happily work all weekend unpaid, if you think it will make a difference.'

Sav shook his head, horrified. 'No, no. It's already gone too far. I can't let you do that, Joe. You've got bills to pay; you need to find something secure, something with prospects.'

'I'll help too,' piped up Hannah. 'I mean, I'll have Alice with me, but she loves being here. Mum, what do you say?'

Maggie's heart swelled with affection. 'Do you need to ask?'

Sav looked pained. 'That's so kind of you all, really, I don't know what to say, but it doesn't change the fact we have no produce and . . .' he checked his watch, 'service begins in six hours. We have no food, and nothing prepped.'

'How many of last night's customers paid in cash, Sav?' asked Maggie, wondering why he hadn't thought of it himself.

Sav looked up at her and she saw the moment it dawned on him.

'A few? I mean, it wasn't a large amount, but I reckon there's a couple of hundred quid in the till, maybe more?'

Maggie shot Hannah an apologetic smile. 'Do you mind if we postpone lunch, love, and cut straight to the shopping?'

Hannah grinned. 'Where are we going and do they sell doughnuts? I'm starving!'

# Chapter Eighteen

## Maggie

After a thorough stock-take of the fridges and the storeroom, Joe stayed back in the kitchen to prep what he could. He also volunteered to phone Ben and explain the situation. It had been decided they would try and manage between them, without involving the teenagers who would be unlikely to want to work on a voluntary basis. Maggie so hoped they could find a way to keep Ben on, as she'd developed a soft spot for the gentle, funny boy and his fierce friend Jade, in their endearing double act.

'Wait up, Mum,' called Hannah, trailing along beside Maggie as she pounded the busy street.

'Time is of the essence, Hannie, we'll be lucky if there's anything left.'

'Are you sure we'll be able to carry everything?' she asked, the empty shopping bags they carried flapping at their sides in the gentle breeze.

'We'll do two trips if necessary.'

As they entered the market square, Maggie halted outside the town hall and turned to her daughter.

'I'm sorry for spoiling our day together. You must be royally fed up with the restaurant taking over everything. I know how precious your weekends are.'

Hannah shook her head. 'Mum, it's fine. Believe me, I don't want to see it fail either.'

Maggie scrutinised her daughter's lovely face. She'd caught the sun in the last couple of weeks and looked healthier than she'd seen her in a long while. There was also something else she couldn't put her finger on, a vibrancy, a spark. Normally by the end of the week, the energy had been drained right out of her by the gruelling toil of her day job.

'Thank you,' said Maggie, reaching across and kissing her daughter's cheek. 'I couldn't even say why anymore, it just feels important not to give up.'

*Because you've got the bit between your teeth, Mags. And because you can do anything when you set your mind to it.* Geoff's voice was loud and clear in her mind. He'd always believed she was the stronger one in the relationship. Had never made her feel she was less because he was the one in the chef's whites and she was behind a desk. There was plenty she *hadn't* been able to do. Life had seen to that. But this? She could damned well try her best.

'Do you understand?' she added.

Hannah nodded.

'Right, have you got your list? You take cheese and fish, I'll take the greengrocer. See you back here.'

With that, they diverged away from the handsome Tudor building watching over proceedings through its stained-glass windows, and Maggie entered the throng of shoppers that had flocked to this place since the twelfth century for the finest local produce.

As she'd feared, seeing as it was close to lunchtime now, Vernon's stall was looking a little thin on the ground.

'Maggie!' he called cheerily. 'Haven't seen you for a while. How are you keeping? I hear you're quite the Delia Smith these days!'

The resemblance between him and Ben was quite extraordinary, and she wondered why she hadn't spotted it straight away, but then again, when she'd first met the young lad, he'd been inclined to hide behind his unruly mop of hair and avoid eye contact at all costs.

'I'm very well, thank you for asking, Vernon. Although I highly doubt Ben has even heard of Delia Smith. He's an excellent little cook himself by the way, you should be very proud.'

'Oh, I am. He's a top lad, and so full of confidence and enthusiasm these days I can hardly keep up,' said Vernon, beaming. 'I've the Kapoors to thank for that.'

Maggie wondered what he meant. Ben hadn't mentioned Raj and Gita much, and he can't have worked there long, he was only just sixteen. Perhaps they were friends of the family.

'What can I get you, love?' he asked, rubbing his hands together.

'Well,' said Maggie, pulling out a very long list. 'Shall we start with brassicas?'

Twenty minutes or so and four bulging bags-for-life later, there wasn't an awful lot left on Vernon's stall.

'You've cleared me out, Maggie,' he said jovially. 'What

on earth are you doing with that lot? Cooking Sunday dinner for the whole town?'

Maggie didn't see the point of fibbing; he'd hear about it from Ben soon enough. 'Actually, this is for the restaurant. Misunderstanding with the wholesalers.'

'A touch of goodwill resolves many misunderstandings, in my experience,' Vernon ventured.

'I believe a considerable amount of goodwill has already been given. You could say we're entering last chance saloon territory here.'

'Ah. That's a real shame,' he shook his head sadly. 'A real shame. Gosh, poor Raj, I had no idea.'

Maggie was intrigued by Vernon's response. 'Do you know Raj well?'

The market trader raised thoughtful eyes. 'Not *well*, exactly. Let's just say he's an extremely kind man who doesn't deserve a rough ride. I owe him a lot.' He sighed. 'Has Ben told you anything about his mum, at all?'

Maggie scanned through conversations she'd had with Ben, but couldn't recall him ever mentioning his mum, now she stopped to think about it. 'Do you know? I don't think he has. Is Ben's mum,' she faltered over how to phrase it, 'no longer with us?'

Vernon gave a humourless laugh. 'Not with *us*, no. Some other sod has the pleasure, or should I say, misfortune.' He scratched his beard. 'Oh, I can joke about it now, but Maggie, believe me when I tell you, that bitch damned near broke me. If it wasn't for Raj that night . . .' He trailed off as a customer approached to pay for a bunch of bananas.

Maggie waited patiently whilst he served the young mother, who peeled one of the bananas and handed it straight to her toddler in a pushchair. Once they had moved away, Vernon pointed to a bench on the far side of the square, next to the post box.

'A few weeks after Ben's mum moved out, without, I should add, so much as a goodbye, I came down here. It was late, after midnight. I do that sometimes, come and enjoy the square without all this,' he waved a hand at the bustling market. 'On this occasion, I might have had a few too many whiskies. Might have been contemplating what it was all for.' He looked up to the green and white striped canvas of his market stall. 'Ben had barely come out of his room. Wouldn't talk to me; blamed me, I think. How could a mother do that to her child?' He screwed his face, incredulous. 'Just *bugger off* without a word? It was a year ago yesterday since she left, and all he's had in that time is one sodding birthday card in the post.'

Maggie remembered Ben's dark mood yesterday and everything clicked into place. Poor lad.

'Anyhow,' he continued, 'I were in a particularly bad place that night, Maggie, I don't mind telling you. Had a bottle of scotch in one coat pocket and a packet of prescription painkillers in the other.'

The rims of Vernon's eyes turned pink.

'I couldn't reach him, couldn't reach my boy. It all seemed so hopeless,' his voice caught.

'Ben is a remarkable young man, Vernon,' comforted Maggie. 'Much stronger than you might think.'

'Oh, I know!' he said, blinking away the painful memory, 'and as I said, I have Raj to thank for that. He appeared that night, as if from nowhere. Must have been out walking, I suppose, they're up late with the restaurant

203

aren't they. Came and sat down on the bench next to me and I ending up pouring my heart out to him – the drink, I expect, don't recall ever having a conversation with him before, other than to order food in the restaurant.' He paused, sniffed. 'Do you know what he said?'

Maggie shook her head, absorbed by Vernon's story.

'He said there was no space in a person's life that couldn't be filled with purposeful intent. All I had to do was get up each day and fill it with useful industry. Go to work. Pay the bills. Do the housework. Feed myself and my son. Rest. Repeat. If the mind and body are employed, he said, there is little room for doubt, and without doubt, we prosper. He asked me if I thought Ben might like a part-time job because he needed help in the restaurant, and since he wasn't getting any younger, could he start immediately? And then he'd turned to me and quoted a proverb which has stayed with me ever since: "We can't change the direction of the wind, my friend, but we can adjust the sails."'

Maggie's eyes smarted and she experienced a rush of fondness for gentle Raj. Hadn't she felt the unbearable weight of her own grief lift just a little in recent weeks, since occupying her hands and mind with new work, new friends, old passions?

She cleared her throat. 'Raj is a lovely man, Vernon. A stubborn one too, as I'm discovering. And Ben is a natural in the kitchen; I'm only sorry it might not work out if the restaurant doesn't get back on track.'

'Isn't there anything I can do?' asked Vernon. 'I mean, I've got to eat, I can't *give* my produce away, but perhaps we could negotiate a discount? I could even deliver first thing before setting up my stall?'

Maggie pondered his words. 'You know, that's not a bad idea, I'll mention it to Sav. We've got this weekend to get through first, mind.'

'Well, I'll be sure to recommend The Golden Crocus whenever I can; you'd be amazed how many tourists pump me for inside knowledge on the town. Not just a greengrocer, me, or a pretty face,' he winked and flashed her his usual cheeky grin, then went to serve a new customer.

'There you are,' exclaimed Hannah, standing outside the town hall, three full bags at her feet, a take-out coffee in each hand and a brown paper bag from the cake shop wedged under her arm. When Maggie put her bags down, she handed her a coffee and an iced doughnut ring. 'I thought you'd gone to harvest the vegetables yourself.'

'Sorry, love, bit of a story. I'll tell you on the way back. How did you get on?'

Hannah checked her list. 'I got everything apart from salmon, they'd sold out.' She winced, 'So I got prawns instead?'

'Perfect. And this is why the ability to adapt a menu on spec is invaluable. So already I'm thinking . . . maybe a take on a prawn chaat puri? Or even a spiced spaghetti dish. It's then just a quick alteration, the press of a button and Bob's your uncle. Speaking of which, the next stop is the butchers, and we can't afford lamb, so we'll be improvising again – otherwise known as flying by the seat of our pants, Hannie.'

As 6 p.m. rolled round in the kitchen, after a busy day of prep and the creation of two new dishes, everyone was surprised and delighted to see Ben stroll in.

'Ben? I did explain properly, didn't I?' asked Joe warily. 'We can't pay you mate. This might even be our last weekend.'

'Yeah,' said Ben, taking a clean apron from the drawer, 'you explained. And I want to be here.'

Maggie wanted to throw her arms around the boy, but didn't want to embarrass him, so instead she passed the garlic crusher and a gnarly lump of ginger. 'Need more paste, love.'

Hannah was outside laying up the tables with Sav. At one point Maggie had popped to the loo and caught her daughter teaching Sav to fashion fans from the linen serviettes in a complex series of folds, while Alice played with her Sylvanian Families at a small table nearby.

'Where did you learn to do that?'

Hannah, who hadn't heard her coming, looked sheepish. 'YouTube,' she shrugged, then carried on, her face a mask of concentration.

Maggie had smirked to herself. A knowing mother's smirk, reserved for the reaching of an observed conclusion, long before their offspring.

The evening was a resounding success. Not without its fraught moments, like when Sav had raced into the kitchen swearing because they'd run out of red wine. The cash-and-carry account was also on stop and booze stocks were running thin. Unfortunately, Ben was too young for this errand, so it fell to Sav to run to Allsave, whilst Hannah held the fort, single-handedly dispatching hot food to multiple tables like a pro.

Jade arrived mid-service, and insisted on helping, even though she was dressed as Batwoman having come straight from her cousin's superhero-themed birthday party – a costume that proved something of a talking point among the customers. Mid-service, when Maggie had stuck her head out of the kitchen to see how many tables were full, she had witnessed a smart-arsed diner attempting to amuse the rest of his party, at Jade's expense.

'Could we get the bill please, Batgirl? And no need to bring your sidekick out, we won't leave without paying. *I'm not into Robin.*'

The customer guffawed with laughter at his own joke, the rest of the table groaned.

'Robbing – Robin – gettit?'

Maggie thanked her lucky stars she was safely ensconced in the kitchen, away from clowns like this.

'If I hear that one more time,' hissed Jade, returning to the kitchen with a stack of plates.

'Cool it, Batgirl,' grinned Ben and then he flicked soapy water from the sink in her direction, splattering her in the face.

'Bat*woman*,' she said, glaring at him through her dripping eye mask, pointed ears standing to attention. 'Different character entirely.'

At the end of a very long day, too exhausted for staff drinks, and with a very sleepy child in tow, Maggie was thankful Hannah had parked her car close by when she'd been home to pick up Alice.

'I think I'm getting too old for all of this,' she said, limbs creaking as she manoeuvred herself from the car.

'Nonsense, Mum. You've got more energy than me and this one put together,' she indicated the back seat where Alice sat in a booster seat, her head lolled to the side, lips parted. 'I mean, obviously, not when she's asleep. Although, from the state of her bed in the mornings, you'd think she'd been having a disco in it,' she smiled, affection brimming from every pore.

Maggie pressed her lips to her fingers in an air kiss to them both, 'Night, darling. Love you both.'

'Love you too, Mum.'

As Hannah slowly pulled away, Maggie traversed the short path to her front door, the bright moonlit sky casting everything in a magical silvery glow. Something looked different. Something *felt* different.

Disorientated momentarily, she slowly turned, performing a three hundred-and sixty-degree rotation until it became crystal clear.

The small patch of lawn had been neatly mown and all the borders weeded, suffocated plants now standing to attention, spot lit by the full moon and saying *look, I was here all along*. Even the rose, gifted by Hannah to her parents for their sapphire wedding anniversary, which Maggie had thought long past it, had been pruned back, its violet petals luminous against terracotta brick.

She glanced along the row, to two doors down. Oscar's house was in darkness, curtains drawn upon his own neat garden. Maggie shook her head and smiled to herself. *Silly old sod*, she thought. Now she'd have to pop by and thank him.

# Chapter Nineteen

## Maggie

For as long as Maggie could remember, the first Wednesday of every month meant one thing. The Women's Institute.

As a child, the small two-up, two-down that she, her mother and grandparents had shared in Croydon was often called upon by well-meaning members.

'I've been baking today, Pat. Thought the little one might like a treacle tart.'

'My Susan's grown out of this now, any good to Margaret?'

Hers had been a warm and loving home, surrounded by strong, dependable women. And although she'd teased her elders relentlessly about their 'mother's meetings', as her grandfather had affectionately called them, it was no surprise to her adult self when she, also, became a member of her local WI.

Maggie had missed the last two or three meetings, her attendance waning at around the same time she'd begun making excuses to Pam. But this month, she felt differently.

Recently, Maggie's cup had begun to overfloweth once more with what Geoff had always called 'the warm and fuzzies', a feeling she hadn't believed possible again. She missed her friends, and more importantly, she owed Pam a heartfelt apology.

She arrived at the church hall early, hoping to catch Pam before the others arrived. Sure enough, there she was, laying out the chairs and sporting a snazzy pink tint on her short hair Maggie had never seen her friend wear before.

'Hi, Pam.'

'Ah!' cried out Pam, dropping the chair she was carrying to the floor with a loud clatter. 'What are you doing creeping around like that, Maggie? You almost gave me a heart attack.' Then, realising what she'd said, she swiftly backtracked in her usual, blustery, word-vomit way. 'Of course, not literally, I mean, at least, I hope things are all ticking along OK in that department, but you never really know of course, as you know only too well, ah, that's to say, um . . .'

Maggie levelled her with the look she always gave when Pam was digging herself a hole, which was a more frequent occasion than you might think, for a woman who volunteered for the Samaritans two evenings a month.

Eventually, Pam stopped talking. 'Too much?'

'Allow me to take your spade away, dear,' replied Maggie, leaning down to right the fallen chair. 'How are you doing, Pammy? Loving the Toyah Wilcox look.'

'It's not too trendy, is it?' she said, reaching up to touch her coloured hair. 'Dave said I looked like I belonged in a Pixar movie.'

'Hmph. What does he know? It looks fabulous, my darling. Really suits you.'

Pam's face broke into a warm grin. 'The girls at work love it – I think it's put me in the cool gang.'

'And how is the world of potholes and fly-tippers?' asked Maggie, remembering her job in council customer services as though it belonged in some distant epoch, rather than just two years ago. How things had changed since then.

'Oh, you know. Colin is still Colin, although I'm pretty sure he's started wearing a toupée. The colour doesn't quite match.'

Maggie laughed, picturing her old boss.

'Samira said she'd seen you in The Golden Crocus a few weeks back, she said you went into the kitchen and never came out. I said she must have been mistaken, because what on earth would you be doing in an Indian restaurant kitchen?'

An edge had entered Pam's tone. As though she perhaps knew more than she was letting on and was waiting to catch Maggie out.

The heavy wooden door to the church hall creaked open, and a group of ladies filed in, each giving Maggie a little wave of recognition when they spotted her.

'I'll tell you all about it afterwards,' she whispered, giving Pam a wink, 'with a weak cup of tea and a rich tea biscuit.'

Pam grinned. It had been their little joke for donkey's years, because despite the considerable sums raised by WI endeavours throughout the year, the powers that be (i.e. Mrs Robinson, head of light refreshments) still never raised the bar above even the most basic of confectionery.

'Well, that was enlightening,' said Pam an hour later, as the evening's guest speaker, an ex-circus performer, began to pack away her props. 'Who'd have thought Judith had it in her?'

'Quite,' agreed Maggie, who had watched on awestruck as timid Judith had hula-hooped her way around the church hall to the chorus of 'Hips Don't Lie' and a steady, rhythmic clap. Although Shakira had probably never experienced the complication of trousers with an elasticated waistband, which didn't fare well under all the jigging. 'And what about Diane, with her balls?'

'Very impressive,' agreed Pam, taking a sip of her tea. 'My Dave used to be able to juggle, would you believe? You name it, he could juggle with it: lemons, potatoes, even melons once.'

Maggie gave Pam's bountiful chest a pointed stare. 'I think he'd have his work cut out these days.'

'So, come on then, enough with all the secrecy, are you going to tell me what you've been up to? And bearing in mind we've just heard the testimony of someone who actually did run away to join the circus, it had better be good.' There was no reprimand in Pam's eyes, only the genuine concern of a friend.

Maggie found her hand and squeezed it.

'I'm so sorry, Pam.'

'Whatever for?' she asked, taken aback by Maggie's unusual display of tacticity.

'I've been a rubbish friend. And you were so supportive, after . . . Well, I shouldn't have pushed you away, but I just haven't felt . . . myself. Not like the Maggie you knew.'

Pam shook her head. 'None of us stay the same, dear.

Life changes us. And your friends go along for the ride. Someone to hold your hand at the scary bits.'

'Hmm,' said Maggie, wondering what her friend had been reading lately. There'd been no end to her wisdom when she'd read Miriam Margolyes' memoir last year, much of it punctuated with ear-popping language. 'Well, I can't guarantee there won't be any more scary bits, but if we must use funfair analogies, I've been enjoying a rather thrilling ride on the dodgems lately and I'd like to tell you all about it.'

Once Pam had been fully briefed on Maggie's involvement at the restaurant and had asked her pertinent questions such as, was Joe single, because a new girl at work was looking for a man and he sounded like such a sweetheart. Another corker was, is it true they put food colourings in Indian food, and if so, didn't all those E numbers make customers hyperactive, eating so close to bedtime? Feeling Pam had rather missed the point, Maggie assured her friend no colourings were used in Gita's kitchen and even if they had been, they were all natural these days.

'Excuse me,' interrupted Judith, who had been loitering near the biscuits. 'I couldn't help but overhear your conversation about The Golden Crocus. Could you tell me how Gita is doing? Is she very poorly?'

Minus her hula-hoop, Judith looked bird-like and reserved once more. Maggie had always found her a little offish if truth be told, which made tonight even more of a revelation.

'She's fine,' assured Maggie. 'Her hip replacement went well and she's just waiting to be signed off by the physiotherapist before they fly home. I imagine it will be some time before she can return to work though.' *If she ever does*, she thought but didn't say.

Judith wrung her hands in relief. 'Oh, that's good news. I was worried something terrible had happened, you hear rumours, you know.'

'Rumours?'

'Well,' Judith faltered. 'Only that the Kapoors' boy was running the place now and there was no sign of the parents, although, from what you've just said, it sounds like it's *you* running the show?'

'Oh no,' laughed Maggie. 'No, no. I've just been lending a hand. Sav is definitely in charge. You should come along and try the new menu.'

Judith nodded vigorously. 'I'd love to. I've been meaning to pop in there for a while. I kind of owe Gita a thank you. Perhaps when she's home I can take some flowers in or ask if there's anything I can do around the house to help.'

Maggie's curiosity was peaked. 'Are you good friends with Gita then, Judith?'

Maggie had tried to convince Gita to come along to WI in the past, to no avail.

Judith's cheeks flushed pink.

She looked about her, to check no-one was listening. 'It's all a bit embarrassing really. After my husband died, I was in a bit of a fix, you know, financially. Terry had always taken care of that sort of thing and then suddenly...' she tailed off, clearly uncomfortable. 'Anyway, it's all sorted now. My son helped me with applying for all the benefits and bits and pieces, amazing what help there is, once you know how to find it.'

Maggie nodded reassuringly, under no illusion at all how difficult it must have been for the poor woman. She had been lucky; Geoff had earned good money and had a hefty pension too, so money wasn't something she'd had to worry about, and she could only imagine the extra stress she'd have been under if things had been different. She mentally scolded herself for not reaching out; you just never knew what others were going through, and it was simply too easy to judge.

'Anyway,' continued Judith, 'one day I was in Allsave with a basket of shopping, just the essentials, you know. There was a queue of customers a mile long and *the worst thing happened*. My card was declined. Twice. I didn't have any cash on me, and the cashier was getting humpy. I've never been so humiliated in all my life. It was only £8.59, but I'm ashamed to say, I began to cry, it was all just so . . . overwhelming.' Judith looked down at her shoes, clearly reliving the moment.

Pam cooed sympathetically, lapping up the unfolding drama.

'Then, before I could stop her, Gita, who had been behind me in the queue, stepped in front of me and without saying a word, handed her card to the cashier.'

'She paid for your shopping. How kind,' said Maggie. 'Did she know you?'

'Never had a conversation with her in my life,' said Judith. 'Terry would only ever eat plain food, could never persuade him to try the restaurant, though I always wanted to.'

'What a lovely thing to do,' said Pam.

Judith nodded. 'I was absolutely mortified. I waited for

her outside and begged her to take the shopping, it was only milk, a few tins of soup and some cereal, but she wouldn't have it. She waved me away, insisted it was nothing, said someone had done the same for her once.'

Maggie was thoughtful, remembering Vernon's story about Raj's kindness.

'Well, Judith, I can think of one way you can repay Gita's generosity,' said Pam, snapping a biscuit in half decisively. 'Get yourself down to the restaurant and make up for lost time – put your £8.59 back in their till with interest!'

Judith nodded her agreement. 'I will. Or perhaps,' she ventured, looking hopeful, 'we could turn it into a girls' night out?'

'That's a jolly good idea, Judith, and we'll arrange something soon. But do you know what?' remarked Maggie, 'I think we can do even better than that.'

# Chapter Twenty

## Hannah

Hannah could only imagine what Laura would say if she knew that instead of disembarking the train at her usual stop, she was continuing straight through to Cambridge. And that she was going to meet Sav.

She wasn't about to volunteer the information either. She could already visualise the athletic work out her friend's eyebrows would be doing.

No, this was a business trip, that's all. One that had tied in ever so conveniently with a pleading text from Darren asking if he could collect Alice from school and take her to meet her new baby cousin.

Hannah wasn't an ogre, she had no desire to keep Alice from her father's side of her family, and she'd got along well with her sister-in-law, Kelly, once upon a time.

Perhaps unwisely, she'd left a key under the potted acer on her front drive, with instructions for Darren to put Alice to bed and wait until she got home. It was far from an ideal situation – the thought of him in her new home gave her the creeps if she was honest – but still preferable to relying on him to get Alice to school on time the next day. As far as Hannah was concerned, this was another test. If he cocked up, it wouldn't happen again. Simple.

When she'd suggested to Sav they check out a trendy Cambridge restaurant she'd read about, she had been slightly fearful he would think she was asking him out on a date.

'For research purposes,' she'd been quick to clarify. 'I gather this place is pretty hot on the Asian fusion scene, it might be good for inspiration?'

'Research,' he'd said, with a curious smile. 'Like a field trip? Perhaps we should all go, in that case? Call it a staff outing?'

Disappointment had balled up in Hannah's throat, but she'd dug deep and given an enthusiastic, 'Sure! Why not?'

Sav's lips had curled into a grin. 'Except, you're not really staff, are you? In fact, you're the only one *not* on the payroll.'

'Neither is Jade,' Hannah had snapped petulantly. And hadn't she spent more hours in that darned place than she had in her own home of late?

'I'm kidding,' he laughed. 'Not that it wouldn't be fun, I can just imagine Maggie scrutinising an artistic smear of wasabi emulsion on her plate as though it were a nasal excretion. And Jade chewing out Joe for his good manners, because apparently it's sexist to hold doors open for women, who knew?'

Hannah pulled a face. 'For the record, I'd like it noted I *don't* find that sexist. For one thing, who wants a door closing in their face? And secondly, my ex-husband was about as chivalrous as a stale bread roll, so a little bit of Joc would go a very long way.'

'He's a big guy, there's plenty to go around,' said Sav, amused.

'You know what I mean. He's a lovely guy.'

'He is,' agreed Sav. 'But, in all honesty, apart from the fact I can't even afford to treat everyone to a Gregg's sausage roll, never mind a slap-up dinner, I'd prefer it if it were just us.'

Hannah's face had burnt under the intensity of Sav's gaze, as a fizz of nerves shot through her. It's not a date, it's not a date, she told herself.

They had settled on Wednesday evening whilst the restaurant was shut, and then when Darren had fortuitously asked to have Alice, it had saved having to involve Maggie, who would doubtlessly have had something to say about the excursion.

Sav had been attending to some business during the day and was meeting Hannah at the restaurant. Then they would drive back to Saffron Walden together in his car. It would be the first time they'd spent any real time alone together, Hannah realised, as she walked quickly through the crowds of students and tourists lining the city's streets.

When she arrived outside The Twisted Duck, she paused to take in the exterior. This was, after all, a reconnaissance dinner. Nothing more.

The building was a period property, as was The Golden Crocus. But whereas the Indian restaurant oozed a rich, warm, crooked cosiness, especially when lit from within at night, The Twisted Duck was all straight Georgian lines and flawless navy-blue matt paint, its calligraphic sign spotlit with a brass rectangular lamp. The ideal balance was perhaps somewhere in between the cracked render and flaking paintwork of the Indian restaurant and the clinical perfection of this place.

Steeling herself with a calm, neutral expression, as she did when entering the courtroom, Hannah was about to push open the door, when an arm shot out to bar her way.

'Oh, please do allow *me*, Madam,' said Sav affecting a genteel accent, eyes sparkling with amusement.

She snorted a laugh and let Sav pull open the door for her. 'Why, thank you.'

'The pleasure is all mine,' he said, conspicuously keeping his eyes on hers, rather than travelling downwards to take in the fitted dress she'd worn to work that day. Which was more than could be said of one of the managing partners who'd openly gawped at her boobs as she'd updated him on a case. Sometimes, she truly hated her job.

'So how did you hear about this place?' asked Sav, once they had been seated at an industrial-looking table that looked to have metal drainpipes for legs.

'Well,' said Hannah, 'I'll confess I'd never heard of it myself. Funnily enough I have neither money nor means to spend my evenings and weekends on the hip gastro scene, but luckily for us, one of my clients does. Caitlin Gallagher, bit of a socialite. Her chief employment? Influencing young professionals to part with vast sums of money on beauty products and dresses. Naturally this requires her to be constantly pictured in swanky hotels, restaurants and holiday locations.'

Sav examined the stainless-steel thermos flask of tap water that had been delivered to their table when they placed their order along with an empty tin can containing chopsticks and thankfully, cutlery. 'This is swanky?' He looked perplexed.

'The Ivy is *so* yesterday, darling. But when I saw this place come up in her Instagram feed, I thought it was worth checking out as we're offering fusion food too. Although, now we're here,' she grimaced, 'I'm kind of homesick for red tablecloths and the cheesy photo of your mum and dad beaming down at us from the wall.'

Hannah tipped her head towards an enormous piece of art on the wall above their heads, which was 80 per cent white canvas, 10 per cent gold frame and 10 per cent a photo of a solitary shitake mushroom.

'Although,' said Sav thoughtfully, 'I do love the idea of pictures of food. I could just imagine some nice bright paintings of chillis, for example, and exotic fruit, something colourful and fun, that doesn't take itself too seriously. Loads of them, covering every wall.'

Hannah nodded. 'I can totally see that. I love an eclectic feel, and I think you have to play to a place's strengths. The restaurant is a piece of Saffron Walden's history, an old, wonky building in a street that's seen centuries of change.'

'I'd swap the old-fashioned tablecloths for Indian fabrics, mismatching table runners and scatter cushions.' Sav's eyes sparkled with enthusiasm. 'Also, I've always thought the name The Golden Crocus doesn't sit right. My parents chose it because saffron comes from the crocus plant, and obviously in our town every other business is called Saffron-something or other, so they had to come up with something different. But it doesn't work.'

221

Hannah nodded. 'Because the crocus plant we get saffron from is purple, not gold.'

'Exactly. There is even a variety called golden crocus, and it doesn't produce saffron.'

'What would you call it then?' asked Hannah, intrigued.

'I'm not sure,' he said, shrugging. 'It needs some thought. Nothing too drastically different, or it wouldn't feel like the same place, just something a bit more modern.'

Hannah smiled. 'So, you do have a vision after all.'

Sav frowned. 'What do you mean?'

'I thought you'd given up on it. Wondered if maybe you were just humouring Mum about giving it another go. Believe me, I know how pushy she can be, once she sets her sights on something. But at the end of the day, the restaurant belongs to your parents, not her. What do they want? What do *you* want?'

Sav was given a reprieve of her questioning by the arrival of their drinks: a passionfruit mocktail for her and a diet coke for him.

'You could have had wine, if you wanted,' said Sav, as she picked up her glass. 'I'm driving, after all.'

'I'll have to collect my car from the station this evening so I can get back again in the morning. But thanks for the offer.'

As she sipped her drink through the straw, she felt Sav's eyes tracking the movement, and self-consciously licked away a stray droplet from her lips.

'Maybe we could do it again some time,' he said, causing her to swallow hard. 'Dinner, that is.'

'More research?' she asked, mortified by how squeaky her voice sounded.

He smiled. 'Definitely more research needed.'

Hannah grinned, feeling disconcertingly hopeful. What was she doing? This was never part of the plan. Not that there had been a plan, other than look after Alice and survive.

'You asked me what I wanted,' he added, eyes boring into hers and making her insides heat up.

'Uh-huh.'

'I want to see my parents into a comfortable retirement, and I want my friends to be happy. And, I used to think I wanted my apartment in Brighton, my gym membership and the 50 per cent stake in the tech company I set up with Greg. That's where I've been today, by the way – I had some business to sort out.'

Hannah felt the air between them thicken. 'And now?'

Sav gave a small sigh and looked down at his clasped hands on the table. 'Turns out, I quite like being a restaurateur, but don't tell my parents, they'll never let me live it down. I haven't had so much fun in years. And it's been wonderful spending time with Joe; I really missed him and haven't kept in touch anywhere near as much as I should have. And Ben is a great kid, super smart and keen to learn. As for your mum, well . . .' He opened his hands in a gesture that said no explanation needed. 'And then there's you.'

Hannah's heart stalled for a moment.

'I've enjoyed being there too,' she said, when what she really meant was she liked being with him.

'It's complicated, Hannah. I know how I'd *like* this to go, but I can also see how it's *going* to go. I can't help feeling it's foolish to delay the inevitable, you know? Perhaps we should just rip off the plaster and then we can all move on with our lives.'

Hannah no longer knew whether they were talking about the restaurant.

'Here's our food,' said Sav, glancing past her shoulder. 'Hope you're not hungry.'

The server presented them with dishes which resembled miniature pieces of art, beautifully presented, but rather scant on calorific content.

'I wonder what Maggie would make of this,' mused Sav, cutting his only scallop in half and spearing it along with a single strand of crispy seaweed.

'She'd probably put down her chopsticks and charge into the kitchen to find out where the rest of her dinner is.'

Sav grinned. 'They wouldn't know what hit them.'

Hannah pushed her chicken wing around her plate. Trust her to order something she was going to smear around her face like her five-year-old daughter did when eating ice cream. 'I hope you weren't too offended that night,' she began. 'I was horrified when Mum got up and walked into your kitchen – it wasn't her place to interfere.'

Sav finished chewing and put down his fork.

'Hannah, the entire place could have burnt to the ground that night and the most memorable part would have been when I saw you sitting there. And now you're sitting here, with me. You don't know how grateful I am to your astonishingly brilliant mother, whatever happens to the restaurant.'

She nodded and felt a curious flurry of emotion. An unwanted sensation of nostalgia for something she feared might already be gone. Which was brutally unfair, because since returning to her hometown, she'd only just realised revisiting her past actually felt like a new beginning.

## Chapter Twenty-One

## *Maggie*

For the third time in as many days, Maggie lifted the brass knocker on Oscar's front door and rapped it loudly.

The man was busier than he ever had been when he'd worked as the local postman, though she suspected his vocation had contributed greatly to the arthritis now plaguing his body.

This time, however, success. Oscar opened the door, and she caught the precise moment his anxious expression changed to cheerful delight. But in that split second, it was enough for Maggie to wonder how much of his joie de vivre was real.

'Maggie,' he enthused. 'What a lovely surprise.'

'You're a difficult man to pin down, Oscar, quite the socialite.'

'Well, you know what they say about idle hands.'

'Quite, which is why I wanted to catch you. To thank you for the splendid job you've done of my front garden.

It was completely unnecessary but also a very lovely thing to do. Thank you.'

Oscar tried to wave away her thanks. 'Honestly, don't mention it. It was a pleasure, I'm always on hand for the odd job here and . . .' He broke off, squinting at something close to Maggie's feet. 'Is that your cat, Maggie?'

Maggie glanced down to find Monty had sidled up to sit beside Oscar's gladioli and was giving himself a good wash behind the ears.

'What are you doing here, you silly sausage?' she said, bending down to stroke him.

And then, just as Monty paused in his ablutions, she heard the tell-tale snarl of a different four-legged friend.

'Banjo!' cried out Oscar, as the little white dog launched itself from between his legs and set off in pursuit of Monty.

Monty bolted across the lawn, easily outrunning the barking dog. Then in a twist no-one could have seen coming, Monty turned on his little white heels and stopped dead, his masked face cocked in challenge, tail standing up like a bottle brush.

Banjo screeched to a halt and gave one pathetic yap, before turning on his heel and ducking back between Oscar's legs, retreating to the safety of home. Monty dived after him, leaving Maggie and Oscar standing there, bewildered.

Oscar moved first, calling out plaintive cries of 'Banjo! Come back here.'

Maggie had a vision of the little dog cowering behind a sofa while her demonic cat clawed at Oscar's upholstery, and she followed in hot pursuit.

'Monty!' she called, charging through the front door

and faltering as she encountered a towering barricade of boxes.

Oscar's house was almost identical to Maggie's, though hers had been extended back in the early nineties. They had added a downstairs bathroom and turned the small kitchen into a large farmhouse style kitchen-diner, spanning the whole ground floor, with Velux windows that flooded the space with light; it was Maggie's pride and joy and the beating heart of the house. Maggie paused, disorientated for a moment by the colourful boxes, which she now realised were jigsaw puzzles, hundreds of them, most of them brand new and sealed in cellophane. Did Oscar have some kind of side-hustle? Was he one of those industrious types who ran eBay businesses out of their box room or garage?

'Monty?' she called again with trepidation, aware Oscar might not appreciate her traipsing uninvited around his home.

The sound of objects crashing to the floor and a whelping Banjo spurred her forwards to the living room, and into a scene of chaos that stopped her in her tracks.

The floorspace played host to seemingly random crates of bric-a-brac. Stems of dried flowers lay crushed beneath a ukulele to her left, and what looked like a potter's wheel and several bags of clay were stacked up against a coffee table to her right. The curtain pole played host to three Morris dancer costumes dangling on coat hangers like the ghosts of country fetes past and if you wanted to sit on the sofa, you'd first have to remove a fluorescent yellow coat and lollipop stick school-crossing sign.

The rug was covered in chunks of broken ceramic,

which must have fallen from the crowded mantelpiece, where other bizarre ornaments stood, including a large mosaic of a fishing boat.

A dining table in the corner was barely visible beneath the piles of junk adorning it, towering stacks of magazines and various crafting tools. A sewing machine was set up, with a large piece of fabric hanging from its jaws, mid stitch. The dining chairs were draped with sheaths of green and yellow material, and as Banjo streaked out from beneath, he took the fabric with him, overturning a basket of brass bells that jingled as they came to rest in a puddle on the floor.

Oscar emerged from under the table, backing out with Monty clasped firmly in his arms.

'Give him here,' said Maggie, wrestling the moggie from him and thanking her lucky stars Oscar looked unscathed. Not that Monty had ever shown her so much as a claw, but after today's turn as a ninja bully, she'd put nothing past him at all.

Swiftly she went to the front door and turfed Monty out. 'I'll see you at home, young man,' she said sternly, before shutting the door in his face.

'I like to keep busy,' said Oscar, as she re-entered the room. The catch in his voice didn't suit the forced jocular tone. 'Can't just sit about all day. Blasted knee put a stop to my Morris dancing, so I offered to refresh the costumes ready for the summer fete. Took a dressmaking course in January so I'm a dab hand with a needle and thread, if you ever need any curtain alterations, that sort of thing.'

Maggie saw the embarrassment blooming in Oscar's cheeks and her heart went out to him. 'I'll bear that in mind. Never could get the hang of it. Poor Hannah did an entire term with the sleeves of her school blazer turned up an inch and stapled into place.'

He bent to pick up the broken pieces of pottery from the floor and winced as he went down on his knees.

'Let me,' said Maggie, hunting around for something to put the debris into before anyone hurt themselves. She grabbed the basket, now empty of bells. 'I'm so sorry, Oscar, I don't know what came over Monty – he's never done anything like that before.'

'Oh, they were just playing. Neither of them would have come to any harm.'

Maggie huffed. 'Well that's more than can be said of . . . whatever this was.' She gingerly held aloft a bulbous tubular object remaining remarkably intact and suspiciously phallic in shape.

'Spout,' said Oscar. 'My first attempt at a teapot.'

Maggie blanched. 'Oh, Oscar, I'm so sorry. Do you think we might repair it?' She looked doubtfully at the jumbled pieces.

'God no, it was one of the ugliest things you've ever seen. I don't think ceramics is my strong suit, probably shouldn't have bought all the kit before I came to that realisation.' He gestured to the equipment in the corner.

Pulling himself to standing, she watched as his shoulders fell in weary resignation.

'Truth is, Maggie, since Mary died, I can't bear to be alone with my thoughts. I know it's got a bit out of control,' he swept an arm around at the mess, 'but if I don't find ways to fill my day, it all becomes just,' he chewed on his lip, 'too difficult.'

Maggie looked about, empathy swelling her chest. 'I do understand, Oscar. Perhaps more than you might know.'

He looked up. 'Really? You always seem so together, so self-sufficient. I can't imagine you desperately filling your week with anything to avoid twiddling your thumbs alone.'

She was about to explain she was doing just that with the restaurant, when she realised something.

'Do you know what, I did exactly the opposite. I pushed all my friends away and stopped going out, gave up my hobbies completely. I don't think there's any right way to deal with it you know, grief. We're all just muddling along and hoping for the best.'

Oscar nodded slowly, thinking about what she'd said. 'I think if I'd still been working, it wouldn't have been so bad. Impossible to be bored when you're a postie.' He looked toward the cluttered sofa. 'I start working on the school crossing next week, though. I'm very much looking forward to that.'

Maggie smiled warmly. 'I think you are an inspiration, Oscar. If you didn't try, you'd never know. That's all any of us can do. Keep trying new things.'

'Well, I think I can safely say I'll be looking for a new home for the potter's wheel,' he laughed. 'And if you fancy broadening your own horizons, Maggie, there's a new art class starting in the gallery in town, Monday week. I've put my name down. Fancy finding your inner Picasso?'

Maggie was about to brush him off, as she did all of his extra-curricular invitations when she stopped herself. Perhaps she *should* push herself to try something new. She couldn't imagine drawing would make her heart sing anywhere near as much as cooking, but if it enjoyed a gentle hum, wouldn't that also be nice?

'OK, Oscar. I'll make you a deal.'

Bemused, he said, 'Go on.'

'I'll come along to your art class if you get yourself over to mine in,' she checked her watch, 'forty-five minutes. And don't come over all unnecessary, dear,' she said at his raised bushy brow, 'I have a few friends coming for coffee, and I think you'll find what we have to discuss a rewarding use of your morning.'

Maggie glanced around her kitchen table at the assembled crowd and felt the familiar glow she always had when entertaining. It had been much too long. OK, so the purpose of this 'mothers' meeting', as her old grandad would have called it, wasn't purely social, though she couldn't deny the pleasure she got from watching her friends tuck greedily into great slabs of homemade Victoria sponge and rocky road.

Diane, of juggling proficiency, was deep in conversation with Oscar about a flower arranging course they'd recently attended together and were discussing the boundless and versatile merits of gypsophila.

Judith was pouring the tea and Pam was updating Vernon and Maggie on what had been dubbed Operation Lamppost by her overzealous nephew Christopher, aka Sergeant Rutherford.

'So, they've linked the paintwork left at the scene to a black Porsche Carrera GT,' she said, 'but without CCTV footage they don't stand a chance of finding it – it's like finding a very expensive needle in a giant haystack.'

'I thought everywhere was under surveillance these days,' said Vernon. 'Isn't Big Brother watching us all the time? It certainly feels like it when Facebook suggests I might want to buy an orthopaedic mattress because I once told a customer I pulled my back lifting a crate of carrots.'

'The one outside Maison Rose was just a decoy, apparently,' said Pam.

'I heard they've been serving up raw food. Gave a woman the trots apparently,' interjected Judith, tutting. 'Well, I won't be eating there any time soon.'

'Doesn't surprise me,' added Vernon. 'The manager's a complete pillock. The best chef he ever had asked him to pop over to my stall to buy some thyme the other day, and he sacked him on the spot for trying to be funny.'

Maggie decided now was the best time to call order, before she added her own opinions of Jacob Green to the mix.

'Right then, everybody,' she announced to the group that included friends from the WI as well as parents she'd known from Hannah's schooldays. She had to repeat herself to get the attention of Diane and Oscar, who had moved on to the perils of floristry wire and were comparing soft-tissue scars. 'Ahem,' she coughed, loudly, finally claiming the room. 'So, as lovely as it is to see you all here today, the reason for this meeting is to set forth our ideas and create a plan of action for The Golden Crocus's fundraiser.'

Oscar looked perplexed. 'The Indian restaurant where you're working?'

'Yes,' nodded Maggie. 'Although I can speak from experience and assure you all it's so much more than just a restaurant. It's the home and business of our friends Raj and Gita, lately in the charge of their son, Sav. It is a place where I've spent the past few weeks nurturing, growing and learning, alongside new friends and where I've been happiest in a very long twelve months. It's where food is created with love and enjoyed with relish. All of that will vanish in just two weeks if we can't turn things around, to be replaced with a soulless monstrosity in the money-grabbing hands of Hugo Wick.'

Maggie waited as gasps of dismay and anger were expressed at her revelation.

'That can't happen!' retorted Pam, who had been on the receiving end of his bullying tactics to force through road closures at the council. 'I've never come across a more odious individual in all my working life. To think what he'd do to that beautiful building. I wouldn't even put it past him to knock it down, its Grade II listed status would mean nothing to him, nothing he couldn't buy anyway.'

'You're probably right,' agreed Maggie. 'But nevertheless, whilst all of these are very good reasons to fight to save our Indian restaurant, I would like to give you all several more good reasons, with Vernon and Judith's permission,' she waited whilst they eagerly nodded their consent, 'why the Kapoors as a family deserve this community's support, even though they've never asked a thing from it.'

# Chapter Twenty-Two

## Maggie

By the time Maggie called order on the meeting and shooed everyone from her kitchen, it was time to collect Alice from school. And it had ended up being such a busy day, with one thing and another, that Maggie eschewed her usual commitment to providing her granddaughter with a properly balanced meal, and instead cooked them both egg and chips.

She hadn't been involved in a meeting of such an emotive nature since someone on the PTA brought up glue sticks. It had turned out no amount of budgeting could prioritise the much-prized resource, which saw teachers poised with empty glue guns at dawn.

Judith had insisted there should be a raffle and had volunteered herself for the role. Vernon had offered a luxury hamper as a prize, and the conversation had veered off course for a good half hour whilst everyone discussed exactly which fruits and vegetables constituted luxury goods.

Diane had suggested a tombola, which had led to a dispute over whether both a raffle and a tombola was needed, until Oscar argued everyone was a winner with a tombola. Maggie wasn't sure plucking a beige ticket from a bucket and being rewarded with a tin of pineapple chunks that had lurked at the back of someone's kitchen cupboard for months, possibly years, really counted as winning.

Joyce, eighty-nine, surprised everyone by suggesting a bhaji-eating contest. 'To attract the youngsters,' she'd said. Maggie had to agree it was a brilliant idea; after all, this was an Indian restaurant, not a day on the cricket green.

By the time everyone left, and she went to collect Alice from school, Maggie had a notepad filled with lists and tasks. All she needed was the green light from Sav and there was a chance this could really work. That they could raise enough to clear the debts and produce a business plan to show the accountants the restaurant was on course for success.

'Granny,' said Alice, pulling Maggie from her thoughts. 'Yes, darling?'

'Seeing as Mummy won't get a dog, do you think she could have a baby instead?'

Maggie gave a surprised laugh. 'Goodness, where is she going to get one of those from?'

Alice looked up from the tea party she was hosting on the patio for her Disney princesses. 'Really?' she asked, in unconcealed disdain. 'You don't know where babies come from?'

She'd walked into that one. 'Yes darling, I do, but what's brought this on? Mummy hasn't mentioned having another baby, has she?'

235

And if she has, she's got more than a *little* bit of groundwork to do on that front first, as well as finding time and energy.

'No, but I saw Phoebe, my new baby cousin last night and it made me really want a sister.'

Maggie seized upon this nugget of information. 'Oh? Did Mummy take you to see Auntie Kelly?' She considered this unlikely, seeing as the delightful woman had called her daughter a 'buttoned-up bitch with her head stuck up her own backside' for not giving her marriage another chance. But Kelly seemed the only likely contender to have produced a baby cousin.

'No, Daddy picked me up from school and we went there. She's so cute, Granny, and she's only four days old.'

'Daddy picked you up, did he?' mused Maggie. When Hannah had messaged to inform her she didn't need to collect Alice from school yesterday, she'd assumed her daughter had taken the day off work. 'Where was Mummy then?'

'She had a business meeting and got home late,' replied Alice, taking Barbie out of a plastic tote and seating her alongside the other dolls at a table formed of an upturned plant pot, 'like Barbie. She's just been to a very important meeting to discuss the rights of women in the workplace. And now she's going to tell the others all about it.'

*Good lord*, thought Maggie, not knowing which part of this revelation was most telling: that her daughter had made such concessions to Darren, or that Alice was sounding like a miniature version of Jade. On reflection, the only disconcerting part was Hannah not mentioning anything about it. Why was that?

After Alice was bathed and ready for bed, they snuggled up on the stylish teal sofa to wait until Hannah got home from work.

'How are my favourite people?' she asked, greeting them both with a wide yawn.

'Can we have a baby, Mummy?' replied Alice, not missing a beat.

Hannah let out a snort of hilarity, before realising her daughter was deadly serious.

'I gather Alice was quite taken with little Phoebe,' explained Maggie. 'She's already decided on names too, though I do pity any poor child christened Citronella, destined to repel all who love her. Although wouldn't she make a great Disney princess – shall I write a letter to Walt?'

Alice dismissed her grandmother and turned her attention to Hannah. 'Did you and Sav have a nice time last night, Mummy?'

Hannah's cheeks flushed pink.

'I told you on the way to school this morning, it was a business meeting.'

Maggie was just trying to rearrange her bemused expression into one of neutral disinterest, when her phone started ringing in her handbag on the floor.

'Not a number I recognise,' she said, frowning at the screen. She decided to answer it anyway, perhaps it was one of the WI ladies. 'Hello?'

'Maggie, Horatio Harding here, apologies for the late call, just finished up with some marking and I wanted to catch you as soon as I could.'

Mr Harding had been Hannah's English teacher back

when she was at high school and in the years that followed, he had climbed the ranks to become Deputy Head Teacher – a very good one, by all accounts.

'Hello, Mr Harding. How lovely to hear from you,' replied Maggie, signalling to Hannah she would take the call in the kitchen.

Always one to mince words, Horatio Harding took quite some time and a couple of wandering anecdotes, to get to the point of his call.

'I've heard on the grapevine you are instrumental in an endeavour to save The Golden Crocus from the hands of Hugo Wick.'

Maggie wondered about the existence of such a grapevine and briefly pictured a leafy stalk wending its way through town. 'Well, I wouldn't necessarily say that. It's more that I'm personally acquainted with the Kapoors and am loath to see them lose their home. Besides, the restaurant has so much going for it. It's quite the town gem.'

'Oh, I agree,' enthused Mr Harding. 'My godson dined there last weekend, said it was the best meal he'd had in years. Did I hear right, Maggie, are you working in the kitchen?'

Maggie felt a rush of pride. 'Just helping out for a while. Gita broke her hip, did you know?'

'Yes, young Ben and Jade told me all about it. You've become quite the talk of the town. Jade even showed me a video of you on TikTok flambéing a Rum baba set to the tune of "Disco Inferno".'

Maggie decided she really must download some of these apps and find out just what Jade was doing with all this footage.

'Anyway,' Mr Harding continued, 'I'd very much like to help out. You may not know this, Maggie, but do you remember back when Hannah was at school, the Year 8 trip to Normandy? Well, I was Savinder's form tutor then, and there were two students whose parents couldn't afford the trip. They were getting a bit of stick; you know how cruel children can be. Savinder must have mentioned it to his parents because the next day, Raj telephoned in and asked if they could subsidise their places.'

'Was that even allowed?' asked Maggie, remembering the red tape around such matters, back in the old PTA days.

'Good grief no, but we did it anyway,' retorted Mr Harding. 'I'll never forget it. Makes you try that little bit harder, you know? When good people set by example.'

'So, what sort of help did you have in mind?' asked Maggie. 'We're organising a fundraiser, and there's plenty of work to go around?'

'I'd be honoured to be involved. But actually, it wasn't *my* help I was going to offer. You see, Ben and Jade came to me with a suggestion . . .'

By the time Maggie had finished on the phone, Hannah had taken Alice up to bed, so she settled herself back on the sofa to wait. She was going to need Hannah's help with this one.

'Fancy a glass of wine, Mum, or are you heading off?' asked Hannah from the doorway, wielding a bottle and two glasses.

'Just a small one then, as I'm driving, but there's something I want to talk to you about.'

Hannah groaned. 'Really? Do we have to do that? I am

239

thirty-eight you know. Do I need to tell you my every movement?'

'Absolutely not. It's nothing to do with me, who you have your nocturnal business meetings with.' She couldn't resist air quotes, around the word *business*. 'But, since you brought it up, there are some developments to tell you about. How do you think Sav will respond to the idea of a fundraiser in the restaurant, a week on Saturday? It's all arranged,' she held her notepad aloft, 'no less than ten willing souls signed up to help out. I think we can really make a difference, Hannie.' She hitched forward on the sofa, her tired mind newly galvanised by Horatio Harding's proposal. 'I think we can raise enough money to get us back in the black and build on the marketing campaign.'

Hannah shook her head in wonder. 'How on earth have you pulled that off?'

'Turns out, there's quite a few folks who feel rather strongly about that old place. Including our very own Ben and Jade who *somehow*, Lord knows how, have managed to convince their Deputy Head Teacher that sending a bunch of students to redecorate the restaurant would be an excellent use of their free time now exams are finished. He's going to mention it in the school leaver's assembly tomorrow. Officially school's out, but volunteering within the community would be great for their CVs, I think that was the angle he was going for.'

'Bloody hell. That's incredible.'

'Isn't it?'

Hannah got back to her feet and took a large swig of wine. She looked totally exhausted, but also slightly wired. 'He's planning to sell, Mum. But I really don't think he

240

wants to. In fact, I've a feeling he wants to take it over himself.'

'Of course he does,' said Maggie.

'But why?' Hannah stared at her incredulous. 'He has a penthouse apartment in Brighton, his own business, a *life* – why would he want to give all that up to come and run an Indian restaurant?'

Maggie smiled. 'Because it's home, love.'

Hannah laughed. 'He was talking about colourful table runners and the pictures he'd put on the wall. This is someone who writes cyber security software programs for a living. He's super clever, wouldn't that be a waste?'

Maggie cocked an eyebrow. 'Are you saying successful careers in catering aren't equally important?'

'No, Mum, of course not. I know how hard Dad worked. And so is working in customer services for the district town council or staying at home to look after your children. I just worry he would be doing it for the wrong reasons, out of guilt or a sense of duty.'

'I think,' said Maggie wryly, 'you should trust Sav to be the judge of that.'

Hannah nodded slowly.

'If it helps swing it at all,' added Maggie, 'I know just the person to knock up some table runners.'

# Chapter Twenty-Three

## Hannah

Somehow, the restaurant had limped through another weekend. True to his word, Vernon had delivered groceries first thing Friday and Saturday morning and had been paid in cash. The menu had been adapted again, very slightly, to reflect the even scanter offering of meat and, yet again, Joe, Ben and Jade had shown up to work their bottoms off, for little more than a free dinner.

Hannah helped with service on Friday evening whilst Alice was with her father and, after fielding nearly two hours of unsubtle eye-jerks, *pssst*s and impatient coughs from her mum, she could put it off no longer. The restaurant, where walls had ears, was not the place for what her mother had tasked her with, and so leaving Jade and Ben to hold the fort, Hannah had insisted she needed Sav urgently in the storeroom.

Sav had looked a little disarmed by the request, and Joe's eyeballs had practically come out on stalks, until Maggie alerted him to the fact he was deep-frying his apron strings.

Apparently, asking Sav if Maggie and her WI friends could throw a full-scale summer fundraiser, complete with bake sale and hook-the-duck, in his parent's Indian restaurant, would sound better coming from her. The mind boggled as to how she could sell the idea any better than the queen of Battenburg's herself. Although the harder part, thought Hannah, as they'd traipsed through the hot kitchen to the storeroom out back, was going to be convincing him Saffron Walden's equivalent of DIY SOS was poised and ready to pounce first thing Monday morning.

Hannah steeled herself and clamped her arms across her chest.

'What is the point of any of this, if you've already given up?'

It probably wasn't the best opener, but those were the words that came out.

Sav screwed up his eyes. 'What do you mean?'

'This.' She casually kicked at a crate of onions, and sent several of them scattering across the floor, shedding their brown skins as they went.

'Whoops.'

She bent to pick them up and his hand shot out to stop her.

'Leave it,' he said gently. 'Tell me what you're trying to say.'

'Why are we here tonight, struggling to feed all these customers, if you've already decided to sell up? Why are we all out there working for free if it's all for nothing? This is just giving everyone hope.'

'Who said I'm selling up?' he asked, confusion crumpling his striking features.

'You did. The other night. You said it would be better to pull the plaster off.'

Understanding dawned on his face, and he brought a hand up to rub at the stubble on his chin. 'I'm a realist, Han. It doesn't mean I don't have hope. And we have until the 14th of July; we should at least be able to make enough to pay all the staff, then it will have been worth it.'

'Huh.' Hannah bit her lip, wondering how on earth she'd got herself so involved with this place, or why she cared so much. 'In that case, I've got some news.' She grinned. 'Never underestimate the power of the WI.'

On Monday morning, as Hannah worked her way through what felt like a gazillion emails, she found her mind kept wandering to the restaurant. Had anyone turned up? What colours were they going to paint the walls? She kept picturing Jade bossing everyone around and trying to persuade Sav what the place really needed was some glitter.

An email notification popped into the corner of her screen and the subject heading caught her eye: 'DNA Test Results'.

She clicked on the email from Caitlin and scanned it quickly.

The paternity test had come back from the lab, and it was conclusive. Bronte and Caitlin were sisters alright.

*Let bitter old Bronte suck on that. I've just booked myself a celebratory holiday in the Maldives. Paid for by myself, I should add. If I do inherit some of my father's millions perhaps I'll set up a charity fund in his name and give it all away to donkeys. Hah, that'll really piss her off.*

Hannah smiled to herself. There was professional impartiality, and there was what she really thought. Donkeys sounded perfect.

*In all seriousness, thank you. You might not have said it, but I know you believed me. I was never interested in my birth father's money, not really, but I wasn't going down without a fight, because you have to do what's right, it was what he'd intended in the end, whether Bronte liked it or not. And this is about the fact my mum fought for him to acknowledge me all my life, although God knows why she bothered. I know you shouldn't speak ill of the dead, but honestly, the man was a git.*

*Anyway, thanks again. I'll buy you a drink, when all of this is sorted.*

*Caitlin xx*

Hannah picked up her pen and began chewing on it thoughtfully.

Doing what was right had always been part of her own make-up; she got that from her mum. That and the doggedness that had seen her through law school. She wanted to be there at the restaurant with Sav and her mum and see Alice when she came out of school, excited to join in the decorating. She wanted to be a part of it all, this huge, final push to save the Kapoors' business and home. And there was so much to do to organise the fundraiser on Saturday.

After ten minutes of daydreaming and realising she was getting nothing done, Hannah pushed back her chair and began striding through the large open-plan space to the office of Richard White.

'Hannah,' greeted Richard, looking up from his computer as she rapped on his door. 'What can I do for you?'

She had every bloody right, she told herself. If anything, she worked harder than many of her colleagues, always feeling she had something to prove. In six years, despite never once using her daughter as a reason to take time off work, she'd been overlooked for promotion time and time again.

'Richard, I'm taking some annual leave.'

He nodded and looked back down to his laptop. 'Uh-huh, going anywhere nice?'

'Home. I'm going to spend some time with my family. I've checked my schedule and with the exception of a court appearance on Thursday, I think I can rearrange most things.'

Richard looked up. 'You're taking *this* week off?'

'Yes. Starting right now.'

The older man looked rather perplexed. She supposed it was rather irregular in their line of work to suddenly down tools.

'It's your workload, Hannah, if you think you can make it work . . .'

'I can.'

Exhilaration bloomed in Hannah's chest as she turned on her heel and went back to her desk for her bag. In her ordered, timetabled world, this felt like one giant act of rebellion.

By 11 a.m., she was making the return train journey. By midday, she had driven home, stripped off her suit and chucked on a pair of denim shorts, her old trainers and a pretty apricot vest top. She put on her sunglasses and stepped out into the warm summer's day feeling like a schoolgirl playing truant.

On the way to The Golden Crocus, she stopped at the bakery and bought a dozen jam doughnuts and a dozen warm sausage rolls, hoping it would be enough.

When she reached the restaurant, she stopped and looked up at the enormous ladder resting against the wall. Standing near the top, sanding the upstairs wooden window frames, was Joe.

'Hello, what's this?' he called down to her. 'Part-timer these days, are you?'

'I'm on holiday, Joe,' she grinned back at him. 'Coming down for a doughnut?'

'Too right,' he said, placing his tools in a bucket and beginning his descent. When he reached the ground, he wiped the beads of sweat from his brow. 'Still got all my tools from the building days, thought I'd put them to use. The render just needs a few small repairs, it's not as bad as it looks. Reckon we'll have it looking brand new in no time.'

Hannah looked up at the building, which looked strangely naked. It took her a moment to realise why: The Golden Crocus's sign had been taken down, leaving a dark patch where it had hung. She wondered if revamping the tired, faded old sign was in the remit for the improvements.

'Any of those students actually turn up?' she asked gingerly. What if after convincing Sav to go for it, no-one had come?

Joe tipped his head. 'Come and see for yourself.'

247

Clutching her bags of baked goods, she went ahead of him and pushed open the restaurant door to an assault on the senses. The smell of fresh paint. Pulp's floor-filling anthem 'Common People' boomed from the restaurant's primitive sound system and at least eleven – no, twelve – individuals Hannah had never seen before in her life, scrubbing at walls from buckets of soapy water or kneeling at skirting boards with masking tape. The furniture had all been stacked in the middle and covered with mismatching bedsheets, leaving much of the balding carpet exposed and its dire need of replacement apparent. At the far end of the restaurant, she spotted her mother on a stepladder working her way around the overhead beams with a feather duster.

'Hi,' said a tall, voluptuous girl beside her, sporting the most eye-wateringly short shorts Hannah had ever beheld. 'Have you come to help?' she smiled widely, then added, 'you need to see Maggie down the end, she's the GEO.'

At that moment, Sav appeared in the propped-open doorway to the upstairs flat where she could see dust sheets covering the stairs, 'Han? What are you doing here?' He sounded surprised, but from the big grin on his face, hopefully in a good way.

'Brought sustenance,' she said, holding up the bags. 'Although from the looks of things, nowhere near enough!'

Sav walked over. 'Isn't it amazing? All these kids giving up their time to come and do this? I can hardly believe it.'

The tall girl interjected, 'Oh, that'll be down to Jade. She's *verrryy* persuasive.' She gave a small, tinkly laugh and turned back to her work.

Hannah shook her head in wonder as Jade emerged

from the kitchen, dressed in a blue mechanics boiler suit, splattered in paint, her thick hair tied back in a yolk-yellow headscarf. She went over to Ben and another young lad with brilliant white-blond hair.

'I'll go and fix some cold drinks,' said Sav.

Hannah put the paper bags down on the bar and made her way over to her mum.

'Hannah? Why aren't you at work?' shouted Maggie when Hannah waved up to her. She was dusting right next to a speaker and squinted so she'd hear better. 'Is everything alright?'

'Everything's fine, Mum, I just fancied some time off. And I couldn't miss out on all the fun and games, could I?'

'Pardon, darling? I can't really hear you. We seem to be in the midst of an impromptu rave. Are the nineties cool again? I keep seeing mullets and *double denim*,' she shuddered in distaste.

'Yep. Everything comes back around.' Casting an eye over the ugly bronze-coloured sandal and sock combo her mother was sporting, she added under her breath, 'You never know, even those Velcro monstrosities might one day be rock and roll.'

Her mum was usually quite stylish, in a casual, understated way. Whatever had possessed her?

'Sorry, what's that love?' said Maggie, curling a palm to her ear.

'I said I brought some sausage rolls, are you coming down from there?'

Perhaps somebody took the hint because the volume went down a few notches as Maggie clambered down.

'I think we have a potential *situation* on our hands,'

said Maggie, mouthing the word situation as though it were code for unexploded bomb. She jerked her eyebrows up and down to indicate behind her.

'Sorry?' asked Hannah, confused. Behind Maggie, it was just Ben, Jade and the other boy, who was helping Ben to peel away a swathe of wallpaper. 'I don't understand.'

Maggie leaned in closer and whispered. '*Blatant* flirting. I didn't think Jade was the sort. She's had both of those boys running around after her all morning. Poor Ben, at his place of work too. You've got to feel for him, poor lad.' She shook her head in dismay.

Hannah pressed her lips into a straight line. Perhaps she should have said something sooner, but it wasn't her business to speculate. However, if she didn't set her mother straight on the matter right now, it had the potential to lead to an embarrassing faux pas.

'Come with me a sec, would you?' she said, heading off to the kitchen.

Moments later, Maggie came through the swing door.

'What's with the subterfuge?' she asked, frowning. 'And you still haven't said why you're here. Is everything OK with Alice?'

'Everything's fine, Mum. I just really wanted to be here. I had some annual leave to take, so I took it.' She held up her hands to indicate it was no big deal. 'But there's something you should know.'

Maggie's eyes narrowed warily. 'Go on.'

'Mum, I'm pretty sure Ben is gay. Him and Jade are best friends, and I think you might find the only flirting going on is between Ben and the rather handsome blond lad out there.'

250

Maggie's mouth dropped open.

'Well, I never. How the devil have I not seen that?'

'It's not something people have tattooed on their foreheads, Mother. It's no big deal.'

'No, of course not.' Maggie looked around her, as though the clues had been lying around in plain sight among the kitchen utensils. 'I just meant . . . How can I have been so short-sighted? Making assumptions like that.'

'Hey, there's no harm done.' Hannah nudged her mum, sad to see her doubting herself.

'I'm just thinking through anything I might have said to offend him,' said Maggie.

'Come on, this is Ben we're talking about,' said Hannah. 'He thinks you're a goddess. Really, that should have been the first sign, right there,' she chuckled.

At that very moment, Ben came through the door with two pieces of paper in hand.

'Hey, Hannah,' he said, as comfortable with them both now as though he'd known them for years. He held up the two paint samples. 'So apparently these are the only options. What do we think? Ginger Biscuit or Wicked Rose? Personally, I think Wicked Rose sounds like it should be in a brothel rather than a refined dining establishment, but what do I know?'

Pam's husband Dave might be a useless so-and-so, but his job at the tip had come in rather handy this week when he managed to procure several cans of trade paint and acres of old linen for use as dustsheets. The only things they'd had to buy were the specialist exterior wall paint, masking tape, rollers and brushes.

251

Maggie sidled up to Ben and to his and Hannah's mutual surprise, planted a great big kiss on his cheek.

'There's nothing refined about us, dear heart, nothing wicked either. Let's go big and bold with the pink, shall we? This place could do with a touch of the Jade treatment.'

# Chapter Twenty-Four

## Maggie

Three days into the refurbishments and the restaurant was unrecognisable. It was simply astonishing what a fresh coat of paint could achieve.

Outside, thanks to Joe's tireless hard work, the period property was now repainted a striking marigold, or to be precise, almost the exact shade of saffron, with freshly sanded and glossed white window frames.

Inside, whilst Sav had worked on freshening up the upstairs flat, the large team of volunteers, which had varied from day to day as new sets of willing hands came forward, were engaged in various tasks. One of the volunteer students, Lin, had a keen interest in woodwork and was about to begin an apprenticeship as a joiner. She'd suggested the structurally sound dark wood tables could be stripped of their decades-old varnish, sanded and waxed to give them a modern feel and was now fully engrossed in the task, taking them outside one at a time to attack with the powerful sander she'd brought from home. Maggie had marvelled at the determination of some of these youngsters, and at how different things were from when she'd been that age, thank goodness. When she had been at school there were limited career paths open to you, particularly if you didn't pass your eleven-plus or go to college.

She had also learned two of the students had provisional places at college where they hoped to take art A Levels, and this had given her an idea. She had called Hannah over from where she'd been supervising a paint-splattered Alice, who had insisted on joining in after school. Lord knew how Hannah was going to get the Wicked Rose out of her tangled hair, but to see her working on her small patch of wall with a tiny paint pot and brush had been heart-melting. Especially when Sav had knelt beside her and used his fingers to dab his initials onto the old paintwork, prompting her to gasp in disbelief and for everyone else to follow suit – marking their presence with a tiny act of rebellion before it was covered over forever. Although some of the hieroglyph signatures, particularly those belonging to Joe and Ben, bore no resemblance to their names and much to what dwelled in their pants.

'Hannie – Ruby and Dylan were just telling me about some of their GCSE art coursework, which sounds marvellous, it's even on display in the local gallery.'

Hannah had nodded along politely, not quite getting the hint.

'Perhaps they might have some good ideas for brightening up the walls?' she decided to spell it out for her daughter. 'Didn't Sav say he fancied bright, colourful canvases? Perhaps the walls could be used to display work by local artists. They could even be for sale – it could attract quite the eclectic mix of pieces.'

A slow grin had spread across Hannah's face. She'd leaned forward and hugged her. 'You're a bloody genius.'

'Well, yes, naturally.'

This morning, after a period of time spent staring down at the sorry carpet which stood out even more amid the clean, fresh walls, Sav had muttered something under his breath then marched determinedly over to Joe's toolbox for a Stanley knife.

'Mate,' Joe had called in alarm, 'what are you doing? You can't afford a new carpet.'

Sav had dropped to his knees in the corner of the room. 'This carpet has been here since I was at primary school. Let's see what's underneath it, shall we?'

A tense crowd gathered in anticipation, as though they were about to set virgin eyes on the ruins of a Roman villa, or possibly even dead bodies. They were most disappointed to see that beneath the orange and brown swirls there was just underlay turned to powder, and more crucially, solid wood floorboards.

Sav and Joe high-fived each other.

'I was expecting concrete, I'll be honest,' said Joe with the wisdom of someone who had undertaken countless restoration projects.

'Let's do this,' said Sav rubbing his hands together with delight. 'Someone ask Lin to get her sander ready.'

Maggie smiled to herself from where she sat at the bar with a notepad and pen as they began rolling the carpet back. There was still a good deal to be organised for the fundraiser on Saturday, not least the dissemination of tasks to various volunteers, the grovelling to local businesses for raffle prize donations and the distribution of posters advertising the event. She and Hannah had a date with the high street tomorrow and she hoped her sartorial sacrifice would pay off. She grimaced at the sandals she had been wearing all week, recommended to her by Diane who'd suffered terribly with bunions for years, apparently. Maggie didn't want to suffer with anything but had to accept that after sixty-five years, perhaps she wasn't completely in control of what various parts of her body had decided for themselves.

A loud rapping at the door interrupted her deliberation over whether to allocate shortbread to Pam or Judith. Pam usually baked it, but Judith had made a song and dance about her family's fourth-generation recipe at their meeting, such was the tightrope she trod.

'I'll get it,' called Ruby.

They'd begun locking it from Monday after being ambushed by potential diners enquiring after luncheon, even though the place was topsy-turvy and filled with Saffron Walden's answer to The Village People brandishing paint rollers as they sang along to 'YMCA'.

'Thanks love, it's probably the glazier come to replace the storeroom windowpane. Tell him to go round the back, would you?'

Maggie scrawled Judith's initials next to the cake on the list, then seeing that everyone else was either embroiled in the great-carpet-removal at the rear of the restaurant, or cutting-in ceilings and skirting boards, got up and nipped through the kitchen to open the fire door.

However, there was no sign of a van on the street, so perhaps it had just been another would-be customer after all.

As Maggie made her way back to the bar and her notepad full of tasks, she was surprised to see an unfamiliar figure loitering there.

'Can I help you?' she asked with caution.

The broad-shouldered man in joggers and trainers turned, revealing a second person behind him. A much smaller and horribly familiar man.

'I'm sorry but we're currently closed for refurbishments,' Maggie said with forced civility. 'We're open from next week if you'd like to make a booking?'

'Thanks but that won't be necessary,' said Hugo Wick.

He flashed her a grin, then slapped the menu he'd been inspecting back down on the bar top.

He ambled lazily past Maggie, then turned and leaned against the wall, crossing his ankles and thrusting his hands deep into his pockets. 'Savinder Kapoor about?'

Maggie drew herself tall. 'Who wants to know?'

She wasn't about to give the arrogant chef the satisfaction of recognition. She had only ever spoken to him on the phone at the council, so he certainly wouldn't remember her. When Geoff had told her how Hugo had trampled his way to fame on the hard work and integrity of others, who all fell by the wayside as he sold them out, she'd already known what to expect. He had lived up to *all* those expectations. But people didn't forget, certainly not in an industry dependent upon teamwork and dedication. His day would come, she was sure of it.

Hugo gave a patronising laugh at her apparent ignorance, whilst his henchman, who hadn't yet spoken a word, merely raised one dubious eyebrow.

The general hubbub from the students began to dim as one by one, they realised who was in the building. Then someone killed the background music.

'Maggie?' called Joe, who had noticed the change in atmosphere and looked up from where he and Sav and Ben were wrestling with the carpet. 'Everything alright?'

Hugo looked in his direction and she heard Joe mutter an expletive under his breath. She also noted, with some delight, that as Hugo pushed himself away from the wall he came away with a smear of deep pink paint along his sleeve. Hopefully there was plenty left for touch-ups.

'Sav,' Maggie said, as he came striding over, wiping his dusty hands on his trousers. 'You have some visitors.'

As though sensing something amiss, Hannah emerged in the doorway from upstairs, where she had been painting the internal doors, her hair and face flecked with white gloss paint. She raised her shoulders in question at something Maggie couldn't yet answer.

'What's he doing here?' asked Ben somewhat audibly, as he'd been sweeping the floorboards with headphones on and hadn't noticed the commotion until now.

'Is that who I think it is?' whispered Tom, the blond boy who orbited Ben like the sun in everything he did.

'Huge Prick,' supplied Jade, also audibly, provoking a twitter among the assembled teens and a death glare from Wick's right-hand brute.

Maggie supposed the prospect of meeting someone off the telly was more than they'd bargained for when signing up for a spot of redecorating so she could hardly blame the kids for being intrigued.

'What can I do for you?' asked Sav, without preamble or introduction.

Hannah found her way over to stand beside Maggie.

Hugo Wick grinned. 'I must say, it's awfully sweet of you to give the place a lick of paint, but you really shouldn't have bothered. My brand is gunmetal grey, not the colour of dehydrated piss, or whatever that is you've plastered on the exterior walls. Only joking. Saffron gold, right? So original. And this is . . .' he gestured at the cheerful interior walls, then stopped abruptly when he spotted the pink stain on his sleeve, 'bloody horrible.' He sighed, rubbing at the fabric and making it ten times worse. 'Is there anywhere a little more private we can take this, Mr Kapoor?'

Sav replied, tight-lipped, 'I don't believe we have anything to discuss. And as you can see, we are very busy, so another time, perhaps.' He gestured towards the door.

'Savinder, Sav, can I call you Sav?' continued Hugo, ignoring Sav's invitation to leave. 'We won't impose for long. You know how it is, once the paperwork side of things is done, everything can move very quickly. I just want to acquaint myself with the building, get a few measurements with my mate Dan here. That alright with you fella?'

Sav visibly stiffened.

'As you very well know, Mr Wick, my parents and I have rejected your offer. The Golden Crocus is not for sale.'

Hannah squeezed her mother's arm in silent acknowledgement of Sav's change of heart.

But Hugo Wick wasn't so easily deterred. He began nodding.

'Right. Well, I've seen this year's accounts, so I beg to differ.'

'You can't have done. They haven't been filed yet.'

Dan gave a menacing cough.

'Believe me, you'll be glad I took this place off your hands,' Wick continued, ignoring Sav's comment and peering beyond his shoulder. 'Solid wood floor. Nice. I'd envisaged manky old carpets stinking of curry.'

'I'm not standing for this, who does he think he is?' muttered Maggie under her breath and making to step forwards.

Hannah placed a steadying hand on her arm.

'This'll have to come down,' said Hugo, slapping the oak beam that divided the small bar from the restaurant. 'And the kitchen will be open viewing, so we'll need to get the surveyors in to see about opening that space up at the back.'

Maggie couldn't help herself.

'Good luck. It's a Grade II listed building, *fella*,' she sneered.

A grin spread across Hugo's face.

'Good job I can afford to do whatever it takes then, isn't it?'

Humiliation and fury turned Sav's eyes inky black. 'I believe I asked you to leave.'

'Mm,' said Hugo, as though considering this statement. 'You see the thing is, your mum and dad own this place, don't they? Not you. And they seemed quite interested in my proposal, so I think we should just wait and see what they decide, don't you?'

Then he winked at Dan and took a step closer to Sav,

adding in a low voice, too quiet for anyone other than the five of them to hear. 'And like I said, I can do whatever it takes. Maybe my good friend Simon Burns suspects there's been some creative accounting afoot.' He paused, then twitched his nose comically. 'Or, maybe, one day, a customer will report a sighting of rats. Do you see where I'm going with this?'

Behind him, Dan smirked.

Hannah, who had become uncharacteristically quiet, suddenly piped up.

'Mr Wick, do you have legal representation?' she asked.

He eyed her with disdain. 'What business is it of yours?'

Hannah gestured at Dan. 'And this gentleman is in your employ, am I right?'

'Again, none of your business.'

'Oh, I think it is.'

Maggie watched as her daughter turned to steel right before her very eyes.

'It would be in both of your interests to vacate the premises immediately, before I call the police, but if you do choose to wait for their arrival, you might wish to contact your legal representative because I am going to advise my client to report you for using threatening language and behaviour.'

Maggie eyeballed Sav, who managed to remain unruffled by her daughter's blatant lie.

'Hannah Lawford, Associate Solicitor of Tucker, Farraday & White,' added Hannah, pulling a business card from her handbag which sat next to Maggie's on the bar.

She stood with the card in her upturned palm whilst

Hugo rolled his eyes and Dan looked between them, doubt having crept into his features.

*So much for the tough guy act*, thought Maggie.

When Wick made no move to take the card, Hannah continued.

'Furthermore, I must inform you that my client has made it extremely clear the property is no longer for sale. You have no jurisdiction here at all and are currently trespassing.'

Hugo laughed. 'Trespassing? It's a restaurant. I was let in by one of your . . .' he flapped a hand in the vague direction of the assembled teenagers, 'child labourers.'

'Sorry,' mouthed Ruby, looking dismayed.

'I should also add,' continued Hannah, 'I will be filing an official complaint against my client's accountant for a serious breach of client confidentiality and implicating you as complicit. There are several witnesses to testify to your admission at having been privy to confidential and sensitive information, so let me assure you – there will *indeed* be claims of incompetent accounting and data management. I will be recommending a full investigation into all of Simon Burns' client accounts, including yours.'

That one struck home and Maggie watched as Wick swallowed down the threat.

Suddenly, Dan began striding for the door. So much for bringing along the muscle.

'Where are you going, you soft prat?' hollered Hugo, still rooted to the spot. 'I want to look upstairs.'

Maggie could take no more of this.

She took three paces towards Hugo Wick and poked a finger into his chest.

'Over my dead body will you take one step into my friend's personal living quarters. Who the hell do you think you are? You're just some sad little man who used to arrange salad garnish on the plates of Leon Lacrois. He was a *real* chef, a Michelin-starred, multi-award-winning chef and one of the nicest men you could meet. I know that because I met him, several times. You hopped from restaurant to restaurant, traded on his name and stole his recipes, stepping over every experienced kitchenhand in the business and making their lives a misery until you'd levered yourself into the role of head chef. Then you worked out that attracting the attention of the media took the focus away from your mediocre food and instead spotlighted your foul-mouthed, arrogant gob. Well, congratulations,' she said, clapping her hands steadily. 'You won the ultimate prize. You are one despicable giant prick deserving of your nickname. I hope all your money buys you some comfort in your old age because you will have precious little else. Now piss off, you vile little bully.'

Hugo glared back at her, rendered completely speechless for possibly the first time ever.

'That means leave,' she clapped her hands again, loudly, in his face. 'Go and ruin someone else's day.'

You could have heard a pin drop as Hugo shook his head in bewildered anger and then finally turned on his heel, joining Dan at the door. As they both stepped out into the street, he doubled back to throw a pathetic parting shot, not realising Maggie had pursued him to the door.

'Before long, you'll be begging me to take this pl—'

The door slammed shut in his face.

Hot-cheeked and furious, Maggie spun around to see over a dozen proud faces staring back at her in awe.

'Wow,' exclaimed Jade, holding her phone aloft in a manner that indicated she had filmed the entire thing. 'You are one mean mother-cooker, Maggie.'

## Chapter Twenty-Five

## *Hannah*

Donning a suit and prising herself away from everyone at the restaurant yesterday to head into London for a court case had been loathsome. She had never resented her job more, which troubled her. She'd gone into law because she wanted to make the world a better place. Could she really do that when every moment, from getting dressed that morning, to travelling into London, to levering herself into a seat beside her client in a hot, stuffy room, had set her teeth on edge?

She had also presumed all those years of study and hard work would mean she could give back to society one day and take on pro bono work. This was not something she was able to do in her current capacity at Tucker, Farraday & White. How ironic that her first pro bono client was going to be Sav.

First thing this morning, Hannah had overseen a Skype call between Sav and his parents, in which she facilitated the process for the application of a lasting power of attorney.

Though Sav's parents were both of sure and sound mind, their physical distance and lack of legal aid left the situation wide open to charlatans like Wick, who were only too happy to exploit individuals in a vulnerable position. They'd all been given a little taster of what that man was capable of, and an LPA would give Sav the power to act on his parents' behalf and was fully reversible when appropriate. Needless to say they'd also appointed a new accountant immediately, and whilst no action had yet been taken against Simon Burns, she had encouraged Sav to make an affidavit, should his testimony be required at a later date.

Gita's world-weariness, and Raj's offended indignation as they listened to an account of what had transpired, made Hannah worry that Sav would decide it was time to chuck in the towel. Especially when he slapped the laptop closed after they ended the video call.

He turned to Hannah.

'Do you think you could ask everyone to gather downstairs?' There was a gritty determination in his eyes she hadn't seen before. He looked just like his father, albeit a far, far sexier version, which was not the image she wanted in her mind as she went off to find her mother.

Maggie was directing Ruby as she proffered her huge canvas up to the wall. The abstract acrylic painting of a sliced open watermelon was exactly the kind of thing Sav had described. It was bright, colourful and fun, and represented one small part of the teamwork responsible for the space's dramatic transformation. Dylan was working on a series of smaller paintings depicting various Indian spices and seed pods; his work was more detailed than Ruby's and complemented her bold, brash style perfectly. They'd made enquiries at the art gallery too and had received quite a bit of interest already from local artists about displaying their work.

'Wow. That's brilliant,' said Hannah, admiring the painting.

'Thanks!' replied Ruby.

'Mum?' said Hannah. 'Sav wants to speak to us.'

'Can't it wait? The clock is ticking and there's still so much to do. What does he want?'

She wasn't wrong; they hadn't even started setting up for the fundraiser tomorrow and it was already lunchtime.

'I don't know, he just said he wants to speak to everyone. Can you tell the others whilst I go find Joe?'

Maggie sighed in resignation, as Ruby placed her picture down on the newly sanded and oiled floorboards.

Joe was outside hanging bunting on loan from the WI. He was balanced precariously on a ladder whilst Pam, who had insisted on accompanying the famed piece of haberdashery to its temporary home during her lunch hour, instructed him to move in increments to the left until it hung in a pleasing way.

'Looking fabulous,' called up Hannah. 'Can I borrow you for a minute? Boss wants a word.'

'Maggie?' asked Joe. 'Please don't say she wants this moving, it's taken an hour to get this far,' he groaned.

'Nope. Your *other* boss,' grinned Hannah, turning on her heel.

Inside, the students began to gather, and Hannah found her mum talking to Ben and Tom.

'Hannie, Ben's just been telling us he's enrolled at catering college, starting in September, isn't that fabulous?'

267

'Really? That's brilliant, Ben. Well done.'

'It's really cool,' added Tom. 'I wish I knew what I wanted to do for a job, like these two do.' He included Jade in his gesture, but she wasn't listening; in fact she seemed curiously distracted by something on her phone.

'Alright, everyone?' asked Sav entering the space, closely followed by Joe and Pam, who trailed in through the front door.

'Right, I won't keep you long, I just wanted to catch everyone before you start heading home. I know Maggie and her A Team are taking over now for the fundraiser tomorrow.'

Hannah saw Pam's considerable bosom inflate at the compliment and suppressed a smile.

'On behalf of myself and my parents, even though they still have no idea what we've got up to in here,' a titter of laughter at this, 'I don't know how I can ever thank you all, for everything you've done. Seriously guys,' he shook his head in wonder, 'it's incredible to think you've all given up your free time to be here, in this old restaurant, bringing it back to life with your frankly weird taste in music and your seriously hard work.'

'The music from the old days is so much better than what we have now,' said impossibly short-shorts, looking sagely at her friends, who nodded their heads in agreement.

'Yeah, I wish I'd been born when you were, before social media, it sounds like so much fun, and like you three are all still friends now. It's so cool,' said Ruby, grinning at Sav, Joe and Hannah.

Hannah wasn't sure how to take the news these kids lumped both The Village People and the mighty Pulp into one broad category of 'olden days'.

'Yes, it is cool,' said Sav, throwing his friends a smile of appreciation.

Hannah felt her insides glow as his gaze lingered on hers, marginally longer than necessary.

'Hopefully Joe, Ben and Maggie will benefit from this huge effort by continuing to work here at the restaurant as we go from strength to strength, but as for the rest of you, I'm sorry but I have nothing to offer you in repayment right now but my heartfelt thanks and the promise of a three-course meal for you and your families when we reopen next week.'

'Cool!' exclaimed Dylan, followed by other remarks of pleasure.

It seemed even this was more than the students had expected, having known they were volunteering to help a good cause.

'And,' Sav continued, 'I wanted to show you all something too.'

He paced over to the bar area and disappeared behind, emerging with something large and rectangular-shaped, wrapped in an old sheet.

'I decided it was high time we rebranded. Especially since Maggie revolutionised our amazing menu and dragged this place into the twenty-first century.' He paused, looking ever so slightly nervous, before unwrapping the sheet and holding the object aloft.

'What do you think?'

The sign he held in his hands was a deep chilli red, with the words 'CROCUS KITCHEN EST. 1981' embossed in gold.

'It's perfect,' whispered Maggie, clasping her hands in

front of her as though she had been presented with a newborn baby.

Irrationally, Hannah felt rather choked. It was seeing the culmination of all her mother's hard work, she told herself. She was just feeling proud.

'Brilliant, mate,' beamed Joe, squeezing his friend's shoulder. 'It's brilliant. Shall I go and fix it up?'

Sav handed it over and the students disbanded.

Suddenly, Ben clamped a hand to his mouth.

'Maggie, I've just realised something.'

'Yes?' she asked, intrigued.

'We have all these people coming here tomorrow to raise money to save the restaurant . . .'

'And?' she asked.

'*And*, shouldn't we have samples of the food we serve available for people to try?'

Hannah watched as the significance of Ben's words land on Maggie's face.

'Bloody hell, you're right, Ben. How can I have missed that?' Maggie rubbed at her cheeks in obvious dismay.

'To be fair, Mum, you've had a lot on your plate, no pun intended,' said Hannah.

'Maybe we can still do it,' said Ben, nodding as he thought it through. 'Let's speak to Joe and see what there is in the freezers. I'm sure we can knock something up, even if it's only canapés.'

'Absolutely,' said Maggie, getting to her feet. 'Come on, no time to lose.'

Hannah found herself standing alone with Sav.

'What do you think your parents will say?' she asked.

Sav laughed. 'About which part? The new menu, the

facelift, or the change of name? They're not coming back here, Han. You saw it in my mother's eyes. She's done with it, no matter what my father says.'

Hannah took in his earnest face, which had lost so much of the tension he'd been displaying of late.

'And you're . . . OK with that?' she asked.

Sav surprised her by stepping forward and folding her into a hug. He smelled of sandalwood and spice, with the turpentine hint of paint.

'I'm right where I want to be,' he said, before pulling away. 'Thank you for today.'

With that, he turned and went outside to help Joe, leaving Hannah with the strange sensation of loss. It had felt good, she realised, being in his arms. Too good.

# Chapter Twenty-Six

## Maggie

Friday afternoon passed in a frenzy.

Pam had gone back to the office, but not before insisting Maggie agreed to join her and some of her former colleagues for an after-work drink in The King's Head.

'But there's so much to do,' Maggie had complained, not knowing how she was going to fit it all in.

'And plenty of helping hands,' Pam had pointed out. 'It's just for an hour, and you promised.'

Joe and Ben had got straight to work in the kitchen. When Ben phoned his dad and explained the situation, Vernon arrived with three crates of produce, enough to prepare several tasting platters for the big day. Maggie felt slightly put out that she couldn't get stuck into the cooking with them, but today she had on a different hat, one she regularly donned with each passing season: organiser of fetes.

Using the plan Maggie had provided, Hannah and Jade, with some considerable effort, heaved the tables into position for all the various stalls. Only for Maggie to go back around after them, straightening them.

Hannah rolled her eyes at Jade. 'Didn't realise we needed a set-square and spirit level to set up for a bake sale.'

'If something's worth doing, Hannie . . .' Maggie had reprimanded, before taking herself off to fold raffle tickets for the tombola.

The volunteer students had now left, each vowing to come back tomorrow with friends and family to support the fundraiser. Maggie glanced around her as she tore at the perforated raffle tickets. They'd done such an amazing job, each and every one of them. The place looked cosy and inviting, like somewhere you wanted to spend time, which was just as well seeing as Maggie spent more time there these days than she did in her own home. Monty would be getting above his station in her absence, swanning about as if he owned the place and divesting himself of his fur wherever he pleased.

A light tap at the front door caused all of their heads to shoot up.

If that repulsive man and his sidekick had the nerve to show up here again . . .

'I'll get it,' said Hannah, heading to the door.

Judging by the exclamation of delight from Hannah, it definitely wasn't Wick, which was a relief. Maggie glanced at Jade for clues as she was in the eyeline of the door, but the girl was engrossed in her phone, eyes wide in disbelief. Perhaps she had just learned *Love-yourself Island* had been cancelled, or something equally as world-shattering. It was a perpetual enigma to Maggie that minds as sharp as

Jade's and Hannah's regularly and willingly submitted to such mush.

'Mum,' called Hannah. 'Come and see what Oscar's brought us.'

*Oscar.* Of course, she had forgotten he'd offered to come along and help.

'Well don't just stand out there, come on in if you're . . .' Maggie reached the door and stopped in her tracks.

Hannah was holding aloft a beautiful satin table runner, fuchsia pink and edged in gold brocade and covered all over with tiny gold embroidered stars. A bulging carrier bag sat next to Oscar's feet, spilling its jewel-like contents.

'I hope they're OK,' said Oscar warily. 'I came across a job lot of second-hand sarees and thought I could repurpose them for the restaurant.' He faltered as nobody rushed to reassure him. 'I can take them away and do something else. I know you mentioned table coverings were needed, but perhaps I, er, should have asked what was wanted, more specifically.'

'More specifically?' asked Maggie, dumbstruck. 'Oscar, these are incredible.' She reached to pull another from the bag, this one was deep turquoise, with accents of navy and silver.

'Sav is going to *love* them,' said Hannah, grinning.

Maggie shook her head. 'I don't know quite how one "comes across" a job lot of sarees, Oscar, but you have truly outdone yourself here. It's like a small piece of India and it's exactly what the restaurant was missing.'

Oscar looked abashed and tried to brush off the gesture.

'No,' said Maggie firmly. 'This must have taken you hours. People will pay very good money for a skilled seamstr—' she faltered, turning around to find Jade, who had vanished. Never a feminist around when you needed one. 'Sewing person,' she corrected herself. 'I think, Oscar, you may have found your new vocation.'

He puffed his chest out and beamed widely.

'I'm glad to have been of some service.'

'Aren't you coming in?' Maggie was conscious of the time and needed to crack on.

'I need to get back for the school crossing this afternoon,' he said. 'See you there, Hannah?'

'Yes, you will, and I promise you won't get tooted at this time!'

She explained to Maggie, 'Alice wanted to chat with Oscar, in the middle of the road, whilst all the traffic built up.'

Oscar tittered. 'They should bloody well learn not to be so impatient.'

Maggie smiled at the image and bent to gather up the bag of table runners.

'Oh, before I go, what's this I hear about you having a viral sensation then, Maggie?'

Maggie's head shot up as though someone had fired a gun.

'I beg your pardon?' she said, aghast.

Hannah sniggered.

'Sounds painful, Mother, do you need to visit the chemist?'

Maggie ignored her.

'Who told you that?'

Oscar squirmed. 'The butcher mentioned something about it and um, there were a few talking about it in the queue at the post office. They'd seen it on Facebook apparently, someone shared it to the Friends and Neighbours Community Group.'

'Talking about *what*, exactly?' Although Maggie had the sneakiest feeling she knew where this was going. She also knew there was precious little that was 'neighbourly' about that group. It seemed to be mostly for the public naming and shaming of bad parking and barking dogs, with the odd philanthropic gesture: I've an abundance of plums, help yourself, and so on.

'So, you haven't seen it yet, then,' said Oscar, looking as though he wished he'd kept his mouth shut. 'Not that I have, either. I don't have one of those smart phones. Do you think it will be on the news?'

Hannah's bemused expression shifted as she turned to her. 'What's he talking about, Mum?'

'I think our dear friend Jade may be able to fill us in, love. Shall we go and find her?' she said, through gritted teeth.

The tablecloths momentarily forgotten, Maggie turned to leave when Oscar called after her, 'Don't forget, it's the art class on Monday! I've booked you a place.'

'Can't wait,' she muttered, wondering what she'd got herself into.

'Mum,' called Hannah as Maggie marched away, 'hold up.'

Maggie came to a stop outside the kitchen where the sound of a clipped, sharp voice stopped her in her tracks. Someone giggled, then the voice spoke the same cold words again. And again.

'No way!' exclaimed Joe incredulously. 'Look at it now.'

Maggie sighed heavily and pushed open the door.

Ben spotted her first.

'Maggie! You're famous, come and see.'

Joe, Sav and Ben were huddled at the kitchen island around a phone. Jade's phone presumably, because she was perched on the counter behind them looking decidedly sheepish.

'Bloody hell,' said Sav. 'It's just gone up by another hundred, in like thirty seconds.'

'Something you want to tell me, Jade?' asked Maggie, fixing the devious minx with her most stern of grandmotherly glares.

Jade made a pained expression. 'I didn't think it would kick off *quite* as much as this. I uploaded it this morning. It just popped into my head, and I thought, why not? It can only be a good thing if it generates publicity for tomorrow, right?'

She looked as though she was seeking confirmation, rather than claiming her genius as gospel, which was rather disconcerting. She must learn to never waiver, not if she planned on taking the world by storm, as Maggie suspected she would.

Maggie stepped towards the group, who immediately fell apart, leaving Joe with the offending phone in hand.

'Show me,' she said, removing her spectacles from her head and slotting them onto her nose.

The video began with Hugo Wick's odious comment about carpets stinking of curry and skipped to when Maggie stepped forward and poked Hugo in the chest. It ended with his parting threat before the door slammed shut.

'I cut Hannah out, in case there was like any legal stuff that could jeopardise her career,' explained Jade. 'But I've got the footage, in case we ever need it. If you turn the volume up to the max, you can just about make out his threats too. The microphones on iPhones are amazing. It's had nearly five thousand views on TikTok already, and it's only been up for a few hours.'

Maggie watched the video through once and then pressed play again. If she could say so of herself, she was magnificent: composed and calm, but cutting. A force majeure in the face of a sneering school bully. *That's my girl*, said Geoff, in her head. *Give 'em hell*. She was really rather proud of herself and knew Geoff would have been too. He'd always hated bullies, especially in the kitchen.

Maggie sniffed. 'Someone could have told me my hair looked greasy. Why did I have to become famous on a bad hair day?'

'You look gorgeous, as ever, Mum,' said Hannah, watching the clip again and grinning at Sav as the views continued to climb. Every user who watched and reposted would have seen the #SaveOurRestaurant hashtag Jade had embedded in the post, along with links to the website, which Sav had thankfully now updated.

Sav visibly cringed as a new comment appeared underneath.

*Someone tell that old granny to put a sock in it. Hugo Wick can take over the shit restaurant in my town anytime he likes.*

Hannah swore under her breath.

'What a dick,' muttered Jade.

Maggie dismissed it with the resilience of one who had

dealt with more than her fair share of irate correspondence over the years. Funnily enough, not many people wrote into the council to express their reverence and support. Topics as diverse as housing, roundabouts and canine excretions had the capacity to reduce perfectly respectable pillars of the community to raving, potty-mouthed thugs on paper, occasionally also in person. Perhaps that was what the younger generations needed before being set loose on social media – a probation period in the council offices to develop skin as thick as whale blubber.

'No such thing as bad publicity,' she rallied. 'Isn't that what they say? Anyway, on to more important things. Show me what you've been cooking up for our big day tomorrow.'

If there had been time this afternoon to sit around thinking about it, then Maggie would probably have worked herself into a bit of a flap about seeing her ex-colleagues again, some of them for the first time in just over two years. As it was, she'd walked directly from the restaurant to The King's Head reciting aloud tasks still left to do on her list like a crazy woman and attracting more than a few turned heads. Breakfast had been bacon rolls, handed out to all by Sav that morning and, she realised, as her stomach growled, she hadn't eaten again since. Her feet throbbed and she still had a Victoria sponge to bake this evening for the cake stall, along with several last-minute phone calls to make. But she'd promised Pam, so here she was. She'd have half a lager shandy and go home. She pushed open the door and braced herself.

'Here she is,' greeted Gary, beaming as she walked into the public bar, 'Saffron Walden's answer to Jackie Weaver.'

*Oh, for goodness sakes, the blasted woman had set a precedent for council meetings everywhere with that sodding lockdown clip.* She had rather hoped a change of vocation might see off the joke. Clearly not.

He stood up and pulled out a chair. 'Sit yourself down, Maggie. What can I get you to drink?'

Maggie took a seat at the table and glanced around, delighted to see all her favourite people were there including Martin, Pam and Samira. No sign of Colin, who'd presumably used up his lifetime quota of fun when he attended her retirement do.

After the initial catching-up and good-natured jibes about Maggie's recent TikTok fame, a gentle hubbub of chatter picked up and Maggie turned to Samira. 'You look well, love,' which was true, she did. Her make-up was pristine, as usual, but she looked different, happier.

The corner of Samira's lips curved bashfully, then she leaned in close and whispered, 'Would you say I'm glowing?' she grinned. 'I haven't told anyone apart from family yet, Maggie, but I wanted you to know. You were so kind to me. Thank you.' She reached under the table and found Maggie's hand, warm skin squeezing hers softly.

Maggie sucked in a breath.

She thought back to the day she'd come across Samira in the toilets, utterly distraught and gasping through her sobs. The poor girl had been so beside herself Maggie presumed she must have received some truly terrible news. She had coaxed her down the corridor and into the first empty meeting room she came across, pulling the blind for privacy, then she had made her promise to stay put whilst she went off in search of tea, the secret stash of bourbons she kept in her desk drawer and a packet of tissues.

Samira had indeed just received news, the kind of news no woman desperate for a child wants to receive, shortly after performing yet another pregnancy test.

'I can't do it anymore,' she'd said through juddering breaths as she fought to compose herself. 'I can't do any of it. Pretending to my friends everything's OK, when all I feel is envy. I don't deserve any friends, Maggie. I watch them with their children, and I hear all about teething and nursery and baby swimming classes and all I can think is, why them and why not me? I'm a horrible person.'

Maggie had got up from her seat and encompassed the inconsolable woman into a hug, holding her tight until the tears began to subside.

Then she'd spoken softly.

'I wanted my career, but instead I fell pregnant, and everything changed. There was no place for a young mother in my line of work. I used to look at friends and colleagues, even my husband – would you believe – with envy back then. Geoff would have been horrified. We can't help what the heart wants, love. But life has a way of tricking us. I fell in love with my baby and was utterly besotted, nothing else in the world mattered at all. Did I not deserve my husband because I was briefly jealous of his career?'

Samira had pulled away and looked up at Maggie, her make-up forming dark rivers down her cheeks.

'What if it never happens?' Samira had sniffed and screwed up her sodden tissue.

Maggie had stroked back a damp tendril of hair from her face. 'I can't promise it will happen, darling. Life can just as easily lift us up one minute and derail us the next. After we had Hannah, I yearned for another child, and it didn't happen. I always believed that was payback for being doubtful the first time round. Utter nonsense, of course. But what I do know is, your friends and your husband love you. They will be there for you, let them do that.'

Now, understanding what Samira was telling her, she looked back into her shining eyes and squeezed her hand back tightly.

'So, then,' said Samira at a normal volume, possibly aware of pricked ears, 'I was having a think about what I could do to help out at the fundraiser tomorrow and I have a suggestion.'

'Oh yes,' enthused Pam, leaning in. 'Samira has the most amazing idea for a stall – you're going to love it!'

# Chapter Twenty-Seven

## Hannah

If Hannah had doubted her alarm clock at all, she needn't have worried, because at daybreak, Alice was leaning over her and prising her eyelids open.

'Mummy, get up! We've got lots and lots to do!'

Hannah grunted and shielded her eyes as Alice ran over to the window and opened the curtain, flooding the room with dazzling sunshine.

'Five more minutes,' she moaned, squeezing her eyes back shut.

She'd been up until gone midnight sellotaping raffle tickets ending in fives and zeros to a seriously random selection of donated items. There had been a hefty proportion of new jigsaws, for some reason, although at least she hadn't had to count the pieces to check they were all intact. But *who* in their right mind had thought a hand-crocheted willy warmer would be an appropriate prize for a family-friendly tombola, for God's sake? It smacked of Judith, if you asked her – the shy ones were always the worst. Needless to say, the offending item had been set aside between finger and thumb with a grimace. Perhaps she'd donate it back to the WI for *their* next fundraiser. Perhaps it had been doing the rounds like this for years, like a perverted game of pass the parcel.

Alice climbed into the bed beside her and snuggled up close, breathing loudly into her ear. She managed about thirty seconds of quiet before asking, 'Mummy, can Daddy come to the fete today? And can he bring Keith?'

Hannah's lack of outward reaction in no way reflected the displeasure her daughter's words caused. Her eyes flicked open to find Alice's huge, grey irises studying her. She'd been expecting something like this. Hannah reached across and stroked a knotty clump of hair away from her face.

'I'm not sure dogs are allowed in the restaurant, darling. But perhaps he can meet you outside when he comes to pick you up?'

Hannah had asked Darren if they could change up the plans this weekend as Alice was quite determined not to miss a minute of the big day.

'But I want to show him my bit of wall,' Alice maintained, vigorously proud of her small part in the Changing Rooms style paint job.

'OK, sweetie. Well, perhaps Daddy could come without Keith, then he can come and look at the stalls and spend some of his money on lots of nice things.'

At least he'd bloody well better put his hand in his pocket, if she was going to have to put up with him imposing on her new patch. She couldn't have said why, but she wasn't overly keen on the idea of seeing him and Sav in the same room together.

After breakfast, Alice picked out her yellow dungaree shorts to wear with a cute white t-shirt embroidered all over with ladybirds. She looked adorable, like a brilliant summer's day. Hannah, on the other hand, spent way longer than was reasonable tugging garments from drawers and getting hot and bothered. In the end, she settled on the very un-Hannah-like floaty tea dress she'd begun with, a garment she'd bought on a whim and never worn. Had never had anywhere to wear it, until now. If you couldn't wear a floaty tea dress to a community bake sale, when could you?

The restaurant was abuzz. The fundraiser didn't officially open until 11 a.m., but from the amount of people inside, it was hard to imagine many more being comfortably accommodated.

She scanned the room for her mum and spotted her laying out raffle prizes on a central table. What was it with jigsaws? There were at least another ten of the blasted things parading as raffle prizes. She made a beeline for her, leaving an excited Alice in the hands of Jade, who wanted to practise her face-painting before paying customers came along.

'Where do you want me to put the tat – sorry, prizes, Mum?' asked Hannah, holding the box aloft.

Maggie glanced up from the task in hand; she was tying a purple ribbon around an enormous basket of goodies: pineapple, melon, kiwis, strawberries, grapes, Prosecco, chocolates, crackers and so much more.

'Look what Vernon dropped in. Isn't it beautiful?'

'Wouldn't mind winning that myself,' agreed Hannah.

'Pam's around here somewhere, she's running the tombola, but I've got something else in mind for you, dear.'

Hannah didn't like the glint in her mother's eye as she looked her up and down.

'Right,' she said cautiously. 'And what might that be?'

'You, my dear, are going to be a model.'

'Sorry, what?'

'Yes, I'm so glad you've got your bits out,' she waved a vague hand towards Hannah's bare legs and arms as though limbs were now classed as erotica, 'I was worried you'd wear one of your suits and then I'd have had to ask Pam and to be quite honest, I'm not sure it would have had quite the same effect.'

'Maggie?' came the gentle voice of a young woman, who came to stand with them. Hannah recognised her straight away as Samira, the attractive young woman who'd worked with Maggie. 'Is there anything else you'd like me to do? I'm all set up.'

Maggie tied the bow with a flourish and turned to them both.

'Yes, this is my daughter, Hannah. Hannah, Samira has very kindly offered to spend the day tattooing, all proceeds to the restaurant. I'd like you to advertise her services, you don't mind a bit of body art, do you love?'

*Tattoos?* Had her mother gone stark raving mad?

Perhaps her incredulity showed on her face, because Samira hastened to add, 'They're *henna* tattoos. And I use all natural dyes, nothing harmful to children or . . . pregnant women.'

Hannah saw something pass between her and her mother and felt the need to state her case.

'Oh, well, I can assure you I'm not pregnant, despite

286

my daughter nagging me to procure her a sibling on an almost daily basis.'

Samira smiled kindly.

Hannah glanced down at her bare arms, imagining the beautiful swirling designs she'd often admired on Asian and Indian women at times of celebration. But something troubled her.

'Are you sure it won't be insensitive, me, swanning around with henna tattoos? I mean . . .'

Samira nodded knowingly. 'I understand what you're saying. But today is a celebration of this wonderful Indian family's legacy. There is nothing inappropriate about joining together to celebrate culture, just as we do when we eat Gita's glorious food. Besides,' she added with a wink, 'I'm still learning, so this is practice. I'm hoping to do my sister's bridal mehndi next year.'

Deciding she quite fancied being Samira's guinea pig, Hannah delivered the tombola prizes to Pam and was surprised to find her old teacher Mr Harding seated at the table beside her.

'Gosh, now there's a face I haven't seen in some years! It does make a chap feel his age,' he chuckled.

'Mr Harding! How lovely to see you. Have you come to help?'

'It seems I have, Miss Lawford. I've been pilloried by many a student at school fetes over the years. But these days, sadly, I don't think my shoulder joints are quite up to the rigour of the stocks. Your mother persuaded me to offer myself up to a different kind of ridicule instead.'

He pointed at a homemade sign featuring an enlarged

photo of his face emblazoned with the words 'Guess my Middle Name – 20p a go'.

There was a numbered chart beside it with space for a guess, the guesser's name and contact number.

'What's the prize?' asked Hannah, already running through various options in her mind. Mr Horatio Harding (forever branded into her juvenile mind as Fellatio Hardon), looked like a contender for a Cedric or Magnus or even a Cornelius. Or had his fiendishly evil parents outdone themselves with the alliteration? Could it be Hubert or Horace?

'Whatever's in here,' he said, holding up an envelope featuring her mother's handwriting: 'Mystery Prize worth £100.'

God. It could be anything. Hopefully not the wine tour vouchers Hannah knew were stuffed at the back of her kitchen drawer, because she'd checked and they'd expired. Not that she blamed her mum for conveniently forgetting about them; it had been a gift for her parents to enjoy together, but they never got the chance.

'Right, well I'd better have a go then. I'll take a pound's worth please.'

After checking on Alice, who was in the process of being turned into a butterfly, Hannah did a circuit of the room, marvelling over quite how many townsfolk had volunteered to help.

Judith and Diane were arranging the vast bake sale table, which was laden with delicious-looking cakes, tarts, cookies and pastries. There was no doubt this would be the most popular stall and the two women had doled themselves up for the occasion, Judith in particular was sporting a lilac shot-silk number more suited to Ladies' Day at Ascot than flogging slices of carrot cake.

Ben and Jade were supervising the much-anticipated onion bhaji-eating contest, which was due to kick off at midday, and a steady pile of them were accumulating on platters as Joe continued to bring them from the kitchen. Nine people had already rung in advance to register and pay their entrance fee and, fortunately, Vernon had provided a never-ending supply of onions.

A young gentleman Hannah didn't know was carefully unpacking a box of objects onto his table, and as she drew level, she saw they were ceramics.

'Hello,' she said, introducing herself as Maggie's daughter.

'Hi, love,' the long-haired chap smiled. 'Oscar suggested we could try and sell the pieces we made in class. You never know,' he picked up a misshapen mug and grinned, 'someone might think it's the next thing in high art.'

'I rather like it. And this,' she pointed to a wonky shallow bowl semi-glazed with a deep purple gloss, 'would look fab on my coffee table. How much is it?'

'Whatever you think it's worth,' he smiled. 'These pieces have all been donated, to help raise money to keep the restaurant. Most of us in the group love coming here, we'd hate to lose it.'

Hannah pulled out her purse to pay for the bowl and instantly regretted not bringing enough cash – this was going to be an expensive day. She'd nip to the cashpoint later.

With her bowl tucked under her arm, she turned whilst zipping up her purse and collided into someone.

'Oh,' she cried, instinctively dropping the purse to save the bowl which had shot out from under her arm.

She grabbed it in time, whilst also grasping a bloody good handful of something warm and firm.

As she looked up into the owner of the torso she'd just groped, she watched a wave of hair fall across Sav's face and the corner of his lips twitch in amusement. She had one palm flat against his stomach, dangerously close to his waistband and the other clamping a bowl into his chest.

'Got it?' he asked.

'Um,' she replied, removing the hand from his stomach, and securing the bowl. 'Yep, all good. You can remove your human bubble wrap from my valuables now.'

'Pity,' he said.

Forcing herself to focus on the hubbub around her, rather than the raging torrent of blood in her veins, Hannah asked, 'All set then?'

He recovered himself and blew out his cheeks. 'I think so. Your mum's been here since stupid o'clock this morning batch-cooking with Joe, we have plenty of samples of the new menu to give out and . . .' he paused to grin, 'as we all know cooking isn't my forte, I thought I'd hone my talents elsewhere and create an Indian-inspired cocktail. I've come up with a mango mojito. Wanna try one?'

'Sav, it's only 11 in the morning.'

He pulled a face. 'Is it? I've been up half the night, feels like the middle of the afternoon.'

Now he said it, Hannah realised how exhausted he looked.

'Everything's going to be fine,' she said, 'and I'll try one later, I promise. But right now, I have a date with a henna tattoo, and judging from Mum's frantic arm-waving, it's time to open the doors.'

# Chapter Twenty-Eight

## Maggie

'EVERYBODY . . . On your marks, get set . . . GO!'

If anyone could command a room, it was Jade. In the immediate wake of her hollering, you could have heard a pin drop, if it wasn't for the repulsive lip smacking, squelching and crunching from no less then fourteen sets of mandibles.

It was enough to put you off eating for life, yet also bizarrely fascinating. Like observing rare and savage beasts in the wild. One chap had clearly opted for the 'hamster' technique and crammed as many of Joe's exquisite bhajis into his cheeks as possible. His fleshy face strained against the unyielding crispy strands; clearly he was more used to the spherical Iceland party platter variety more closely resembling cotton wool balls than an authentic taste of the Indian subcontinent.

'God, that's gross,' remarked Hannah from her side.

'Isn't it? Although, remarkably cost-effective. Even after paying out the winnings, this contest alone will have raised over a hundred pounds.'

'I meant him,' she said, nudging Maggie so she looked to where Hannah had been watching Darren devour one of Mrs Robinson's cupcakes. Half of the buttercream was attached to his nose.

'You found him attractive once, dear,' commented Maggie, unable to resist adding under her breath, 'Lord knows why.'

She was met with a shudder in response.

'Why did he have to come here today and ruin it for me?' Hannah sounded like she had whenever she'd been asked to tidy her room, aged twelve. Maggie hoped she wasn't about to start slamming doors.

'Well, instead of resenting him for it, perhaps we should be grateful he's making the effort, for Alice's sake. Look how happy she is.'

This was quite true. Her dear granddaughter, who looked as cute as a button, with the iridescent wings of a butterfly painted on her cheeks, was nibbling at a cake at his side, possibly her second or third cake, not that she was telling Hannah.

'Two minutes to go!' shouted Jade, who stood on a chair adjudicating the contest with all the gravitas of a Wimbledon umpire.

'Gosh, Martin's doing well. I've counted at least thirty disappear down his gullet,' said Maggie. Perhaps her former colleague moonlighted as a competitive eater.

'It's pretty close,' said Hannah.

As the contest entered its final minute, the crowd grew rowdy, calling out support for their friends and family. What they should have been doing was preparing themselves for the ensuing fracas. Maggie didn't know for certain, but she was pretty confident upwards of thirty onion bhajis was a recipe for pandemonium in the lower intestine.

'We have a tie!' declared Jade, as puce and perspiring entrants slumped back in their chairs.

Maggie decided she couldn't watch as Martin and Hamster Cheeks prepared for their deciding battle. It was making her quite queasy.

Instead, she strolled over to the front door to look out into the street.

It was a gorgeous day, the higgledy-pickledy rooftops of the street stark against a turquoise blue sky. Families strolled by, children skipped along, parents with pushchairs navigated the narrow lanes and high curbs. It was *too* nice really to be stuck inside, but the restaurant didn't have a courtyard, like some of the other properties. Briefly, she wondered how Raj and Gita had managed all these years without a garden. But then again, she thought, as her gaze alighted on picnickers and walkers crossing the street to disappear through an entrance way in a high brick wall, they'd had the beautiful Jubilee Gardens on their doorstep. Such a shame they couldn't have held their fundraiser outside today, but then the whole point had been to raise awareness of the restaurant and promote its delicious food.

She wondered if it would be enough. More and more stories of the Kapoors' kindnesses had come to light as townsfolk had stepped forward to offer their help. But the restaurant wasn't a charity, Sav was right about that; the business was only worth saving if those same individuals used the restaurant regularly. Use it or lose it, wasn't that the saying?

Sav hadn't shared with her the magic figure they needed to raise to pay off the creditors and start afresh. And that was before he managed to repay his own savings. She hoped he hadn't done anything silly, like remortgage his flat in Brighton.

Maggie returned to the restaurant just in time to see Martin crowned Baron of Bhajis to much whistling and whooping from the council crowd.

*How Geoff would have loved this*, she thought, allowing herself a moment to soak up all the lovely, good feeling and warmth. Children darted in and out of the stalls, faces disguised variably as bumble bees, lions and monkeys. She was pretty sure the two boys sporting the frankly disturbing clown face paints were Laura Garcia's twins. They looked like they'd stepped from a horror movie, what bizarre choices. Joe and Ben were circulating among the visitors, with platters of complimentary food, offering various dishes on paper plates with wooden forks, some hot, some cold. Oscar was chatting to his friend from the pottery club, having broken the news he wasn't going back, although how bad could his work really have been, judging by the items set out for sale? Hannah had obviously taken pity and purchased the most hideous bowl, bless her heart.

Oscar had taken the brave first step in reducing his house of clutter and donating his mountain of puzzles as prizes. He didn't even enjoy doing jigsaws, he'd confided, and besides, he'd found his calling elsewhere if his beautiful table runners were anything to go by.

She picked out Hannah at the bar, taking a glass of something vibrantly orange from Sav and testing it through a straw. He watched her intently, as he usually did, especially when she wasn't looking. For someone so hugely intelligent, her daughter could be downright dense sometimes. She looked absolutely stunning today. A different woman entirely from the one who had reluctantly moved home earlier in the year. Her skin glowed from all the time she was spending outdoors now; it was entirely unnecessary to get a dog of their own because she and Alice spent so much time walking Banjo. Oscar had privately confided his gratitude for this, as his hip had been giving him jip. The henna tattoos created by Samira swirled up and down Hannah's arms, complementing the pretty floral tea dress and accentuating her natural beauty. She took another sip of her drink and giggled at something Sav said, making Maggie smile.

'Are them two seeing each other or something?' came a voice behind her.

'Are the two of them seeing each other,' corrected Maggie, unable to help herself. 'And it's absolutely none of my business, nor is it yours, Darren. Where's Alice?'

She spun on her heel, seeking her out.

'She's over there, playing with Laura's boys.' Darren looked pained. 'Maggie, I'd really hoped with us all being here today, like a family again, it might make Hannah rethink, about us, about me. But she's barely said hello.'

Maggie sighed. She really didn't want to be having this conversation.

'Look, Darren . . .'

A noise outside distracted her.

The front door was propped open and there appeared to be a small crowd gathering outside in the street.

'Yes?' prompted Darren, oblivious, as people who had

been milling about around them began trickling outside to scc what was occurring.

'Hold on a minute,' said Maggie, craning her neck to see. 'I'll be right back.'

She stepped out into the street to see a throng of people, who had appeared as if from nowhere. Someone was speaking at the heart of the crowd, but she couldn't see over their heads.

'Maggie!' came an urgent voice, and she turned to see Jade racing out of the restaurant towards her. 'It's him, I've just seen it on Instagram, he's doing some kind of interview. He announced it this morning.'

'Him? Who do you mea—' but before she'd finished her sentence, she'd understood.

Hugo Wick.

Of course.

What the devil was he up to?

'Grab Hannah and Sav will you please, Jade,' she asked, before diving forward and elbowing her way through the clustered bodies.

'We're here in the pretty Essex town of Saffron Walden today to hear from the star of *So You Think you Can Cook* – the infamously blunt Hugo Wick.' The woman with a microphone in hand was your typical local news reporter, hair coiffed enough to make the cast of *Dynasty* jealous, thick calves and a boucle jacket, even though it was twenty-four degrees. 'Mr Wick, we understand from your tantalising Instagram reel a little earlier you have some exciting news for the community, is that right?'

*No. Bloody. Way.*

No, no, no, what was he up to?

297

A jostling and a loud *excuse me*, announced Hannah's arrival beside her, Sav too.

Hugo preened. He was wearing tight black jeans and a grey polo shirt with the name of his own show embroidered across the chest.

'That's right. I'm here today to make an exclusive announcement.'

Maggie watched him scan the crowd until finally his eyes landed on hers, then Hannah's and finally Sav's. He smiled widely.

'I wanted all my fans, and the people of this charming town, to be the first to know I've chosen Saffron Walden as the location for the first restaurant in my brand-new chain of high-end gastronomic establishments, Wild Wicks.'

He paused for applause and Maggie's heart was only partially lifted by the half-hearted effort.

Wick continued regardless. 'I foresee our restaurants completely revolutionising the high street when it comes to innovation in food. You can expect big, bold flavours and the culinary fusion of entire continents as we bring the tastes of Asia, America, Africa and Australia to your doorstep in ways you've never seen before.'

Maggie watched on, horror-struck, as Hugo formed the shape of a gun with his fingers and extended his arm.

'Your tastebuds are going to explode.' He pointed his metaphorical gun at Maggie and pulled the trigger.

'Wow, that sounds exciting indeed,' commented the reporter. 'And since we're here, I was hoping I could ask you about a certain video that went viral this week on TikTok – can you tell us more about that?'

Hugo arranged his face into a rare picture of sweetness

and light. 'Nothing to tell. Just a misunderstanding with an OAP whose views differed from mine. You can't please all the people, all the time,' he added with a sardonic smile.

An *OAP!*

Hannah placed a restraining hand on Maggie's arm, which did nothing to dampen the unprecedented rage that tore through her veins. How *dare* he?

She considered launching herself at the pair of them, perfectly happy to end up on the evening news as the deranged grandmother who bludgeoned a celebrity chef around the head with a bum bag full of 50ps, which was the only weapon at her disposal, when he spoke again.

'Anyway, I'd like to say to everyone here today, enjoying this extraordinary British weather, that I'm going to be just over there in the park signing my latest recipe book and very happy to take photos and chat. After all,' he grinned widely, 'we're going to be neighbours.'

With that, he turned on his heel and the crowd parted for him as though he were Jesus.

And then, one by one, the treacherous souls began following him into the Jubilee Gardens. One woman could be overheard asking her husband to run to the shop for a bottle of wine and grab the camping chairs from the car, as they may as well make a day of it.

'The unscrupulous bastard,' hissed Hannah. 'He's deliberately hijacked our customers. And why the hell are they all following after him like doe-eyed groupies?'

'Because he's famous, plain and simple. And most of the general public have no idea what he's capable of,' said Maggie, humming with quiet fury. 'They think his unpleasantness is just for TV.'

'Come on,' said Sav, his voice tight with barely controlled fury, 'let's get back inside and salvage what we can of the day.'

Maggie stood rooted to the spot, watching as one by one, the onlookers drifted into the park.

'Are you OK?' asked the reporter, who was waiting for her cameraman to pack away his kit. 'You look a little unwell.'

She shook herself out of her trance and barked, 'Fine, thank you,' to the reporter before turning to go back inside.

At the cake stand, Pam was wide-eyed with hysteria, while Judith and Diane looked flustered.

'You are *never* going to guess who just picked pink number 135 on the tombola and won a set of bamboo chopsticks? I mean, could it have *been* any more appropriate?'

From the way she was wringing her hands together, Maggie could only presume it was the Emperor of Japan himself.

'No, you can't guess, can you?' squealed Pam, who hadn't even given her a chance. 'Only flipping Jamie Oliver!'

OK, so granted, Maggie hadn't been expecting that.

'What? How? Why? Where is he?' she spun around.

'He's gone now,' supplied Judith, whose voice had gone all quivery, 'but he said my shortbread was the best he'd ever tasted.'

*Oh, for God's sake, get a grip, woman.*

'Can you believe it? I can't believe it. I really can't.'

Just then Hannah came rushing over.

'Mum, you'll never guess who was just in here?'

'I've heard.'

'Joe said he tried the food, reckoned it was even better than he remembered. He asked after Raj and Gita too.'

Though she was still hopping mad, a small smile spread over Maggie's lips. They'd better make sure the picture of the Kapoors with the man himself was put back up on the wall post-haste, and in pride of place. Perhaps Raj hadn't been exaggerating, after all.

What a shame the media attention had been focused out there on that weasel, rather than the hugely successful, and talented celebrity chef who had been right under their noses. Perhaps that had been the point, a quick scoot around whilst everyone else was distracted. Well, he was long gone now, and so, unfortunately, were all their customers.

'What we need is a jolly good downpour,' remarked Hannah, reading her mother's mind. 'That'll soon send everyone rushing back in here.'

Maggie was inclined to agree. There couldn't be more than ten people left besides the stall holders, and their friends and family constituted most of that headcount. She hadn't yet sold even half the raffle tickets and there was so much food left.

'Excuse me,' came a voice at her side, as Hannah went off to find Laura and Alice. 'Are you Maggie?'

Maggie spun around to find a face she vaguely recognised. The man looked older than he probably was, his teeth were yellow and his hair thin, but his skin still held the elasticity of youth.

'Yes, I'm Maggie,' she said expectantly.

'Oh good,' he said. 'The ladies over there told me what you've been doing. To try and save the restaurant.'

Maggie smiled, though she felt like sobbing. She'd tried, but thanks to Wick, even her best efforts had been thwarted.

'I just wanted to say,' continued the man, 'that unfortunately I can't spare any money right now, but if there's ever anything I can do, I'd really like to help. I owe this place a lot.'

Something in the way he cast his eyes downward triggered Maggie's memory banks and she remembered where she'd seen him, but not for quite some time.

'What's your name?' she asked, aware she couldn't refer to him as the rough sleeper often to be seen hunkering in doorways and in parks.

'Nigel,' he replied. 'I spent a bit of time on the streets a few years back. I'm sorted now, I've got a flat in Haverhill. A job too. But back then, Raj used to bring me plated dinners most evenings. Kept me alive, I reckon. I'd leave the empty plate by the back door every morning. Couldn't wash it up, of course.'

Maggie nodded. 'I have to say, Nigel, your story doesn't surprise me. They are good people. The best. That's why we're all here, trying to make sure the restaurant doesn't close.'

He smiled. 'I saw one of posters, thought I'd come and say hi. I didn't realise they wouldn't be here.'

Maggie pointed to Sav. 'That's Raj and Gita's son, Sav. I'm sure he'd be delighted to meet you.'

Nigel thanked her and turned away just as Alice ran over. The very sight of her granddaughter was enough to lift Maggie's mood, which had swung wildly throughout the day from hopeful to murderous to quietly contemplative. Suddenly, the germ of an idea popped into her head.

As Hannah approached, she tested the water.

'Hannie, how would you feel about a touch of child exploitation?'

Hannah's eyebrows rose in alarm.

'If Mohammed won't come to the mountain, well, you know how the saying goes, send the cute child to the park instead. Where's Darren got to? It's time he made himself useful.'

Once a rather bewildered Darren had been briefed on his task (to smile adoringly at his daughter and sell raffle tickets like his life depended on it), they set off to the park hand-in-hand.

Ben stood hugging a full platter of bite-size balti pies to his chest. 'Shame we can't take this food over there too, it seems like such a waste.'

Maggie and Hannah looked at each other, mischievous smiles reflecting on each other's faces.

'Ben, be a love and tell Joe to keep the food platters coming, would you? Now then, let's find ourselves some volunteers.'

It was decided Judith and Diane would keep watch over proceedings in the restaurant, with Mr Harding on hand should things perk up.

Sav, Ben, Hannah and Jade armed themselves with silver platters and stepped out into the street, whilst Pam followed with a tray of plates and serviettes. Maggie and Oscar completed the attack strategy, coming up the rear with a stack of A5 flyers specially printed for the occasion, featuring the restaurant's new menu on the front and a discount voucher on the reverse.

They filed through the gateway into the park and were

met with a sea of bodies. It was immediately obvious from the snaking queue of people that Hugo Wick was holding court in the Jubilee Garden's Bandstand.

Hannah snarled when she spotted him brandishing a hardback book on the stage like the great bard himself, and it spurred Maggie forwards. This bloody man! He might have money and sway, but he did not have the Lawford family's stubborn gene, which had been proven time and time again to surmount anything in its way.

'Let's split up,' directed Maggie. 'Half of us take the queue, the others take the green. He might have books, but *we* are bringing the picnic.'

'You know what we need?' whispered Oscar to Maggie.

'A strategically directed meteorite?' she hazarded a guess.

Oscar chuckled. 'I was thinking of something a little more community-minded. Give me five, I just need to make a quick call.'

# Chapter Twenty-Nine

## Maggie

The look on Hugo Wick's face when he spotted Maggie handing out restaurant flyers, and her daughter doling out food, to the very people queuing to get his autograph, was absolutely priceless. Maggie resolved to hold the memory close to her chest, to bring it out and hug to herself whenever she thought of the despicable man.

'Mmm, this is fantastic,' raved a man with a baseball cap Maggie hadn't seen before. He'd just sampled a portion of Joe's biryani stuffed peppers and was now tucking into a sweet samosa devised by Ben, bursting with banana, honey, nuts and fruit. 'You wouldn't believe how hard it is to find really tasty vegetarian food; so many places just add in a couple of dishes as a token gesture without really thinking them through.'

'Oh, well, you must come to Crocus Kitchen then, because our junior chef here,' she indicated Ben, who smiled shyly, 'as a veggie himself, has created many of our vegetarian and vegan options.'

'I will,' said the man, tucking the leaflet into his back pocket. 'We live out of town and only came here today because the wife saw his announcement this morning. She's crazy about him.' He jerked his head towards the bandstand and gave an eyeroll when his wife wasn't looking. 'Got all his books. *Tries* to cook all his recipes.'

How any self-respecting woman of the twenty-first century could find his arrogance attractive was baffling indeed. It put Maggie in mind of the manager of Maison Rose, Jacob Green. No doubt he idolised everything Wick stood for and would serve up his own grandmother as canapés if it meant he achieved such stardom.

As they continued their circuit around the park, they chatted with families lounging on the grass, parents soaking up the afternoon sun whilst children ran riot with ice creams from the nearby kiosk. Many of the folk were day-trippers, drawn to the town to visit the castle or museum, and finding themselves within the midst of a celebrity.

'How's it going?' asked Maggie as they passed by Darren and Alice.

Darren held up the raffle ticket book in reply. 'One page left.'

'Brilliant!' said Maggie, her estimation of her ex-son-in-law rising above its current low bar. 'Well done, sweetie,' she said, ruffling her granddaughter's hair. 'You've done a super job.'

'A-ha,' said Oscar, standing to attention at a disturbance in the north-west corner of the park, 'I think it might be showtime.'

They all stopped what they were doing and watched as

eight men and women in white and green costumes filed onto the grass, coming to a stop right in front of the bandstand in a practised formation.

Maggie shook her head in wonder and side-eyed Oscar. 'You sly old dog.'

'What?' he asked innocently. 'It's a public place and they regularly perform at community events. This is a community event, wouldn't you say?'

The age-old strains of a concertina filled the air along with jingling bells as the Morris dancers began to move.

'You've done a lovely job of the costumes, Oscar,' said Maggie.

'If it wasn't for this blasted hip, I'd be up there shaking my stuff,' he said wistfully, testing the water with one ankle.

Perhaps there were benefits to be had from growing old and decrepit; they'd all been spared that spectacle, at least.

As the onlookers realised what was happening, many stood and began to clap. The queue to see Hugo Wick began to disperse as the time-honoured stalwart for many centuries of fetes gradually became the main attraction.

Jade swooped over and deposited a stack of empty platters by Maggie's feet.

'Just gonna go and film this,' she grinned, holding up her phone. 'Hugo's face is a picture.'

It most certainly was. If it were possible to vaporise human beings by evil glares alone, the entire park would be dust and bone.

'I suppose I should go and check on Judith and Diane,' said Pam. 'Check they've not eaten themselves into a coma, with all the surplus cake.'

'Hold up, Pam, isn't that your Christopher, making his way over?'

Maggie pointed to the uniformed police officer cutting a path through the crowds towards them.

'Christopher,' gushed Pam, who was obviously delighted to see him.

'Sergeant Rutherford when on duty, remember, Auntie,' he said, attempting a light-hearted tone, but coming off as a bit of a dickhead, in Maggie's humble opinion. And to think she'd harboured hopes for him and Hannah.

'Of course, sorry,' said Pam, suitable chastened.

He pulled himself tall. 'Would any of you ladies happen to know who the dented black Porsche Carrera illegally parked on double yellows belongs to, because I would very much like a word?'

'No, sorry,' said Pam. 'But we can ask around for you, if you like.'

'That would be helpful, thank you. It seems rather busy in town today. Whoever it is has a large box of hardback books on the passenger seat.'

Maggie's head shot up.

'Did you see what kind of books?'

It couldn't be . . . *could it*? Was life really that serendipitous?

'Yes, they seemed to be recipe books of some kind. Stern chap on the front cover.'

Hannah burst out laughing.

'Oh, this is perfect. I think you'll find the car belongs to the guy on the bandstand who looks like he's lost an applauding audience and gained a dose of the clap.'

Sergeant Rutherford looked a little bewildered, and

clearly had no idea who Hugo was, which was hugely reassuring.

'His name is Hugo Wick,' supplied Maggie. 'Never met a nicer chauvinist in my life; a little light dangerous driving probably comes with the job title.'

As the police officer made a beeline for the bandstand, they all drew closer to get a better look.

Jade turned and gave them a grinning thumbs-up, to remind them she was capturing the entire event on screen, though she was far from the only one. All around them phone screens directed at the Morris dancers shifted slightly to film the spectacle taking place behind them on stage, as though orchestrated just for their enjoyment. It was like something out of *Midsummer Murders*, as Wick's indignation mutated swiftly into temper and ultimately to his arrest.

Back in the restaurant, Judith and Diane were most put out to have missed such drama and watched Jade's footage with awe.

'What a pillock, I hope he gets his comeuppance,' tutted Judith.

'I hope he gets the rulebook chucked at him,' said Hannah. 'That could have been a person he hit, instead of a lamppost.'

'Well,' said Maggie, exhausted. 'I suppose we should draw this raffle, before everyone disappears off home.'

'Mind if we get off now?' asked Darren. 'My sister's bringing the baby round this evening to see Alice.'

Hannah drew Alice into her and gave her a big squeeze.

'You've been such a good girl today, sweetheart. I love you,' she kissed her cheek and came away with glitter on her lips. Then, taking both Darren and Maggie by surprise, she leaned forward to give Darren the briefest of hugs. 'Thanks for today, it meant a lot to Alice that you could be here, and we really appreciated your help, didn't we, Mum?'

'Oh yes – much appreciated,' spluttered Maggie, thrown by the sudden thawing of her daughter's disdain for her ex.

He smiled thinly, and rather bravely, Maggie thought.

'Thanks,' he said, placing a hand on Alice's shoulder. Then he turned back and added, 'I can see how happy you are here. I'm pleased for you. See you, Hannah. Maggie.' He nodded at them both, then took Alice's hand and left.

As everyone began packing their stalls away, Ben and Jade volunteered to take the raffle prizes over to the park for the draw; after all, as Jade said herself, she did have the biggest gob.

'Did anyone guess your middle name?' asked Hannah of Mr Harding.

Mr Harding smiled as he got to his feet. 'I'm happy to report nobody did. So, the prize remains unclaimed.' He handed the envelope to Hannah.

'But you're going to tell us, right?' asked Joe.

'Joseph Butler, where is your foresight? If I divulged, we couldn't do this again.'

He tapped the plastic tub on the table.

'Fifty-seven pounds and forty pence. Not bad for a few hours spent in the delightful company of these fine folks eating cake and drinking tea.'

Judith laughed coquettishly. How interesting, thought

Maggie, eyeing her friend with suspicion. Was she witnessing a budding romance?

When everyone else had left, Maggie picked up a broom to begin sweeping the floors when she felt a hand on her arm.

'Have you got a sec?'

It was Joe.

'What's up, love?'

He looked about him, checking to see if anyone was listening.

'I meant to say something earlier, but it's just been so busy. I popped into Beckingdale Antiques the other day, to look for something for my mum's birthday, and I can't be absolutely certain, but I think the Kapoors' Indian tea set is on display in the back room.'

Maggie frowned.

'How do you know it's the same one?'

'I don't know for sure. But it's really distinctive, silver and engraved with elephants. I remember when I was a kid, Gita was always polishing it.'

'Silver?' asked Maggie, astonished. 'I'd assumed it was china.'

Joe shook his head sadly. 'Are you thinking what I'm thinking?'

'That it was probably worth considerably more than Beckingdale Antiques would have paid for it?' she said, saddened.

'Undoubtedly.'

The front door opened and in filed Ben and Jade, minus all the raffle prizes.

'Shall we have a count-up then?' asked Maggie, jingling her bum bag.

'Yes!' enthused Jade, 'We must have made loads.'

Sav didn't look quite as enthusiastic; he looked more like a prisoner being led back to their cell.

Come to think of it, whenever Maggie had seen him today, he'd seemed distracted.

Everyone gathered around a table where all the various kitties had been assembled whilst Hannah went to the bar for a notepad and pen.

'What's the magic number then, mate?' asked Joe, as coins and notes were upturned onto the tabletop. 'Where do we need to be, to get straight with all the suppliers?'

Not for the first time, Maggie found herself wondering why Sav hadn't already shared this information. It wasn't as though they didn't already know the finances were a mess. That was the whole point of this fundraiser.

Sav shifted in his seat and chewed his cheek.

Ben and Jade were both suddenly very interested in their phones, which Maggie was fast learning was code for uncomfortable situations or boredom. This could frankly be either.

'Sav?' asked Hannah, more gently, her pen poised.

'A few hundred. Shall I take the fives?' He started filtering out the five-pound notes and collating them into a pile.

'I'll take tens,' said Joe.

'I'll take twenties,' said Ben, plucking out the only four twenty-pound notes on the table.

'I'll take the pound coins,' said Jade.

'I guess that leaves me with the shrapnel then,' tutted Maggie, who was well used to the metallic stink and grubby fingers one got from totting up takings after a fete.

Hannah noted down the totals in the columns she'd

drawn, as everyone finished counting. It was the work of seconds using the calculator app on her phone to add together the sums.

'Blimey,' she said, looking impressed. 'Eight hundred and thirty-eight pounds and fifty-five pence. That's amazing!'

Maggie had to concur. Considering everyone had scarpered off to the park for the majority of the afternoon, it wasn't bad at all.

Joe looked thrilled. 'Brilliant. Surely it's enough to set the wholesaler straight?' he asked Sav, who grimaced in reply.

'Almost,' he said, in a tone that implied there would be a but.

There was a but. A considerably large one.

'It *will* just about pay the wholesaler. But then there's also the meat delivery guy, the cash-and-carry, the wine merchant, the business rates, the VAT, the electricity, the gas, the water, the building insurance, the overdue PAT testing and of course, the wages.'

Joe's face fell.

'When you said a few hundred?' he asked what everyone else had been thinking.

Sav squirmed. 'Um, like, around one hundred and thirty-three hundred.'

Jade's mouth dropped open. 'Thirteen thousand, three hundred pounds?'

Hannah looked confused. 'Sav, you didn't seriously think we could raise thirteen thousand pounds at a bake sale?'

He put his head in his hands and let out a long sigh.

'No,' he said, his words muffled. He dragged his palms down his face, then looked each of them in the eye. 'I didn't think we'd raise more than a few hundred pounds, which I thought I could give straight back to you all as a bonus. I decided just over a week ago that I wanted to take this place on myself.' His earnest gaze fell on Hannah. 'You made me believe I could do it. That, unbelievably, I *wanted* to do it.'

Maggie saw compassion fill her daughter's eyes and had to swallow down a small lump in her throat.

Sav continued, 'I knew there was no way this place could continue. That we would have to sell eventually. Until, that is, I decided it could be *me* who buys it. Think about it,' he said. 'My parents still need somewhere to live. An income too. If I was going to deny them the chance to cash in on Wick's over-the-top offer, then it had to be worth their while. The only thing, really, that would make it worth their while, would be seeing me take over the family business. That would make them happy. And I want them to be happy, as happy as you guys have made me, these past few weeks.'

His eyes glazed as though he was fighting to stave off tears. 'My business partner was going to buy me out of our firm. We set the wheels in motion last week. There would have been enough to clear the decks and invest in the business *and* the property, and to set my parents up somewhere new.'

Hannah reached out a hand and wrapped it around Sav's, the soft, swirly tendrils of her tattoo snaking around his fingers like a promise.

'But I found out this morning his funding fell through.

He can't raise the money, certainly not in time to deal with the court summons we've received this week from HMRC, or the notice of disconnection from the electric company. I couldn't say anything, not with all the work that's gone into making this happen today, besides – best to go out on a high, right? I'm going to have to go back to Brighton and focus on the business, I can't leave Greg coping alone any longer. This place . . . will have to be sold.'

And there it was.

The punchline.

And boy did it feel like a punch, right in the gut.

By now, Maggie knew there was no way she could have kept this up.

Ever since she stepped through the doors to this restaurant for an unplanned meal with her daughter, she had been on a non-stop rollercoaster ride of adrenalin and emotion. This restaurant and the people in this room had galvanised her and inspired her, brought her back to life. The work had steamrollered through her grief and reignited her love for cooking again. She now thought of dear Joe, and sweet Ben, and feisty, indomitable Jade as extended members of her family.

But she was completely and utterly exhausted. Her feet hurt and were in urgent need of attention, her joints ached, and she was starting to remember all the small complaints Geoff had made, as retirement had grown closer. He'd never been a whinger, and perhaps deep down, he'd always known how Maggie had envied him his career. Perhaps he'd resolved to never take it for granted; it would have been typical of his sensitive and kind way. But she'd seen the pain in his face some mornings as he'd stretched his back and inserted memory foam insoles into his shoes. The physical work of being a chef took its toll, and she couldn't have sustained it for long at her age, and that was OK, because now she knew what she *really* wanted to do.

'Sav, love,' she said, reaching across the table and rubbing his other hand. 'You've done everything you can. And I'm sure I speak for us all when I say we wouldn't change a thing – it's been quite the journey.' She smiled warmly, feeling immeasurably thankful for having had this time with these wonderful people. 'Maybe it's time to let it go, huh?'

Joe let out a deep, world-weary sigh.

'I'm so sorry, Joe,' said Sav, voice thick with emotion. 'You've done such an amazing job – all of you have. I hate letting you down like this. If there was anything more I could do . . .' He trailed off miserably because there wasn't anything more anyone could do. They'd tried everything and it hadn't been enough.

There were those who maintained business should never be mixed with pleasure, but here, around this table were several exceptions to the rule. Of all the emotions struggling for dominance on Joe's expressive face, *love* shone through. They were best friends, and that trumped anything else.

Joe reached across and squeezed Sav's shoulder hard.

'Maggie's right, mate. It sounds like we might all need to accept we've reached the end of the road here, and it's nobody's fault. It's just life. It's shit, but we can't say we didn't try, huh? And no matter what happens next, today was a good day, one to remember.'

Sav tried to raise a smile, but everyone could see he was heartbroken.

'Just promise us one thing . . .' added Joe.

Sav looked up.

'For the love of God, don't let that prick Hugo Wick get his hands on this place. I'm not a violent man, but that could quickly change where he's concerned.'

Sav shook his head vigorously. 'I can't promise much, but I *can* promise that. Certainly not whilst it's ours to sell, anyway.'

'I'll really miss working here,' piped up Ben. His eyes shone with sincerity. For Ben, perhaps as much as for Maggie, this place had been safe harbour. A place of refuge during stormy seas. And now they would ready themselves to set sail once more.

'Well, perhaps it's time for a final toast then, before I instruct an estate agent. Mango mojito, anyone?' asked Sav.

Jade made a strange, anguished noise, as one might imagine a tortured cat to sound, then, looking horrified at her own fallibility, attempted to disguise her tears with the hem of her top. 'Sorry, sorry,' she said, rubbing furiously and throwing in a yawn for good measure. 'I'm just tired.'

'You have absolutely nothing to apologise for,' scolded Maggie. '*Never* apologise for caring, my girl.'

In the tenderest of gestures, Ben swung an arm around his friend and pulled her into a hug.

Hannah met Maggie's eye and they exchanged the smallest of smiles. It was one that acknowledged the sheer volume of feeling in the room, and love for the small family they'd become. For them, those feelings far outweighed the brick-and-mortar of the restaurant. But for Sav, of course, it was quite different. For Sav, and for his parents, this was the end of an era.

'Want me to walk you home, Jade?' asked Ben.

She nodded mutely.

'I'll get started on the kitchen,' said Joe, pushing back his chair. 'It's a bit of a mess.'

'No,' Sav said forcefully. 'Leave it. It can all wait until tomorrow. Just get yourselves off home, it's been a long day.'

Joe hesitated.

Hannah glared helplessly at Maggie, who decoded her daughter's message, as though it had been transmitted straight into her frontal lobe and knew instantly what to do.

'Come on then Joe, love. You can run this decrepit OAP home if you like?'

The reference to Hugo Wick's slur lightened the mood enough for everyone to get to their feet.

'Coming, too Hannah?' enquired Joe, dangling his car keys.

Maggie almost cried out her objection, fumbling for an excuse, but as it turned out, tactics weren't needed, because Hannah and Sav both spoke at once.

'No, thanks Joe—'

'I'll run her home—'

Even Joe took the sledgehammer-sized hint, taking Maggie's arm in his and steering her to the front door.

# Chapter Thirty

# Hannah

'Just us then,' said Sav, as they moved to sit at the bar. Hannah slid onto one of the high stools, whilst Sav set about making their drinks. 'Although I suppose, technically, nearly 50 per cent of our staff *are* underage for drinking these. I shouldn't have even suggested it.'

Judging by the strength of the one he'd made earlier, Hannah was inclined to agree.

'Although if memory serves me correctly, by their age most of our year at school were pissed on cider at weekends and fumbling with each other in the park,' he said, scooping ice into two glasses.

'I've no idea what you mean,' said Hannah, although ironically, she didn't, not really. She'd never really been part of that scene, always too studious and focused to let herself go completely, something she had lately been coming to regret. 'Speaking of school, I wonder what Hardon's middle name is,' said Hannah wistfully, spotting the unclaimed prize envelope sitting on the bar top. 'I put literal money on Cornelius. What about you?'

Sav laughed. 'Well, I know what it is, so it would have been rather unscrupulous of me to guess.'

'What?' exclaimed Hannah. 'How the heck do you know?'

'My dad told me. Believe it or not, they knew each other years ago, back in London when they briefly shared the same lodgings. He used to see his post in the hallway.'

Hannah waited, ears cocked, but Sav still didn't expand.

'And . . .' she urged.

Sav shrugged, pretending not to know what she meant. 'And, what?'

Hannah grabbed the nearest thing, which happened to be a dried-up slice of lime from the tray of cocktail garnishes and lobbed it into his face, striking the end of his nose with precision.

'What is his middle name, you moron!' she laughed.

Sav faux-tutted and plucked up the lime segment between thumb and forefinger, 'No need to get fruity, Lawford. You only had to ask nicely.'

'If you don't tell me right now,' said Hannah, sliding the tray towards her menacingly, 'I'll get fruitier than a Del Monte factory in Hawaii.'

Sav's eyes glittered and a thrill hummed through her.

'As tempting as that is, Han, I'll tell you anyway. Mr Horatio Harding's middle name is Horatio.'

'What? Who calls their child Horatio Horatio?'

'No-one, apparently. His actual name is John Horatio Harding.'

'John?' Hannah was scandalised. 'All this time and his

name is *John*. For the love of God, *why* would you choose to go by Horatio when your name is John? It doesn't make any sense. Especially if you're a teacher and open to ridicule on an almost hourly basis.'

Sav shrugged. 'Reinvented himself at university, apparently.'

Hannah fingered the envelope.

'Wonder what's in here then?'

'Open it and see. It's not like it matters now.'

Hannah slid a finger under the seal and popped the envelope open. Inside was a small printed card. She tugged it out and read aloud.

'This voucher entitles the holder to a one-to-one course of cookery lessons. Fall in Love with Food Again.'

The card went on to give Maggie's email address and telephone number, and was signed off, *Maggie*.

Hannah glanced up at Sav. 'OK, so it looks like Hardon isn't the only one reinventing himself.' She shook her head in wonder. 'Mum never ceases to surprise me. Dad would be so bloody proud; he was always telling her she should teach. I don't think she believed she could.'

Sav placed two mango mojitos on the bar, then slipped around to take a seat beside her.

'In India, the Alphonso mango is in season between March and July. They are like nothing you've ever tasted, super rich and sweet. Difficult to get them here, so Mum and Dad used to buy it pulped and it was my favourite thing as a kid, especially with yoghurt. Don't tell your mum, but this mango is out of a tin.' He held his glass aloft. 'So then, a toast to this place, and whatever it becomes,' said Sav, clinking his glass against hers. 'I hope the new owners love it as much as my parents did, and yours too.'

Hannah clinked back. 'It'll always be The Golden Crocus as far as I'm concerned, even with your fancy new sign.' She pointed to a table in the corner. 'And I'll always picture Mum and Dad sitting just there, fighting over the last piece of a garlic naan. Something that probably never changed in over thirty years.'

They sipped at their drinks in silence.

Hannah found her mind kept snagging on something.

'Sav,' she said, twirling her glass. 'Remember when we were having dinner in Cambridge, you said you knew how it would probably go, that it would be far better to, what was it you said? Rip the plaster off now.'

'And I was right. Today has been like rubbing salt in an open cut, and that was before your ex-husband turned up and mooned about after you all day.'

Hannah decided to ignore the comment, though she hadn't missed the way Sav's eyes had tracked her whenever they'd been near to each other. Hadn't missed the electrical current surging between them when her body had been pressed up against his. Hadn't missed anything much, when it came to Sav.

'You said you'd been to see Greg that day. Is that when you approached him about buying you out?'

Slowly, Sav nodded. He lifted heavy eyes to hers. 'I put the proposal to him, and he didn't seem keen. Said he'd need to think about it. That's why I couldn't get my hopes up. Then the next day he rang to say he wanted to do it, and that he'd found a way to raise the money.'

'I'm so sorry,' she said, meaning it. 'I honestly thought

322

you were just doing what you needed to, out of duty to your parents.'

'To begin with, I was,' he replied. 'Then you came along, and we did all of this,' he indicated the space around them, 'and I guess I got carried away with a fantasy.'

'None of it was fantasy, Sav,' she said, her voice coming out like a whisper.

He fixed her with a steady gaze.

'You have no idea what I fantasise about.'

She swallowed. 'I don't. But I do know that ever since you came back into my life, I find myself thinking about the first time a boy ever kissed me, twenty-two years ago. And how it was still the best kiss I've ever had in my life, yet somehow, the boy doesn't even seem to remember.'

Sav reached out and traced a finger along the lines of the tattoo on her arm. Every nerve ending in her body stood to attention.

'You seriously think I don't remember?' A smile played on his lips. 'I spent the next year of my life contemplating ways I could make it happen again, but you were so absorbed in your studies I never really found myself alone with you again, so I figured it was a one-time fluke. And I was happy with that.' His face broke into a genuine grin. 'On that day, the girl of my dreams chose *me*, how could I be sad about that?'

'You're alone with me now,' breathed Hannah.

Sav leaned closer, so close she could see flecks of gold in his conker brown eyes.

'And in less than a week, I'll be gone.'

Hannah closed the gap a few inches more.

'Nothing to lose, then,' she said.

323

Need burnt in his eyes, and he closed the remaining space between them, bringing his lips to hers and murmuring, 'Only everything. But what the hell.'

# Chapter Thirty-One

## Maggie

Standing among parents at the school gates the following Friday, some of whom she'd become quite friendly with over the past eight months, Maggie wondered if Samira would also be standing here in four years' time. She was getting ahead of herself, admittedly, but her heart filled with joy to know her former colleague and friend had been blessed with the only thing she'd ever wanted. Samira was going to make a fantastic mother.

There was only another week left of school pick-ups before the end of term. Maggie looked forward to the summer holidays and lots of quality time with her granddaughter, but she also worried, perhaps for the first time, if she had the energy for it. Working in the restaurant kitchen had shown her that whilst her mind was agile as ever, her body was beginning to fall slightly behind.

Oscar was standing in the street, commanding the traffic in his hi-vis gear, lollipop stick at the ready. Perhaps she'd have to take him up on his yoga for the over sixties' class, after all, keep her limbs supple and active. At the sight of Oscar, she remembered the art class she'd attended on Monday and a physical shudder ran through her at the memory. Dear God, please smite the image from her mind and pray she never see such a thing again.

'Mum!'

Hannah startled her from her thoughts, waving as she walked briskly towards her, looking, quite frankly, ridiculous in a grey skirt suit and pink Skechers.

'Hannie, what are you doing here?'

'Knocked off early, thought I'd come and meet you both here.'

Hannah leaned in to kiss her mother on the cheek.

'That's lovely. Alice will be thrilled,' said Maggie.

'Also, Sav has asked if we can go to the restaurant. Kind of a farewell thing, I think.'

'Ah, yes,' sighed Maggie. 'The dreaded date: 14th of July. No doubt that crooked accountant has rubbed his hands together with glee and scoured his books for other prospective buyers. There's no way on earth that man wasn't getting a sizeable backhander from Wick all along; he'll just sniff out someone else with money.'

'Probably,' Hannah agreed, in an all too cheerful manner for Maggie's liking. Since their fundraiser last weekend, the closure of The Crocus Kitchen, had sat heavy on her shoulders all week. As though there *had* to have been something more she could have done. As though, beneath it all, she was responsible for its failure. Perhaps in a way, she was, for charging in like a bull at a gate and offering hope to poor Joe, who was now out of a job, and to Ben, who had just been getting his life back on track after his mother had so cruelly deserted him.

'So will we go straight there?' asked Hannah, as the babble of children's voices and Roadrunner-style exits signalled the end of the school day.

'Hmm?' asked Maggie.

'To the restaurant, shall we go straight there, or did you need to go home first?'

'Whatever you think best, dear.'

Maggie held up a hand to wave to Alice as she saw her blonde head appear. She wasn't keen to go back there at all, if she was being brutally honest. Why prolong the misery?

But a glance at Hannah told her all she needed to know. It was written there on her anxious face. Though her daughter hadn't said a word, there were quite clearly feelings of a different kind when it came to her and Sav. Maggie mentally kicked herself for being so insensitive. She may have lost an inspiring job and a brand-new work family, but Hannah was losing someone she'd grown to care about, who would be heading back home to Brighton any day now.

'Granny! Mummy!' cried Alice, her eyes lighting up to find them both there waiting for her. Maggie smiled at the thought that in just a few years, seeing them outside the school gate would probably yield only cringeworthy embarrassment. She remembered those days well; the tricky path to negotiate between childhood and teenagerhood when anything you do is precisely the wrong thing to do. She hoped the close relationship she had forged with her granddaughter would calm those angry waters and provide a place of sanctuary, just as she had found with her own treasured Gran and Hannah had with hers.

'Am I still going to Daddy's tonight?' asked Alice, perhaps a little thrown by the change to routine.

'Yes, sweetheart, he's coming to pick you up a bit later. But first, we're just going to pop to the restaurant to see everyone for a little while, is that OK?' asked Hannah, taking Alice's bag.

'Is Joe going to be there?' she asked, her idolisation of the big man having never waned.

'Yes, and Sav and Ben and Jade too,' answered Hannah.

Maggie was struck by a deep melancholy. It was like her retirement party all over again, except this time perhaps all the exciting days really were all behind her. *Every day's an adventure with you*, Geoff had said once. *I don't need anything else. Just my girls.*

Well, that was all Maggie needed too. Her girls were more than enough to sustain her, and lately her family had grown. So long as she got out of bed each morning and found ways to connect with others, that would be adventure enough. And perhaps friendship was the greatest adventure of all.

'Actually,' she said, coming to a halt on the pavement. 'You two go on ahead and I'll meet you there.'

Hannah wavered. 'Do you feel OK? Do you want us to come with you?'

Maggie dismissed her with a shake of the head. 'I'm absolutely fine. Just remembered something I need to do, that's all. Won't be long.'

She turned on her heel before Hannah could quiz her further and set off in the opposite direction, hoping she wasn't too late.

First, though, she was making a quick detour home

and sent up a silent apology to her disapproving daughter, patron saint of law-abiding citizens – or perhaps that was the old Hannah, for the new one was so chilled out she'd apparently abandoned all notion of dress sense and skipped off work willy-nilly. She'd never seen her so happy as in recent weeks. If only Geoff were here to see it, although ironically it was probably only Geoff's passing that had brought her back home; maybe if they'd still be galivanting around in their campervan, Hannah would simply have battled on alone in London. How fickle life could be, offering up in one hand and taking with the other. One simply had to ride the flume, to use another of Pam's insightful theme park analogies, and be prepared to get soaked along the way.

Almost an hour later, Maggie arrived, breathless and sore of feet, to The Crocus Kitchen. She rang the bell and waited.

It was Ben who opened the door, almost dazzling Maggie with a newly acquired piercing in his left ear, a small square diamante stud, which she had to admit brought out the mischief in his eyes.

'Are you off somewhere frightfully hip this evening, Benjamin?' she enquired, following him into the restaurant. 'You're looking rather suave.'

'Fab, isn't it?' commented Jade, who was in her usual position of bum on seat, feet on opposite seat, phone in hand. 'He was going to just get a boring old stud until I convinced him sparkles are for every day, not just occasions.'

'Bit extra for a Friday afternoon, I think,' muttered Ben. 'I'm going to feel like a right melt when I go to the dentist or somewhere else equally as dull.'

'Well, I'm afraid I have to disagree,' said Maggie. 'I go all out for glamour when *I* visit my dentist: jewellery, lippy the lot. He's a total dreamboat. Got to be an upside to the fortune I've doled out over the years on root canal and denture bridges.'

'Mum!' cried Hannah in outrage. 'Tell me you're not serious.'

'About which bit, sweetheart?'

'Any of it! You and Dad were with the same dentist for over twenty years.'

'Oh, don't be such a prude, Hannie. Even a happily married woman can enjoy a bit of eye candy once in a while, especially when the confectionery in question is literally in your face.'

Sav sniggered from where he sat nursing a cup of tea.

'I am *not* a prude,' said Hannah sulkily. 'I'd just rather not hear about my elderly mother's crushes.'

'What's a prude?' asked Alice, looking to each adult for the answer when none was forthcoming. 'Is that when a plum goes all dry and wrinkly? We learned about that at school.'

'*Exactly* like that,' Maggie said quickly, quaking with suppressed mirth under Hannah's glare.

With rapier wit, Hannah reversed the spotlight onto her mother. 'Why don't you tell everyone all about your own very recent encounter with dry, wrinkly prunes, Mum?'

In a quite visceral reaction, mere mention of the experience had Maggie shuddering again with horror.

'I can't bring myself to,' she said. 'Too awful for words.'

'Then allow me,' said Hannah with glee. 'You remember

Oscar, the elderly gentleman responsible for these beauties?' she said, fingering the table runner, the others all nodded. 'Well, Mum finally relented and accompanied him to an art class earlier in the week – he's been badgering her to go along to one of his clubs for ages, hasn't he?'

Maggie mutely nodded.

'Did you do colouring, Granny?' asked Alice, who was herself creating a fine masterpiece on a piece of paper Sav had found for her.

'Drawing, darling,' replied Maggie.

'*Life* drawing,' expanded Hannah. 'And when the nude sitter cancelled at the last minute, it seems Oscar was only too happy to offer up his services.'

'No way!' exclaimed Jade, a look of unbridled disgust creeping across her face. 'That's properly *gross*.'

'Yes,' agreed Maggie, 'it wasn't a feast for the eyes. More like a dog's dinner.'

'I can't believe you didn't keep the drawing,' spluttered Hannah, beside herself with laughter.

'Why the hell would I want that?' cried Maggie, aghast. 'I'm having enough trouble looking the man in the eye as it is, without a memento of the awful experience.'

'He's certainly full of surprises,' said Sav. 'Must be something in the water around here, everyone hits retirement age and decides to start reinventing themselves.'

'Speaking of which, let me give you all one of these,' said Maggie, delving into her handbag. 'Spread the word, tell your friends. If I've learned one thing from working here over the last few weeks, it's how much I've enjoyed the shared learning experience. It might be a little late in the day, but I am going to teach.'

331

She handed around some of the small cards she'd had printed, advertising her cookery classes.

'I've registered for a food hygiene inspection, so I can open up my kitchen. Oscar, very much fully clothed, is going to be my first guinea pig. The poor man's been living off an array of toppings on toast for nigh on a couple of years. You'd think with all his clubs and classes, he'd have thought to try baking, really.'

Though she knew, from personal experience, how easy it was to make do, when simply getting through the day was an effort.

'This is a brilliant idea,' said Ben. 'I've learned so much from you and Joe.'

'Isn't Joe coming?' she asked, disappointed he wasn't here. Perhaps he'd already found a new job. Maggie hoped so. He was far too talented not to be working in a kitchen somewhere, but still, she'd hoped to see him today. Had counted on it, in fact.

Sav said, 'Yeah, he's just out back tidying a few things up. He won't be long.'

'Oh great, I'll just pop out to say . . .'

Sav jumped to his feet. 'Can I get you a drink, Maggie? Coffee, tea? Something stronger?'

Was it her imagination or did something pass between Sav and Hannah just then. The slightest hint of panic.

'I'll have a cup of tea please, Sav, thank you,' she said, feeling slightly wrong-footed.

As he turned and made for the kitchen, Hannah became all animated and asked Alice to tell Granny all about her sunflower's progress. She knew her daughter and knew when she was hiding something, but she leaned in to

332

listen to Alice and tried to ignore the niggling feeling something was off. It better not have anything to do with that imbecile Hugo Wick, or she was in peril of losing any shred of dignity still within her possession.

When Alice had finished her lengthy and unfortunate anecdote about Tabitha's sunflower snapping in half when she'd decided to scale it like Jack and the beanstalk (this had predictably led to two grazed knees and tears), Maggie glanced up to see where Sav had got to with her tea. Possibly, he'd nipped to a Sri Lankan plantation; he'd had just enough time.

'What's in the bag, Mum?' asked Hannah, motioning towards the large bag Maggie had brought in with her.

'Oh, just a few bits,' she said, brushing away the question. If Wick was even within sniffing distance of this restaurant, she'd be rethinking the leaving gifts she'd brought in for everyone.

It was all just so damned disappointing, particularly as the restaurant had never looked nicer. The freshly painted walls were cheerful and inviting, the ad hoc pictures gave the place a homely feel and Oscar's colourful table runners were the piece de resistance – it felt eclectic, bohemian and interesting. Sav had obviously staged the restaurant for estate agent viewings and photography, the tables were laid and fresh flowers in shades of red, saffron and lemon spilled from a vase on the bar. Was it too much to hope Sav might find a buyer who would take it on as it is? Not that she could bear the idea of dining here ever again right now. Memory lay upon memory upon memory. Perhaps that would change in time, if the place was still standing by then. Unless the proprietor was Wick, of course, in which case she could be tempted to facilitate in its untimely demise.

'I've been working on a new dish, Maggie,' said Ben, looking terribly pleased with himself.

'Really? Do tell all.'

Maggie was thrilled Ben was as enthusiastic about cooking at home as he had been at work. It was the measure of a true cook; to never cease exploring, creating and honing their passion.

'Fajita's, Indian style. I used chapatis for the wraps, with spiced veggies and paneer cheese, but you could use chicken, beef, anything. Oh, and like this mega tasty coleslaw as a side. It tasted amazing.'

'Ooh,' agreed Maggie, her tummy gurgling at the thought of it, 'and I presume your dad was chief taster? Did he enjoy it?'

Jade snorted.

'There was tasting alright. And I don't think his dad got a look in.'

Ben flushed to the exact shade of the wall. Wicked Rose. How apt.

Maggie took a shot in the dark. 'Tom, perchance?'

He nodded but couldn't stop the silly grin from spreading across his face.

'Hi, Maggie!' greeted Joe, emerging from the kitchen trailed by Sav and a trayful of teas and coffees.

It was odd to see him without his chef's whites; he looked almost undressed in his t-shirt and jeans. He placed the tray on the table and Sav began dishing out mugs and a pot of milk and sugar.

'Coke, Jade?' he asked, remembering she found all hot

drinks to be the very sputum of the devil. *It's a hot sunny day, why would I want to put molten lava inside my head, where it's already hot as hellfire,* she had argued once, fairly convincingly.

'Yes please,' she said, swinging her legs to the floor. 'So, before all the *it's been nice knowing you, have a nice life,* or whatever we're here for, can I please show you guys my report?'

'Report?' asked Maggie. 'A school report?'

Jade scoffed. 'God no. Why would I want to show you that? I can give you the bullet points if you like.' She affected the plummy accent of Mr Harding and said, 'If Jade applied herself to her studies with half as much *diligence* and *zeal* as she did her social media accounts, she would doubtless have the makings of a promising scholar.'

They all laughed. Then, looking like the cat who got the cream, Jade explained, 'I mean an actual report. Like a news report. We have to do them as part of our college coursework next year and this is my practice piece.'

'Can't wait,' said Maggie, hitching forward in her seat.

'Hang on,' said Hannah, reaching down to the floor. 'Let's watch it on here. Bigger screen.'

She brought her work laptop out of its case and opened it up, then began typing into the keypad.

'How do you know about it?' asked Maggie.

Hannah grinned. 'I saw it on Jade's Instagram. Trust me, you're going to love it.'

They all shifted their chairs so they could see the laptop screen, and then Hannah pressed play on the video.

# Chapter Thirty-Two

## Hannah

The video ended and they all sat in stunned silence, though Hannah had by now seen the video many times.

'What did you think?' asked Jade, a rare trace of doubt in her tone.

Maggie turned to her and shook her head in bewilderment.

'I think it's . . .' She scrabbled around for words. 'It's professional, it's arty, it's simply *magnificent*, Jade.'

Jade had pieced together several pieces of film featuring the delightful Hugo Wick, including the showdown in the restaurant, and his thinly veiled insults tossed at her mother, and interspersed it with snippets of TV footage. The innumerable instances of swearing had been bleeped out, which only served to further highlight his foul mouth. Overlaid was a solemnly spoken narrative by Jade, questioning the ethical stance of TV companies in giving a public platform to this sort of man. Most cleverly, certainly from a legal standpoint, she did not accuse him of effectively bullying a person of colour, or threatening the elderly, but moreover the facts spoke for themselves in the actions of the man himself, there for all to see.

A montage showcased clips of the fundraiser and soundbites from familiar voices emphasised what they loved most about living in the town.

'There's a real sense of community here. We are so lucky to have family-run businesses like this. It would be a crying shame to see yet more soulless chains run the locals out of town.

'A recent survey suggested as many as 57 per cent of small UK businesses will face closure this year and Crocus Kitchen is just one of them. Perhaps the question we should be asking ourselves is – at what cost to the community? Do we really want to lose the places where memories have been made, to those who would stand on the shoulders of others to further their own career? Perhaps as a nation we should be doing more to support our local businesses, although sadly it looks as though the support has come just a little too late for the much-loved Crocus Kitchen. I'm Jade Johnson, thank you for watching.'

'Come here, you clever thing,' said Maggie, getting up and wrapping her arms around Jade's shoulders. 'If you're not on the BBC news within the next ten years, I'll eat my hat.'

'I don't think I've ever seen you in a hat, Mum,' interjected Hannah. 'Not even at my wedding.'

'I'll buy one especially. Something big and flouncy and befitting of the fact I will *never have to eat it*,' she emphasised for Jade's benefit.

'Do you think it was OK?' asked Jade, still completely unaware of the consequences of her work. 'I wasn't sure whether I should have put it out there in the public domain, but I didn't say anything slanderous, just used existing footage that's already been out in the world. It's up for the viewers to decide what it all means.'

'Oh, I think the meaning is crystal clear,' said Joe, raising his mug of tea in salute. 'Jade, you rock.'

'I'm seriously impressed,' said Ben. 'I can't believe you hadn't shown me yet. It's awesome.'

'Well maybe I would've if you hadn't been so busy sticking your tongue down—'

'Er . . .' Hannah interrupted, before Alice got the gist of where Jade was headed.

'It's wonderful, Jade. And, well . . . now seems as good as time as any.'

Maggie reached down to the enormous bag she'd hauled in with her and pulled out something small, wrapped in tissue paper. She handed it to Jade. 'This is just a little thank you for all you've done, you know with all your social media jiggery pokery, and what have you.'

Hannah watched, intrigued, as Maggie added, 'I had these in the eighties, living in London and filled with a similar fiery passion to stamp my mark on this world. I thought you might like them, seeing as you insist on wearing all things garish and clashing.'

Jade unwrapped the tissue paper and held up an earring. Her mouth formed an O shape, almost as big as the bright orange hoop between her fingers. 'These are *awesome*! They must be *really* old. Are they like Bakelite or something?'

Maggie gave a snort of distaste. 'Darling, they stopped using Bakelite before I was born. They are your bog-standard variety of plastic, guaranteed to still be around long after the world has polluted and Botoxed itself into annihilation.'

'I *love* them, they are, like, *so* cool. Thanks, Maggie,' said Jade, turning on the self-facing camera function of her phone so she could thread them through her lobes immediately.

*Huh*, thought Hannah. *Who knew Mum was such a paragon of style?*

Hideous sandals aside, perhaps she should start raiding her wardrobe.

'And Ben,' continued Maggie, delving into her bag of tricks again, 'you might well decide cooking isn't the career for you, but I suspect you'll always enjoy it. I bought something like this with my first-ever wage as a trainee chef.' Maggie handed him a small, leatherbound notebook. 'I wrote every recipe I was shown in here, couldn't get enough, then filled another, and another. If I'm honest,' she confessed, 'collecting recipes has always been a bit of an obsession. Don't tell Gita, but I've copied all hers down too, including her famous cardamom biscuits. Although I may have used underhand tactics to get that one.' She winked at Sav.

'That's such a brilliant idea,' said Ben, handling the book like it was a rare butterfly.

'Revolutionary,' agreed Maggie, rolling her eyes. 'Next they'll start printing recipe books with pictures.'

'Silly Granny,' piped up Alice, proving to all she *was* listening, despite appearing as focused as Picasso on her masterpiece. '*Of course,* you can get cooking books with pictures in.'

Hannah snorted a laugh. *That's my sweet, sassy girl.*

But what was Maggie doing? It looked awfully as though she was handing out leaving presents. She should have known she'd do something like this. Even with little to no notice, she had still managed to pull something, quite literally, out of the bag.

'Sav, love.' Maggie placed an unwrapped object on the table in front of him, a silver teapot, engraved with elephants. 'This one's for Gita, and I'm sorry if I've over-stepped, but I couldn't stomach the idea of her losing this place after sacrificing something as meaningful to her as this. I couldn't carry the whole set; it weighs a blinking ton. But it's all arranged with Beckingdale Antiques – you can collect the rest tomorrow.'

'But how . . .' Sav faltered, looking down upon the teapot, dumbstruck.

This had to be the tea set his parents had pawned, realised Hannah. How *on earth* had her mother tracked it down?

'We haven't managed to save the restaurant, love, but it's only right your parents get to keep something they always treasured. We can do that for them, at least.'

Sav gawped and opened and closed his mouth like a goldfish. Then, he pushed back his chair and got to his feet, bending to enfold Maggie into a tight hug.

'Hey,' said Maggie, rubbing his back. 'It's alright, love.'

Sav released her from his arms, eyes shining. 'I don't know what to say, Maggie. This is incredible, I'm certain Mum will be over the moon to be reunited with it. I still can't believe she was prepared to part with it if I'm honest.'

'Maybe they were always intending to buy it back, love. Many who pawn their valuables hope it's only a temporary measure. That's how they bring themselves to do it at all.'

'Maggie, this is so generous. But I think there's something you should—'

'It's alright. I'm almost done,' Maggie interrupted. 'Then we can get on with the unpleasant business.'

'But Mum—' tried Hannah.

'Just one moment, love,' said Maggie.

'Joe,' she continued, smiling at him. 'I just want to say it has been an absolute pleasure cooking with you in this kitchen. You are a damned fine chef and don't ever let anyone tell you otherwise. So, I want you to have these.'

She delved back into the bag and pulled out the familiar rolled canvas containing Geoff's Japanese knives.

Unbidden, a small noise of surprise escaped from Hannah and Maggie shot her a fearful glance. Perhaps she was worrying whether it was painful for Hannah to see something of her father's given away to someone else. Perhaps she also now wondered, too late, if Hannah may have wanted them for herself one day, even if, despite her mum's best efforts to instil a love of cooking, she relied almost exclusively on the varied wares of Messrs Marks and Spencer. She *was* emotional, but not for the reasons her mum feared. The moment was poignant, and more so than Maggie realised.

When Hannah spoke, her voice was thick. 'It's a brilliant idea, Mum. Apart from the fact you carried them into town, although Sergeant Rutherford attempting to arrest *you* is something I'd pay good money to see. Dad would have wanted you to have them, Joe.' She grinned at him and blinked away the moisture in her eyes.

Joe shook his head.

'I can't take these,' he looked up, bewildered.

'Yes, you can,' asserted Maggie. 'And you will. I want you to use them and enjoy them.' She leaned across the table and placed a reassuring palm over Joe's. 'Besides, I can't have them lying about in my kitchen at home if I'm going to have novices cooking there – that's just a recipe for catastrophe and far too much blood. Now, as soon as you've sorted yourself with a new position, I want to hear all about it, because I'll be first in line to book a table for dinner.'

Joe ran an appreciative hand over the case, before sniffing away his emotion.

'I'm afraid I can't do that, Maggie,' he croaked.

Maggie's face dropped. Hannah knew she was probably imagining Joe abandoning catering and drifting back into the building trade again, after all this. That would hit her hard, the idea of all that passion and talent thwarted again.

'Oh,' she said, trying not to let her disappointment show. 'Well, try not to worry, dear. There's plenty of time and opportunity. You're still a spring chicken.'

Joe sat up straighter.

'No. I mean, I can't let you book a table for dinner because I need you in the kitchen . . .'

'Joe, I'm flattered, truly I am, but wherever you're working next, I can't come with you – even if any of the kitchens around here would have me, which I can assure you from first-hand experience is highly unlikely. Besides, I've realised,' she shot her daughter a grateful smile, 'that whilst being a professional chef might have been my first love, it certainly wasn't the love of my life. My husband, my darling daughter, my scrumptious granddaughter,' she scrunched her nose at Alice who was quietly watching proceedings, 'and all my friends past and present have been my greatest achievements. *And*,' she added, 'it turns out my knees aren't suited to bearing the brunt of my ambitions for eight hectic hours a day. I'll keep a hand in with the cookery classes, if I'm lucky enough to attract any clients, and it will be far more rewarding to teach than to slog away in the kitchen of someone who doesn't know a frying pan from a fish slice, like that dreadful Maison Rose chap.'

Joe smiled. 'No. Maggie. I don't mean I need you in just any kitchen – I mean I need you in this one right here.'

Maggie gave a small, dismissive laugh.

'Oh, he's perfectly serious,' said Sav.

Jade and Ben both shrugged, just as confused as Maggie. The ambiguous statements flying around were interrupted by a firm rap on the windowpane.

*Oh, not now!* What terrible timing. Hannah went to get up, but Sav beat her to it.

'I'll get it,' said Sav, pushing back his chair and sprinting over to the front door.

'Is that Daddy?' asked Alice, craning her neck to peer between Maggie and Jade's shoulders. 'I don't want to go yet, Mummy.'

Hannah said, 'No, sweetie. I asked him to come a tiny bit later today, so he won't be here for another half an hour.'

'Good. Because I'm not going until we've done the thing you said,' she said decisively, picking up her crayon and resuming her magnum opus. Marvellous. You could always rely on a five-year-old to be discreet.

'What thing?' enquired Maggie, raising an eyebrow at Hannah.

'No idea what she's talking about,' said Hannah, who hid her face away behind her laptop and began furiously tapping away.

'Don't look at me,' said Jade, when Maggie turned to her. 'All I'm saying is I hope there's cake. There should always be cake.'

Behind her, Hannah heard the exchange of voices out in the street, before Sav came back in and closed and locked the door.

'Everything alright?' asked Hannah, looking up.

'Fine.' Sav bounced on his heels, as wired as a comedian about to perform their debut act in front of a rowdy, leering crowd, for things had gone quite beyond *fine*. 'Look, I think we're going to have to wrap this up now.'

Hannah pulled the lid on her laptop shut as Sav crossed to the bar and reached behind it.

'We got you a little something too, Maggie,' he said, handing her a small, soft package.

'Ah,' said Maggie, 'so *this* is the thing. A gift, how lovely.'

She carefully peeled open the paper, to reveal a folded piece of red cotton fabric. Her face crinkled in curiosity as she unfolded it then shook it out, to see the garment was an apron. A very smart apron, embroidered in gold across the chest with the words:

*The Crocus Kitchen*
*G.E.O.*

'Oh, I don't know what to say,' said Maggie, hand going to her mouth. 'What a splendid memento of a wonderful adventure. I shall wear it *always*.'

Hannah experienced a warm glow of gratitude. Even if this had gone differently, the journey they'd all been on together had been special. *Had* been something to celebrate.

Joe pulled himself lazily to his feet and rubbed his hands together.

'Right then, Maggie, pop that on then, and let's get cracking, shall we?'

Confusion clouded Maggie's features. She did a double take. Glanced at her daughter.

Hannah grew aware that if her grin got much wider, her teeth were in danger of falling out.

Ben's eyebrows shot skyward. 'Eh? What's going on?'

'Anything pressing planned for this evening?' asked Sav. 'Either of you, Ben? Jade? Because there seems to be something of a queue outside and I only have the one pair of hands. I even had to unplug the phone before you lot arrived because it hasn't stopped ringing all day.'

'What? How? But, I'm not wearing the right clothes!' exclaimed Ben, who was in jeans and a t-shirt.

'Er, hello!' said Jade, pointing at her own inimitable style, which today happened to consist of a leopard print top and white leather shorts, finished off perfectly with the orange earrings.

Sav dismissed them with a shake of the head. 'I want everyone who comes here to feel like they're home from home. Anything goes, guys. Just be yourselves.'

Maggie got up silently from her chair and crossed the

restaurant floor to the window. She peeked outside and gasped at the sight of the queueing customers snaking up the street.

'What the heck?'

Hannah drew up alongside her.

'There's been a bit of a development this week, Mum. We didn't want to get your hopes up, but everything was finalised yesterday. Just in time to haul Joe back into the kitchen and get the orders in with the suppliers.'

'What kind of development?' asked Maggie, incredulous.

Hannah twisted her cheek. 'Let's just say there's a silent partner. And everything is going to be sorted, *more* than sorted. Crocus Kitchen is very much open for business and if today has been anything to go by, it will be fully booked for weeks.'

Maggie narrowed her eyes. 'A silent partner? Please don't tell me it's anything to do with Wick.'

Hannah scoffed. 'Sav would rather tear the place down with his own bare hands than let that dickhead within fifty feet. Besides, I'd like to think Wick's evil plans for world domination have been sidelined by a dangerous driving offence. Such a shame they couldn't get him on the drink driving charge, even with Baz's testimony.'

From the look on Maggie's face, her mind had gone into overdrive, puzzling as to who the mysterious investor might be. Probably she suspected someone from the community who despised Wick as much as they did. Or another chef perhaps? She'd tell her eventually, once everything had settled down, but for now, did it really matter?

'I'm so proud of you, Mum,' said Hannah, wrapping an

arm around her. 'I know what you sacrificed to give me and Dad a happy, loving home, I don't want you to think for a minute that we weren't both grateful. I'm so sorry for doubting you when you said you wanted to go back to work in a kitchen. This is exactly where you should be.'

Maggie rested her head against Hannah's. 'Oh, love. There is nothing in this world more important than my family. But that doesn't mean I don't want *you* to follow your dreams. Don't ever let the fact I'm on my own now hold you back. Dad wouldn't have wanted that, and I certainly don't. I'm doing OK. Besides, if Oscar has his way, I'll never know a minute's peace. He was blathering on about a beekeeping course the other day. Might give that a go actually; no danger of catching sight of his meat and two veg with all that venom about, one would presume.'

Hannah laughed. 'Just be careful what he signs you up for. And for the record, I'm not going anywhere.' She turned and shot a look in Sav's direction. He was leaning over Alice as she pointed out the various elements of her extensive artwork and doing his best to look impressed. It made her heart race, just seeing them together. As though she'd had a glimpse into a future that made sense.

'I think Dad would have approved, don't you?' she asked, though perhaps it was her mum's approval she sought.

'Dad would say the same as me. You deserve to be happy. *No settling*,' Maggie's eyes crinkled with warmth. 'He's a lovely man, with a kind soul, like his dad. Like *your* dad.'

Hannah swallowed hard. 'I don't know how you've

managed, Mum. Without him.' Tears burnt her eyes, but it was impossible to tell whether they were sad tears or happy ones. Both, probably. 'It was only being a mum myself that got me through. I felt like if I just kept all the plates spinning, then I'd be alright. But I couldn't do it, I had to come home. And it's *you* that's got me through, you're a bloody inspiration.'

Maggie squeezed her tight.

'Well, you know what they say – what doesn't kill you makes you stronger. We're tough, us Lawford girls.'

Together they watched as Ben and Jade dragged themselves to their feet at Joe's cajoling and gathered up the cups from the table, complaining loudly as they headed off to the kitchen that he was a slave driver and how did he know they didn't have anything better to do on a Friday night?

They turned back to each other and grinned, before Maggie slipped the apron over her head.

Things might change, they always did, but for now, there really wasn't anywhere else she'd rather be than here with friends and family, whilst her mum cooked yummy dinners for paying customers, as her daughter had so astutely predicted, all those weeks ago.

# Epilogue

## Maggie

*Six weeks later*

Maggie paused in the open doorway to the bathroom, where Hannah was running a brush through her untamed hair.

'Alright, love?' she asked.

Hannah found her eyes in the mirror and smiled.

'Yeah. I am, Mum.'

In the weeks following the restaurant fundraiser, there had been some significant changes in her daughter's life; seismic, one might say. It was a Friday afternoon, and she wasn't dashing for the 17.37 train from London Liverpool Street. Nor was she racing home to kick off her heels and swap her tailored suit for joggers, before falling into an exhausted snooze on the sofa before the evening had even got started. For one thing, she was already home, having spent a lovely day at the zoo with Alice and Maggie. The sun-kissed face in the mirror – with a sprinkling of freckles across her nose and eyes, bright with intent – was happy and relaxed. Hannah was no longer uptight and stressed, as it seemed to Maggie she had been for so long.

Having an entire fortnight off work to spend with Alice in the school holidays had been an unexpected gift when Hannah had handed in her notice at Tucker, Farraday & White. She'd been put on immediate gardening leave, which couldn't have worked out better if she'd planned it, as the small family law firm in town she'd just joined as junior partner had wanted her to start as soon as possible.

'I'll see you downstairs,' said Maggie, turning to leave.

'Mum?' asked Hannah, halting Maggie as she reached the top of the stairs.

'Yes, love?'

For a split second, she looked just as she had done the evening before her and Geoff had driven her to the university campus all those years before, a mixture of trepidation, excitement and nerves.

'I've made the right decision, haven't I?'

Maggie understood at once what she was asking.

Was she doing the right thing in giving up a high-flying city career, to take a lower paid, less illustrious position in a small, family-run firm in her small hometown, to have more quality time with her family? It was a question she had asked of herself, once upon a time. Of course, she knew now, without a moment's hesitation, she'd do the same a hundred times over. But she would never have wanted to influence Hannah.

'Well,' she began carefully. 'In my experience, it's rarely a case of questioning whether something is the right thing or the wrong thing to do, Hannie. The only thing that really matters is whether it feels like the right thing for you.'

Hannah began to nod, her warm smile slowly growing.

'You're going to love Alison, Mum. As batty as a fruitcake, so you'll get on like a house on fire.'

'Cheeky madam,' tutted Maggie.

Apparently, from the minute Hannah had stepped into the office of Alison Knightley, she'd warmed to the woman, whose outward appearance was as chaotic as her desk. Her small practice specialised in every aspect of family law but had been desperately in need of someone with Hannah's level of expertise in wills and probate. Of particular importance to Hannah had been Alison's assertion, upfront, that she liked to dedicate a proportion of her time to pro-bono cases and hoped Hannah might feel the same. It had been the work of a handshake to seal the deal and by this coming Monday, the small, rented office in Gold Street would have a new sign above the door, one that read Knightley and Lawford Solicitors.

It made Maggie's chest swell with pride just to think of it.

The office was only round the corner from Crocus Kitchen, which was where all three of them were headed for the evening.

'Which shoes did you decide on then, sweetheart?' asked Hannah, as they both entered the lounge. Alice had brought two different pairs with her to Granny's as she'd been simply unable to choose.

'The sparkly ones like Jade wears,' she said decisively.

Maggie could think of no better role model for her granddaughter, who had even begun babysitting Alice on occasion now Hannah and Sav were dating.

'Perfect. Right then, shall we go?'

It was almost the end of August; the school holidays

were coming to a close and it seemed to Maggie as they strolled into town there was a sense of new beginnings in the air. Alice was very excited about going up to Year 2, and they had enlisted Oscar to alter her new school uniform, which was miles too big for her – *so* handy having a talented seamster, which she hadn't even realised was a word until she'd googled it, on speed dial. He'd refused payment, of course, although they still walked Banjo regularly and even when Maggie was alone, sometimes she found herself popping along to see the old duffer and his mutt, for a cuppa and a chat.

The town was bustling as some finished work for the day, and others made mad dashes for last-minute items. The market square hummed with tourists and shoppers, walkers, families, commuters, children and teenagers alike, and Maggie felt the pull of home and the memories of the past settle over her like the warmth of sun on skin. Everything she wanted was right here. Well, *almost* everything, and not quite everyone.

Sav appeared at the door to Crocus Kitchen before they even had chance to ring the bell, flinging it open with a wide grin.

He looked rather handsome in jeans and a pale blue shirt that brought out the gold tones in his eyes. Hannah seemed to have persuaded him the head-to-toe Milk Tray Man look really wasn't for the height of summer.

'Hey,' said Hannah.

'Hey,' he replied, restraint written across his face, still conscious of displays of affection in front of Alice; such a thoughtful chap. 'The others are here, go on through.'

'Joe!' shouted Alice, spotting him towards the back. 'Hi,

Sav,' she said, before setting off at a sprint to where the others were gathered.

'Hmph, I see I still can't hold a candle to our head chef,' grumbled Sav good-naturedly.

'Never fear, his heart is set on another,' Maggie lowered her voice so Joe couldn't hear. 'Apparently he was spotted in town with a *woman* last week,' she said conspiratorially.

'Wow,' agreed Sav, for this was news indeed. 'Just when I was starting to think he had the hots for you, Maggie.'

'Oi!' scolded Hannah, flicking him on the shoulder. 'I could've done without that mental image, thank you very much!'

'Charming,' said Maggie, who fancied she wasn't *quite* beyond the scope of toy boy territory.

Out of the corner of her eye, Maggie clocked Sav catch Hannah's hand as she passed, and she smiled to herself as she left them to it and made her way over to the others.

'Mummy!' hollered Alice, disturbing their private moment anyway. 'Come and see what Joe's made. It's so cool!'

A table was laid for eight, with water, wine glasses, champagne flutes and small dishes of raita and mango chutney to accompany the starters. On a small table beside it were ice buckets containing wine and champagne, and an enormous celebration cake, consisting of four separate layers of sponge, oozing with summer fruits and thick cream. The top was decorated in shortbread pieces, kiwi and strawberries and dusted with icing sugar. It looked way too perfect to eat, as though it were from the pages of a food magazine.

'Wow,' said Hannah, echoing Maggie's thoughts.

'Isn't it awesome?' agreed Jade.

353

'Well, it's not every day we get to have a triple celebration,' said Joe.

'Er, quadruple,' corrected Ben, wrapping an arm around Tom's shoulder.

'Sorry, Tom,' said Joe. 'Quadruple celebration, I keep forgetting you're the same age as these reprobates. You seem so much more sophisticated. I can't imagine what you're doing going out with Ben here,' he winked.

Joe ducked the backhand that shot out from Jade and retreated, chuckling, to the kitchen.

Jade joined Ben and Tom, who had been examining one of the latest art installations on the wall, an eye-popping neon nude, with a price tag of nearly one thousand pounds. Surprisingly enough, it had become an unexpected revenue stream, with the restaurant taking a 10 per cent commission on every piece they sold. It seemed artists countywide were queuing up to get their artwork into Essex's most popular restaurant.

'Right, can I just borrow everyone for a few minutes,' asked Sav, commanding the room to attention with his deep, silky voice. 'It'll only take five minutes if you could just gather round. I'll never hear the end of it otherwise.'

Everyone duly rallied at the bar and Sav spent some time ensuring everyone was seated or standing so they could be picked up by the camera, then he went and tapped on the kitchen door.

'Got a sec, Joe?' he shouted through the gap, then jogged back to the group.

The dial tone rang out six times, before the call connected and the screen was filled with a giant silver-flecked beard.

354

'Hello, Dad,' said Sav, shaking his head as the beard moved from left to right, before shrinking away to reveal Raj's beaming face.

'Ah, son, can you hear me?' he shouted, as though his voice was required to project across the entire hundred miles separating them.

'Sit down Raj, you're blocking the screen,' came Gita's chastising voice from behind.

'Hi Mum,' said Sav, smiling at his long-suffering mother.

'Have you lost weight?' asked Gita, when Raj had shuffled back to sit beside her on the stylish black leather sofa.

'Probably,' shrugged Sav. 'I'm on my feet twelve hours a day.'

Raj waved a hand in understanding. 'Radox bath salts, my boy. The blue one for tired muscles, best thing for it.'

'The blue one. Got it,' grinned Sav, who was, by now, used to his father's well-meaning hints and tips for being a successful restaurateur.

Not that he needed any help, in Maggie's humble opinion – he was absolutely rocking the gig.

'So, what have you both been up to this week?' he asked.

Gita became animated.

'Today we went to the Royal Pavilion. Why did you not tell us, Savinder, that it was used to treat Indian soldiers in World War One? It was a most fascinating excursion.'

Sav shook his head. 'Didn't know that either, Mum. Never been there.'

Gita tutted. 'All this history on your doorstep. You spent so long with your nose in a computer you forgot you had legs and eyes.'

Hannah laughed, enjoying Gita's good-natured scolding, which never ceased to amuse her.

So far, the new arrangement was working out perfectly. Sav had effectively swapped homes with his parents, who since returning from India were enjoying their retirement in Brighton and cramming a lifetime of skipped holidays, days out and trips to the beach into their every waking moment.

'So, what is on the menu tonight then, Maggie?' asked Raj, who despite his initial misgivings about retiring had embraced it wholeheartedly and had nothing but praise for the revamped restaurant.

'Well,' said Maggie, who hoped Joe had ordered in everything she'd requested. 'How does fillet steak with a spicy masala sauce and wilted greens sound?'

Raj visibly drooled on screen.

'How are you, Maggie?' asked Gita, beaming at her friend.

'Very well, thank you,' said Maggie, 'though I'd better get in that kitchen if we want feeding before opening time.'

'It's Maggie's night tonight,' explained Sav. 'She guest-cooks for us on Friday nights.'

'Most popular night of the week,' chipped in Joe, who just then appeared behind her.

'Oh, nonsense,' dismissed Maggie. Although it did seem that The Crocus Kitchen was permanently fully booked, which probably had less to do with her cooking and more to do with Jade's media coverage. Her cookery classes also had a waiting list, and she even used the restaurant kitchens to teach in, when it was closed from Monday to Wednesday. Jade's piece of journalism had much to answer for.

'This lot have offered to be guinea pigs tonight, so hopefully the dish will pass muster,' said Maggie.

'We're having a meal together, before the restaurant opens,' explained Sav. He motioned to Ben, Tom and Jade. 'To celebrate Hannah's fantastic new job *and* because these three superstars got their GCSE results yesterday. Tom's staying on to do A Levels, Ben got a place at catering college and Jade here, was accepted onto her media studies course.'

Gita clapped her hands together, 'Oh, marvellous. Well done to you all. You are all such hard workers.'

'Huh, I don't know about that,' mumbled Ben under his breath. Maggie knew he hadn't done quite as well in his exams as the others, which was little surprise if you considered that partway through the year his mother had walked out on him and his father without a backward glance.

She hissed in his ear. 'Don't be hard on yourself. You've done amazingly well to find something you're so good at. So many people never find out what they're capable of, let alone something they love to do.'

'Well, don't let us keep you from your delicious dinner,' said Gita, before leaning forwards conspiratorially, 'besides, believe it or not, Sav, your father is taking me out tonight on a date!'

Sav pulled a face of disbelief. 'A date? Who are you and what have you done with my parents?'

Raj looked sidelong at Gita with so much love and admiration, it made Maggie ache for Geoff. Involuntarily, her eyes slid to their old table in the corner. How proud he would have been of his family. Of his brilliant, compassionate daughter and his inquisitive granddaughter. He'd be jolly pleased with Maggie too, she knew. Could almost hear him teasing her about luring all the boys to her kitchen with the promise of a treacle tart, and he'd have had a point – at least 75 per cent of her cookery students were men. And half of those were single, some were dads, most of them embarrassed they barely knew how to pierce the film on a microwave meal, let alone plan a balanced meal. By the time she'd finished with them, they were cutting petals out of pastry to decorate their pie lids. Although she made sure never to show them her shepherd's pie, the original family secret. That one's just for you, she silently promised Geoff.

They ended the Skype call with goodbyes and promises to send photos of their meal. Maggie wasn't sure Raj and Gita would ever move back to their flat above the restaurant, now they'd dipped their toes into a new chapter. It was a feeling she could relate to, having had a taste of it, in that precious, fun-filled year with Geoff. Lately, she'd even found her mind wandering to the campervan, still sitting in storage at a local site. She had never been able to bring herself to sell it, because maybe one day, just like herself – it might be unretired. Called into service for another grand adventure. It was an exhilarating, if scary, thought.

Maggie's gaze fell on the silver tea set she had rescued from the antiques shop. It had pride of place in a cabinet behind the bar, among bottles of booze and elaborate goblets. It matched the bohemian mismatched interior brilliantly and served as a reminder to all that even when everything seems lost, it can also still be found.

Next to the cabinet, also in pride of place, was the framed photo of the Kapoors with a certain Mr Oliver, who had been the source of much speculation among those who were surprised by the restaurant's sudden turnaround of fortune.

Maggie, herself, had fallen foul to such circumspection, until only a couple of weeks ago when Hannah had taken her aside.

'I want to tell you how the restaurant came to be saved,' she'd said, 'but you must never tell another soul.'

Maggie had listened as Hannah told her how one of her clients, an influencer called Caitlin Gallagher, had seen Jade's film on TikTok. She'd recognised Hannah from the footage and contacted her to see what it was all about. Apparently, she's well known in hospitality and is regularly paid to promote restaurants, bars and hotels, as well as a whole raft of products. Who knew one could make a living out of simply swanning about?

'She has a *lot* of money, and is about to inherit more,' explained Hannah. 'Money she's looking to invest in small businesses and ventures that would otherwise be overlooked. She came from nothing, Mum,' said Hannah, who clearly had a soft spot for the woman. 'Found a way to earn her own money, even though she was an outcast to her own extremely wealthy and obnoxious family.'

Turned out Caitlin had another motive, too. She'd been, rather publicly, on the receiving end of Hugo Wick's vitriol when he'd called her the *kind of cheap trash he didn't want anywhere near his dining establishments* on one of her own Instagram posts.

Maggie hugged the thought to herself, that whilst Wick

scrabbled around for airtime and drew a blank on every property he attempted to purchase within a thirty-mile radius, The Crocus Kitchen was thriving.

And Wick would never know about Caitlin Gallagher's involvement because she wasn't a partner in the restaurant. Hannah had been astute with her advice about that.

Restaurants *did* come and go. It was a simple fact of life. And who knew what the future had in store? No, much safer to invest in the ever-changing world of cyber-security and help to grow one of the most successful tech start-ups in the last ten years. The small company Sav had set up with Greg was going places; he'd just had a change of heart about going with it. Mainly because his heart had been very successfully stolen by a determined solicitor and her five-year old daughter.

Caitlin had bridged the finances in the restaurant until she officially replaced Sav as co-director with Greg in an amicable parting of ways, meaning Sav was now the official and proud owner of Crocus Kitchen.

Caitlin watched on silently from the sidelines, sometimes from a ringside seat as she had become a regular fixture at the restaurant, a presence that had no doubt boosted its popularity ten-fold, and yet still no-one had twigged. She and Hannah, and Laura too, had all become rather good friends – another thing Maggie loved to see. Perhaps she'd ask if her and Pam could tag along on one of their girls' nights out; she suspected it could be eye-opening, and besides, her green Hobbs dress was overdue an outing, and quite ready to make new memories.

But right now, there were eight hungry mouths to feed, including her own. She'd practised her guest dish at home in the week, and if she was allowed to say so herself, it had been bloody tasty. Good job, because she'd be cooking upwards of a hundred of them over the course of the evening, thank goodness it was just once a week.

She took her red apron from her bag and slipped it over her head, as the others all poured themselves drinks and chatted about their week.

'Come on then, Chef,' she said to Joe, looping her arm through his. 'Dinner won't cook itself.'

'Oui, Chef,' he said, grabbing a bottle of white wine from the small table as they passed it. 'What?' he said, when she cocked her head in question. 'You've never heard of one for the pot and one for the chef?'

'Of course I have, dear.' She tugged the bottle back out of Joe's hand and plonked it back in the ice bucket. 'And surely *you* must have heard of chef's privileges.'

Maggie winked as she looked around the room at the faces of her new friends, then swiped a bottle of Dom Perignon instead, before flouncing off into the kitchen before anyone could think to stop her.

## Author's Note

The quaint Essex market town of Saffron Walden is the setting for this story, and whilst the historic Cross Keys Hotel, castle ruins, market square, town hall and Jubilee Gardens are genuine historic landmarks, all other places and establishments mentioned are entirely fictional. Jamie Oliver bears no real-life connection to this story, or the fictional people and places in it.

# Maggie's Keema Shepherd's Pie

A different take on Geoff's favourite dish, bringing
together the hearty flavours of an aromatic keema
curry and buttery mashed potato to create
the ultimate comfort food.

*Serves 4*

**INGREDIENTS:**

500g best-quality minced lamb

1 large red onion, finely diced

2 tomatoes, chopped (or half a tin)

1 tbsp tomato puree

50ml vegetable oil

1 green chilli, deseeded and chopped

1 tbsp fresh ginger and garlic paste

1 tsp salt

1 tsp ground turmeric

1 tsp chilli powder

1 tsp ground cumin

2 tsp ground coriander

½ tsp red chilli flakes

1 tbsp dried fenugreek leaves

1 handful fresh coriander

100ml water

100g frozen peas

500g potatoes, peeled and chopped

85g butter

3 tbsp milk

Optional – squeeze of lime juice and fresh mint

## METHOD

1. Heat the oil in a pan on medium heat, then add the diced red onion and cook for 4–5 minutes until softened.
2. Add the garlic and ginger paste, and chopped green chillies then sauté for a further 2–3 minutes.
3. Add the mince, break apart then cook for 6–8 minutes, until browned.
4. Add the salt, chilli powder, ground turmeric, chilli flakes, ground coriander and ground cumin and cook for a further 3–4 minutes.
5. Add the chopped tomatoes, tomato puree, frozen peas and 100ml water to the pan then cover and simmer for 20 minutes on a medium heat.
6. Finally, add the chopped coriander, dried fenugreek leaves and, if desired, a squeeze of lime and chopped fresh mint to taste. Set aside.
7. Meanwhile, bring the potatoes to the boil in salted water, drain once cooked, then mash with the butter and milk until smooth.
8. Place the keema mixture into an ovenproof dish, then top with the mash, ensuring full coverage. Use a fork to rough up the surface of the potato.
9. Bake for 20–25 minutes at 180C / 160 Fan / Gas 4, until browned and the meat is starting to bubble at the sides. Serve with steamed fresh seasonal vegetables.

# Joe's Peach and Pomegranate Tart

Crisp shortcrust pastry, with a rich frangipane filling, topped with fresh, colourful peaches and jewel-like pomegranate seeds — Joe thinks this makes a great centrepiece.

*Serves 8*
**INGREDIENTS:**

*For the Pastry*
200g plain flour
100g chilled butter (cut into cubes)
50g caster sugar
1 egg yolk

*For the Zesty Frangipane Filling*
110g softened butter
110g caster sugar
110g ground almonds
35g plain flour
½ tsp baking powder
2 beaten eggs
Zest of half a lime

*For the Topping*
4 ripe peaches, sliced
Seeds from 1 pomegranate

4 tbsp apricot jam to glaze
Small handful of flaked almonds

## METHOD

1. Sift the flour into a mixing bowl and add the cubes of butter. Using your fingertips, rub the butter into the flour until the mixture resembles fine breadcrumbs, then add the caster sugar and briefly combine.

2. Add the beaten egg yolk then mix all the ingredients together to form a soft dough. Add 1 tbsp of water if needed to help to bind the mixture.

3. Wrap the ball of dough in cling film and refrigerate for up to one hour.

4. Grease a 9 inch / 23cm loose bottomed flan tin.

5. Roll out the pastry dough on a lightly floured surface to around the thickness of a pound coin and large enough in diameter to line the flan tin. Carefully line the flan tin with the pastry and refrigerate whilst you make the filling.

6. Preheat the oven to 200C / 180 Fan / Gas 6. Cover the flan case with baking parchment and fill with ceramic baking beans. Blind bake for 15 minutes.

7. Remove from the oven and carefully remove the beans and parchment. Leave to cool.

8. In a mixing bowl, make the frangipane filling by combining the flour, ground almonds, eggs, baking powder, sugar and butter. Beat until light and fluffy. Add the lime zest. Mix briefly.

9. Pour the mixture into the cooled flan case, then stud the mixture with pomegranate seeds, pressing them down into the filling. Arrange the slices of peach in concentric circles. If desired, decorate with more pomegranate seeds, filling in any gaps.

10. Bake for 30–40 minutes, until golden.
11. Remove from the oven and brush with warmed apricot jam and sprinkle with flaked almonds. Allow to cool completely before serving.

# Ben's Indian-Style Paneer Fajita's with Mint Raita

Inspired by a popular street food snack, whip up this veggie dish in no time and enjoy. (You could even buy ready to eat chapatis, just don't tell Maggie.)

*Serves 4 (2 x fajitas per person)*
**INGREDIENTS:**

*For the Chapati Wraps*
100g plain flour
100g wholemeal flour
¾ tsp salt
1 tbsp olive oil
150ml warm water

*For the Fajita Filling*
500g paneer (Indian cheese)
2 red peppers, sliced,
2 green peppers, sliced.
2 red onions, sliced.
1 tsp ground turmeric
1 tsp ground coriander
2 tsp ground cumin
1 tsp chilli powder
1 tbsp olive oil

*For the Mint Raita Dressing*
20g fresh mint
30g fresh coriander
Pinch of ground cumin
Pinch of salt
350g natural yoghurt

## METHOD

1. Make the chapati wraps. Add all the ingredients into a mixing bowl and use a wooden spoon or your hands to bring together into a dough.
2. Knead the dough on a lightly floured surface until smooth. Divide into eight evenly sized balls and leave to rest.
3. Slice the paneer into strips, place in a large dish. Add sliced red onions and sliced peppers. Add the spices and the olive oil and stir to coat, then leave to marinate.
4. Next, prepare the dressing. Roughly chop the mint and most of the coriander, and blend (or grind with a pestle and mortar). Add the cumin and salt, then mix into the yoghurt. Refrigerate until ready to serve.
5. On a floured surface, roll out the dough balls into thin circles, approx 15cm in diameter. Add more flour if the dough begins to stick but brush off any excess before cooking.
6. Heat a heavy-based frying pan to a high heat, then grease the surface lightly. (Brushing with a little oil ensures a thin and even layer.)
7. Place the first chapati in the pan and cook for around 30 seconds, or until it begins to blister and brown. Flip and cook on the other side for another 30 seconds. Repeat until you have cooked all the chapatis. Keep warm whilst you cook the fajita filling.

8. Heat a splash of oil in a large frying pan and add the marinated paneer and vegetable mix. Stir frequently and fry for 5–6 minutes, until the paneer is browned, the vegetables softened.

9. Serve with a sprinkle of chopped coriander, the stack of cooked chapatis and the mint and coriander raita so that guests may assemble the fajitas themselves.

# Sav's Mango Mojito's

If, like Sav, cooking's not your thing, bring out the show-stopping cocktails instead. Sweet and zingy, this tropical mojito is made for sunny days. Omit the rum for a tasty mocktail.

*Serves 4*
**INGREDIENTS:**
- 2 ripe mangoes, chopped (Alphonso mangoes when in season) OR, cheat, like Sav, and use a tin of sweetened mango pulp/ puree
- 3 limes (2 cut into wedges, 1 juiced)
- 4 tsp caster sugar
- Small bunch fresh mint, leaves picked
- 120ml white rum
- Crushed ice
- Soda water

**METHOD**
1. Prepare the mango puree by blending the chopped mango with the juice from 1 lime. If using mango pulp, allow around 90g per cocktail.
2. Place 2–3 lime wedges into the bottom of 4 high ball glasses, along with 1tsp caster sugar and 5–6 mint leaves.
3. Using a cocktail muddler, or the back of a long spoon, lightly crush the mint and lime together to release their flavours.

4. Divide the mango puree between the glasses and add 30ml white rum and a handful of crushed ice to each. Stir well to mix. Top up with soda water and garnish with mint or lime. Sweeten to taste.

# Gita's Cardamom Shortbread Biscuits (Nankhatai)

These traditional Indian biscuits have been enjoyed by many generations. Gita shared her recipe with Maggie, eventually . . .

*Serves 12*

**INGREDIENTS:**

125g plain flour, sieved

50g chickpea flour, sieved

75g caster sugar

75g ghee (or softened butter)

½ tsp baking powder

½ tsp ground cardamom

Pinch of salt

1 tbsp chopped pistachios

1 tbsp chopped almonds

**METHOD**

1. Preheat Oven to 200C / 180C Fan / Gas 5.
2. Mix the flours together in a bowl and add the baking powder, ground cardamom and a pinch of salt.
3. In a separate, large bowl, beat the ghee and sugar until pale and fluffy. Add the sieved flours and mix to make a dough, add a splash of milk, or water if needed.

4. Mould into 12 equal-sized balls, and space apart on a lined, greased baking tray. Flatten slightly and cut a small cross in the centre.
5. Bake for 7–8 minutes.
6. Remove from the oven and sprinkle chopped nuts in the centre of the biscuits, then return to oven for another 7–8 minutes, until lightly coloured.
7. Leave on a wire rack to cool completely.

# Acknowledgements

There are a few fine folks I would like to thank for their involvement and hard work in the publication of this, my debut novel.

Firstly, the very lovely Rachel Hart, Senior Commissioning Editor. Bringing a book to publication is down to the collaboration of many, and Team Avon are a fantastically creative and diligent bunch whom I've thoroughly enjoyed working with. Thank you to Assistant Editor Raphaella Demetris, Marcomms Executive Ella Young, and Production Controller Francesca Tuzzeo. Thanks to Bodil Jane and Toby James for their brilliant work on illustration and cover design, and to Laura Sherlock for Publicity. Thank you to Anna Nightingale and Clare Wallis for their thorough copyedit and proofread. Thanks also to the rest of the Avon Team: Helen Huthwaite, Sarah Bauer, Maddie Dunne-Kirby, Amy Baxter and Elisha Lundin. A huge thanks too to the bloggers and reviewers who have given their time and support. And to you, Reader, for picking up a copy, thank you so very much. Thank you to my literary agent Kate Nash, and the wider agency team, for taking a chance on me in Book Camp 2020 – it was truly exciting to find industry professionals who believed I could write.

Thanks to the brilliantly talented and endlessly encouraging Book Camp Mentees. Beta readers, senders of gifs, cheerleaders, friends and general good eggs, thank you: Jon Barton, Annabel Campbell, Ina Christova, Joanne Clague, Adam Cook, Kate Galley, Nicola Jones, Katie McDermott, Georgia Summers, Laura Sweeney, Helen Yendall and Kathryn Whitfield. Extra thanks to Imogen Martin for always going the extra mile.

Thanks to Julie Reilly for her thoughts on legal elements of the story (any mistakes are my own).

Thank you to the RNA Cariad Chapter, who accepted me into their ranks, despite my closest link to Wales being that I once climbed Snowdon. You're a fab bunch.

Thank you, Pop Tarts, dear friends, for your enduring support, and Prosecco-fueled fun times xxx. Thanks to all my family and friends (especially my parents), for being so understanding whilst I neglected you for months on end to write and edit this story. But biggest thanks of all to my husband, who has been at my side throughout my writing journey; listening, brainstorming, beta reading, problem solving, tasting and testing the recipes in this book and celebrating every small success. Love you, Jimbob.